DRIVEN

THE FOUNDER'S SEED BOOK 3

DRIVEN

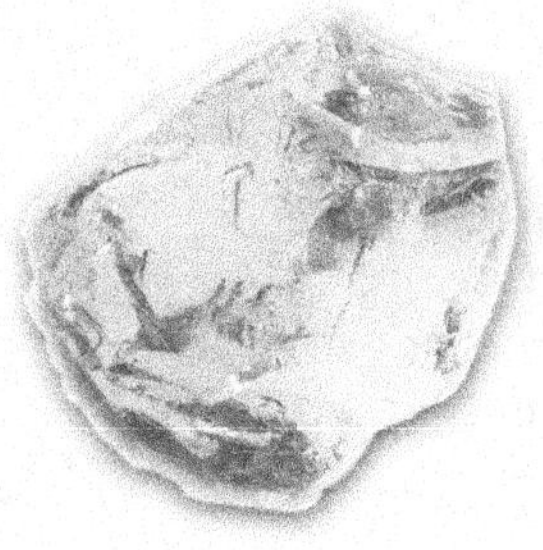

DREMA DEÒRAICH

NIVEYM ARTS LLC

Print ISBN: 978-1-958461-12-9
Ebook ISBN: 978-1-958461-13-6
Audiobook ISBN: 978-1-958461-15-0

Book Cover Design by 100 Covers.
100covers.com

Interior Design by Niveym Arts, LLC.

Published by Niveym Arts, LLC
Norfolk, Virginia 23509
www.niveymarts.com

First edition : June 2025
10 9 8 7 6 5 4 3 2 1

For my readers. You are the reason I write.

New Canaan, Harajüd

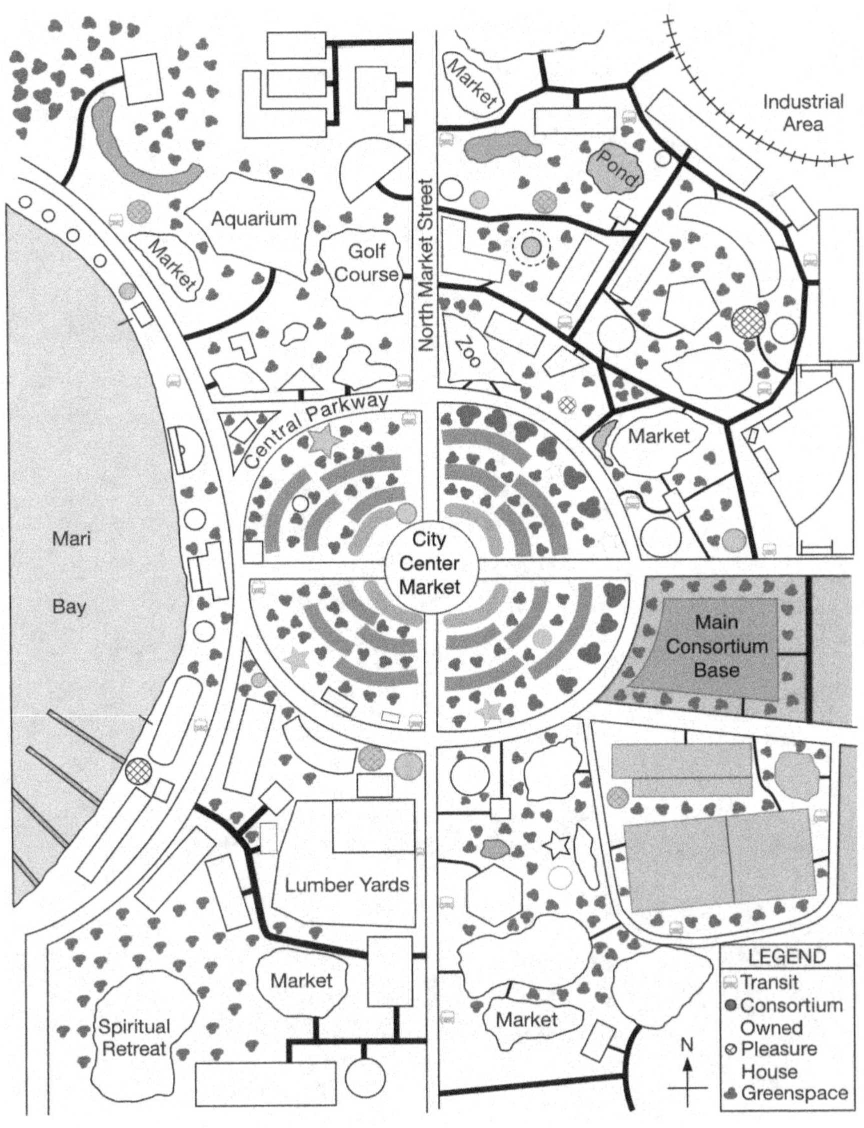

Tuneloras, Saacharis

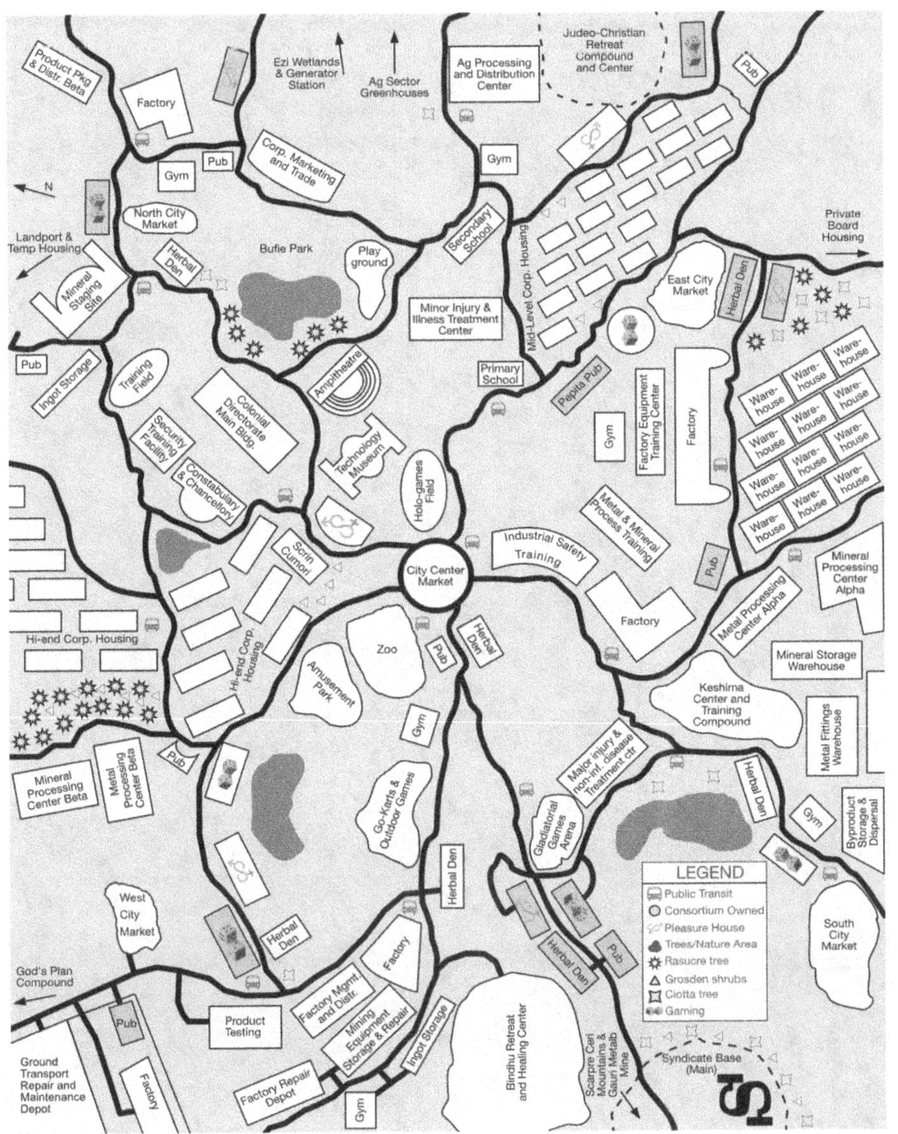

Bejami (B)

Onlebaar Island
(unofficial name)
Verregandor
Haradhalen
Canyon
Mandoslóna
Ysigdo Channel
Vestibulum
Cubozoa
found here
Eredras
Canyon

LEGEND
Ice, Snow
Jungle
Land (undefined)
Mountains
Mountains-Polar
Open Water

N

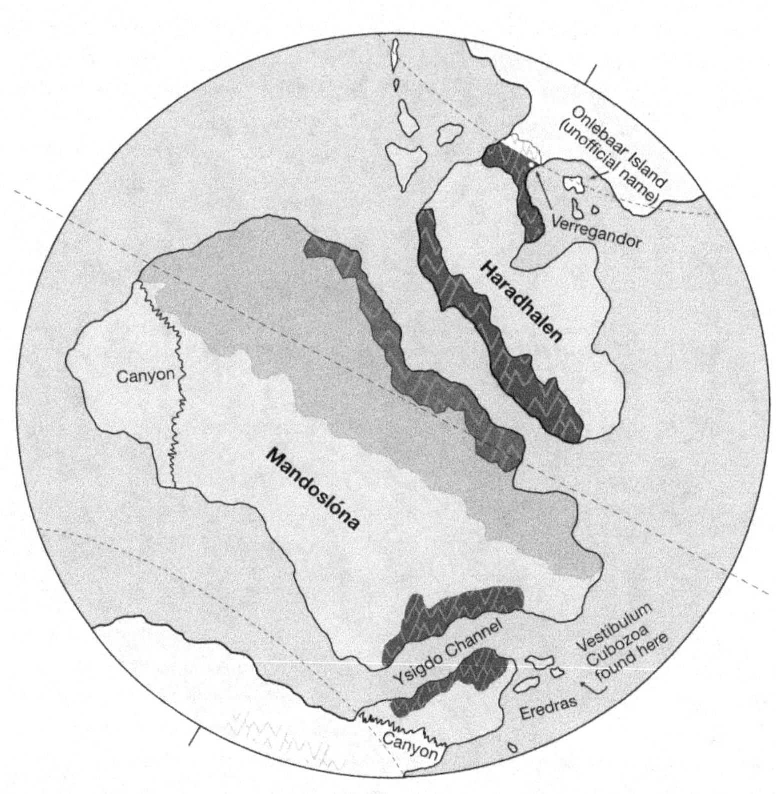

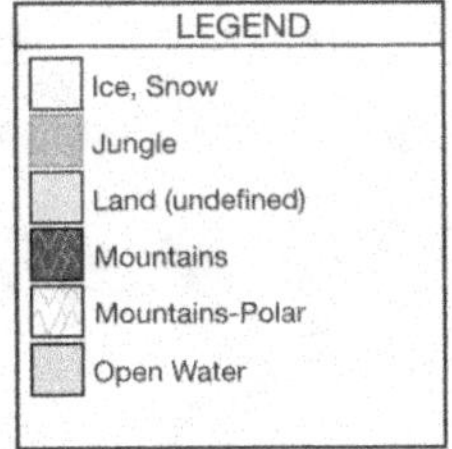

Bejami (A)

Canyon
Firnos Underwater Ruins
Stawanel Mountains
Bregaina
Dairnen Bay
Bel-Rhovan
Baisken River
Dorucuin
LEGEND
Bog
Ice, Snow
Inland Water
Jungle
Land (undefined)
Mountains
Mountains-Polar
Open Water
N

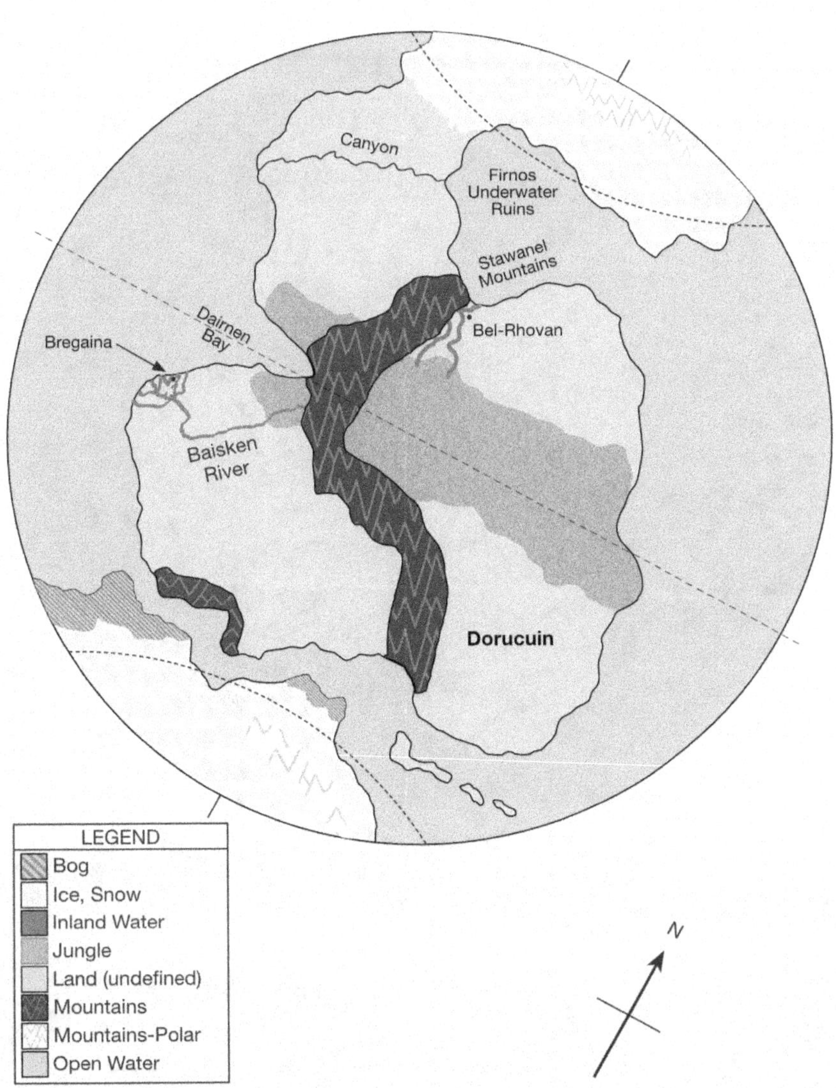

Zebalu

Utatikra
Daima Ocean
Binka
Batikri
Jaudgin
Cara'antra Sea
Matakri
Bantali Sea
Pelarr
Duakela
Lapua
Achitina
Kekalu Ocean
Gulf of Busala
Seladik

LEGEND
Bog
Ice, Snow
Inland Water
Land (undefined)
Mountains
Mountains-Polar
Open Water

N

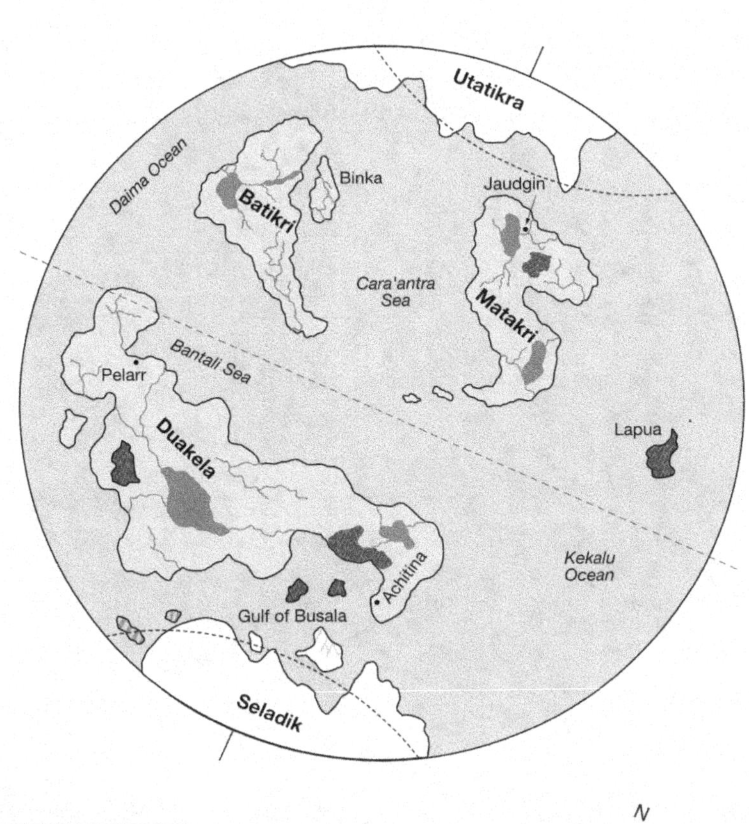

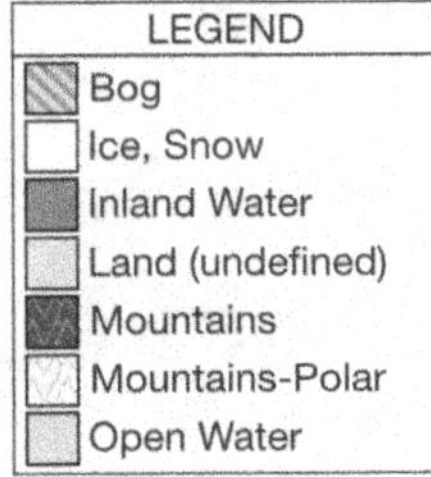

Part One

chapter 1

Haven, Danua
<u>Clan Trader Base, MedFac 6</u>

CAPTAIN KNØFA'S BREATH SOUNDED LOUD inside the mask as he bent over his Iridosian subject with the laser scalpel. His knife was every bit as capable, but this job required sterile tools. It wouldn't do to have the squib die of infection before he was finished with it. With steady hands, he sliced off a long, thin layer of the epidermis along its upper back, adding a bit of the dermis near the end. Its unconscious body lay unresponsive, save for that all-over white color display.

He wasn't yet sure what purpose this would serve in his larger experiments, but the sample stayed white even when separated from the body. Maybe that tissue would hold a clue to the source of its dermal colors. Once, the squib had even hidden in plain sight by changing its skin hues and patterns to match those of its surroundings. For all he knew, the same physical mechanism that operated its variable pigmentation could be essential to the squib's ability to shapeshift.

He had told Admiral Tsurin his suspicion, that the colors were connected to its emotions in some way. So what did white mean? Given the prisoner's current situation, it might convey fear, or maybe pain. He just needed the *how* of it in order to find the proof Tsurin would want.

Blood—red, like a human's—oozed from the sliced skin and the assisting med tech pressed against the wound with clean gauze. Knøfa placed his sample in a lab dish and covered it, then returned his attention to the specimen. He'd already completed a surface exam the first time they gassed it. 142 centimeters in height. Hairless, save for colorless eyelashes. Pale flesh, almost translucent beneath all those colors, with ribbons of dark blue just beneath the surface, too many to be all blood vessels. Its epidermis had to have a resting color, one untouched by these reactive affectations, but Knøfa had yet to see it. Large eyes, silver irises. Maybe they saw better in the dark? Slim shoulders, small breasts—female, perhaps, though its external genitalia weren't quite the same as a human's—wide waist, wider hips, legs thickening as they progressed into wide, almost flat feet. Nails similar to humans.

The med tech removed the gauze. The bleeding had already stopped. When she pulled a bandage from her kit, Knøfa stopped her.

"Wait," he said. "Watch."

They stared at the wound, which had already begun to heal. Edges on either side of the slice thickened and spread toward each other as if the squib's skin cells had minds of their own.

Knøfa frowned. How did it do that? Could he interfere with the process? He glanced around, grabbed a small medical clamp, and laid it in the still-open segment of the cut. Seconds later, the foreign body began to wiggle, slight jigs of motion as the flesh in the layers beneath it healed, pushing it up and out of the wound. Capillaries and other dermal structures reformed themselves as if there were no barrier. Within moments, the clamp lay atop—and outside—whole, unblemished skin.

Eyes wide, he drew upright, staring down at this medical miracle. If he could figure out the squib's healing mechanism, he could find a way to make it work for humans. Whether it was a genetic code that needed to be injected into a human or a technological device that affected healing on a patient's body, the Clan could then license it to others. Especially if it was healing in the form of an injection that was required more than once, even regularly for the rest of the patient's life, charging credits for each and every "treatment" would push the Clan to the forefront not just of the factions, but all twelve corporate worlds, as well. That would be even better than Tsurin's desire to bump them up the Trader food chain.

But this squib was a gold mine for other reasons, too. If they could understand the mechanism behind its ability to shift the dermal pigment in such an effective camouflage, his people could potentially put that knowledge to use in the development of cloaking technology for their ships, maybe even whole bases. Of course, *that* knowledge would never be shared. Not when it could give the Clan such a clear advantage over the other factions.

Even the ability to shapeshift could conceivably benefit the Clan. Not soon, granted, but if they could learn how to incorporate that ability in the womb, new Clan crewmen could be raised from birth to serve the faction as agents who could carry out otherwise impossible missions, get away with almost anything, even impersonate corporate directors or officers long enough to run corporate espionage. Imagine if one of their people could look like the chairman of Danua's corporate government while perpetrating such crimes. With evidence to "prove" it was a colonial official, think how much the Clan could charge for blackmail, either against the chairman, or the colonial government overall. What would they pay to keep their secrets quiet?

Oh, the possibilities that ran through his mind while he worked. His heart beat a little faster. He couldn't wait to tell Tsurin about all this.

He gave the lab dish to the med tech. "Get this down to the lab. Tell them to find whatever mechanism in this skin makes it change color. I want answers. And pump fresh gas in here on your way out. I don't want our guest waking up before I'm finished with it."

The tech left at once, her bronze face pallid and a bit green.

Knøfa sneered. Some of the med techs were too squeamish for this type of work and he guessed he at least knew why, even if he didn't understand or share the feeling. Tsurin had tried to explain to him that compassion was a good thing, in moderation, and that he should hesitate to resort to torture without a damn good reason. But it wasn't like that's what he was after here. If he was going to make Tsurin proud of him, he needed answers and would do whatever it took to get them. Blood was blood, and everything eventually died. Where was the harm if one death could save dozens or hundreds of others? It might be painful for the squib, sure. That's why they'd gassed it, so it wouldn't suffer. That and the fact that when it was conscious, it had a way of screwing with people's heads.

He had to admit, though, that there were a few of the Clan's med techs who might actually enjoy this kind of wetwork. Knøfa couldn't fathom why. He didn't feel anything one way or another. Any given lab experiment was much like the next, as far as he was concerned. This was part of his job. A messy one, perhaps, but once he'd accomplished his goal, he'd stop. Simple as that.

He watched the squib breathe. What should he examine next? Figuring out the bioluminescence would be a start. Still, the ability to look like another person, another *being*, didn't come from something in their skin. There had to be something else, something more in the squib which gave it such a unique ability. He expected to dig quite a bit deeper before he uncovered that mystery. Start on the outside and work your way in. Less chance of missing something.

So. Healing. He squinted at the prisoner. How deep did that ability go, anyway? Mending a slice was one thing. What about regrowing a finger? Or a toe? Could it do that, too?

Only one way to find out.

He stepped closer to the table and set to work on his next experiment.

chapter 2

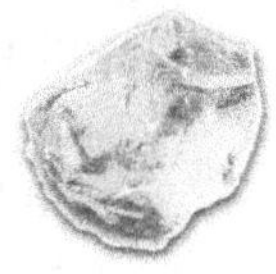

New Canaan, Harajüd
<u>Consortium Trader Base, Admiral Baldric's Office</u>

CHIEF HARLAN DOWNING, HEAD OF Harajüd House Unlimited's security forces, snapped his fingers. "Hello? Are you in there?"

Admiral Thrace Baldric blinked and focused again on Harlan's annoyed face. "My apologies. You were saying?"

"I was explaining," he said, "that the Consortium has been cleared of slaving."

"I'm glad to hear it." Thrace forced her smile to remain steady. "Can you share why you've reached this conclusion?"

Harlan blew a sigh past his thick lips. "Please don't make me repeat myself."

Thrace's second in command, Captain Mira Cohen, cleared her throat. "HHU has found evidence on the surface of Iridos to implicate the Cartel, specifically minute traces of a Cartel ship." She glanced at Harlan. "Does that sum it up, Chief?"

"Yes," he said. "Thank you. Looks like the Cartel tried to cover up their presence, but there's always something left behind. And while we're on the subject of ships, where are the Iridosian haulers? None were found on Harajüd. None of the other corpgovs admitted finding one at their landports, either. So, I can't help but wonder what happened to all those boats." He squinted at her. "You wouldn't know anything about that, would you?"

Took him long enough to ask. Thrace had considered handing them over when she first reported Skalar for the destruction of Iridos. But it could have had negative effects on Rizzo's shipbuilding secrets, so she'd kept the ships' whereabouts to herself. Nothing had changed, and if Harlan knew she had them, he'd never stop hounding her.

"No," she said. "I don't." She was getting good at lying. It didn't even bother her much now. Not that he'd believe her.

"Sure you don't." He snorted. "If you hear anything—"

"I'll certainly let you know, Chief." Weariness dragged at Thrace's voice, weighed on her limbs, her spirit. Slow changes in the shifting blue light from the nanopanel reflected her mood.

Mira peered at her. "Admiral, would you like me to handle the rest of this briefing so you can finish what you were doing?"

Thrace managed to nod. "Yes, thank you, Captain. Chief Downing, please forgive my distraction. I have a lot on my mind. Can I make it up to you with a beer at Dagons later today?"

Her empathic senses felt him waver on the verge of acceptance.

Instead of agreeing, though, he smirked. "A beer isn't going to make us friends, Baldric. We're always going to be on opposite sides, you and I."

"Of course. But the offer stands. Anytime." Thrace got to her feet. "Thank you for coming, Chief. Mira will hear the rest of your update."

Thrace watched them go, then stared out the window at the glimpses of water beyond the City Center. Outside, Lakaya shone its midday face on the city's residents, its light sparkling and flashing in the choppy water of Mari Bay. Even with the turn of early morning tides, boaters still cruised out beyond the bay's sanctuary in search of fish, a simple day of pleasure, or perhaps an interlude of peace outside the sprawling city.

It made her think of Botha. He, too, found solace on the water. How was her friend faring now, surrounded by coastlines but unable to pass beyond them for moments alone in his treasured boat?

And Alira. Had she progressed? Had Botha been able to reach her, or would Thrace be called upon to end her suffering?

Thrace's breath caught in her throat and she squeezed her eyes shut. Her mind veered away from that potential future and she bent it toward a distraction. Any distraction. Like the latest report from the outpost.

Tiral and his crew of unammi outcasts and mitigants had finished repairs on the landing bay and reported significant progress on a working shield for the new unammi city on Earth. Two pilots were still working their way around Earth's atmospheric buoys, checking the status of the biohazard alarms, boosting the distance at which they would begin their warnings, and servicing the buoys when necessary, though it proved difficult to simply repair them as they were. Where they could, the crew had nudged the mechanicals at a quantum level to effect minor repairs, but more than a few had required an infusion of new tech to bring them up to full functionality once more. Thrace had no objection to doing this, as long as it wasn't immediately visible or detectable to a passing ship. They couldn't take the chance that an anomaly like centuries-old devices with contemporary readings would draw the curious close enough to investigate.

Besides the shield and buoys, the outpost remained the only guardian between humans and the last of her—of Galen's—people. The longer Thrace spent in the Consortium admiral's chair, the more convinced she became that it wasn't enough, reliant as it was on maintaining an unammi as leader of the Consortium. Her people lived much longer lives than humans, true. But when Galen had taken over for Alira, he had painted an enormous target on his primary human persona's back and stepped into a constantly shifting position with tenuous security. Anything could happen to take Thrace out of the equation, which could introduce an even bigger threat to the unammi. If Thrace died in the presence of humans, they would witness her body's reversion to Galen's natural state, further revelation of unammi secrets.

Even if no one saw, her sudden removal from the faction would set things in motion that threatened the unammi survivors. Without Thrace as a buffer, traditional Trader faction process would kick in. Mira would take over and the fate of the outpost would be at the mercy of a human, one who knew nothing of the unammi, not to mention their last remnants now living on Earth. Thrace wanted to confide in Mira, bring her over to their side. But that captain was still an unknown element. She probably would not betray the unammi, but Thrace couldn't take that chance. Not yet.

For now, the Consortium still ranked top among all six factions, but fierce competition could change that at any time. The strongest factions got the most work in edgy, off-the-books jobs that paid fabulous sums in both colonial credits and favors owed, which were often far more valuable. All the other admirals would be after the Consortium's favor among the colonial governments. Thrace hadn't the inclination to trick and scheme like her counterparts in other factions, and so she sought other ways to cement her elite place in the Trader hierarchy. Strengthening her faction's relationship with the Syndicate helped, but that friendship didn't guarantee Rizzo would be on call for Thrace's safety, or that of the remaining unammi. Rizzo's people had to come first for Rizzo. Thrace would need to think outside the normal parameters on this. At least her alliance with the Syndicate offered potential for the same with Admiral Bardo, of the Levyron Order, and the somewhat precocious Admiral Georgeanne, of the Rubene Federation.

That left the Danua Clan and the Zebalu Cartel. She still hoped the Cartel would be more reachable, now that Hannah had taken Bellamy's place. But the Clan might be a different story. According to Rizzo, that faction's current admiral was Tsurin, a reasonable woman. But apparently no one had heard from Tsurin in weeks. Rumor was that she'd been injured on a job and her second, Knøfa, had taken over. No one knew much about that captain, other than that he was a giant of a man, and that he had a cold streak as wide as the legendary Ysigdo Channel on Bejami. Not a comforting thought. Hopefully, she would not have to go against someone like that.

She still had hopes for closer ties with HHU, too, but that would rely on Harlan. HHU's board chairman, Logan Roucharde, had been mysteriously quiet in the few months Galen and Alira had masqueraded as humans here. Nor had he reached out since Thrace took over as admiral. She knew he'd had a prior business relationship with Skalar, so she couldn't quite figure why he hadn't tried to touch base with the new faction leadership. Maybe she could learn this from Harlan. If he wouldn't tell her outright, maybe she could sense it in his emotions? Feel her way to a resolution? Maybe she should buy him that beer after all.

"TICS, locate Chief Downing."

A soft chitter preceded the response. "Harlan Downing is in the west conference room, level twelve, with Captain Mira Cohen."

"Message Captain Cohen that I'm on my way. They should wait for me there."

She stared out at the city. The light had shifted by at least an hour. She hadn't meant to get so engrossed, but these were not small details, and every one required a considered resolution.

Thrace murmured a Bindhu mantra of protection, one specific to her own Shidara sect. When she'd finished, just to be on the safe side, she added a prayer.

Na'Staani, don't abandon us now. Speak through my voice, guide my actions, so that your people will remain safe.

All things had a season. Birth, life, death, respite, rebirth. Thrace headed for the door, holding tight to the hope that the unammi's season did not near its end.

chapter 3

Tuneloras, Saacharis
<u>Pepita Public House</u>

ADMIRAL RIZZO STEPPED THROUGH THE door and into the crowded pub. A multiplicity of food aromas laced with perfumes assaulted her senses as she passed through the knots of patrons surrounding the central bar. Light gleamed off the gilded rays of Saacharis's star in the mosaic above, and Rizzo squinted.

Heads turned as she passed, and the patrons made a path for her, closing behind as if she were parting the waters with a thought. Usually she ignored them, but tonight it raised one corner of her mouth into a half-smirk. She'd earned their respect, and probably more than a little of their fear, both through her actions and through rumors that followed. A small amount of fear could work in her favor, but terror would put a kink in the works. Terrified people did stupid things. Terrified people got themselves, or others, hurt. So, she'd also earned their admiration through giving back. The Syndicate may not follow the letter of the law—or even remain on the same continent in some cases—but her faction also helped aid children and women, as well as a few men, who fell through the cracks of Saacharis Aggregate's corporate maw. People talked. They remembered. Rizzo remembered, too. She'd been one of those children on Zebalu.

She broke free at the edge of the bar and crossed into her private dining room, where her second in command, Captain Bailey Madden, waited. A murmured word from Rizzo brought down the privacy screen at the door. Staff could pass through, but patrons outside this space could not hear or visually track what happened inside. She sank into the seat across from her second and picked up her chopsticks.

"Report." Her fingers worked the sticks with practiced ease on the short rice noodles. She took a bite.

Bailey's intense blue gaze focused on Rizzo. "Our shipment of salt came in short this time. I had a word with the contact. I don't expect it'll happen again."

Rizzo nodded.

"Ruma University sent their thanks for your donation, and promised to use it for outreach, as you requested."

"Good."

"We've signed three new clients for small ship fleets." The captain leaned forward, one lock of long black hair sliding past her shoulder. "I set two of them up to meet with the design teams next week, but one was so eager to have her fleet as soon as feasible, I squeezed her into the schedule three days from now."

Rizzo swallowed. "Don't put yourself or the designers out like that. If potential clients aren't content with your timetable, they can go elsewhere."

"I just didn't want the Syndicate to lose the business."

"Plenty of others will fight for her place." Rizzo picked up another bite. "What else?"

"Still no reports of any children in Gauri Metalb. Operations in the mine are clean."

They should be, after her "visits" with Reyes and Michels, and all those they'd named in her shower. If it was still slave-free now, five months later, Rizzo could breathe a little easier. For a while.

"Good. Keep surveillance running. I want regular reports."

"Of course, ma'am."

Rizzo gestured for Bailey to continue.

"I saved the worst news for last. We received confirmation from our folks on Danua," Bailey said, her tone flat, "that Admiral Tsurin was injured on a job. No one seems to know how."

So the rumor had been true. "How bad?"

"Brain damage. Possibly permanent. Captain Knøfa's now in charge of the Clan."

Rizzo finished her bite. "I thought Jansen was Tsurin's second. What happened to him?"

"His shuttle's guidance failed. Crashed him into some isolated rock they were using as a drop site, from what we can tell."

Rizzo grunted. If she were the betting type, she'd take odds that was no accident. "What about Michael Trask? He should be up next."

"Apparently not," Bailey said. "Tsurin promoted Knøfa to second sometime in mid-Octomen. Captain Trask took over security. Too bad. He would've made a much better admiral."

"Indeed," Rizzo said. "Eat."

"I will, ma'am, as soon as you're updated."

"Eat. I'm thinking." Rizzo picked up her bowl and scooped the last of the noodles into her mouth.

All her intel said that Tsurin had taken Knøfa in as a child, raised him as her own, taught him the trade. It stood to reason this would be the next logical step. It just didn't happen to be convenient or expedient for Rizzo's needs.

Had Knøfa popped Tsurin? Was that how she got "injured" on a job? Knowing that little tidbit might help her put together some of the other pieces in this puzzle, see the picture they made. Regardless, Knøfa's new role might be bad news for all of them. No doubt Bardo, Georgeanne, and Hannah already knew of this development by now.

Did Thrace know?

Rizzo sipped her water and considered sending word to the Consortium. But if she played messenger now, she stood the chance of being once more sucked into that drama. No thanks. She'd had plenty of that cleaning up Alira's mess.

Still, despite her annoyance with being suckered into the whole thing, Rizzo had to admit to a hint of admiration for the woman, if that's what she called herself. Yes, she'd been taking stupid risks with too few guarantees of success. But she'd done it for all the right reasons, despite knowing what it might cost her. Was that little troublemaker still alive? If anyone could help her, it would be Botha. Rizzo had satisfied her own urge to assist by connecting that baba with Georgeanne and Bardo, and by providing a sturdy pop-up shelter. Even if they were still on that godsforsaken island so close to the polar zone, the pre-fab would keep them warm for a year. Maybe more. Would all their efforts be worth it? Would the baba be able to drag Alira away from the abyss?

Rizzo pressed her lips together in a tight line. Not her business. Neither was Thrace, nor the Consortium. If that faction's admiral wanted to know what was going on outside her own walls, she could damn well send out her own spies. Maybe Thrace had already done so, and her spies were already reporting on Syndicate activities. Probably. It would be the smart thing to do. Thrace wasn't stupid. Foolish, yes. Emotions, like those the Consortium's admiral held for her troublemaking lover, brought nothing but problems. People got themselves killed over such things.

"Where are you?"

Bailey's voice cut through the haze of Rizzo's thoughts. How did she always know? Rizzo huffed in amusement. "Pepito's."

Bailey cut a sideways stare at her admiral. "You know you can trust me, I hope."

Rizzo put down her water, placed her elbows on the table, and looked into her second's eyes. "I trust you with my business. My faction. My life."

"But not your secrets?"

"It isn't my secret." Rizzo sighed. "Otherwise, yes. Without question."

"Okay," Bailey said, a lock of hair falling past her shoulder. She tucked it behind her ear. "Just…I can tell something is weighing on you. Has been for a couple of months now. When you're ready to tell me, I'm here."

"Understood." Rizzo cleared her throat. "What are the latest figures on imports?"

Bailey threw some numbers from her TICS into the air over the table. Rizzo focused on the holo-projection like a laser, and shoved her doubts about troublemakers into a deep, dark box in the recesses of her mind.

chapter 4

<u>Onlebaar Island, Bejami</u>

ALIRA PUSHED HER BOOTED FEET through the snow and stopped outside the habitat, a bucket in each hand. She noted Botha's tracks leading up the slope to the meditation circle. Last night's howling winds, almost as crazed as she'd been when Botha first brought her here, had eased in the last hour. She offered a word of thanks to Na'Staani for that small favor. The winds on Iridos, fierce though they were, had nothing on those here. In winter, Bejami's star didn't rise much above the horizon this far north. Daytime temperatures warmed by a blazing eight degrees.

This small spit of rock had plenty of trees crowding together in its southern territory, along with thick tangles of undergrowth beneath their boughs. They would've had to clear an area there to set up camp on the lowland. Alira hadn't been present enough to have a say at the time but she agreed, later, with Botha's choice to set them on higher ground. No trees and more wind, but easier to manage as a site, and easier to pack it up and move it out when they finished here.

If they finished here.

Those early weeks were a blur. The first clear memory, after Admiral Bellamy's death and Alira's scrambling escape from the Cartel, was waking in the low lights of the hab to the sound of singing. She thought she had died and lamented the fact that no one had called her name. Then Botha had held a cloth against her face, dampened with something that smelled of sweet herbs. She'd opened her eyes, and he'd said something typically Botha-like—she didn't recall his words now, probably something about a boat—and smiled at her. When next she came to awareness, he had been feeding her hot broth, talking as if he believed she would hear and respond. Instead, she had panicked, slapped the cup out of his grasp, stretched her fear into his throat and tried to throttle him. He had reached her, helped her stop seconds before he passed out. After he'd caught his breath, he helped her remember who she was, who he was, where they were, and why. Then he'd left her alone in the hab for many hours. She'd begun to think he wouldn't return.

That was more than a month ago. Yet even now, when she thought about what she'd almost done…

She blinked away the memory and followed the hab's outer wall to a spot well off the path and apart from the trodden ice. There, she filled the buckets with fresh snow, carried them inside, and set them next to the central cookstove to melt. She straightened and looked around at the temporary home Botha had arranged for them. The hab itself, circular in shape, was pre-fab, easy-up and easy-down, Botha said. The floor, raised off the actual ground on which it sat, carried heat from the central unit, using some sort of sustainable human technological magic she did not understand. Botha explained that their composted waste from food byproducts and bodily functions helped to supplement the power source, but that was the extent of her knowledge. She could have mined her harvested human voices for the information but did not. That might wake them, get them all talking again. No one wanted that.

Their sleeping pallets sat on raised platforms, opposite one another across the hab, each surrounded by a curtain for some semblance of privacy. Shelves next to their beds held clothing, and a row of pegs next to the door held four other coats, two of varying weights for each of them. Alira had recovered enough to mimic coverings on her own, now. But it would take far more energy to do so. Unless there was an emergency where she had to shift or quickly don a disguise, she was happy to have the added warmth. Large rugs covered segments of the warmed floor, granting even more of a cozy feel to their shared room. The central cookstove, also circular and usable from all sides, dominated the smallish space. Even the slight hum of the air recyclers felt like home now. Botha never seemed to hear it, but for Alira, it offered comfort of the known.

Rizzo and her allies had provided the hab, the clothes, even their early food and camp provisions. Botha had seen to the rest.

Alira had no illusions about where she would be without Rizzo, without Botha. She thanked Na'Staani for them every cycle.

every day

She squashed the quiet suggestion of human terminology and moved on. She rifled through the food bins and came up with several strips of protein jerky and a small packet of dried fruit, which she stuffed in her coat pocket. Then she filled two bottles with the fresh melt and walked out into the dim daylight to follow Botha's tracks up the slope of the little bowl in which their camp sat.

On the plateau above the hab, fingers of rock stood clustered in small groups like sentinels staring out at the surrounding sea and distant land masses. Botha's meditation space sat amid a trio of boulders near the far edge, where they helped to block the wind. From here she could see the treed wilds in the lowlands, but today they held no interest. She pushed on and squeezed between two of the sentinels to find Botha waiting. It no longer surprised her how he always knew when she was coming.

"You are here to mark Lynju's passage with me today, eh?" He pointed at that star's trek across the dim sky. "It's good you came out early or you might miss her. She keeps her boat close to the shore in the cold months."

Alira passed him two pieces of the jerky, some dried fruit, and a bottle of water before she sat. She bit off a piece of the leathery protein, chewing in silence while she stared at the sky. Stars still shone in the shadowed portions near the horizon opposite Bejami's star. Were any of these same stars visible from Iridos? Probably not.

"The green in your skin tells me you are ashore with me, my friend, and not swimming the deeps."

"My feet are dry today, Botha." She grinned at him.

"Ah." He peered at her. "Now you give me a new color. I haven't seen that one before. It is pale, like sand along the shores near Bel-Rhovan, but not the white of fear and pain you've shown before. What does it mean?"

She took another bite to buy time. Sands on Iridos were different colors in different places, but none matched her current color. Had she seen the sands of Bel-Rhovan before? Maybe, but just now her mind was blessedly blank. "I'm feeling a closeness with you, a friendship where we can laugh together. One where I feel safe." She watched him. "I hope you'll soon feel as safe with me."

"That day is coming, Gelaboot."

"You've used that word before," Alira said. "What does it mean?"

He wagged his head. "It is a shortened combination of two word elements that mean 'patched boat.' My people use it with those in the process of healing. To us, it is like a rune of hope."

Alira repeated the word, tasting it on her tongue. "You have my thanks, Na'apa. For the rune, for the rescue, for everything."

He stretched his legs and crossed them at the ankles, his leathery face tilted toward the sky. "When a fish escapes a net, I do not think he thanks the currents that saved him from the trap."

"We are not fish."

"Neither are we currents." He looked askance at her. "But we are all carried by them. No matter the world, this is the way of the river, the way of the ocean. You can fight it, but why would you waste your energy on such a futile task? If you are patient, and watch the tides, you will see where the water is taking you and can make the best of your journey."

Alira frowned, digging into the meaning of his words, their concept so similar to her own belief in Musju, and the way of Na'Staani, the Great Mind. Personal experience had taught her beyond doubt that struggling against that force was pointless.

Botha sat up to place his elbows on his knees. "The current carried you across my bow for a reason. Whether that was a lesson for you or for me, I do not know. But now we are in this boat together. If one of us sinks, the other does too. It is better to help than to drown. Yes?"

"So, your actions were selfish?"

"Not in the way you mean. But do you ever cast a line without some hope of a catch?" He finished his jerky and chewed on a piece of fruit.

She'd never thought of it that way. Before she could respond, he changed the subject.

"We should go for a ride to one of the villages on Haradhalen today. Maybe the market in Verregaandor."

What? He wanted to take her out among people? What if she shifted in a public place? What if she lost control of the voices? What if she—

"Not a long cruise, Gelaboot." His voice soothed her. "Just a short voyage, a quick visit. A boat must risk the water if it is ever to sail."

In the back of her mind, her Companion shifted, murmured, and she strained to hear Its words. A rustle of Presence, too long absent from her world, echoed off the stone pillars around them along with a whispered *yes*. She scanned their small meditation circle, searching for the shifting, amorphous image of her Companion, but It did not appear.

A wrinkle knitted Botha's brow. No doubt white flashes in her dermal display were catching his attention.

"You're right, Na'apa," she said. What sort of human mask should she wear for this test? "It's time. I'm as ready as I ever will be."

chapter 5

Haven, Danua
<u>Clan Trader Base, Captain Knøfa's Office</u>

THE THREE-DIMENSIONAL PUZZLE HOVERED in the air above his desk. Additional segments floated around it in a colorful array, each drifting in a lazy rotation to show all angles and sides to the player. Knøfa stared at the unfinished game, at each piece, then at the jagged space near the top. The block that filled that gap would be unique. He observed each part, nudging first one, then another, jockeying them about for a better view.

Ah. There.

He dragged one fragment over and watched as it snicked into the odd gap, its color switching to match the overall yellow of the completed portion. When he laid the last chip in place, the whole thing would change color—green, maybe—and the next puzzle would be harder to solve. Good. This one was too easy, though not quite as much as the levels before had been.

A new element popped in where the old one had hovered. The finished image might be anything. No way to know yet. Just now, it had an ovoid shape, with protrusions rounding the surface near the top. Those, too, awaited matches.

Tsurin had given him this game, a solo player version that would keep learning and advancing as he did so that he could play it for years without growing bored. He'd thanked her, as she'd taught him, and managed to avoid saying it was a much better gift than the items of decor she'd bought him before to make his office more "homey." Who cared about the room's ornamentation? If its layout and furniture served their purpose, he gave it no further thought.

This, though…

He squinted at one of the floating pieces, his gaze flicking to the unfinished surface of a protrusion. So close, it had to be a match. He dragged it over and released it, only to have it zip back to its floating position.

Not a match. Okay. No problem. He reexamined the available pieces, his eyes never leaving the display even when his TICS chittered.

"What?"

"Sir," one of the medfac doctors began, "we're almost ready for the exploratory examination of the prisoner. Should we start? Or—"

"Negative. I want to observe. Five minutes."

"Of course, sir." The TICS chittered and fell silent.

Knøfa frowned at the game, dragged a different piece to the protrusion, and it snicked into place. "TICS, save and close program."

He left his office and walked down the hall toward the medfac. This squib was like the puzzle. Sooner or later, he'd find the right connections to piece together an understanding of how it worked. Once he did, they'd be able to heal Tsurin. Not only that, he'd have found the Clan's newest specialty. So far, they'd kept things surface level. Skin samples, clippings of the eyelashes and nails, shallow incisions. Nothing meaningful had come from those, but it was still early in the game. His geneticists had the cell and skin samples so they could keep working to fit the pieces together.

This experiment, though, would give them a lot more data.

By the time he got to the medfac, the squib was sedated and face up on a table in the next room, behind a clear pane of plaz. The surgeon, his assistant, and two technicians were scrubbed and ready and, at Knøfa's nod, they began.

"TICS," said the surgeon, "project surgical action for the theater and begin recording." He picked up a scalpel.

"Wait," Knøfa said. "Why are you going old school on this? Wouldn't it be better to use higher tech tools than a metal blade?"

"I don't believe so, sir," the surgeon said. "I'm not sure what we'll find in there, so I want to take it one delicate step at a time. The equipment would take longer since I'd have to experiment, find the proper settings to avoid cutting deeper than necessary. I'd rather feel my way through this and hopefully avoid any accidents, if you have no objections."

He gritted his teeth. "Whatever. Proceed."

The surgeon made a shallow incision that began to close almost as soon as he stopped cutting. He straightened and glanced at Knøfa with wide eyes. "That's incredible."

It *was*, but Knøfa kept that to himself. He didn't have all day to stand in amazement.

The surgeon leaned over the squib once more. This time he sliced a thin section of skin and pulled it back from the wound. He gestured to the assistant. "Surgical pins."

The assistant obliged, and the doctor pinned the skin in place. He opened and pinned another segment, and continued in this way until the entire abdominal cavity had been exposed. Bleeding had already stopped. The surgeon uttered something about miracles, but didn't slow the procedure.

"Very similar to a human peritoneal cavity," he noted. He manipulated a few organs, using extreme care, to look beneath them. "This resembles the human liver. This must be the stomach." He bent closer, pulling a magnifier into place. "I'm not sure what this is," he said, pointing at a small gray nodule, "but it's where the gallbladder would be on a human. Maybe it serves the same purpose? And this," he indicated a mass of dark blue tissue to one side, "I don't recognize at all."

"Can't you even take a guess?"

The surgeon only shook his head, staring at the specimen before him.

"Maybe the organ has something to do with it being a female."

"No," the surgeon said. "I don't think so, sir. I see her uterus, fallopian tubes, and ovaries right here. Or at least what I suspect is the Iridosian equivalent." His fingers prodded the blue organ with gentle pressure. "We just know far too little about their physiology to make a guess."

"Could you figure it out given enough time?"

"Maybe," the surgeon said. "But it would take a while. Months, probably, since I wouldn't know where to begin." He swung his gaze toward the plaz screen.

The man wore an odd expression. Knøfa tried and failed to interpret what it meant, what emotion it might imply. He took a deep breath, then let it go. Months? Tsurin needed answers now. Still, it might not be a bad idea to pursue it, just in case. "Then you better get started."

The doctor looked down at the table.

"One other thing," Knøfa said.

"Yes, sir?"

"It has a working reproductive system, you say?"

"Well…" The surgeon leaned in again, peered down into the squib's opened torso. "The tissue appears healthy, or at least what I imagine healthy organs would look like in an Iridosian. Just a surface glimpse wouldn't tell us, though. We'd only know if we cut it open, or if she got pregnant."

Knøfa blinked. A squib fetus. How many could it produce? But no. Without a male squib, he couldn't fertilize the ovum. Besides, if it was pregnant, he wouldn't be able to experiment on it. He would have the fetal tissues, of course, but that might not be the same.

Then a new thought occurred.

The squib's physiology was unknown, true. But what if they fertilized a squib ovum with human sperm? Would it work? His eyes narrowed. If it did, maybe they wouldn't need to understand how the *squib* did what it did. They could see quickly, in a matter of months, maybe a year at most, whether a genetic cross would produce the same traits in half-human offspring. And *that* might bring them closer to science they already understood. It was worth a shot anyway.

"Is the squib biologically compatible with a human?" Knøfa asked.

"I…don't know, sir. It's possible, I suppose. Why?"

"I want to try something. You can harvest her ova, right? We have the facilities and equipment to store them on base?"

"Well…" the doctor said. "Yes…sir."

"And do we have human sperm samples on ice?"

The surgeon frowned. "No, sir."

Knøfa grunted. "Then find some. Extract as many of the squib's ova as you can without harming it. Store most of them but keep a few out. Fertilize them with human sperm. If they produce viable zygotes, I want to know about it."

"But…but…sir," the doctor said, "who…where…we would need suitable surrogates. Implantation would need to take place soon after fertilization."

"Leave that to me."

"Sir…"

"What is it?"

"I don't know if this Iridosian has fertility cycles similar to those of human females. I'd have to take it for granted she does, and work on blind assumption that we're starting at the right point in that cycle. Beyond that, in vitro fertilization isn't an immediate process. We need to harvest the eggs first, which may or may not take some time, depending on how the patient's ovaries process the ova. Then we'd need the surrogates so we can regulate their hormones and prep them for the implantation. We'll need to obtain the drugs required to help them carry any viable fetuses safely to term—"

"How long?"

The doctor's mouth opened and closed like a fish taken from the water. "I'm not a specialist in that field, sir, so I'll have to research the matter, but I would guess at least a standard month before we can even harvest the eggs and prepare the surrogates, and two before we'll know whether it was successful."

Knøfa sighed. "There's no way to speed up the process?"

"Not that I know of, sir, but I'll check into it."

"Right." Tsurin's voice murmured in his mind. *It'll take as long as it takes.* "Start the process. If you can make it happen faster, do so. Keep me informed."

"Yes, sir."

The doctor murmured instructions to his team, then unpinned the squib's skin, and pressed it into place. Within a minute, the slices had healed shut.

Knøfa watched the doctor work while he spun out possibilities. He'd need some willing women, but that wasn't going to be very likely. Not once they learned what kind of fetus they would be expected to carry. He frowned. Even an indentured worker wouldn't be a good bet for this task. He might have to contact the Cartel. That would've been a sure bet under Bellamy's admiralty. But Hannah's position on slaves had yet to be clarified. He'd soon find out if they were still in the business. Tsurin wouldn't like that he'd used slaves, at least not at first. But if he could show her viable genetic crossbreeds that could serve as lab rats for the Clan—he'd have to soften his pitch a bit, make it fit her language so she would be more likely to accept the idea and not lock him up in the brig like she'd done when he broke the rules as a kid—she'd come around.

One of the techs brought a hypo and injected the squib.

"What was that?"

"The first step in regulating her reproductive cycle," the doctor said. "Assuming she has one."

Knøfa grunted a response. So many pieces to this riddle. So much to consider. What would a half-human, half-squib look like? Would it carry the skin color of its sperm donor? Would it light up? Would it heal as quickly as this squib, or be able to change shape? Would it have the same mental abilities to screw with the humans around it? Hmm. He could just imagine a squalling infant, mad because it didn't get its bottle on time, but unable to control that mental twist of the humans within reach. He'd need to take extra precautions with any that came to term.

chapter 6

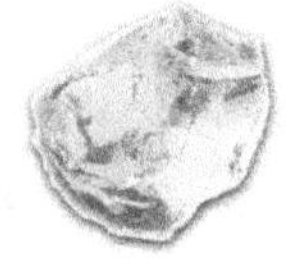

<u>Onlebaar Island, Bejami</u>

TRAVERSING THE PATH DOWN TO the forested woodland took all of Alira's concentration. Rocky debris littered the trail, threatening to twist an ankle or throw her balance. She stopped once to survey the area, but Botha seemed to know his way well enough and was soon far ahead of her. She didn't tarry long.

Their boat waited at the bottom of the crag, pulled into a tiny cove and camouflaged with scrub. Together, they pulled away the branches and set them aside on the shore. No small thing, this craft. Its overall size dwarfed the enclosed passenger compartment. The hull, constructed of some heavy material that appeared impenetrable, echoed their footfalls when they boarded, as though the whole thing were hollow. Alira tried to remember riding in it before. Big as it was, though, they couldn't have brought the hab this way. That would've required a jumper.

Inside, sheltered from the cold wind, Botha started the power and pulled out into the wider channel. Chunks of ice littered the deep green water around them, slowing their progress for a while. Once their path was clear, Botha gained some speed, lifting the craft off the surface to skim past the shoreline to their right.

Alira watched the mountains for signs of human habitation. Once they got closer to other villages, she would need to adopt a human persona. Not one of her harvests, and not the same one as the last time they'd gone to the village. Someone new. Someone random.

"Is this how you brought me here?" she said. "This boat?"

He laughed, a rich warm sound that made her smile. "Oh no, my friend. You were too big an anchor even for a boat this size. We brought you by air."

Movement behind them in the compartment caught Alira's attention and she whirled in her seat.

Her Companion stood in the rear of the craft, Its form stable in the guise of Elisul. Long coppery hair fell in waves down his back. Green eyes pierced her soul.

She gestured at him. "*There* you are. I've missed you."

Botha shot a look at her, slowed the boat, stopped it altogether, and pivoted his seat. "I thought we were alone." His pointed glance at the spot she'd indicated spoke volumes.

Alira sighed. She shouldn't have spoken aloud to her Companion. But she also shouldn't keep secrets from Botha. How could she explain?

"You know that my people have many gifts not available to humans. Healing, shifting, that sort of thing."

"Yes," he said.

"Those come about through symbiosis with a tiny organism we call the Iri that lived in the rock walls of our temple and training caverns. The interaction causes special crystals to grow—"

A glimmer of understanding dawned in his expression. "The blue stones Thrace sent with you."

"Yes. We call them irolium. They are responsible for our gifts. Without them, we lose our special abilities. All unammi have access to this."

"Do all unammi speak to invisible friends?"

"No. That's my own specialty. You already know, Na'apa, that I am…" She paused to choose the right words. "…different from others of my people."

"Yes."

"One of those differences makes me able to communicate with the tiny organisms that create the blue stones."

A slight wrinkle furrowed his brow. "But we are not in your temple."

"No. We aren't." She stared at him, willing him to understand.

He blinked at her. "They are here? On the boat with us now?"

She grimaced at her Companion, whose form began to shift. "This is your fault. You need to work on your timing."

Her focus swung to Botha, who seemed to be watching her with care. She stared through the windows of the boat's cabin. They were surrounded by water. If she lost control out here, he might be forced to hurt her to save himself. Given what he must've seen while she was possessed by the voices, she understood his fear.

"I'm still patched, Na'apa. I promise. But this is difficult to explain to someone outside my own people." She took a breath. "The Iri are not here on the boat. But they are not entirely of this world. A part of them, their spirit, you might say, comes from outside our world. That part of them acts as a communal organism. They all act and think and present as one. Since I can communicate with them, or more like they can communicate with *me*, they can become visible to me wherever I am." She waved in her Companion's direction. "You don't see them, I know, but they're standing right there."

Botha shot a quick look toward the rear of the boat, then to her, concern written in every line across his skin. He didn't yet believe her.

She turned an exasperated frown on her Companion. "Don't just stand there. Tell me something that will convince him."

Its silence held while It shifted through its forms and settled on the human face of Elisul. "Ask him why he is afraid of the water."

Alira whirled and gaped at Botha. "You're afraid of the water?"

Color drained from Botha's cheeks. He lurched to his feet so fast he collided with the ceiling of the compartment. He flinched and sucked air through his teeth before he gaped at her, his lips parted. For once, he had nothing to say.

"Elisul says to ask you why."

Botha peered out the window. He rubbed his close-shorn scalp, then covered his mouth as if he feared what might come out. Long moments passed while he digested this revelation. At last, his green gaze found her face.

"Four summers into my life I fell from a platform in my village. The tide was high, nearly at flood, three fingers below the deck. I died that day. Six people fought to revive me." He stared at the floor a moment. "I wanted to never go near the water again."

Alira realized she was leaning forward, hanging on his words. "But you love the water."

"Now, yes." He straightened, rubbed his head. "But the tide is a fickle lover who will caress you one moment and kill you the next. Fear is a healthy response to such a one, is it not? I love her no less."

"I would never have known."

He shrugged. "My fourth summer was many years ago. That river's course has shifted." He gestured. "Your friends told you my secret?"

"Yes," she said.

"They are here still?"

"Yes."

"Do they have a face you can show me?"

Her Companion settled into Elisul's form with a nod.

"Elisul says it's okay." She made a little "turn around" motion, and Botha gave her some privacy. She didn't want him to see her shift. Would he be horrified? Disgusted? Frightened? Not a risk she wanted to take.

She stretched her body to Elisul's height, pumped up the musculature in arms, chest, and legs. Male genitalia bulged in the space between his legs, and a tickle ran across his scalp as coppery waves of hair sprouted and hung longer, longer, to the middle of his back. Eyes shifted into a green two shades lighter than Botha's emerald ones. Alira-as-Elisul took his time, getting it exactly right, but the clothing was of his own design. Those Alira's Companion wore in Its human form would stand out in this world.

"I'm ready."

Botha spun by slow degrees, as if not sure what he would find. When he saw her

him

Botha gasped. "My magtig…" he whispered. "That is you, Gelaboot?"

"Yes."

"This is your magical friends, too?"

Alira-as-Elisul laughed. "The Iri always appear to me as a single entity that I call my Companion. It has many faces, but this is the one I know best." He looked down at himself. "Maybe I'll stay in this form for our outing. I'd have to choose a human disguise to go to the market anyway."

"Shall I still call you Alira?"

"No. Not in front of others. But how about Eli?" he said. "Short for my Companion's nickname, Elisul." That would be easy enough to remember, since Alira had called her Companion "Eli" ever since she'd identified the Founder's face among its shifting multitudes.

"Eli." Botha still gaped. "You are a wonder."

"That may be." Eli grinned. "But if you still want to go to the market, we should go soon, before I lose my nerve."

"Then why are we bobbing about like a lazy bok?" He started the boat and pointed them toward their destination, then shone a wide, white smile on Eli. "Let us see how your patches hold today."

chapter 7

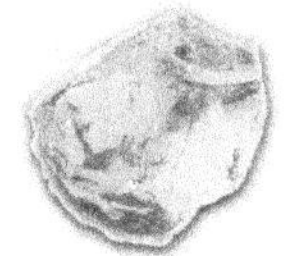

Haven, Danua
Clan Trader Base, MedFac 13

KNØFA PACED BESIDE THE BED, staring at the floor in front of his feet. Only four days since he'd set the surgeon to start the in vitro process with the squib's eggs. That would take weeks just to set up its reproductive system and ready the surrogates, not to mention the term of the pregnancies. They couldn't rush it even with tech, not without risk to the only test subject available. Okay. He could live with that enforced delay.

But the lab techs with the first squib skin samples had been working for eight days, and still hadn't found anything he could use. He'd even tried again three days ago. That time he'd dug a little deeper, into the meat of the squib's leg. Still nothing. What was taking so long?

"I'm not convinced they're doing their best." Knøfa scratched his beard. "But I can't tell what they're thinking. Not like you could." He paused to regard his prone admiral. All their medical equipment and knowledge, yet she still lay connected to life by the thin spans of tubes. Automated machines carried away her waste. The silver had taken over most of her hair, though its shine had long since fled. Flesh on her neck and arms sagged. The green of her eyes had taken on a sickly gray-green hue. Their color reminded him of that fungus he'd sometimes found on spoiled food. Why wouldn't she look at him?

"I wish I could take you to the lab and show you what I mean." Of course, then the techs might let slip about the egg-harvesting process. That would not do. He didn't want to tell Tsurin what he'd done. Not yet. She might call a halt to his plan before they could see whether it produced usable results.

He resumed his trek beside the bed. Tsurin's grasp of those on her crew, her uncanny ability to read their expressions and body language, to know the right words to encourage or chastise them, comfort them or make them do what she wanted them to, seemed magical now. She'd tried to teach that skill to him, along with all her other training throughout his life. He'd managed to grasp a few small things about the art of people-reading, based on details that didn't vary. Like the unmistakable signs of fear.

But people displayed their emotions in so many differing ways, a plethora of facial twists and contortions. One person's concern was never conveyed in the same way as another's. A furrowed brow, squint, or tense shoulders could mean any number of things. When you combined all those tiny little clues into a confusing jumble, he could never make sense of them. How was he supposed to remember and interpret those myriad combinations when he had trouble enough deciphering the basics?

Frustration rose in his chest like the afterburn of a bad psuka bean dinner. Tsurin tried to convince him from the beginning that he could learn to be like everyone else, just another crewman in the Clan. He'd tried. Oh, how hard he'd tried. He'd followed every exercise she gave him, took every test, listened to every lesson, endured every price for the times his anger took over and he stepped over the line. He'd managed, to a degree, to bring himself under control, but Tsurin was wrong. He would always be different from his crewmates.

But why? Yes, Tsurin had him evaluated. Yes, there was a clinical name for it. Yes, he'd done the research and understood it as well as anyone else. Yes, doctors pointed out valid possibilities for why he got confused sometimes, or why he felt no strong emotion other than occasional anger. Tsurin had asked, but none of the doctors could say for certain whether it was genetic, or due to something that happened before she took him into her care. One thing they all agreed on—they knew of no "cure."

Knøfa had heard it all, numerous times, and didn't buy it. Medical miracles had been taking place for generations, so why couldn't the doctors fix him?

Rage surged through his veins, its mood as chilling as the rapid advance of winter. Its brewing tempest drew a shadow across the light around him and narrowed his focus to a small window of vision.

"Why can't I read them like you did?" he rumbled, his voice growing louder as he spoke. "I've worked hard to master that skill. I should be able to do it by now." He pounded the side of his skull like he could shake loose something that had gotten stuck. "What's wrong with me?"

A wayward step brought his knee into sharp contact with the visitor chair, and he sent it clattering across the floor with a savage kick. It landed upside down, and he snatched it from the floor and pulled its parts one from the other, growling, until nothing remained but useless hardware fit only for recycling.

Heavy thumping in his chest brought him back to the moment. The sight of the demolished chair made him stop and remember where he was. Tsurin's past lessons whispered through his memory, and he forced himself to practice the calming exercise she had taught him.

Slow, even, deep breaths. In and count, one, two, three, four.

Hold and one, two, three, four.

Out and one, two, three, four.

Hold and one, two, three, four…repeat.

Repeat.

Repeat.

When he could think straight, he pushed the bits out of the way and tried to remember destroying it. "I want you to hear it from me first," he said over his shoulder. "I've accepted the role of admiral—just until you're on your feet—and I appointed Michael Trask as my interim second. I know you trust him." He pointed at the bed. "And if you do, then so do I."

He waited, as always, for her to respond, then paced to her side. That little scar near her hairline on the left side of her forehead stood out. She'd told him it came from a struggle with a john in the pleasure house when she was nineteen, before she joined the Clan. The laugh lines around her eyes and mouth had deepened in the last two months, even though she hadn't told a single bad joke. If she told him one right now, no matter how awful it was, he would laugh.

His fingers, lying on the bed, drew into a meaty fist, pulling and twisting the sheets into a bunch around his hand. Why didn't she wake up?

"Did I mention that the squib heals in seconds? Well, sometimes it's minutes, depending on the injury. Can't regrow its parts though. I checked." He released the sheet. "Don't worry. I only took the one digit. It can still manage its food and what little activity it can muster in the brig."

No reaction from Tsurin. Knøfa frowned.

"We performed a simple exploratory and ran it through the scanners. Its internals are mostly like ours, but it has a few organs we don't. Structural imaging neuroscans showed lumpy nodules nested around the brain stem, but we haven't yet run a functional image. We always have to sedate it before we work because if it can see us, it can affect us somehow. We haven't figured that out yet. I've got a team working on a new lab in the medfac, one with a central chair, neuroimager, and other scanners that can be worked remotely without the subject being able to see the operators. Once that's complete, we'll be able to tell more." He paced the few steps to the foot of the bed. "This squib is the key to enhancing the Clan's profile. I know it." He spun and pointed at her. "You'll see I was right."

From this perspective, Tsurin's line of sight seemed to focus on a random point somewhere above him. An image of her towering over him that first day flashed through his mind. He'd come into the kitchen as he always did when rising. That morning, though, his mother and father were weeping, babbling to the strangers who held them motionless while Tsurin had questioned them. He'd waited in the hallway, watching while she lost patience and killed them both. Knøfa had seen them fall just as Tsurin turned. Her face had changed when she noticed him standing there, but he didn't know what it meant. He just knew he was hungry. Tsurin had taken slow steps toward him, towering above while he asked in his four-year-old voice who was going to make his breakfast now.

Knøfa scowled. In all the years since, he'd never known her to be weak. She wasn't weak now. Just broken. And broken things could be repaired. If her brain's connections to her body had been severed, as the med tech had explained, then he needed to figure out how the squib's healing process worked so he could initiate the process in Tsurin. She could then regrow those neural pathways and wake up on her own.

He inhaled, slow and even. "This is no different than any puzzle you ever gave me. I'll figure it out. You know I will. And when I do, I'll make you better. You just need to hang on a little longer."

chapter 8

New Canaan, Harajüd
<u>Consortium Trader Base, Admiral Baldric's Quarters</u>

GALEN LEANED OVER HIS LOOM, focused on the rhythm of his work. Distractions caused mistakes. Mistakes meant wasted hours, since he would need to pull out all his work and start over from the point of error. The last time he'd done that was two months ago, when Alira was on Zebalu under Bellamy's nose. His life had been nothing but distractions then. Not that it was much better now, but since that time his—rather, Admiral Baldric's—crew had grown more settled under the new command. Taking a few hours of down time to do something like this no longer felt like a huge risk to his security on the base. Weaving was almost spiritual for him. Working with his hands in this rhythmic way kept him centered. Relaxed. Sane.

When the comm chirped, he paused. "Who is it?"

TICS replied in a gender-neutral voice. "Spencer Kilbee."

"Accept. Voice only."

"Admiral," Kilbee said. "We need to meet. In person. I can come to you, if you have a few minutes?"

"It's important?"

"Yes. And I'm not alone. I know it's your leisure time, but you'll want to meet this guest, preferably in your quarters, apart from crowds or cameras. We're nearby."

"Very well. I'll have the gate send you through when you arrive."

"Acknowledged. Be there in ten."

Galen sent a verbal order to the gate and bent to his loom. For a while, his mind flowed in rhythm with the shuttle. He'd tried a new incense today, one not quite so intense as before. Not similar to muñise resin at all, but more grounded, like the smell of moist soil or humus in the Bindhu retreat's garden. He'd considered bringing in a pot of growing things to his quarters, something that flowered maybe, just for the novelty of it. But from what he could tell, those kinds of lifeforms required a great deal of care. He wasn't ready to commit to it, then fail to meet all its needs.

Like he'd failed Alira.

Before he could sink into that self-defeating mood, the comm chirped once more. Galen heaved a sigh and straightened at the loom. "Who is it this time?"

"Adjutant Andrea Sweeney."

"Very well, voice only. Receive."

Her voice came on at once. "Sorry to disturb you, ma'am, but you have an incoming communique from Chairman Roucharde. I know you've been hoping he would respond. Should I tell him you're busy? Or put him through?"

Finally.

Galen spoke in Thrace's voice. "Give me two minutes, Andrea, then put him through."

"Will do."

Galen fastened his work where he'd left off and laid the shuttle aside before moving into the main room, morphing as he went. "TICS, lower flute volume by twenty percent. Receive next incoming comm in main room." Music dropped to a pleasant background trill, too soft to interfere in a conversation.

The comm chirped, then Chairman Roucharde appeared in the corner. "Admiral Baldric, thank you for taking my communique. I know we haven't yet been formally introduced."

"You need no introduction with me, Mr. Chairman. Chief Downing speaks very highly of you. How can I help?"

Roucharde grinned. "I wanted to personally thank you for the delightful gift. I was quite surprised, and grateful. How did you guess I have a fondness for mead?"

Thrace laughed. "I admit to cheating. I wanted to gift you with something you would actually like, so I asked Chief Downing." It had taken three beers, but he finally divulged this small bit of intel, that a special gift would soften Logan's attitude toward the Consortium's new leadership. Finding and *purchasing* the mead, however, had taken a bit more finesse. "I take it the package arrived intact?"

"Yes, less than an hour ago." Roucharde held a bottle to one side with great care as if afraid it might shatter under his very nose. He gazed at it like the prize it was. "Apple Blossom Meadery has always produced my favorite wines, but Honey'd Spiced Apple is the best of the lot, and this particular batch marked the peak of their production for at least the last ten years." He beamed at her. "How did you manage to find a whole case? I thought the last bottle was long gone!"

Thrace gave him a small, secret smile. "Come now, Chairman Roucharde. You can't expect me to unveil my mysteries in our first meeting. I only hope it will help to open the door between your office and mine. I look forward to working on more friendly terms with Harajüd House Unlimited."

Logan put the bottle down gently. "That's my hope as well. I trust you'll join me for a glass of this delicacy in the near future?"

"Thank you. I'd be glad to join you for a visit, but I don't consume alcohol. Perhaps you could offer tea, instead?"

"I think that can be arranged."

The door chimed.

"Very good. I'm glad you like the gift. I'll have my adjutant contact your staff to set up a time for our visit. Now if you'll excuse me, there is another matter that requires my attention. Be well."

She signed off and called out. "Come."

The door opened to admit Kilbee and a man she'd never seen. Thrace could see security outside the door. They were taking no chances with the safety of their new admiral. Good.

"Mr. Kilbee, how can I help you and your guest?"

"Are we as safe here as before?" Kilbee murmured. "Are your quarters secure, ma'am?"

"Yes." Thrace looked from Kilbee to the stranger and back. "Why?"

"Because our friend isn't quite accustomed to wearing this persona yet." Kilbee shifted to Tiral as he turned to the stranger, who'd also begun to morph. The unammi who stood beside him afterward flashed a confused tangle of teal, blue, and lavender with spots of white. "This is Betron. You might want to hear what he has to say."

Thrace's form flowed into Galen's natural state, and he led them to a pile of cushions, taking one for himself. "Please sit. I'm listening, Betron."

The guest lowered himself to the floor with a frown. "I'm afraid it isn't good news. The council is pressuring the remaining survivors with more stringent requirements than ever. I'd heard rumors that they were going to relax some of our strictures, be more accepting of new ways and ideas. And to some degree, they did." His skin flushed blue with small yellow spots. "What few younglings we still have are being introduced to multiple disciplines, as always, so that they can choose wisely when their time comes. But now the frem are also being allowed to do so. The council's grudging toleration of that change makes it awkward, though. Some of the frem avoid the extra training so they won't alienate the councilors."

"But not all of the frem are unhappy about it?" Galen asked.

"No. Many are excited to learn something outside their own areas. It's interesting. It's new. It's a distraction from the current hardships and challenges of our new world."

This was surprising. He never would've expected the frem to enjoy learning outside their own guilds' parameters. That much was good news.

"But…" he prompted.

"Everything else is tighter than before. It's as if they want us to behave the way we did before the humans destroyed our city. Before everything changed." Betron leaned forward. "No, it's worse than that, because they want to restrict us even more than before."

Galen squinted at him. "Can you give me an example?"

"For one thing, we aren't allowed to discuss the Fall of Iridos. Or any of the outcasts or mitigants who've gone to the outpost. Their names are anathema."

"Tell him the rest," Tiral urged.

Betron's colors shifted to lavender, streaked with red. "When I objected in an open session to the council's decision to censor our speech, they put me on notice. Rakalesh herself told me that we were too vulnerable to allow dissension to take root. That I should follow their guidance, as the unammi have always done, and do what was best for the whole." He huffed, his shoulders shaking. "I had no doubt what that meant. Stay quiet or we will force the issue."

Galen frowned. "She said this to you in private?"

Betron shook his head. "She said it in front of everyone. Made me an example." He paused, staring at the floor between them. "When the news reached us half a season later about Alira's breakdown, the council reported it to us in an open meeting. They said ugly things, claimed she'd always been unstable, said they should have mitigated her when they had the chance, and that she was no longer one of us."

"Is the entire council unified in this new direction?" Galen asked.

"I don't have the council's ear, so I can't be sure." Betron's features twisted, mirroring the uncertainty displayed across his skin. "But I think Yoloron, at least, disagrees. There was some talk to indicate she had defended Alira in their deliberations. And despite the dutiful green in her skin during that open council session, it seemed to me that she was struggling to stay on the path defined by the louder voices. Regardless, the council's overall stance was firm. They declared Alira a criminal, and forbade anyone to speak of her, even to say her name."

No surprise there. After the way she'd almost fallen to the harvesting malady, and her refusal to submit to the council's demands for genetic samples and the holovids of her unammi harvests, he at least understood the reasons for their antipathy. But it was more than that. Rakalesh had never liked Alira. Nor had Dyson. Alira's willing, almost eager, divergence from her people must have made them feel justified in their judgment of her. Everything that happened afterward was a bonus for them, a reason they could point at her and say, "See? We were right all along."

Still, it would've been hard for some of the survivors to hear. Harder yet to obey. "How did the people react to that?" he said.

Betron sat up straight, his gaze boring into Galen's. "I don't know about everyone else," he said. "But I stood up and spoke in her favor. Asked those who are supposed to be leading us with wisdom and experience how they could condemn the person who'd given up everything she loved—her friends, her people, her world—and sacrificed her own sanity, maybe her life, so that we would be safe. We should make her a hero, I said. And then…" Betron's jaw worked. "Then I spoke her name. Over and over, like a chant, and I tried to rally those around me to do the same."

Galen found that he had covered his mouth. He spoke between his fingers. "Did they?"

"Huh." Betron picked at a thread on his cushion. "I could see a lot of vacillation in the dermal displays, those who aren't sure what the right thing is. But only two others stood up for her. After all she did for us." His face closed, grew hard. "It isn't right. Them trying to squash us into meek servile followers. I won't do it. Not any longer."

"What did the council do?" Galen asked, breathless.

"They mitigated me. Right then. Rakalesh called the remaining healers forward and they mitigated all three who spoke her name, right there in session with everyone watching."

Horror splashed Galen with white blotches that shifted and glowed. Bad enough that they would do such a thing at all, but to do it in front of everyone! Rakalesh had lost all perspective. For her, it seemed, things were no longer a matter of what might be best for the people, but that the survivors fit themselves into her version of right and wrong. Their society would not last long under a rule such as that, and they could not afford to split.

"That must have been harrowing."

Betron shuddered. "It was."

"Do you want to tell me about it?"

"No."

"I understand," Galen said. "But you're here now. I take it the treatment didn't last?"

"That's right." Betron's expression, though grim, showed triumph. "And as soon as I was in full control of my own mind again, I told everyone who would listen about the treatment, how it felt, how I had overcome it, how they, too, could speak their truths and come away whole. How if enough of us spoke up, we could change things for the better."

Galen closed his eyes. "Oh, Betron."

"I refuse to let them win by those sorts of methods. We deserve to be heard. Our society needs to change. Rakalesh knows that. So does Dyson. They all do. But letting go of what they know, abandoning the old ways, is as desirable to them as a blind leap into the void. Their fear hinders all of us. We can't continue in that way." Red speckles skittered across his skin. "Someone will need to relent, and it isn't going to be me. I'll stand for Alira, and for the best hope for our people. And if that means leaving the new city and its infuriating council, then so be it."

Alira would like this person. "I take it you were outcast."

Tiral spoke. "He was sent to the lunar base with the next genetics team rotation, with instructions to never return. But we're running out of work for the outcasts and mitigants we already have. And even with a shield, if we keep activating larger segments of that base, it may bleed through. If anyone comes near, they could see."

Alira had always assured Galen that was an empty fear, humans would never venture so close to Earth. And that world *was* outside the normal travel range for the colonies. But Galen wasn't convinced, and neither was Tiral, apparently. The two of them had spent far more time among humans than Alira. They knew the curious nature of these aliens, and had no doubt that, sooner or later, humans would approach Earth. The unammi would not be safe there forever.

At this point, too, how long would it be before Rakalesh cut the outcasts off entirely, refused them not only a landing on Earth, but access to the irolium? What better way to control their people than to threaten their supply of the one essential thing for continued unammi existence? He was surprised she hadn't done it already.

"Tiral, in all those worlds the pilots lined up as potential homes for the survivors after the attack on Iridos, were there any that would've made a perfect fit for the Iri, but not for the unammi?"

"Of course," Tiral said. "Why?"

"See if you can barter with Rakalesh for some of the seedstones from our migration," Galen said. "Let's see if we can start our own supply of irolium, outside of Rakalesh's control." It would be a long shot, since the unammi always theorized it was the symbiosis between the races that caused growth of the irolium. But it was worth a try.

"She isn't likely to agree to much of anything with us."

"Then try to reach Yoloron." Galen hated the words as soon as they emerged from his throat. "Get her aside if you can or find someone who can take her a message. Tell her you need a couple of the stones. If she asks why, tell her that given the council's direction of late, it's time we non-conformists started making an alternative sustainability plan. I think she'll know exactly what you mean."

Tiral's skin blotched with sudden patches of blue and purple. Galen loathed putting his friend in this position. Rakalesh was Tiral's ama. It would not be easy for him to go against her in this blatant a fashion.

But it was worse than just asking a friend to do a hard thing. If this plan worked, and Yoloron cooperated without telling Rakalesh what she'd done, her actions would eventually be discovered. That would irreparably divide the council, and it would be Galen's fault. What had begun as a division based on ideas for a better path forward would end on a political split based on betrayal fomented by him.

Galen gritted his teeth. He hadn't asked to be put in this position. But he couldn't stand by and allow the council's reckless decisions to destroy the unammi altogether. Some, at least, might live on, *if* he acted now.

"I know this is a hard task, my friend." Galen stared at Tira, and offered a hand. "But will you do it?"

Tiral swallowed hard, and didn't speak for a long time. At last, he took Galen's hand and nodded.

"Thank you. In the meantime," Galen gestured at Betron, "we should bring our new ally up to speed on life in human colonies. Take him to the outpost for now and begin his lessons. If he's going to live on a colony world, he'll need to know how to act."

chapter 9

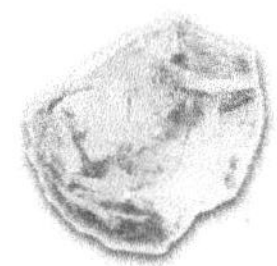

<u>Verregaandor, Bejami</u>

MOUNTAINS FILLED THE BACKDROP IN Eli's view when they stepped off the boat at the pier. In the shadow of those massive peaks squatted a village that served as a market center for the whole region. Every slip held a boat, while new arrivals clamored for the next open spot. Humans departing their watercraft made quick progress down the docks to join those already crowding the street.

Eli hesitated, focusing on the milling crowd. "What if something happens?"

Botha swept his hands out to the side. "Something always does. But until you jump in the water, you cannot learn to swim."

Ironic, Botha offering that platitude, and Eli smirked at him before anxiety turned his attention to the humans once more. Alira's Companion rustled in his mind, but did not make an appearance.

"We came before, *Eli*," Botha said, emphasizing the name of Alira's newest human persona. "You did well. You will be stronger today."

"That time we didn't stay long," Eli murmured. "This time you want to shop. Barter. Talk to people."

"We need supplies." Botha touched Eli's shoulder. "You are stronger than you think, Gelaboot. Your patches will hold."

"If someone dies in the market…" Eli shot Botha a quick look. "I don't intend to hurt anyone. But if someone dies, even of natural causes, I might harvest them. Neither of us could stop it. And people would see." Like when Alira had hidden behind Bellamy's divan. Like how the harvest had slammed into her with the force of a speeding skimmer. A shudder ran through him, chilling his skin even further.

Botha peered at Eli. "People die all the time. On Haradhalen, Mandoslóna, all over Bejami. On all the worlds. How is it that you do not take all their spirits?"

"I'm not sure." Absorbing a whole world of voices… She shuddered. That would be the stuff of nightmares. "Maybe they were too far away."

"How far is 'too far'?"

Eli blinked. He hadn't considered that. All his prior harvests had been practically at his feet. He shrugged. "I don't know."

"And so you will keep a world between you and them," he gestured at the market, "out of fear?"

How to answer that? It didn't matter what she did or what face she wore. As long as she lived, Alira risked another harvest.

"Today, it will be hard." Botha lifted a crate from one of the seats. "Next week, it will be no easier. Wait a year, and you will always find a reason to remain apart from others. I think even your people would not be happy living alone for long. Yes?" Botha wagged his head from side to side. "It is true you have shown me your difference from them but," he leaned close to Eli's ear, "unless you so love Onlebaar you never want to leave its shores, you must take this step." He straightened and stepped onto the pier. "I will leave you to decide."

He winked and walked away, his lanky form moving in the direction of the crowded market, a box of preserved fish under one arm.

"Dammit," Eli muttered. He took one step in that direction when Botha's voice drifted over his shoulder.

"Don't forget the other crate."

Eli grumbled, his jaw tight, and ducked inside the cabin for the other box. This one held dried fruit. He had no idea where Botha had gotten it. Food and supplies just showed up in their hab every few days. Probably Bregaina or Syndicate contacts made regular drops but he'd not asked. He caught up with Botha and walked beside him.

"You're right. I need to do this."

"I know."

Eli glared at him a moment, then focused on the imminent challenge before him.

Inside the market, booths lined both sides of the dirt walkways, hard-packed from the frequent passage of so many feet. Row after row of them stretched inland toward the village proper. Woodsmoke, along with aromas of cooking fish, spicy peppers, curing meat, and unwashed bodies assaulted Eli's nostrils. People on all sides shouted, haggled, laughed, called to one another, and his harvests stirred, murmured.

He made a fist

shut up

while he struggled to calm himself. It wasn't this busy the last time they'd come.

"Loud, isn't it?" Botha took in their surroundings, then stared into Eli's eyes. "Remember to listen for what you can't hear."

The man wanted Eli to meditate *here*? Before he could object, Botha winked.

"The water around the boat is not always calm, Gelaboot. Sometimes peace must come from you." He pointed at Eli and walked off toward a booth.

Eli watched him go. Listen for what you can't hear…could he do it? Meditate here in a crowd? Without losing his form and drawing all manner of unwanted excitement?

He stumbled forward in the direction of Botha's wake and tried to do as his teacher suggested. He listened. Not to the raised voices or scrabbling feet or scraping and clanging that filled his ears but for the silence *between* the sounds

there's no silence here

between *all* sounds, those from without or within. He frowned, straining with the effort, reaching for success as if it were a physical prize he could grasp with his fingers. Surrounding noises took on a brassy tone, echoing in his mind and falling, falling into gray silence, and—

"Gelaboot."

He jumped at the sound of Botha's voice, snapping out of his own thoughts and into the noisy market.

Botha stared at him, his brow creased. "So, you can meditate in a crowd after all, eh? That, then is a success. But such a deep dive here in the market is unwise, my friend. The waters here teem with predators." He touched Eli's back and guided him forward. "Come. Let me teach you how to barter."

chapter 10

Haven, Danua
<u>Clan Trader Base, MedFac 6</u>

ON THE OTHER SIDE OF the clear pane, two Clan surgeons stood across from one another at the table where the squib lay under heavy sedation. The skin of its chest and belly had been pinned open, same as the last few exploratories they'd done.

Most of the squib's organs had been lifted and examined, poked and prodded by now. In the observer segment of the theater, Knøfa clamped his teeth together to keep from pushing the surgeons to do something different, move faster, take chances. The tests they'd run so far offered no concrete answers, but there was only so much they could do before stress on the patient provoked her life sign readings into erratic patterns, which happened faster now than it had before.

Without a replacement subject, it probably wasn't wise to take chances with trial and error.

Med techs and physicians had theorized that the healing was a dermal-level mechanism, though they had not yet unraveled its mysteries.

The shapeshifting and color changes were likely associated with those organs beneath the brain. One said it seemed likely that the dermal patterns were triggered by the portions of the brain that controlled the squib's emotions. Postulation was all well and good. But without proof, none of it was worth a single credit for the Clan. He was failing at his assignment, the last one given to him by his admiral.

Maybe once they could run waking neuroscans on the prisoner, they'd get clinical evidence of where, exactly these special abilities originated in the body or brain. At least that would help to guide the surgeons' blades when they performed an exploratory on the squib's brain. That was still at some nebulous point in the future. Once they commenced cutting on that delicate tissue, the rest might shut down. As much as he wanted answers, they had no choice but to save that organ for last.

Meanwhile, Tsurin slid farther away by the day, as did his patience with this squib, the med techs, and this whole damned situation.

A loud expletive from one of the surgeons caught Knøfa's attention in time to see the squib's body seizing on the table. "What's going on in there?"

Both doctors worked over the body. One held it down while the other unpinned the flaps of skin. Neither responded.

Knøfa bellowed and slammed his fist against the plaz. "*Answer me!*"

The surgeon working the patient's skin spun sideways, hands still on the squib, and glared over his shoulder. "Sir, with all due respect, I can explain what's happening, or I can save the patient. I can't do both."

Knøfa's jaw went slack, then clenched. "Save it."

The surgeon returned to his work, but the squib's legs began to spasm. The second doctor shouted for assistance, and another med tech rushed into the room with a hypo. She held it to the squib's arm where it hissed its load into the seizing body. Within seconds, the patient quieted. One of the doctors smoothed the sliced skin into place and pulled back to wait for it to close. A minute later, they both hunched forward, peering down at the squib.

"What's wrong?" Knøfa said.

The lead medic shook his head. "Her incisions aren't closing like they did before."

"Why not?"

The doctor swung around to give Knøfa a strange look.

What did that mean?

"I don't know, sir," the doctor said. "But I'm going to have to suture it."

Knøfa gestured for them to get on with it, then paced in front of the window, checking every few seconds to make sure they were doing their jobs. So many things depended on this squib.

When they finished, both surgeons stumbled away from the table, huge wet spots under the arms of their surgical scrubs. One's hair covering was soaked with sweat. He wiped his face with a forearm.

"She almost died, sir."

"Why?"

The surgeon struggled to keep his countenance from changing. Knøfa squinted at the man, trying to understand.

"Because, sir, repeatedly cutting it open is traumatic. Invasive. Unless there's good medical reason to do so, it's inadvisable."

"I'm aware." Did the man think he was stupid? "But if we're going to trace its unique biological processes, it's unavoidable. You're one of the best surgeons on Danua. In the colonies overall. This shouldn't be beyond your skill."

The doctor pulled off his hair covering. "I appreciate your faith in me, sir, but it isn't just the trauma of the surgeries. She's not healing as fast now. Those colors in her skin are dimmer, slower to react." He rested against the counter. "I don't know what's changed to make this so. It could be the fertility drugs, or the human hormones we're giving her. Even the sedatives could be damaging her physiology. I know I've said it before, but we know far too little about this species, medically speaking, to understand what we've seen thus far. I'm compiling notes and results from our experiments, as you instructed. But as of now, they mean very little."

"Did you learn anything new in this surgery?"

The surgeon huffed. "No, sir."

Knøfa grunted and stood with arms akimbo. The doctor was right. The squib's color, mostly white at the moment, appeared dull. Muted. Knøfa frowned. If he was right that those dermal displays were connected to the squib's emotions, he'd probably find it easier to read a squib's emotional manifestations than those found on human faces. Ironic. "It's still alive?"

"Yes, sir. For now. I suggest we take a break. Give her a few days to recover."

Knøfa sighed. "Fine. Meanwhile, I want to be clear, doctor. That squib is a key element in our ability to help the admiral. It's also fundamental to the Clan's future competition in the colonial market. Not just with the other factions, but with the corpgovs. If anyone else finds out they can do these things, and reaches those answers before we do, this all will be for nothing. Do you understand the importance of this matter?"

"Yes. I do, sir."

Tsurin would tell him to go easy on the doctor, but she wasn't here. Knøfa was. "So, here's what I want from you. Give the squib a week's rest from surgical procedures. You and the remainder of your team start researching the latest developments in genetic development, neuroscience, and anything else that'll help you to solve this mystery. The next time the squib comes under your knife, I'm going to want some answers."

The faded body on the table seemed to be half-dead. Without that squib, they had no chance of healing Tsurin, and the very simple task she'd set before him prior to her accident would be a lost cause. Because none of the other ideas he'd put forth—not the ones she approved, anyway— would bring the Clan to success that came within a light year of this kind of potential. That squib had to survive.

Maybe some added incentive would help the doctor be more vigilant. Focused. He locked eyes with the lead surgeon. "Take note, doctor. This is the only squib we have. Obtaining another would be problematic. Until we can harvest its eggs and produce additional subjects, I need it alive. Therefore, that patient's health status is now tied to your own. Understood?"

The surgeon sagged, then nodded.

chapter 11

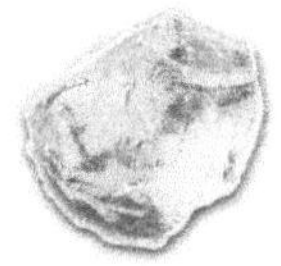

Tuneloras, Saacharis
<u>Syndicate Trader Base, Admiral Rizzo's Office</u>

BAILEY ENTERED AT RIZZO'S CALL. "I have those plans you wanted." She pulled up the file on her TICS pad and threw it to the holoprojection above the desk.

Rizzo stood and inspected the design. "You examined it for weaknesses?"

"Yes, but my view isn't as experienced as yours, ma'am. Most of it seems serviceable enough. I do see one problem." She pinched the projection, pulled it out to either side to expand the magnification, and pointed. "See this connection? I suspect it's too delicate a join between the chambers. If it breaks, leaks would ensue. With a solid or non-hazardous cargo, that would present a minor inconvenience, simple enough to repair. But if it's toxic or could potentially create a toxin by combining with another substance in the adjoining holds, the whole crew could be endangered. If it happened in a port…" She left the rest unsaid.

Rizzo expanded the design layout further. Bailey's point was valid. The join needed to be reinforced. "Good catch." She shrank the expansion to its normal size and scanned the blueprint. Overall, it was a good design. Sleek, efficient. "Where is the client's list of requirements?" She reached for Bailey's pad.

Bailey touched the screen, then passed it to her.

The TICS chittered. "Incoming voice communique."

"Receive," Rizzo said, still skimming the notes on Bailey's pad.

"Admiral," a breathless voice said, "Knøfa has an unammi prisoner."

Rizzo's gaze jerked up to stare straight at Bailey, who gaped in shock.

"I don't know where he got it, ma'am, or how long it's been there, but I think he's using it like a lab animal."

Bailey paled.

Rizzo pressed her lips together. She should've asked for a point of origin before playing it in Bailey's presence, damn it.

"I'll send more when I can."

And the comm ended.

The silence that followed made Rizzo's ears ring.

"But I thought there were no survivors! How…" Bailey fumbled over her words.

Rizzo frowned. "It's probably a pilot who's been in hiding."

"Why would Knøfa do such a thing?" Bailey's features pinched, as if she was trying to find logic in anything that madman did. "He has to know that if any of the colonial governments find out he's imprisoned an Iridosian pilot, the Clan will be forfeit. Danua Textiles has too much to lose to let him escape charges for that."

Bailey didn't yet know the half of this mess. "The Clan's continued operation is the least of my worries right now." Rizzo grimaced. "Get my ship ready."

"You aren't going after Knøfa, ma'am?" Bailey's eyes still showed their whites. "Or thinking of forming a rescue attempt? Not on the Clan base?"

If only she could do that. But going against another admiral on their faction's home base would be suicide. This unfortunate unammi was beyond her grasp. "No."

Her second calmed a bit. "Estimated departure?"

"Immediate."

"Copy that." Bailey left the room.

"TICS," Rizzo said, "record communique for Admiral Thrace Baldric, Harajüd Consortium. Urgent news for you and the baba. No comms. Meet me at the landport on Botha's world, in front of jumper rental, in three days." She paused. "We will go together to his camp, where I'll fill you both in. I leave it to your discretion as to whether you involve our mutual friend, once you hear what I have to say. Rizzo out."

She sent the comm, pulled the ship blueprint into a file and secured the display, then stepped into her private lift.

"Quarters." The lift started down.

It might be wise to keep a bag packed on an ongoing basis, as long as Alira and the unammi were a continued presence in her life. One part of Rizzo's mind hoped this would be the last time. But another part, a tiny piece she only reluctantly acknowledged, felt justified in her efforts to do what she could. In all humanity's reach since they went to the stars generations ago, the unammi were the only other sapient species they'd found. Isolationist though they were as a race, unammi individuals she'd encountered had all proved to be interesting beings, in possession of more integrity than most humans Rizzo had met. She'd been grateful to learn that Skalar's attempts at genocide had failed, even though she didn't know where the survivors now hid.

But if Knøfa had one in custody, then he was no doubt bringing Alira's greatest fears to reality. If he didn't already know of the unammi's secret gifts, he soon would. Rizzo could only hope that the one in his custody would die soon and that Knøfa wouldn't find the others.

The lift opened in her quarters, and she stalked into her bedroom to pack.

Whatever came of the Clan's prisoner, Baldric needed to know so that she could alert her own people.

The Clan contact's timing could've been better, but that was Rizzo's own carelessness. At least it was Bailey who overheard, and not someone else. Bailey was trustworthy. She would not speak of what she'd heard, but she also wouldn't let it go or forget it. This would probably come back to bite Rizzo later.

Either way, done was done. She had a much bigger emergency, and the faster she could get off-world, the faster she could deal with whatever came on Bregaina.

chapter 12

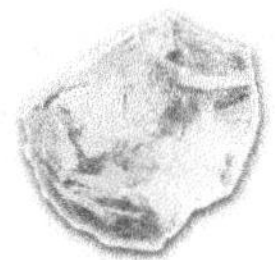

New Canaan, Harajüd
<u>Consortium Trader Base, Admiral Baldric's Quarters</u>

GALEN STUMBLED OUT OF BED and watched, half-awake at first, the message from Rizzo. Brief as it was, by its end, Galen stood wide awake and speckled with white. Rizzo did not strike him as the type of person to send a message like this lightly, so her implied urgency underscored the gravity of her news.

His fingers clasped one another as he stared into space in his sleeping quarters. He shouldn't leave. Mira wasn't ready to run this base by herself yet. But Galen couldn't ignore this message, either, not with so much balanced on the point of a pin.

"TICS, locate Captains Sa'abah and Cohen. Override privacy. Have them meet me in the landing bay at once. Comm the landing bay. Instruct them prep the *Nebula*."

He donned Thrace's face and scanned the suite for anything that needed attention before she could leave. The weaving project should be fine, but she would need a supply of irolium. In her sleeping quarters, she opened the safe and pulled out enough to last a week—plus some extra for Alira, in case her supply was low—placing the stones with care into a small case along with a few other essentials, then locked the vault once more. She gave the quarters a final glance for telltale clues that might hint at her true identity, then headed down to the landing bay, her mind racing.

Had something happened to Alira? No...surely Rizzo would have revealed that in some fashion. Botha? No, that would also involve Alira. Besides, Rizzo's message made it sound like it was something outside the two of them. What, then? The surviving unammi? Rizzo didn't know where they were, or where the outpost was, for that matter, unless...

A chill shot through Thrace. Had someone found the outpost, or the city? Or both? She covered her mouth, then immediately dropped her arm to her side lest someone see Admiral Baldric in a state of near panic. Until she knew what this was about, she should stay calm.

Easier to say than to do.

The lift door opened. Thrace cut a fast pace to the *Nebula,* which had first been Skalar's, then Alira's. Now, it belonged to Thrace, as much as any faction ship belonged to any admiral.

Mira and Sa'abah waited outside the hatch. She greeted them, indicated they should follow her inside, then stepped aboard. In control, she dropped her bag behind her seat and set up the parameters for flight, leaving out the destination just yet. That done, she turned to her officers.

"This is for your knowledge only. Do not share. Understood?"

"Of course, Admiral," said Sa'abah.

Mira's eyes went wide.

"I need to go offworld."

Sa'abah shifted on her feet. "Ma'am, is that wise at this point?"

"Probably not." Thrace scowled. "My meeting last week with Chairman Roucharde went well, so HHU is beginning to accept my presence. We might eventually have a friend there, but they won't yet step in to help us if something goes wrong. That's why I'm asking you to keep this quiet. I wouldn't go if it weren't urgent."

"What's going on, Admiral?" Mira asked.

"I'm not sure yet, but an ally has called for an in-person meeting," Thrace said. "I'm leaving you both in charge. You are to lead the faction *together* while I'm gone. Is that clear?"

Both women nodded, but Thrace felt Mira's hurt.

"Captain Cohen, I want you to understand something. This order has nothing whatsoever to do with my trust in you, or my faith in your abilities. The only reason I ask Captain Sa'abah to work with you as a team is that she has done it before and has a great deal more experience at running the base than you do, *thus far*. That will change, I've no doubt. But for the time being, you have a lot to learn. Sa'abah is a first-rate mentor. Listen to what she says, watch her example, but the two of you should make decisions together."

Mira's hurt feelings eased. "Understood, ma'am. How long will you be gone?"

Thrace sighed. "I don't know. But I'll be in touch when I'm on my way back." She looked from one to the other of them. "Any questions?"

"No, ma'am," Mira said.

"Good. Then I should be on my way. Close the hatch on your way out, if you would."

When they were gone, Thrace cleared her flight with base and planetary air control as if her planned itinerary was multifaceted. No one would question a change in direction with such a complicated flight plan. Moments later, she received a transfer signal for satellite tracking to ensure her path remained clear of collision potentials

She followed the set course for a time, then veered south and flew until she was past the constant trackers. Only then did she set her destination and jump to interstel.

Thrace shifted to Galen's form, his hands already gripping one another above the controls. Two and a half days before he would know what this was about. He could lose his entire mind with worry in that length of time.

chapter 13

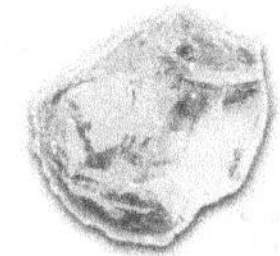

Onlebaar Island, Bejami

ALIRA FELT IT BEFORE THE shifting presence manifested behind her on the path she'd made through the thick, white-dusted undergrowth. She didn't feel the need to speak. A mellow silence followed her through the frosted lowland tangle, broken only by the natural sounds of the woodland. The light source she wore strapped around her head probably confused the wildlife. To them, this was the time of long nights, and dim days. Were they mystified at this minor miracle outside their norm?

The basket Botha had sent with her snagged on a prickly shrub. Alira stopped to free it from the foliage before picking a handful of its berries. Not too much, Botha had directed. Leave most for the animals, the birds, the insects. This is their home, not ours. We are guests. He had come with her last time, pointed out what was safe to eat, and what she should avoid, but she had wanted to be alone this time. It felt a bit like the windwalks she'd taken at home. What she wouldn't give for a rufesh or two right now!

Alira stopped and stood still, listening. Birds hooted, squawked, and trilled above and around her, but she'd not been able to match each sound with its maker yet. The breeze that filtered through the wood felt cold, but gentle, and she swayed with its passage, appreciating its touch on her cheeks. Something made a dry, rattling sound less than a meter distant. She pointed her light toward it. There, a large scaly insect balanced on its rear pairs of appendages and flapped wing-like protrusions, its forelegs stretched up and out. As she watched, it took clumsy flight across her line of sight, disappearing into the shadows to her right. The sound—had that been its wings?—followed it and soon stopped.

She grinned. So much life here, even in this cold place. Last time, she'd seen a small rodent-like animal that made her think of a fealle sprite, only much smaller. Long, legless creatures with scaly flesh and flicking tongues like the atlish—Botha called them snakes—also made a home here, though they didn't see those very often. Too cold for them now. Scaly insects, lumpier than the one that flew past, clung to the bark and made music by rubbing their legs together. Once, from up on the plateau's edge above the forest, she'd seen a furry bird with leathery wings that flew above and around the trees in quick, erratic paths. Botha said it was hunting.

"What do you think of this place, my friend?" she asked, still picking her way through the brush. It didn't answer, and she glanced back. When she did, the voices rose in a confusing jabber, like a bubble from beneath the water. Fear shot through her in white veins that splashed their own colors onto the vegetation near her face. Her breath jittered in her throat, which tightened and pushed out a squeak as the voices began to surface, their clamor squeezing her chest and widening her eyes.

In a second, her Companion stood before her as Elisul, Its form stable, Its face a blaze of clarity, Its presence releasing the band around her chest. But the voices clawed at her calm, and she forced herself to reach into her memories—*hers*, not *theirs*—for Botha's lessons. What was the first step in control? His voice rose above the others, though his was a memory, and not an intruder.

Look at what you can't see. Her physical gaze remained pinned on Elisul's face, yet she reached inward for the mental framework Na'apa had helped her build. Structures of light, energy channels, stood steady, a scaffold on which her growing sanity hung in trembling defiance of the voices. It was still there. The voices had not yet razed its support. A quivering sigh of relief escaped her lips, and the power of the clamor seemed a little less formidable.

What next? *Feel what you can't touch.* Alira gave a minimal nod, as if anyone would see or care or understand, and reached for the connection to her own life force. The flow of blood, the functioning of her body's parts, the processes taking place inside her at this moment. But strongest was the constant, subtle buzz of her pithasia, the eternal connection to Na'Staani that linked to the cells in living organisms. She brought the sensation forward in her consciousness and let it comfort and calm her.

The last part, the piece of her lesson that almost revealed her in the market, was *listen to what you can't hear.* Listen for the silences between the sounds. She relaxed, let the voices come as they wished, and focused her rapt attention to finding the minuscule gaps. There. The peace emanating from her own life force grew brighter, clearer, more pervasive, revealing the portions of the clamor that came from her own mind, and exposing those that did not belong. Alira listened to the silence, until the voices faded into the background, a low hum she could hear or ignore at her whim.

When it was done, she stood swaying, as she had before, the cold wind caressing her cheeks. Elisul awaited the return of her awareness, and she smiled up at It. This was the first time she'd managed the exercises and banished the voices without Botha's help. Maybe, she let herself believe, he'd been right. Maybe there was some hope for her after all.

chapter 14

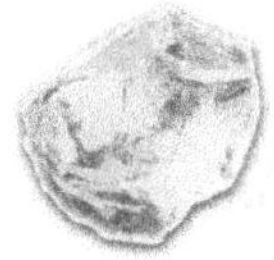

Haven, Danua
<u>Clan Trader Base, MedFac 6</u>

KNØFA ENTERED THE OBSERVATION ROOM, peering through the plaz and past the doctor in the examination room to the squib stretched out on the gurney. Its skin still appeared dimmer. Like the lights had gone out. "It doesn't seem any better today."

"No." The surgeon was already sweating. "I'm not sure she is, sir. I don't think she'll heal completely in our care. She isn't eating or even drinking fluids. I expect she's given up."

"Given up on what?" Knøfa frowned.

There was that weird look again. The doctor's face puckered, like he'd bitten into something sour.

"On living, sir. She has to know she's never leaving here alive, and these experiments can't be pleasant for her. I think she's willing herself to die, so her suffering will be over." He gestured at his patient. "The drugs and lack of sustenance are probably messing with her mental capacity, too, making it harder for her to cope."

"Put it on forced sustenance and fluids, effective immediately. Sedate it if necessary and feed it intravenously every few hours." Knøfa squinted at the doctor. "You remember what I said would happen if she dies?"

The surgeon sighed. "I do."

"Good," Knøfa said.

The door to the observation room slid aside to admit Trask. Knøfa acknowledged his second before turning to the doctor.

"What are we doing today?"

"We're going to try something new." The doctor's voice sounded brisk. Efficient. "I began to think about the layers of human skin, how different physiological mechanisms are sandwiched between them. We reexamined the skin samples you took early on. Its layers are different from those in our skin. Thinner. Not more delicate, but definitely more flexible, more puncture- and abrasion-resistant, like an ultra-fine surgical glove. This time, I want to try and dive into the dermis, one microlayer at a time. See if we can uncover anything we missed last time."

"Very well. Begin."

Projections of their work popped in above the table. Trask stepped closer to the plaz. "She's so small. Almost like a child."

Knøfa snorted. "Tsurin thought the same thing. That's how it fooled her. Don't fall for it. If the squib was awake, none of us would be safe."

"Of course, sir," Trask said. "I read the reports. No word yet on how it does that, I presume."

"Not yet." Knøfa grunted. "We'll figure it out. Once they get that new scanning lab complete, I want to send a human test subject in with it and watch what parts of the squib's brain light up while it's messing with them."

Trask crossed his arms. "Have you decided who the test subject will be?"

"Not yet." He wasn't ready to sacrifice his own people, not when he might still need them, and when Tsurin would be asking questions of his decisions once she got out of that bed. He'd already reached out to the new Cartel leader, Admiral Dupré, and established that they were, in fact, still in the slaving business and could provide for this need. He'd placed an order for a dozen females of breeding age, so they'd be ready for the surrogacy, assuming that came through. Maybe one of those would serve in this capacity, too. She didn't need a functioning brain to carry a fetus to term. "But that's at least a week away. Maybe more. We have time."

"Sir," the surgeon called. "I found something."

Knøfa looked at the projection. "Magnify. Three hundred percent."

The visual zoomed in to show minute, almost cell-sized nodules nested among other sub-dermal skin cells. Barely visible threads led from each one to interweave with others around them and other structures in the surrounding tissue, almost like a thin web of mycelia.

"I don't think that's something you'd find in human skin," Trask murmured.

Knøfa grunted. "What do you make of that, doctor?"

"I don't know, sir." The doctor peered through the magnifier at his work. "But I have to wonder if it's connected to her dermal colorations."

"There are nerve networks around them, yes?" Knøfa frowned. "To carry neural signals?"

"Of course."

If that was so, then maybe they weren't receiving a strong enough signal. That would explain the duller color. "Try hitting one of them with a minimal electric pulse."

Techs swung the equipment into place. The surgeon touched one of the probes to the exposed dermal structures.

The squib's whole arm flushed white, its skin webbed with bright veins that dimmed the moment the pulse was removed. The doctor repeated the charge three times, all with the same result.

Finally, a solid answer. Or at least a partial one. If he was right, those signals to activate the lights came from the squib's brain. Now they needed to learn which facet of its neurology determined emotions or emotional reactions to physical stimulus.

"I wonder," Trask said, almost as if he were talking to himself, "what evolutionary purpose that serves."

"It's not the first development of bioluminescence in lower animals," Knøfa said, "though I'm not familiar with any land mammals who display this characteristic. It's a type of communication. In this case, probably an indication of emotional status."

"Of course, sir." Trask cleared his throat. "But the Iridosians aren't animals. They're sentient. Sapient. We know they can speak. I've heard they are shrewd negotiators. They interact with the human colonies on a regular basis. Why would such a being require this sort of communication?"

"Just because they can talk doesn't mean they're intelligent," Knøfa said. Tsurin once told him about a bird kept as a pet in one of the pleasure houses, where the workers had trained it to speak. The bird would still eat its own shit if you mixed it with food.

He thought for a moment that Trask would say more, but the man held his peace.

"Doctor, vary the power levels in both voltage and amperage. See what that produces."

For the next fifteen minutes, the doctors experimented. The only color to emerge was the same white, though higher amperages made the arm glow brighter. At the high end of their test limit, the arm flickered. Trask retreated from the window, and the doctor reduced the power.

Knøfa shook his head. Maybe, as he'd postulated before, white indicated fear or pain. If so, then he'd been right. The colors must be tied to its emotions. Could also be hormones or neurochemical signals, both of which affected—or fed—its emotions. "How much longer before the squib's special lab will be finished?"

The doctor shrugged. "I haven't checked, sir. I've been focusing all my attention on these tests, and the research you assigned."

"Captain?" Knøfa asked Trask.

"I'll find out right now, sir. Will you excuse me?"

Knøfa waved, and Trask exited the room a little faster than seemed warranted. If only Tsurin was awake, he could ask her what that meant. She would know.

"Take that sample you have there off of her arm and see if you can still get the same electrical result," he told the doctor. "If so, try treating the sample with dopamine, serotonin, and epinephrine. See if that changes the result."

"Do you want to observe that process, sir?"

How many neurochemicals were there? Probably dozens. Which ones performed what tasks? "No. I'll leave you to it. Keep me informed."

Knøfa swept out into the corridor outside the medfac and touched his wristcom. "TICS, compile a list of all known human neurochemicals and what systems or functions they affect or control. Send to my office as soon as the file is completed."

His wristcom chirped an affirmation, but he was already on his way. Of course, the squib's neurochemicals would be different, and who the hell knew how many of them there might be? Those from humans may not even affect the squib in his lab, but at least it was something they hadn't tried. If even one of those tests produced a positive result, his one known fact would be complete.

chapter 15

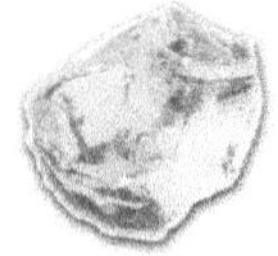

<u>Onlebaar Island, Bejami</u>

RIZZO CIRCLED THE ISLAND, KEEPING watch on the approaching clouds as she landed the jumper on the bluff, a short distance from the bowl in which the hab sat. Galen had pressed her more than once to enlighten him about the purpose of their trip, but she had declined to share. Yet. She hoped to tell this tale once. Let them all hear it at the same time.

Even after he'd accepted her silence on the purpose here, he had peppered her with attempts at conversation. Suggestions for potential joint faction endeavors. Probing queries on the Syndicate's history with the Consortium. Tentative questions about her past with the unammi. At the moment, though, Galen's silence told her he understood the difficulty of landing even a small ship like this one on such a tiny spot.

Through the windshield she saw Botha coming up the bowl to meet them. Her jaw worked. A baba belonged with his people, not coddling someone who hadn't the sense to stop her reckless dash toward a precipice before she went over the edge.

Rizzo muttered a curse at herself. That wasn't even close to fair. Given Alira's total lack of experience among humans, it was almost easy to understand her actions, even if Rizzo didn't like or agree with them. Alira let her passion, rather than careful planning, drive her actions. Years ago, Rizzo might've done the same. In fact, she had done exactly that on several occasions. One of those had almost cost her life.

Now? No. She'd given up passion. Logic, cold reason, and practicality accomplished more without so high a price.

Except here she was, on a remote island, with nothing more than the sure knowledge that the information she carried was essential to the survival of a devastated populace, and that it should be shared with those who could best use it. What was that, if not some form of passion? Perhaps she and Alira had at least that minuscule thing in common. Rizzo sighed.

"Are we going to sit here until he knocks?"

Rizzo answered with a grunt. She locked down the jumper, stood, and opened the hatch.

Botha waited. "Wat het jou so lank gevat?" he said with a grin. "I expected you before now. Your dinner grew cold, so I ate it for you."

Rizzo frowned as she stepped off the craft.

Galen laughed. "He's joking. Botha, I would've come sooner, but I didn't want to interfere with your progress." He gazed out over the encampment.

"She is wildcrafting, down below. We have a moment to speak." Botha peered into Rizzo's face. "I think your words are not for her?"

Galen's blue veins and splotches said all he did not.

"I bring news from my Clan contacts. Knøfa has an unammi prisoner."

"Ag nee," Botha breathed.

Galen flushed white. "Do we know who?"

"No," she said. "Nor do I know how long he's had them." She raised a brow. "Long enough, I expect."

"So, he knows about us." Galen's voice, hushed though it was, quivered.

"He knows about your shapeshifting, I'm sure," she said. "From what I know of him—and that is inconclusive—he probably knows about unammi healing abilities, too. Your people may have few secrets from this man by now."

Botha muttered something in his own language. "There is nothing to be done, then. The fish is out of the net."

Rizzo gave them a minute to absorb this news before she moved on. "Are you going to tell Alira?"

"I don't know." Galen's fingers twisted together in front of him. His features pinched. "Probably. She'll need to be told sooner or later."

"Oh, my friend," Botha said, gripping Galen's shoulder, "think hard about that. I know you want good things for her, and right now this will knock another hole in her boat."

Galen puffed out his cheeks. "I'm glad you told me first. I need to consider it with everything else."

"How is she doing?" Rizzo asked.

"She is much improved. But…" Botha shrugged. "There is still much water between her and the shore. Carrying such a heavy load takes a toll. I was surprised my rope could reach her."

"So am I, Baba." The corners of Rizzo's mouth curled down at the memory of Alira bloody and sitting in her own waste. If it had been up to Rizzo, she would've ended the pitiful thing's suffering then and there. Perhaps it was just as well it hadn't been her choice.

"Has she been off the island at all?" Galen asked.

"Yes. We went to the village market at Verregaandor." Botha rubbed his pate. "The first time was easy, but we did not stay long. The second time, she had a moment that made us both quake. We went a third time, a few days ago, and she did well."

Rizzo shuddered to think what might've happened in a crowded market if Alira lost it there. "Do you think her recovery will hold?"

Botha tilted his head. "That is up to her. But if she survived that nare adder, that *Bellamy*," he almost spat the name, "she might live through anything. She fears the other passengers in her boat will wrest the oars from her again. I cannot blame her for that. It is rational, healthy. I can only teach her to quiet their noise so her own inner voice can be heard."

Scrabbling footsteps sounded by the plateau's edge, along with the sound of falling scree. "Na'apa, I saw a ship! Who—"

Rizzo pivoted in time to see Alira's expression change to one of unbridled joy. Yellow streaks and splotches colored every bit of exposed skin, which wasn't much, given the climate here.

"Galen!" Alira's delighted voice carried across the rocky plateau. She clambered up the last few steps and ran the short distance to collide so hard with Galen he almost lost his footing.

They weren't near the edge, yet it seemed unwise to have so enthusiastic a greeting here. The lowlands were a long way down. So was the icy water. Yet he looked as happy as Alira. His face was splotched with yellow, too.

Botha's laughter resonated in Rizzo's bones just as a frigid wind whipped across the plateau from the direction of the polar landmass to the north. He pulled his coat closer around his neck. "Rizzo has gifted us with a warm shelter. We should not waste it." He gestured to the others. "Come. We can share food and a fire."

Rizzo and Galen grabbed their packs from the ship, then followed Botha and Alira down to the hab as it began to snow. Rizzo checked the sky. She'd hoped to be in and out, on her way home before nightfall. But that was clearly not in the works. If only she could blame Alira for the snow. But no. Even gifted troublemakers couldn't control the weather.

Inside, Rizzo stood to one side, awkward in this setting. She'd spent many a night in just such a hab, or a smaller version, just big enough for a roll-out cot and a supply pack. This one, though…they'd made it cozy. Homey. Such a place was not something she'd ever known in her youth and now, with all her thick walls and sharp edges, these soft touches made her teeth ache. She took in their setup. Why did they need rugs on a heated floor? And privacy curtains. It wasn't likely either of them would lust after the other. Why put up such a thing? These extras just meant it would be harder and take longer to pack out. No leaving in a hurry, unless they left most of these things behind. The inefficiency of it offended her sensibilities.

Botha gathered cups and rifled through their stores for food.

Galen and Alira had disappeared behind her curtain—maybe that one would come in handy, at least—but came out to help with food.

"We'll need more water. Come sit, Rizzo," Alira said, pushing Galen toward a cushion near the central stove. She called over her shoulder, "I'll scoop more snow, Na'apa."

Botha came with a basket of food. "This is the happiest I've seen her." He bit into a stick of protein jerky. "Don't take that from her. Not yet."

Galen grimaced.

Rizzo lowered herself to a cushion and accepted a jerky, peering at Botha. "What are you going to do?"

The door opened to admit Alira, accompanied by a cold wind and a miniature blizzard. She placed two snow-filled buckets near the stove, then dropped to the cushion between Galen and Rizzo and plucked a jerky from the basket. "It's so good to see you! But why are you here? Aren't you still running the Consortium, Admiral Thrace?" she said with a teasing lilt.

Rizzo shot a look at Galen. The baba sat cross-legged, taking in every detail. Did he ever miss a thing? Probably not.

"I left it in capable hands," Galen said, avoiding the question. "You've accepted my decision, then? You're no longer angry?"

"That wasn't me," Alira said. "That was Skalar. And Crow. They convinced me I was the only one who could stand in that role and—" She stopped, as if jolted by what she'd almost said.

And what? What was she going to say?

"And protect the outpost," Alira said.

These two were hiding something. The survivors of their people, Rizzo had no doubt. It couldn't be on any of the colony worlds. Not the way humans often refused to recognize boundaries. Or rules. Or laws. She almost grunted a laugh. She was a big one to talk.

"And now?" she said.

"Now," Alira said, "I'm learning to tell the difference between their voices and my own. And to keep them quiet." She lifted one shoulder. "There is one downside, at least for now."

"What is that, Gelaboot?" Botha took a bite of fruit.

"If I keep them all quiet all the time, I can't get helpful intel from them." She gestured at the stove. "A few weeks ago, I was curious about the tech that runs the power recycling system in the hab and wanted to mine my voices for details. But I'm not sure if it's an all or nothing exchange. If I open that door even a crack, I'm afraid I won't be able to close it."

"The system works on—" Rizzo said.

"That's okay," Alira said. "You don't need to explain. I've made my peace with not always knowing what I want to know. What I *do* want to know is why you've come." Her attention swung to include Galen. "You're avoiding my question."

Galen glanced at Rizzo and Botha.

He should just wave a flag while he was at it. Rizzo watched Alira's display, both facial and dermal. She knew they were keeping something from her. Would she push it?

"I wanted to bring you more irolium," Galen said. "And to tell you I'm thinking of arming the outpost."

Arming a base? No colonial government would allow that. Rizzo frowned. Where was this place?

"Skalar—well, Skalar and I," Alira said, "suggested that months ago. I think it's a good idea."

"It would need to be a faction. Colonials disapprove of these kinds of things," Galen said. "The Consortium could do the job. We have the resources and the means, but perhaps a multifaction effort would work better to mask the end results and their intended use. I don't want anyone asking questions I'm not prepared to answer."

"What about the Syndicate?" Alira said.

Rizzo's lip curled. Of *course* they'd want more from her.

Botha chuckled. "You thought to get out of the boat, eh?" He winked at Rizzo. "But I think you are still holding an oar."

Alira's and Galen's skin flashed and winked in shifting hues. What did those colors mean? She grunted. "What kind of weapons are we talking about?"

"The last resort kind," Galen said. "Surface-to-air. But I hope our shielding will make them unnecessary. There's a passive sensor system to warn us of any approach. I want a plan B. Just in case."

So many questions crowded her mind. They weren't likely to give her a location. But without seeing the base, how could she devise a weapon system? "And you want me to work on this project without prior knowledge of the base layout, atmospheric conditions that might affect its output, or any of the dozens of other details relevant to such a construction."

"I'll provide you with all those details," Galen said. "I only want you to design the thing. Maybe build pieces of it. I'll spread parts of the work to other factions."

"Be careful who you trust with that. You," Rizzo nodded at Alira, "already have some limited experience with the new Cartel admiral. But," she eyed Galen, "my contacts tell me the Clan's prior admiral is badly injured. She may never recover, so the Clan is under new leadership, someone named Knøfa. If it had been Michael Trask, he would've been reasonable, but Knøfa…" She showed her teeth. "He's cold. He won't care if he steps on you or your people. Take care in your dealings with him, especially you," she said to Alira. "You do not want this man in your head."

White speckles flitted across Alira's skin and were gone. "I hear you."

"Bardo is a good choice for something like this," Rizzo went on. "So is Georgeanne. Both The Order and The Federation have experience and will do a good job for a reasonable price."

Alira leaned forward, her elbows on her knees. "What about you, Rizzo?" she asked, her voice soft. "Will you help?"

Rizzo snorted. "I've already done so. Numerous times."

"True." Galen cleared his throat. "But you advised Admiral Baldric to recruit allies. And your faction is a business, is it not? This is a paying job, not just a favor. This is added protection for a Consortium base which just happens to be protecting the rest of the surviving unammi. I'm glad to bring Bardo and Georgeanne into the mix, but they don't know the reasons behind why we need this level of protection. You do."

Rizzo looked away. She knew this would happen. That they'd drag her into their drama. She probably should've stayed out of it, stayed on the base running her life, her business.

Even as she completed that thought, pangs of conscience niggled at her selfish boundary. If Esther had felt the same way all those years ago, stayed out of Rizzo's drama and kept to herself, Rizzo's life would have taken a ruinous turn. Were it not for Lourdes and Esther, Rizzo would've abandoned the inclination to trust anyone. Ever. She could almost feel Esther standing nearby, watching her with those dark blue eyes, crinkles at the corners even though she would not be smiling. Rizzo could almost hear the reproach in the woman's voice, whether or not she spoke a word.

Of course, given the fact that Alira's mind now housed both Ijydin and her human persona, Esther, then Rizzo's old friend *was* nearby, and *would* have a strong opinion about this situation. She'd been unammi all along.

Rizzo sighed. She had no illusions about what Knøfa was doing to that prisoner in his brig. It wouldn't be pretty, and the longer it was there, the more Knøfa would know about the unammi's secrets. More to the point, the prisoner wasn't going to last forever. When it died, he would be hunting for another. She couldn't sit back and let that happen.

Galen was right about one thing. The Syndicate didn't decline a paying job without good reason. And right now, she couldn't think of a single damn one. She didn't yet know if she would throw herself on the altar of the unammi to save them, but there were plenty of other things she could do without sacrificing her own safety or that of the Syndicate.

Like design weapons for their base.

"Okay," she said. "I'm in."

chapter 16

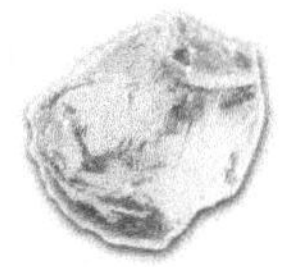

Haven, Danua
<u>Clan Trader Base, MedFac 13</u>

KNØFA SHOVED THROUGH THE DOOR, startling the med tech on duty who stumbled into the wall and almost fell. "Get out."

The tech exited at once. Knøfa paced at the foot of Tsurin's bed, hands on his hips. True, the lead surgeon had made good progress, finding those nodules. None of the neurochemicals or peptides they'd tried on the sample had changed the skin color, but Knøfa agreed with the man that some chemical trigger likely determined the tones in its dermal display.

Then just now, in another exploratory under a different doctor's direction, they'd almost lost the squib. That made three times—*three*—in the last nine days. He wasn't finished with that prisoner yet. It still had too much to teach him. If it died, his promise to the surgeon would be carried out. It mattered little that the doctor had almost collapsed from lack of sleep and had taken a few hours to rest. Ultimately, the responsibility was his.

"Are you upset?"

The voice from the bed stopped him cold. He whirled, his mouth agape.

Tsurin appeared awake, as she often did. But this time, she looked *at* him, not *through* him. She'd aged so much! He stepped closer. "Hey. It's about time you woke up and did your share of the work around here. You've been slacking off too long."

The tubes in her nose pulled down one side of her smile, made it crooked, but Knøfa didn't care about that.

"So," she said, her voice raspy from disuse. "What has you pacing in my room rather than out doing your job?"

He pushed his hair back. "It's that damned squib. The one who hurt you."

A slight wrinkle formed between her brows, like she was listening hard. Trying to focus.

"I've got it in one of the labs. You should see what we've seen. Did you know squibs could appear human? Disappear by shifting their skin pigments to blend into the background?" He gestured toward the door, where a crewman peeked in through the window. At his glance, the tech withdrew from sight. "Heal themselves like magic?"

"You're making this up."

"No." He shook his head with vigor. "I'm not. I swear. When you're better, I'll show you myself. If the med techs don't kill it first."

"What do you mean?"

"The squib keeps almost dying." He paced. "Twice, it actually flatlined, and we had to resuscitate it."

"Why?"

He frowned at her. "I just told you why."

"No," she closed her eyes for a moment, as if gathering her strength, "I mean why is it dying? What are you doing to it?"

"I'm examining it. Like I told you weeks ago."

"You mean you're experimenting on it."

"Well," he stared at her, confused, "I suppose you could call it that, yeah. We're learning as much as we can about it. Three days ago, we found nodules in its skin with roots that spread out through the whole dermal layer. An electrical charge makes them light up, but we don't know how it makes the color changes. If I can figure out how it shapeshifts or makes itself blend into a wall, or heals in seconds or minutes, that can be our thing. That can be the answer you told me to find that helps bring the Clan forward in the faction ranks. Hell," he said, "even if we could just figure out the healing bit, we'd be out in front of the colonials *and* the factions. We might be able to fix you, too. Except," he paused a moment, "it isn't healing as fast now as it did in the beginning." He could still see the docs stitching it up that first time it didn't heal its own incisions.

She sighed. "Knøfa…"

"What?" Why was she getting all worked up? "I wouldn't have done anything like this to a person. I know how you feel about that. But this is different. It's just a squib."

"You know," Tsurin said, "their race has a name."

"So?"

"They call themselves 'unammi.' You should call them that, too."

He scoffed. Wait. She was serious? "Why?"

"Because it's the honorable thing to do."

Knøfa stared at her. What did honor have to do with this?

"Come sit," she said. She cut her gaze at the chair beside the bed.

Ah. A lesson. She always asked him to sit when she had something to teach. He sat and listened like the good son she'd never had.

"When you were little, Henri tried to talk me out of raising you. Did you know?"

He hadn't. Why would Henri—

"He said you weren't human. That you were broken. Unfixable. A danger." She stared at his features as if she watched for his reactions. "How does that make you feel?"

Good question. Knøfa tried to feel something. Anything. Just so he could give her an answer.

"He was right that you were broken," Tsurin said. "Doctors told me you would never show any improvement, that shustithymia is an 'incurable condition.' I can't say that I agree with that assessment. You've come a long way since you were a child." She reached toward him, and he took her hand into his own. "But the important part is that Henri was wrong about the rest. You are a human man. You should not be called anything else, because *that's who you are.*"

Her lips worked as she tried to form the right words that would make him understand. He recognized the motions. He'd seen them enough times in his life.

"When someone calls you a danger, an animal—"

Someone called him an animal?

"—it demeans you. It robs you of the dignity you've worked hard to earn in your time here. It would be the same thing as if someone robbed you of your position as my second. Or of the ship you fly. You can't see your dignity. You can't touch it."

"I know what dignity is," he muttered. "I'm not stupid."

"Of course you aren't. But knowing isn't the same as understanding."

He frowned. Sometimes saying nothing was easier than trying to argue, especially with Tsurin, who liked to imagine she could change him. Make him better. That fantasy meant a great deal to her, so Knøfa listened as if it would make any difference at all.

"Your dignity is an intangible asset more valuable than anything else you could ever own. Even if you have wealth beyond measure, without your dignity the rest is worthless. It should be your most prized treasure. Do you understand?"

She stared at him in a way that made him know she was after something specific here, attempting to teach yet another Life Lesson so that he might more readily fit in with others.

So, he tried. He turned her comments over, flipped them around in his mind, tried to see what she meant. He understood the concept behind the word she was attempting to explain, but not how it would feel to have this nebulous treasure. Not what having or losing it might mean, beyond reading or hearing the words expressed by another. He knew its loss wouldn't hurt, not physically. He understood that dignity was defined by subjective perception, based on values determined by both the bearer and by others in the related peer group.

But why did it matter what others thought of him? Should he base his self-worth on nebulous opinions that could change in a blink? It made no sense why Tsurin would believe he should accept the judgment of others over his own views of himself and his actions. That would never change. Wouldn't that be a more stable benchmark for such a valuable thing?

He could follow this reasoning for days and still not have any clue what she was trying to say. So he looked straight into her face and lied.

"Yes."

"That's what you steal from the unammi when you call them 'squibs.' That's what they lose when you cut on them like animals. You're robbing them of their most precious possession." She smiled.

Maybe a nod would satisfy her, so he offered one. "Okay." He squinted. "But now I'm concerned."

"Why?"

Why? It seemed to him a simple enough deduction. Squibs were a threat to security. He blinked at her. "Because if they can come across as human, how am I supposed to tell a squi—" He stopped, restarted. "How will I know an unammi from anyone else?"

"I don't know of a way," she said, "except that maybe if you treat them better, they won't feel the need to hide from you."

Yeah. Okay. Enough of this. Time for a change of subject. He stood up and crossed his arms. "Do you remember me telling you that Trask is acting as my second until you're on your feet?"

"No." She watched him in that way that said she knew he was redirecting the conversation. "He's a good choice, a man you want to have on your side."

"Yep. I knew you'd approve. Anyway." He jerked a thumb toward the door. "I should get to work. Don't want my admiral to catch me slacking." He twitched a brow at her. On his way out the door, he patted the tech he'd scared earlier, in the same manner he'd seen Tsurin do in the past. "Good job, in there. She's coming along nicely."

The tech stared at him, but Knøfa kept walking.

chapter 17

<u>**On Approach to Bregaina, Bejami**</u>

ALIRA WATCHED BOTHA AS THEY approached his village. The light in his eyes seemed brighter, the crinkles at their corners more pronounced. He swiveled in his seat to peek out the front of the craft, then the sides, until Rizzo barked at him.

"Baba, if you want us to arrive intact, sit still."

He laughed, a sound that warmed Alira to her core.

"I cannot help myself. I have missed these shores, these people." A crooked smile lit his face. "I have missed my women. I hope they have missed me as well."

"Women? Plural?" Rizzo said.

"Yes." He turned a quizzical expression on her. "Why?"

"And are you their only mate?"

He scowled. "Oh no. I cannot imagine that." He laughed again. "We are too happy, too filled with love. One person cannot hold all the love from another. There is too much. We would burst if we could not share it with others."

Below and in front of their jumper, the village came closer. Galen had told her about this place, how the structures sat above the tideline so the water could come and go unimpeded. Hearing it was one thing. Seeing it was another. She was excited to explore a bit. For now, the waters were out. People crowded the constructed walkways across muddy channels between buildings and on the platforms above the marsh. All of them waved at the craft.

She sighed. She was the reason Botha had been absent from his village.

Rizzo landed the jumper on the platform without a bump, and Botha was on his feet and opening the hatch before she'd even locked down the craft. Galen stepped out of sight and exited the craft as Thrace, following close on Botha's heels. He, too, had friends here, though they didn't yet know Thrace.

Rizzo stood and started after them. Alira stopped her.

"Thank you for doing this."

She grunted. "I'd leave him here if I could. But he won't hear of it. A visit, he said. Then he's off to the island, with you." Rizzo glared at her. "Tell me you're worth the Baba's sacrifice."

She was right, of course. Maybe they could take Alira to the island and leave Botha here. He could come for visits, to check on her, then come home to his village. She would give a lot to be among her own people, despite the differences between them that made her stand out. It pained her to know she had caused Botha that same grief.

"I—"

"Never mind." Rizzo pushed past Alira on her way to the hatch. "Show me, instead. Prove him right."

Alira pressed her lips together, shifted to her Eli persona, and stepped onto the platform.

Outside, Botha was surrounded by a mob of people, all crushing forward to touch him, to speak to him, to hear his voice. They, and Rizzo's passengers, paraded through the briny air along the walkway, around the pilings on which the building platforms rested, toward a large gathering space she'd seen in the center of the village. He expected them to lift Botha off his feet and carry him on their shoulders. What would that feel like, to be so adored by so many?

At the rear of the throng, Eli took in his surroundings. Iridescent green birds perched in the low scruffy brush that thrived atop peaks of the ribbed mud, almost at the same level as the platforms on which the villagers lived. The birds stared at all the activity, staying well out of reach, sometimes calling to one another in a croaking *grawk* that echoed across the mud. Perhaps they waited for these intruders to depart so they could hunt or forage in the mud along the walkways. Above them, other birds soared. Silhouetted against the pale blue sky at such a great distance, he couldn't see much about them at all.

Platforms dotted the marsh. Surfaces of the nearest ones sat far above Eli's line of sight, though on the ones farther off and out to the sides, he could see the curved tops of dome-like structures—dwellings, perhaps. In several spots, wide platforms covered on top with pots full of green growing things or fruiting plants sat atop the mud, each platform buoyed by floats along the bottoms and anchored by ropes attached to much shorter poles driven into the marsh's basin. The Bregainans could grow their food whether the tide came or went, then.

Shouts drew his attention to their destination. Other villagers stood atop a central space, waving and shouting in joy. Those who had greeted Rizzo's jumper reached the platform and began to climb the ladders along the pilings. Botha climbed along with everyone else, as did Thrace. Rizzo walked about ten paces in front of Eli and climbed the first ladder she saw. Eli followed, with no idea of what to expect. Would this be like a Telling? Would they share stories or sing songs?

Before he even reached the platform, the noise beat at his ears. Music, laughter, shouting, talking, and Botha at the center of it all. Eli was glad for his friend, but this experience overloaded his senses. He skirted the crowd, careful not to get too close to the edge—it was a long way down— toward the shelters that lined up along the far perimeter. People gathered there, too, but he found a spot beside the wall where he could at least be protected on one side. Before him, younglings raced between the taller humans, playing some game with rules Eli didn't know. Everyone wore bright colors, feathers in their hair, no shoes on their feet. Bodies in shades of brown from light to dark gleamed with the sheen of sweat, despite the frequent breezes that wafted past the marsh.

Someone strummed a stringed instrument. Another joined in with a drum. Another with something like a canara. Before long, the platform vibrated with the rhythmic, jumping steps of the participants. Eli watched, rapt, trying to make sense of their movements, to understand why it brought them such joy.

Rizzo joined him, standing nearby. "Don't tell me you've not seen this before."

Eli shook his head, a small frown creasing his features.

"It's called dancing," she said.

"Is it a ritual?" Eli asked. "A mating behavior?"

Rizzo scoffed. "Something like that. Humans do it when they are happy, or when they celebrate, or yes, sometimes when they're feeling sexual." She looked at Eli. "The unammi don't dance, then."

"No," he said, his voice so low he wasn't sure she would hear him. "But they should."

Thrace came to stand with them, a huge smile fattening her cheeks, sweat trickling down her brow. She clearly knew about dancing. He opened his mouth to mention it when another sound started, a thrumming beneath the heartbeat of the drums. Thrace apparently heard it too.

"Ah hell," Rizzo yelled, shoving him and Thrace under the shelter's cover so hard they rammed into a table full of food. "Hide!"

A shiver raced up Eli's neck, a feeling of something…not right.

Alira's Companion appeared before him, Its form shifting so fast Eli couldn't make out any of Its faces. *"Hide!"*

Its urgent warning hissed into Eli's ears and he dove behind one of the tables, dragging Thrace with him.

Before they even hit the ground, the sound had exploded in the sky above the platform. From his vantage point, peeking over the top of the table, he made out the lower portions of some sort of shuttle craft, its rear hatch wide open. In the yawning hole, several pairs of human feet were visible, but he could not see what the intruders were doing.

Until a net came flying down out of the sky, wrapped around one of the villagers, and snatched her up into the maw of the ship. Another, a young man this time, was snatched up off the platform, in a different direction. Two ships, then. Other villagers ducked and ran, yanked up the younglings and threw them under the shelters, pulled the tables over, food and all, to serve as a barrier to these snatches. From the hatch he could see, two humans dropped down to the platform, cables attached to harnesses on their torsos, and swung clubs, fists, whatever it took to stop the other adult villagers from interfering, as long it wasn't lethal

a corpse doesn't bring in as much profit

before dragging the now-compliant humans into the ship.

He half-stood, shuffled closer to the opening of the shelter and peered up into the sky. Two ships. Far fewer villagers. Maybe they had escaped down the ladders. To one side, Rizzo had her blade out, swinging it at the cabled intruders, but not having any luck. They were too fast. What—

A few meters over, near the edge of the platform, Botha bent over a fallen woman, trying to lift her in his arms, even as a cabled man approached him from behind.

No…*Botha!*

Eli leaped out of the shelter and raced toward the intruder. Somewhere in the recesses of his conscious thought, he heard Thrace

and the rest of us, squib

calling him to stop, but the commands did not register enough to make his legs obey. He got to the intruder at the same time the man lunged for Botha. Eli grabbed the intruder's shoulders and twisted as hard as he could, flinging the man aside. As he tumbled and fell, the cable that attached him to the ship rewound, jerking his body up. Eli heard the man's neck snap

No!

and couldn't stop it from happening and the harvest crashed into Eli

not again

and he gritted his teeth, faltered the next few steps, his whole body shuddering, but he kept going. He picked up Botha and the woman and carried them both under the shelter then ran out to help the others.

By then it was over. The ships were lifting higher into the clear sky, their hatches closing. They'd gotten what they came for. Eli stopped in the center of the platform, searching for a place where he could be most useful. Wails and calls came from below, people who had fallen in their haste to escape, maybe. Others lay injured on the platform where moments before they'd been dancing. Limbs twisted at macabre angles. Bloody gashes and other injuries, Na'Staani only knew how dire, scattered among those who'd been left behind. The biggest wound, though, the one that would take the longest to heal, was the loss. The grief. Eli stumbled forward, still processing the harvest that had happened so fast, as tears rolled down his cheeks.

Rizzo came close. "Are you…"

"I'm—" Eli gulped in a deep lungful of air, hiccupping with shock. He forced his mind through the steps of his mentor's meditation, working to focus, to keep the rallying voices at bay and not

lose his shit

shut up

fall apart.

"Alira," Rizzo hissed.

He closed his eyes. "My name, at the moment, is Eli." He regarded Botha with his woman. She still lived

or she'd be in here with the rest of us

yet what of the others, who'd fallen to their deaths below the platform? They must be too far away to harvest.

"I told you to hide." Rizzo studied him, as if trying to peer beneath his surface and determine motives. "Why did you come out here? It was a foolish risk. What if they had grabbed you? Or Baldric?"

Her words jittered him out of his confusion. His lip trembled. "They were going to hurt Botha." He gestured around him. "They *did* hurt Botha." The tears came harder. "This is my fault."

Rizzo frowned. "No. This had nothing to do with you. They were after human cargo. They would've hit whether you were here or not."

Then his newest harvest spoke up, and Eli felt all the blood rush out of his face. His chest heaved, fighting to inhale deeply enough to cleanse him of this abrupt, crushing dread.

"What is it?" Rizzo said.

Eli tried to form the words. His throat tightened, air wheezing in and out. He stopped. Took a breath.

"I know who they were."

Part Two

chapter 18

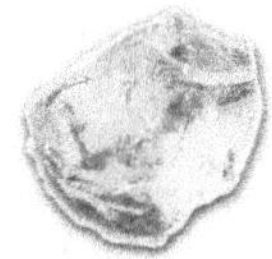

THE SHUTTLES HAD BEEN STANDARD make and model. No identification or registration numbers on their sides, from what Rizzo had seen. Could have come from anywhere. None of the colonies would trade in a human market. This was a faction job. Not the Federation. Not the Order. The Clan, under Tsurin, no. Now? Under Knøfa? Possibly, though the Cartel was the most likely suspect. Her frown deepened. "Who was it?" Rizzo stepped closer. "Tell me."

Alira—*Eli*—waved Rizzo off and shook his head as if denying the knowledge even to himself. Instead of answering, he hurried toward Botha, then squatted beside him. Eli and Thrace exchanged words, and Thrace scrambled to another of the injured.

Rizzo muttered a curse and evaluated the scene. The ships hadn't even landed, so the platforms and nearby buildings were still standing. All the damage wrought had been to the residents of those structures. Around her rose the wailing of those left behind. Children called, weeping, for a parent who did not respond. Cries of the injured, or shouts for help.

Villagers bent over the fallen, helping where they could, grieving where they could not.

This was bold, even for the Cartel, if that's who it was. Even when she was taken as a young girl in Pelarr, the colonials overlooked that sort of thing, since the snatchers yanked only street kids or adults found in the homeless encampments. Those "supposed victims" were not technically colonial citizens, after all. They didn't provide work or other resources to the larger community. They took what they could steal or con out of hardworking citizens who *did* follow the rules, and blah blah blah. This, however, was a whole level up from taking unregistered residents. Bregainans were registered. They didn't work for the colony. Instead, they paid a certain percentage of their fishing and marsh-picking in exchange for limited colonial support like building materials and health care, when needed.

So, what would make the Cartel—or whomever—suddenly snatch resources from a colonial government's lands?

She glared at Eli, still squatting beside Botha's partner, who was sitting up now. Alira, or Eli, or whoever the hell she was, knew what this was about, and Rizzo would have the truth from her. Soon.

Rizzo rubbed her chin. At least the snatchers hadn't grabbed Eli or Thrace. This mess was already bad. That would've made it even worse. One unammi at the mercy of an enemy was enough. Even though Eli hadn't known about that, he *did* know what was at stake for the unammi. Yet he had thrown himself in harm's way, for Botha. And for the Bregainans.

She snorted. Foolish little troublemaker, yes, but she had to admit it's what she'd have done. Maybe Alira was worth the baba's sacrifice. Maybe. Rizzo would reserve judgment for the time being.

She glanced over the edge of the platform. A number of villagers had fallen in their frenzy to escape. She climbed down, helped others carry those who couldn't climb to the top on their own. The tide would return soon. The villagers needed to be out of the way before then. The dead would be moved to the recycling platform later, when they could be mourned and processed. For the moment, those still living were the priority.

When Rizzo stopped to catch her breath, she noticed Thrace and Eli moving from victim to victim, staying with them a moment, sometimes longer, before moving on to the next injury. What were they doing? Those they visited were soon up and on their feet, mobile, and joining the rescue efforts. Rizzo looked around. Far fewer people lay broken or bleeding. One woman had blood on her clothing, though no visible injury.

Were the unammi…*healing* them? Was that even possible? Yet another question on the growing list for her new allies.

For another hour, those with able bodies helped restore what order could be managed. Still, it would be a long time before the Bregainans would feel safe in their own homes. By the time the water once more lapped at the pilings beneath the platforms, all the villagers had been moved from the mud below. Most were healed—if not completely, then to a more comfortable state—and those who remained outside their homes gathered in small knots atop the community space.

Rizzo found Eli sitting with Botha and Thrace. Weariness rode them all, especially Eli, who'd gone a little gray. Thrace watched him with obvious concern. Botha seemed smaller, his presence shrunken, as if his bones had been sucked out. So much of his world, of all that gave his existence any structure had been ripped from his hands and the rest hung in tatters from his grasping fingers.

She crouched beside him.

"Baba, are you well?"

His cheeks puckered as he stared at the deck before his knees. His body shook. His eyes were blank as if in denial even now, confronted by the aftermath, that this could happen. "We were dancing, the four of us. It had been too long since we stepped to the drums. Jaru was with the children. We had just waved to her when the noise broke our sky. When we looked up, they grabbed Bika and Yele. Oni tried to stop them taking Bika. Her arm got caught in the net, and when she freed it, she—" His lips quivered and he swallowed hard. "She fell, cut her head. She wouldn't wake up. Until you," he raised his gaze to Eli, "called her back with your magic."

Rizzo's focus shifted with a jerk to Eli, who winced.

"It isn't magic, Na'apa. If I could, I would teach it to you." Eli touched Botha's arm, then aimed her attention at Rizzo. "His hurt isn't one I can heal. Not like the others. But I can help *you* do it."

"How?"

"Those ships were Cartel."

She muttered a curse. No surprise there. "Then you can help shut them down. You've been inside. You know their operations."

"No," Eli said. "I don't. The closest I ever got to Bellamy and Hannah was Captain Rook. They didn't tell her much, especially once they began to suspect I wasn't who they thought I was."

"Then what can you offer me?"

He tapped his temple. "The one I harvested, crewman Angus, had a lot to say about the changes Hannah has made. She's no longer intent on selling. Nor is she satisfied with taking street folk. Thinks they're too malnourished, too unhealthy to be worth much on the market. If she can bring in healthy, strong adults, they'll fetch more in a long-term lease."

"So she's building a worker resource," Thrace said.

"Yes." Eli gritted his teeth. "She knows she'll get more business that way. Fewer colonials will balk at 'indentured' workers than they would at slaves."

"She'll need to stick to small communities," Rizzo said. "If they'd tried a snatch like this one in someplace like Bel-Rhovan, those shuttles wouldn't have made it out of atmo." Unless this effort was being sanctioned by someone in the corpgov. Like Saacharis Aggregate's implicit approval of the children in the Syndicate's mine. Except here, Rizzo couldn't put those responsible in her shower. Her jaw tightened.

"There's more."

Rizzo peered at Eli, whose skin seemed almost translucent.

"The Clan is involved somehow. Angus didn't have the details."

Thrace grimaced.

"When do you go to Zebalu?" Rizzo said.

She would swear Eli's face went pale, as Alira's might have done. His eyes flew so wide they showed the whites all around.

"No. Absolutely not," Thrace said. "We just pulled her from the brink. She's not ready to dive in as before, especially not with a mess like this."

Even Botha sat up, caught by this change in subject. "Thrace is right. That may not be wise."

"Do either of you have a better idea?" Rizzo asked. "I don't mean to reopen your wound, Baba. But if we are to rescue your people, we need more information. Alira—or Eli, or whoever—can get that for us."

"Rizzo, it was hard enough to harvest one more human," Eli murmured "I don't think I could endure another. I'm not ready."

"This," Rizzo said, her voice deliberately harsh, "from the person who leapt to the defense of Baba, of his whole village, without a thought for whether or not she was 'ready'."

Botha's countenance twisted in a confusion of grief, uncertainty, disapproval, and anger.

"Baba, you know Alira is the only one who can do this."

"What about you, Rizzo?" Eli said. "Can't the Syndicate send a team?"

"I'll have the contacts already in place do their part. The rest of my people would be recognized." Rizzo gestured at Thrace. "Baldric could do it. She's got your special talents. But as I understand it, she's got her own gates to guard right now."

Rizzo watched Eli's expression, the way his body pulled in on itself as if he were trying to disappear. She scowled. This instigator had brought a cargo hold full of annoyance and inconvenience into her life. Why did it bother her so to press Eli into service that might end him?

"Infiltration of the Cartel was unsuccessful the last time you attempted it despite the small gains you managed. Hannah's seen you do it once. She'll catch you faster next time. I'm suggesting something a little easier."

"Like what?" Eli said.

Thrace's lips puckered. "She wants you to assess the fringes."

Botha frowned.

"Just so." Most of the others had left the community platform to pole their boats home to their dwellings. Except for a few survivors still cleaning up the mess and trying to salvage any of the food, they were alone. "I shouldn't have to tell you," she said, speaking softly, "that this will happen again. In another village, maybe on another world, two more ships will sweep in on unsuspecting victims and shred their lives, too, unless we work together to stop her."

"This is about more than the Bregainans, isn't it?" Thrace peered at her. "For you, it's personal."

Rizzo waved her words off. "My story is my own. Yours," she speared Eli with her glare, "involves us all. You have the unique ability to blend in, see how things are in both colonial and faction businesses around Pelarr. You're the only one of us who can do this."

"I can't," Eli said, voice small. He shrank in on himself as if his whole body were pleading with her to desist. Let him be.

Rizzo held her ground. "Yes, you can."

Botha sighed. "My boat is empty. There is no water to keep me here. If you choose to do this, Gelaboot, I will go with you in case there is a problem."

"Botha…" Thrace said.

"What about your other partners?" Rizzo asked.

"They will help each other. Eli will have no one."

Eli's features twisted, as if he were arguing with himself—or one of those dozens of other voices he carried around. Would he refuse?

She had just begun to formulate another plan when he nodded. "Okay," he said. "I'll go."

"Give me a few hours to check on the others," Botha told Rizzo, "and ensure they are as well as they can be. Will you fly us to the landport?" He pushed himself to his feet, his movements slow, lethargic, as if he were sleepwalking.

"Yes," she said. "Of course."

Thrace got up. "I'll leave for New Canaan from there."

Eli stood, took one step, and stumbled. His form…winked.

Rizzo's eyes went wide. "Eli, you're fading."

He shook himself, as if to reawaken his limbs. "I need rest. And irolium."

"Did you bring some on the jumper?" Thrace asked, leaning in close to him.

"No."

"Rizzo," Thrace said, "we need to go to the island."

"Why?" Rizzo frowned. "What is this irolium? Why—"

"They're stones that feed our abilities." Thrace scanned the area, but no one was close enough to hear. "Without regular exposure, especially given what we've all just been through and Eli's latest harvest, he won't be able to heal himself or even maintain his human form. If you want him to go to Zebalu, he'll need those crystals."

Rizzo's jaw clenched. The others could probably hear her teeth grinding. Still, it was her, after all, who pushed this on Eli. The least she could do was get him the resources he needed to start the task. He couldn't help anyone if he couldn't even hold a form.

"We could make the trip, pick up their belongings, and pick Botha up in a few hours," Thrace said. "He said he needed some time, anyway."

It would take longer than a few hours to make that round trip. "It'll be dark soon. Help Alira—*Eli*—to a boat. I'll be there in a minute."

When they were out of earshot, Rizzo turned to Botha. "Are you sure, Baba?" She gestured at the platform. "You have other concerns right now."

His smile was devoid of warmth. Only weariness and grief rested there. "You want this trip to succeed, yes?"

"Of course," she said, her tone more curt than she'd intended.

"Alira will need me." He blinked, his movements slow, ponderous. "She has no identification papers for this Eli, I imagine?"

"I don't know."

"Then she will need a new disguise, just in case. Maybe she could wear Bika's, carry her identicard. That will get her through the ports, yes?"

He was right. They had no way of knowing what Alira would run into, and since her ability to change personas was the very reason they wanted her to take on this task, it might be best to have a selection of alternates for her to choose from. Bika's identity would be a start.

"Yes." Rizzo squinted at him. "You'll want others, too, even of some villagers who died here tonight."

Botha's mouth twisted as if he'd bitten into something bitter.

Rizzo's conscience prickled. "I'm sorry to impose on your losses, Baba. It's just that Alira may need to change her appearance before this is over. She'll want as many backups as possible. I advise you not to report this assault yet. Don't tell them about the deaths, or Danuagov will deactivate those idents."

Botha's lips drew tight, and a tear eased down the side of his face. "The others will want to spit out that bitter herb. I will convince them. Somehow. We will gather as many cards as we can." He walked toward the ladder. His stride was that of an old man, bent and worn.

Rizzo frowned. She'd done the right thing. Hadn't she? Her words held truth. This would not stop unless someone stepped in. But did it need to be these two?

She swallowed her doubt and followed Botha to the boat.

chapter 19

<u>**En Route to Bel-Rhovan, Bejami**</u>

GALEN WATCHED ALIRA SLEEP, CURLED into her seat in the rear of the jumper. Restless dreams had plagued her all the way to Onlebaar, even brought her gasping into wakefulness at least twice. Now, a fat blue crystal clutched in her fist, she seemed more peaceful. He hoped so. She would need all her faculties when she and Botha arrived in Pelarr.

He pushed out his lower lip. Thank Na'Staani he hadn't yet told her about Knøfa's prisoner. She was already dealing with enough. Rizzo's plan would triple that pressure, even though it did have merit. Galen just didn't want to admit it.

"Alira and Botha are both too important to lose," he said, his low tone pitched to Rizzo's ears only.

She cast a glance at him. "Are they more important than the Bregainans who were taken? Or the surviving unammi you're trying so hard to protect?"

Galen's fingers twisted 'round one another. "I know. It's just—"

"Are they more important than the prisoner in Knøfa's brig? What about the humans Hannah's people will take next? If they ask me some day why we did nothing even though we knew what was coming, is that what I should tell them?"

He glared at her. "That isn't fair."

"'Fair' is not a factor in this equation," she said, her tone flat. "The situation is what it is."

Her words cut deep. She'd probably intended them to. Sometimes, the best way to wake someone was with a splash of cold water. Unpleasant, but effective.

Galen grunted and stared out the window. This was so frustrating. Two unammi faces floated in his memories. Bishtari and Faraad, the pilots living on Danua. Neither of them had shown up on Iridos after the fall of the city. Galen hadn't known Bishtari well, but Faraad had been a dear friend. He'd found a joy similar to Galen's in weaving, and they often compared techniques and experiences with different materials. When word came from home that Faraad's ama had passed, Galen had come to Danua to call her name, and to share a private Telling with his friend. Faraad had never once chastened Galen for seeking a partnership with Alira and, in fact, had encouraged him to pursue it.

Which of the pilots was still missing? Which had ended up in the Clan's brig? It felt wrong to wish for the demise of another, whether he knew them or not, but death would've been the kinder fate, even with no one there to call their names. But when he thought of what Knøfa would do to a captive unammi…

He shuddered, rubbed his arms. If appearances were any indication, Alira had taken that last harvest well. She hadn't lapsed into her old behaviors, not yet anyway, nor fallen apart as she had after Bellamy's death. Oh, she would be angry when she found out he'd known about Knøfa's prisoner and didn't tell her, but he agreed with Botha. Again, Galen peeked over his shoulder at his i'shin's sleeping form. Almost as if she'd felt him watching, she shifted in her sleep, clutching the crystal even tighter than before.

In front of her, Botha was awake and staring out the window. He, too, seemed to see something other than landscapes or passing cities. Was he remembering Oni lying on the platform? or Bika and Yele being yanked into those ships? Maybe he saw the sadness in the other villagers, or the weeping children whose parents were now prisoners of the Cartel.

Galen swallowed hard at the notion of Alira going to Zebalu, to Pelarr, the home of the Cartel. He still saw Eli dashing out into the chaos to save Botha and Oni, how he had dragged them into the relative safety of the shelter, then raced out a second time to help. Thrace's own heart had pounded in her throat as she leaped to help Eli bring Botha into safety, but by that time, the ships were gone. It had happened so fast, but Eli never thought twice about risking himself.

Galen feared for Alira's sanity, for her safety, but in so many ways, she was the same as always. If she knew about the unammi in Clan custody, she would insist on trying to save them, which would put all their people at risk. He admired her courage, even as he acknowledged the danger it posed. Such a rescue op would be hopeless. As long as that prisoner was on a faction base, it was out of their reach. Unammi pilots were always expendable. But now that their secrets were revealed to humans, Galen couldn't let Alira risk herself, or any other unammi. If they were to rebuild their society, their species, each and every individual was a priceless resource.

She would find out about the prisoner, sooner or later. Whether or not she would forgive him for making this choice on her behalf remained to be seen. He had already been forced to put some distance between them before she left to go to Zebalu. It still hurt to remember the things she'd said to him, the way she'd treated him before her breakdown. It had been Skalar's face. Skalar's voice. One of her harvests, true, and she hadn't been in control of the voices then. He was being unreasonable to resent it, but there it was. How much farther apart could they drift and still be i'shin? Maybe they would never find their way back to one another. His mind churned, and he turned to watch Bel-Rhovan grow larger through the window.

chapter 20

Haven, Danua
<u>Clan Trader Base, Landing Bay</u>

KNØFA ARRIVED IN THE LANDING bay to find that Trask had already unloaded the Cartel slaves. Twelve women of varying ages stood in the bay, flanked by security on all sides. He evaluated them as best he could, though he had to admit he had no idea what details would be important.

"Do you have kids, Captain?" he asked Trask.

"Yes, sir."

"Were you present during their mother's pregnancy? Or even at their births?"

"Of course," Trask said. "Their mother and I were married then. I was with her the whole nine months, both times. And yes, I was by her side when she gave birth. I even got to 'catch' the second one."

Knøfa squinted at his second. "'Catch' it?"

"Yes sir." Trask smiled a little. "Haven't you ever seen a birth, Admiral?"

"No." He'd never even thought of watching something like that, but it probably would be a good idea. It would help him know what to expect when the squib hybrid fetus came to term.

"It's a beautiful thing. To 'catch' the baby means you're standing at the gate, so to speak, during the birth. When the mother pushes the baby out, you 'catch' it and put it on her chest or belly. You're the first one to touch it."

It sounded unpleasant, but there was no mistaking the grin on Trask's face now. Even Knøfa could tell the memory of this catching thing made his second happy. For the first time in his life, Knøfa wished he could feel, like others did.

"Why do you ask, sir?"

Knøfa regarded the new slaves. "Because the surrogates for the squib fetuses will be chosen from these women. Since you went through the whole gestation period with your woman for two different offspring, you would be better able to determine suitability among these potentials."

Trask's smile faded. "Are we certain that their reproductive organs are intact?"

"They'd better be." Knøfa had paid dearly for that option.

"We should probably have the medlab test them to be sure there are no drugs in their systems, and to check for diseases, physical conditions, or genetic malfunctions in their physiologies that might interfere with carrying a pregnancy to term." The man's voice sounded flat. Toneless.

Knøfa ignored it. "Good thinking. What else?"

"That's about it, sir."

"Should we use the youngest ones?"

"That doesn't matter, as long as they're not past menopause. The med techs should include that as part of the women's health assessment."

"Very well. Take over this part of the project. See that the slaves are cleaned up, housed, and fed, and that each one is examined as you've laid out. I'll want your recommendation on the best candidates by the time the doctor is ready to start treating them for the surrogacy."

"Yes, sir."

Before Knøfa could leave, his wristcom chirped.

"Yes?"

"Medlab here, sir. We started ovarian stimulation on the prisoner, as per our reported schedule."

"And?"

There was a pause. "Well, sir, the doctors are not sure whether this'll work given the patient's alien physiology. She's not responding well."

"Explain.'"

"Her life signs have dropped significantly."

Hmm. "This is following the normal protocol and dosages for an average human female?"

"I'm sure they compensated for her size difference. The doctors suspect that the drug may not be suited to her body chemistry."

At this rate, he could lose it before he finished his tests. Knøfa ground his teeth. What puzzle piece were they missing?

"Acknowledged. Tell the lead surgeon my promise stands, and that he should continue as planned. Whatever it takes, he is to keep that squib alive."

"Understood, sir."

His wristcom chirped and went silent.

"Admiral," Trask said, his voice low, "I think I understand what you're trying to accomplish with this experiment. But if the human drugs are affecting the unammi prisoner so badly, it's possible that any unammi fetus will have a similar effect on a human surrogate. Are we prepared to lose all seven subjects?"

"Seven, seven hundred, what's the difference if we gain knowledge that could save seven thousand? Seven million?" Knøfa would be happy to save one at the moment. He leaned closer to his second. "We are serving the greater good, Captain, and striving to enhance Clan influence in the process. Changes that big are bound to carry costs."

Trask frowned.

"You don't approve?" Knøfa asked.

"It's not my call, sir," Trask said, avoiding Knøfa's eyes. "But it just seems like an enormous risk for such a nebulous potential return. I hope we're doing the right thing."

"'Right' by whose standard? Yours? Mine? Theirs?" Knøfa gestured toward the Cartel cargo, then straightened. "You are a Trader Captain,

Michael Trask. Clearly, you don't agree with all the laws laid before us by Danuagov, or any other colonial world, or you wouldn't be here. What is the difference between crossing that line and stepping over this one? Treading beyond the boundaries of some outdated moral limitations leads us into new terrain, new discoveries. Right?"

"I suppose so, sir."

"That's what we're doing." If this didn't work out and people died in the process, Tsurin would be most unhappy. Trask didn't need to know that, though. Besides, that wasn't going to happen. "Whenever your conscience makes noise, just imagine how humanity will benefit if we are able to harness the abilities of that squib."

Trask nodded.

"It has occurred to me that given the fact the squib could affect humans within sight of it, we might want to create a way to isolate any newborns with the same abilities. We can't have an infant breaking people's brains because it's uncomfortable in a pissy diaper."

"Right." Trask looked away.

"See what you can come up with for ideas. We have some time, but we don't want to wait until the last minute."

"No, sir."

"Good. Carry on."

Trask pivoted back to the cargo, speaking into his wristcom as he did, something about medlab exams.

Knøfa left him to it and walked out of the landing bay.

chapter 21

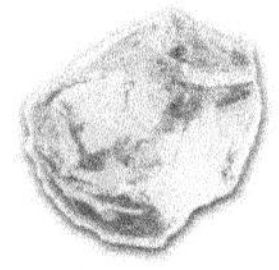

<u>Bel-Rhovan Landport, Bejami</u>

AT THE MAIN CONCOURSE, RIZZO stopped and considered her fellow travelers. "You know where to go from here?"

Botha nodded. "I will secure our seats so that Bika—it feels so strange to say her name and know that it isn't her—and Thrace can say their goodbyes." He pressed his hands together and bowed slightly in Rizzo's direction. "Tussen goeie vriende is daar altyd 'n kortpad."

Rizzo frowned.

"Between good friends there is always a shortcut," Galen translated.

"Thank you, Admiral Rizzo," Botha said.

Rizzo's jaw clenched. What answer could she give to that? You're welcome, sorry it wasn't enough to stop them from taking your people? At least you got to see them for a while before they were gone? Nothing seemed appropriate. She stuck to her standard response. Silence.

Baba set out in the direction of the ticket kiosk, and Rizzo looked at the others. "Don't stay here too long. The presence of Admiral Baldric is sure to draw attention. And you," she said to Bika, "be careful. Don't take unnecessary chances. Intel only." She suppressed the part she really wanted to say—don't get yourself, or Baba, killed. "Aes te nalya."

Thrace and Bika answered in unison. "Nalena t'staani."

Rizzo walked toward her ship's docking station. They were on their own, now.

She tried to focus on the coming trip, but her mind kept replaying everything that had happened over the last few days. Waves of travelers came and went as transports docked and passengers boarded or disembarked. Rizzo kept close to the wall and apart from the throngs with their heavy perfumes. She would be glad to get home, even though she'd once again been sucked into someone else's trouble. But this time it was her own doing.

Almost immediately, she grunted in amusement at herself. The day she'd signed on with the Syndicate, she'd known her life would be a never-ending stretch of drama. Might be a bit hypocritical to blame someone else for it now. Regardless, she regretted nothing. If Alira hadn't been inside the Cartel, she wouldn't have had the necessary know-how to track down what they were up to, but Rizzo would've pressed this task on her anyway. She was the only one of them who might have a chance of getting in and out without being caught. Rizzo hoped Alira would be smart about it and not throw herself at any challenge that might arise without thinking it through, which seemed to be her modus operandi.

Cleaner tech whirred at one bank of windows, sloughing off the layers of grime from outside and inside. The sound created a familiar background hum as she passed. This problem with the Cartel required a multi-pronged solution. Alira and Botha alone could do little, if anything. Even Rizzo would be unable to stop it entirely, though she could be on guard for tendrils of Hannah's new indentured workers web on Saacharis. She'd need to get others involved, pull in all the Syndicate's allies. Maybe, if they could tighten the market and keep Hannah's workers out, she would stop doing this.

But Rizzo didn't have eyes and ears on all the worlds. No doubt Fashere and Gadney, two worlds heavy into farming and animal husbandry, would welcome the opportunity for temporary workers who wouldn't be a long-term "burden" on the colonial resources. Their shelter, food, medical, and other needs would be the responsibility of their handlers. Ranafta, too, could have any number of uses for day laborers. With their enormous natural game reserves, Hannah might approach them right after Zebalu's needs were met. Phejoss was too small to need many extra inhabitants, though additional workers might prove useful in the semi-annual move from one continent to the other. Shemonaea? She squinted. No, never. All the spiritual havens there would surely reject such a resource. Besides, there were plenty of devotees in the various retreats to do whatever work those needed. Would Harajüd take them? Baldric would watch for that, of course, but a world as big as that one had so many industries both on-world and off, it could happen right in front of her, and she may not see.

Another thought made her falter and miss a step. What about Iridos? On that mineral-rich, unexplored world, the need for workers would be endless, a great gaping maw.

Her mood darkened further, and she veered in at her berth without slowing. At the controls, she cleared her flight path with the port, awaited her chance, and launched the *Kris Cross* into the air. She flew past the satellites, hit interstel, and recorded communiques for Georgeanne and Bardo with information about the Cartel's snatch in Bregaina, and asking them to guard against connected activity on their worlds and through their networks. Any ideas about how they could collaborate to stop this were welcome. She deliberated for a moment, then decided not to tell them of Knøfa's prisoner, or the abandoned unammi world. Until there was a good reason to share that info, she would keep it close.

For a moment, she considered reaching out to Trask but quickly discarded the thought. He had no reason to trust her word. Besides, if Knøfa learned of the comm, his second's life wouldn't be worth two credits. No, Trask would remain a wild card for now. With luck, he wouldn't play his hand against her or the unammi.

chapter 22

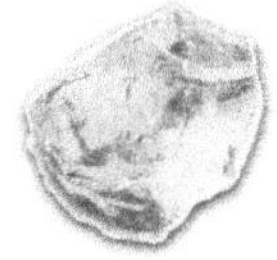

Haven, Danua
<u>Clan Trader Base, MedFac Office</u>

KNØFA SHOVED HIS WAY PAST the door and into the medfac, Trask right behind him. On the monitor, the squib—unammi, whatever—lay limp on its bed, tubes from a child-sized ventilator hooked up to its face. That was new. Except for that discoloration along its belly and chest where the surgeons had opened it up a couple of weeks ago, its skin had lost most of its colors, almost as if the squib were already dead.

The doctor stood beside the monitor, while his assistant cringed by the far wall as if she were trying to be invisible. Knøfa might've been able to help her with that, if only the doctors had managed to uncover the mechanism behind the squib's dermal display functions, and then successfully implemented them in a human.

"What's going on?" he said.

"Our patient lapsed into a coma a few hours ago, sir." The lead surgeon pointed to the screen. "We waited, gave her the usual treatments to bring her out of it, but there's been no response."

"Bottom line it for me, doctor."

The doctor stared at the screen so long Knøfa thought he wouldn't respond. At last, the man met Knøfa's eyes. "I've performed all the tests and confirmed an absence of pupillary response or facial muscle movement in the presence of painful stimulus. There was no pharyngeal or tracheal reflex response. Blood pressure and body temperature are slightly lower than when she was first brought to us." He shook his head. "A few moments ago, just before I had the staff comm you, I performed an apnea test on the patient. Respiratory movement was absent, confirming my diagnosis."

Knøfa wished the man would just get to it. "Which is?"

The doctor swallowed so hard it made an audible sound. "The patient is brain dead, sir."

Trask shoved his fingers in his hair, and paced farther back as if the news would sound better from there.

If it was brain dead, they would never be able to scan that organ while it performed all its tricks. "There is no treatment," Knøfa said, his voice carefully even, "that'll restore it to health? No stimulant or chemical cocktail that will jump-start the neurological functions?"

"Even if there was, I'm not sure it would be a good idea, sir. It may even be the human reproduction stimulants that pushed her this far."

"You do remember what I promised you." Knøfa heard the edge in his voice. Tsurin would accuse him of being impatient. She knew better than he did how to manage people, so he listened to her imagined guidance and shut up.

"Sir," the doctor said, "given your orders to harvest her ova, and the lack of time to know how best to do that on an Iridosian, I don't know what we could've done differently. There's no way of knowing how anything will affect her until we try it. In this case, it was a one-shot deal. We can't undo it at this point."

Knøfa clenched his fists and stepped closer to the doctor. "So it's my fault?"

The doctor blanched. "What? No! No sir…that's…that's…not what I meant. I… I…"

Knøfa focused on the monitor. The squib's chest rose and fell as the ventilator pumped air into its lungs. "Its heart is still beating, though?"

"Yes, sir."

"How long can we keep this up?"

"Well," the doctor said, "I've seen records of human cases where the body was kept alive for years. In this case?" He rubbed a shaking hand across his jaw. "I have no idea. All we can do is try."

"Then do so." Knøfa stared at the doctor. "How much longer before those eggs can be harvested?"

"More than a week," the doctor said. "Seven, maybe eight days."

Trask's nostrils flared, as if he'd smelled something foul. "What's that discoloration on her stomach?"

"That last exploratory we did…" The man frowned. "She got an infection." He indicated the darkened skin around the incisions, the long fingers of dark bluish black that spread outward from the cuts into the surrounding flesh. "We're still treating the sepsis, but we need to settle for gentler medications than we normally would use so as to not damage the ova."

His second grunted.

"What special medical procedures are required," Knøfa asked, "to keep the ventilator running, and the fertility drugs flowing to the squib?"

"None, really." The doctor pointed at the monitor. "The ventilator will run on its own as long as it has power. Now that she's comatose, the drugs can be delivered with a simple hypo. Her medical record has a schedule of what medications she is to receive and when, so that her eggs will be harvestable by—"

The doctor's words abruptly cut off as he realized what he was saying. He retreated a step. "However, since I'm the one who's been supervising all along, it would be best if I—"

Knøfa closed the distance between them and punched the side of the surgeon's skull. From behind him, Knøfa heard Trask suck a breath in through his teeth, even as the doctor flew to one side and crashed into the wall before he crumpled to the floor. Knøfa knelt beside him, touched his neck, waited a moment, then covered the doctor's mouth and nose and gripped the back of his head. In seconds, the doctor regained his senses and began to fight. Knøfa held tight while the man's struggle weakened. When the surgeon fell still, Knøfa counted in his mind from one to one hundred in a slow, methodical rhythm. Only at one hundred and one did he let go.

Again, he checked for a pulse. Satisfied, he got to his feet and watched his second. Trask's features, twisted into some unrecognizable moue, went blank. His gaze rose from the dead doctor to fix on the admiral.

Trask cleared his throat. "With all due respect, Admiral, that was one of our most skilled surgeons. Was it necessary to waste a resource like that?"

Knøfa shrugged. "I told him if the squib died, he died. I'm a man of my word." He turned to the med tech, who stumbled into the wall with a squeak. "Get this body out of here. And inform the rest of the staff that this squib is now their number one priority. They are to keep it alive until the egg harvest is complete. Every other physician on base should start polishing their knowledge on that procedure. They are now standing in this doctor's shoes. Clear?"

She nodded, her whole body trembling, and Knøfa left her gawking. Trask followed him out, staying two steps behind. Knøfa gestured over his shoulder. "Keep up."

Trask sped his pace to match the admiral's and walked beside him.

Together, they passed through the corridors to Tsurin's room. Knøfa pushed past the guard at the door, Trask behind him, and told the med tech on duty to leave them alone with the patient. Inside the room, Knøfa confronted Tsurin.

"I told you they weren't trying hard enough." He waved toward the hallway. "That stupid surgeon let the squ—unammi die. You told me I could trust him. See where that got us?" He began to pace and caught a glimpse of Trask staring at him.

"She's dead?" Tsurin asked.

"Well," he muttered, "its body is still alive, but its brain isn't. Now we'll never learn how it shifts or heals or any of the rest."

"I'm sorry to hear that." Tsurin pinned him with her gaze. "You've always been impatient. Ever since you were little. People sometimes fail. It's part of being human. We make mistakes."

"Yes, and sometimes those mistakes get us killed."

Her eyes went wide. "Knøfa, you didn't."

"I certainly did. I told him what would happen if it died. The idiot did something that affected the prisoner's healing abilities, then let it get an infection. In the medfac of all places, which should be a sterile environment. Only an incompetent could've done that."

"Or maybe," Tsurin offered in a reasonable tone, "it was that the reproductive stimulants weren't a good match for her body chemistry."

He stared.

"Do you think there is a single thing that goes on in this faction that I don't know about?" She gave him a lopsided grin. "Don't worry. I'm not angry. It's not what I would've done, but I understand why you're doing it."

Knøfa grunted. "Well good. Then I won't need to fill you in later. Still, even if it was the drugs, that doctor should've been able to compensate." He planted his hands on his hips. This complication could ruin all his plans. "Now what am I going to do? I wasn't finished with the damned thing. I still don't know how it could heal, or change shapes, or anything else. All I have left are questions and its offspring won't be viable test subjects for at least a few years." He peered at Trask. "Can you offer any suggestions, Captain?"

"No, sir," Trask said. "Sorry, sir."

"You should know," Tsurin said, scowling, "that I don't agree with most of what you're doing in the labs, but if it can help you find a way to get me out of this bed, I'll go along with it. For now." She thought a moment. "While you're waiting for hybrid offspring, maybe you could get another unammi directly from the source, at least until you find a way to 'see' one who's disguised as a regular human." She grinned again. "And if the Clan learns something we can then share with the colonials, so much the better. You'll have found 'our thing.'"

Knøfa set his jaw. "I knew you'd eventually see it my way." He swung toward Trask. "The admiral's got a point. Let's get right on that."

Trask blinked. "Sir?"

"You heard the admiral. Send a ship to Iridos. Grab another—no, make that half a dozen unammi so we can continue our work."

Trask glanced at the bed, then at Knøfa's face. "Of course, sir. If you'll excuse me."

Knøfa stared at the door after Trask had gone. "You were right about him. He's a good officer." He winked at her. "A bit slow. Took him a minute to know what you meant."

She smiled, though she looked tired. "Give him time. He'll catch on."

chapter 23

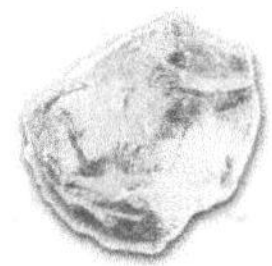

<u>Pelarr, Zebalu</u>

BIKA SCANNED THE ROOM SHE would share with Botha. Human living spaces felt so boxy to her, so confining. Interesting that she would think this, given that she spent so much of her life in natural caverns, walking through unammi-crafted tunnels, working and living in grottoes carved ages ago into the bones of her home world. But enclosed as those were, they had never felt constructed. They just felt…natural. Unammi underground spaces held few sharp angles. Instead, their walls, floors, and ceilings curved with the grace found in the outside world around them.

She moved farther in, granting Botha space to enter behind her, and explored the room's furnishings. Shelves for personal items, a separate room for washing and elimination, a small table and two chairs, one bed large enough for two sleepers, and a window that afforded a view of the port to one side, the recycling and composting field to the other, and the landscaped grounds and permanent residential towers beyond that. In the far distance, she thought she saw the sparkle of light on water. On the wall opposite the bed and table, a panel held controls for the entertainment holos or communication system. Bika inspected the ceilings, climbing onto a chair to peep into the upper corners and ventilation units.

"What are you doing?" Botha sounded weary.

She glanced at him. He had never seemed so old. "Checking for cameras." She gestured at her body in a clumsy communication she hoped he would understand.

"Ah." He sank into the other chair. "There will be no cameras here, Gelaboot. Out there, in the corridors, out on the streets, yes. But in this room, you are safe." He peered up at her. "I hope you brought your blue stones this time."

"Yes."

"Good. You should be your true self here and save your strength for when you must wear a mask."

Bika hesitated to shift in front of him. She still remembered Rizzo's shock the night the admiral had come to kill Skalar, and Bellamy's rage when Rook had shifted during their struggle in Bellamy's office. She shuddered. She did not want to alienate this human. He had already been through enough on her behalf.

As if he'd heard her mind, he smiled. "Show me your magic. I am not afraid."

She twisted her lips to one side, hopped down from the chair, and shifted, watching his face. The usual sensation, that familiar tingling of the corporeal transformation down to the cellular level, started at the top of her head and raced across her skin down to the soles of her feet. A tickle spread across her scalp as Bika's hair retracted. The outlines of Botha's features, and the objects around him, twisted and wavered as if seen through a heat shimmer. The clothing Bika had worn transformed into a replica of the silk wrap she'd seen Lurien wear so often. Her view of her surroundings slid lower as her shorter, natural form reasserted its shape. Through it all, Botha's expression filled with wonder. When the transformation had completed, she waited for him to speak.

He regarded her form, his mouth slightly open. "Geeste van lug," he whispered. "How do you do that?"

"It's a function of unammi symbiosis with the Iri. Elisul and his kind." Should she mention the unammi-human connection? No. She'd save that for another day. "The interaction affects us on a cellular level. The specifics would be difficult to explain, Na'apa. I'm not even sure I fully understand it."

"This is a thing worth protecting." He nodded as if he were absorbing all this new information. "Do you not feel alone here? With no one like you, no one who understands what you endure, you must feel afloat on the vast sea, surrounded by dangers, with no boat and no shore in sight."

A pang pierced Alira's core. Blotches of lavender in her skin reflected on the chair and the floor beside her feet. She struggled to bring her emotions under control before she dragged the chair to the table.

"Yes." She climbed into it and sat facing her mentor. "Sometimes." Every time she stopped to think about it.

"Why do you live apart from them?" he asked. "Is it only to protect them from outside? Like a jakkal standing between the young of its pack and the hungry lênask?"

She had no idea what those were. "That's part of it."

Botha put his elbows on his knees, brought his eyes to her level. "What is the rest?"

"Unammi society is based on strict conformity to the rules of the social structure. Of the guiding council." She sighed. "You might have noticed I'm not much good at conforming to others' expectations."

"A bit," he said. "Tenzin—I am sorry, Galen—told me this, too, before your city fell. But your people are few now. And your gifts make you as vulnerable as a bala hatchling at low tide. Still they shun you?"

"I'm used to it." She shrugged, tugging at that old grief. "It doesn't bother me now."

"Oho," he said, almost in a laugh. "I would sooner believe you no longer breathe air. You cannot find peace in this life until you confront its sharp teeth as well as its soft purr."

"I know." She tried a smile. "I'm working on it."

"Yes, you are." Botha sighed. "I watch you with *bewondering*, with *respek*. What is the word…" He paused, muttering to himself, then snapped his fingers. "With awe. I do not think I could pilot my boat through your waters, even were all my people with me. But even on a calm tide, I would not want to live without them. They are my flesh, my bones, my heart."

All his people.

Flashes of dancing, singing, laughing villagers rang loud in her memory and, for a moment, she was back on that platform in the heartbeats before the ships came. Alira had been unprepared to encounter such a vibrant, cooperative community. What would it be like to grow up there, surrounded by support and love? How might she have flourished, if she'd had the opportunity to thrive in that kind of environment? The open and trusting nature of the Bregainans made the wound inflicted on them by the Cartel so much worse. How would the villagers—those taken and those left behind—suffer if Alira failed in her goals on this trip? How would Botha grieve their loss?

Alira's throat tightened. She stood and moved to the window, standing far enough away that she wouldn't be visible to anyone on the ground twelve floors below. Behind her, shuffling sounds told her Botha was crossing the room. A second later, the window shifted to privacy.

"No worries now, my friend." He stood behind her. "Step as close as you want to the view."

"I'm sorry I didn't stop them from taking your people, Na'apa." Her voice trembled. "I should've—"

"You could do nothing, Gelaboot. You did not send those parasites to our door. Don't knock a hole in your own boat. We are too far from the shore for that."

They stood in silence for a moment.

"It is selfish of me," he said, "but I am grateful that you are here. I hope you can work your magic, and we can find my people."

"I hope so, too. But I'm afraid of what I might be forced to do to bring them home."

"Can your Companion not help you?"

She leaned her forehead against the pane. "It's complicated."

Botha made a soothing sound. "Then free the worry from your net. We will cross this marsh one mud flat at a time."

chapter 24

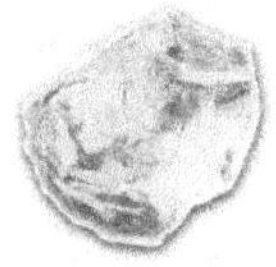

New Canaan, Harajüd
<u>Consortium Trader Base, Admiral Baldric's Office</u>

THRACE STOOD AT THE TABLE in her workroom, sorting through the latest batch of counterfeit idents when Spencer Kilbee's voice sounded from the main office. "Admiral?"

"Workroom," she called. Thrace pulled a smudged card from the pack and tossed it aside. That would never pass the port scanners. She could understand how an occasional card could be missed, but her crew needed to pay closer attention before sending them to her for inspection. If that card had gotten out, no telling what trouble might've ensued.

Muffled footsteps padded through the office and stopped in front of the door. She glanced up. "Aes te nalya, Tiral."

"Nalena t'staani, Galen." Kilbee stepped into the workroom and stood across the table from her. "It's nice to hear that kind of greeting in this office. Thanks for that."

She grinned. "As long as no one else is around, it's a given." She bent to her task. "What's the status at the outpost?"

"Shields should be completed in a week. Maybe less." He pointed at one of the idents. "That one's crooked."

Thrace tossed it aside with the other botched card. "What about the buoys?"

"Those aren't as easy."

"What?" She eyed him. "Why?"

"I ran tests on the ones with new tech," he said. "Those read differently, of course. Granted, the anomalies are small. It might fool someone with little experience in that sort of thing. But anyone with a lick of technical expertise is going to see it."

"How close would they need to get to notice the aberrations?"

"Closer than would be smart in a biohazard zone. And every buoy within range of its approach will be setting off alarms on the ship."

"So," Thrace said, "they'd have to be willing to get closer than they should in the first place."

"Yes…It's the best we can do without access to working parts from that era. We searched the base but didn't find anything we could use. It's possible, I suppose, that I could set some of the mitigants or outcasts on a search of the planet's surface, see if they can find the parts we need. But I don't know. It's a long shot. I doubt there's anything like that left."

"Do it." She worked a moment longer. "How are things in the city?"

"About the same. Not entirely balanced and serene. Those who favor change are restless." He shrugged. "I even had a little run-in with a couple of the younglings during my latest visit."

Thrace froze. "Which younglings? What happened?"

"Trumo and Folmir," he said. "I reentered my ship to get something and found them in the control center with their hands on the weapons system." He huffed, the sound somewhere between a laugh and a sigh. "If I hadn't come back when I did and caught them there…"

She stared at him. "What did you do?"

"I gave them a strong lecture about the harm they could've caused to themselves and others and then asked what the hell they were doing there. Trumo…" Kilbee grimaced. "He says he wants to be a pilot, so he can help defend the unammi like Alira did. His words, not mine."

Great. Just what the unammi needed, another Alira. "What did the council say?"

"I didn't tell anyone. I think I got through to them, convinced them to wait until they were older and could get some real training. Meanwhile," he said, "I gave them a tour of the ship, pointed out the different controls and bays and tried to explain what everything was used for. Even though there's no way they understood it all, it seemed to satisfy them. For the moment, anyway. I'll be locking down my ship every time during future visits."

Should she tell Alira about this? No. Not yet. She'd keep it to herself for the time being. It would only alarm Alira to hear she was having this sort of effect on the younglings, especially Trumo. Galen's i'shin—was Alira still his mate?—didn't need anything else to worry about.

Thrace finished the idents, set the sellable ones in their tray for distribution, and returned it to the vault. Three bolts of silk came down next, followed by a crate of supplies boosted from a hauler before it could leave the landport in Ranafta. She set down the crate, with the silk on top. "There's your delivery to our client on Phoenix. Tell them their coffee has been delayed."

He nodded, but didn't move to pick up his items.

Thrace peered at him. "Is there something else?"

"Couple things."

He fidgeted, as if he were unsure how she would take the news, and worried her reaction would be unpleasant. Like Alira's would've been. A small, tight angst squeezed her heart at that thought.

Her lips curled in the suggestion of a smile. "Skalar isn't here, Tiral. Speak your mind."

"Okay."

He hesitated. Maybe he was searching for the right words, even though he'd had eight days' flight time to come up with them.

"The crew's identified three suitable planets for the survivors, just in case we need to evacuate them."

"That's wonderful news!" Except that he showed a total lack of jubilation. What had she missed? She frowned. "Unless it isn't?"

"Depends on your perspective, I suppose." He leaned against the table. "They're a long way off, Admiral. Beyond easy reach. Even if they went to the closest one, we wouldn't be able to see them often. They would be pretty much on their own. And it would take weeks of round-trip travel to resupply our irolium."

Thrace winced.

"Yeah." He massaged the nape of his neck. "And if we run out, and can't get there in time…"

"Ouch." She searched his face. "Have you told the council yet?"

"No. Wanted to tell you first."

"What about our little experiment? How is it going?"

"We only set it up a couple weeks ago," he said. "It hasn't been long enough to show any results yet. To tell the truth, I'm not sure it will. We aren't there often enough to interact with the Iri."

Thrace blew out a long breath. Would Alira's Companion be able to help with that? If the Companion was the voice of the Iri in Alira's ear, and she was in danger of dimming and losing that connection with them, wouldn't they want to take action on their end to change the process? Of course, if the irolium came about devoid of symbiosis with the unammi, the stones might not even work the way they did now.

Perhaps it didn't matter yet, since at the moment they couldn't ask Alira to speak to her Companion on their behalf.

"We have to try," Thrace said.

"I know." Kilbee sighed. "The other outcasts don't want to share this news. They still hope the council will come around, loosen the reins a bit. Stop driving the rest so hard. If they'd do that, we could all go to one of these new worlds and be safe, together."

"That," Thrace said, "and the outcasts are afraid."

"That too. If they leave and we don't go with them, there won't be enough of us left behind to avoid a bottleneck. We might not have enough genetic diversity to sustain a separate population."

"And if they keep sending mitigants and outcasts into your ranks," she said, "neither will the rest of the survivors."

"Exactly." Kilbee stared into her eyes, as if he might find an answer there. "I don't understand why they risk so much."

"Neither do I," Thrace said. The councilors' reticence was a mystery they would need to solve before they could save the unammi. Until they could remove that obstacle, all their efforts would be futile.

chapter 25

Haven, Danua
<u>Clan Trader Base, Knøfa's Quarters</u>

KNØFA ROLLED OVER IN HIS bed and tried to ignore the chirping of the comm. It persisted, like those minuscule biting night flies so prevalent in Spring. The ones he always seemed to attract, unless he wore tech to repel them. This fly came again and again, as if buzzing by his ear until he pulled his pillow over his head to shut it out. Still he heard its annoying intrusion.

He lifted the pillow without rolling over. "Answer, voice only. Make it good, I'm trying to sleep."

Trask's voice came through. "Sorry to wake you, sir, but I thought you'd want to hear this sooner rather than later."

Knøfa waited. "Well?"

"I'm…" Trask said, "…not sure whether this is safe on the comms, sir. May I come to your quarters?"

Knøfa groaned and sat up, swinging his feet over the edge of the bed. "Yes. Lights, eight hundred lumens."

He rubbed his jaw, ran fingers through his hair, and pushed to his feet. This is the kind of thing Tsurin had warned him about all his life. She used to wake him in the middle of the night, when he was training, and give him so-called critical tasks, just so he could see how it felt to be fully focused within a matter of seconds. And though this was the first time it happened with an actual problem he needed to address, and not one of her tests, Knøfa swore that if he was ever needed to help stop some world-shattering apocalypse, the call would surely come while he was trying to sleep.

He crossed to the washroom and splashed water on his face. He was still drying it when the door chime sounded. "Come."

The door panel swished open, then closed. "Admiral?"

Knøfa stepped out into the larger room.

Trask stared at him.

Knøfa glanced down at his naked form. What was the man gawking at?

"We, uh," Trask said, stuttering out his report, "received word from the ship you sent to Iridos, sir."

"And?"

"They…" Trask seemed to be struggling to keep his eyes on Knøfa's face. "They…ran into patrols from Harajüd House Unlimited and were told that Iridos is now HHU property and that they were trespassing."

Knøfa scowled. *"What?"*

"That's the gist of the report, sir. I've sent you an encrypted copy of the entire message."

"Did they run life-sign scans on the surface? Were there still squibs down there?"

"The captain said no. Only human."

"How the hell did that happen?" Knøfa shouted. "And where did the squibs go?"

"Unknown, sir." Trask held his ground. "But I'll start digging around, see what I can find."

"You do that." Knøfa paced, one fist still on his hip. Now where was he going to get a squib?

This also meant price increases on hematium, and therefore ship parts and construction. Which didn't make sense, because HHU didn't need to pay for the resource now, beyond the expense of extraction and transportation anyway. And all that had been built into the price from the beginning, long before HHU took ownership. But they'd raise the price anyway. He'd bet credits on it.

Halfway across the room, he stopped.

Hematium. That was at the heart of this latest mystery. It had to be. Pieces of a puzzle he'd believed unrelated fell into place to create an unexpected shape. "This is tied to Skalar somehow, some way."

"Ex…cuse me, sir?"

Knøfa pointed at Trask. "The Consortium's under new leadership. A new admiral, new second."

"Yes."

"Think about it," he said, snapping his fingers several times as if to wake Trask up. "All the clues are right in front of us. Skalar's disappeared, along with Crow, and now, suddenly, the colonials on Skalar's world have exclusive access to the only known source of hematium."

"But Skalar and Crow vanished months ago, sir."

"Your report made it sound like HHU's already entrenched there. Is that an accurate assessment?"

Trask nodded.

"That didn't happen overnight." Knøfa grunted. "That's probably why our hematium shipments were delayed a few times." His mind raced. Too convenient to be a coincidence, and an unnerving precedent. "A new admiral *and* a new second, both replaced at the same time. They could be HHU tools, evidence the colonials are trying to take over the Consortium."

"If that's the case," Trask said, frowning, "then how soon until their scheme is replicated by other colonial worlds? If the Danua Coalition thought they could replace you, sir, and Admiral Tsurin…"

Knøfa pointed at Trask. "And you. But forget it. They're not seizing the Clan on my watch." He clenched his jaw. They couldn't, could they? The Clan had the freedom to do things the Coalition could not without clear violation of the Intercolonial Charter. The colonials needed the Traders.

Didn't they?

Tsurin had told him once that even Traders could conceivably go too far and be removed from the playing field. The legal leeway granted to Traders hung on the unspoken understanding that the colonials would suffer them only so long as they kept their activities low-key. Blow up a building, kill someone in broad view of witnesses off base, leave behind incriminating evidence at a scene, and corpgov wouldn't be able to ignore their deeds. Citizenry of the colonies expected corpgovs and their assigned security to keep their cities safe. Crime-free, or close to it. Make too much noise and it could even upset everyone's boat enough to bring down the entire Trader network. All six factions could fall if even one admiral did something bad enough to warrant it. The other factions would never let that happen. They'd step in first, take care of the problem themselves. Their own continued existence depended on it.

So…did HHU step in and replace Skalar and Crow, as he'd theorized? Or did they go too far on their own world and one of the other admirals took them out?

"I need to think about this. Meanwhile, since we don't know where the squibs went, I have a special project for you."

"Of course, sir."

"Let's follow Tsurin's other idea."

"Which…idea…would that be, sir?"

"Find some way to tell a disguised squib from an actual human, some device that'll reveal who they are. Task our best tech experts with this. Wake them right now and get them started. I'm not partial to how they do it, whether it's a device I can point at someone and tell if they're human, or one we can hide in the ports to find squibs moving through among the other passengers."

"Do you have any ideas on how they might do that, sir?"

Knøfa pursed his lips. Hmmmm. The color shifts, the pigment-level camouflage, the dermal structures they'd found that reacted to electrical pulses, those details alone indicated a cellular, maybe even chromosomal difference between squib and human. But his own medics suspected those abilities were triggered by the squib's brain structures. "Research crew records for anyone who has training or experience in genetics. Also neurological specialties or related research. Maybe there's a way they can scan for those nodules we found. Let them know the medfac has a skin sample they can use as a test material. We'll let them figure it out." He huffed a frustrated grunt. "Was that it?"

"For now, yes, sir."

"Good. Get to work." Knøfa pointed at the door. "I'll want a beginning report over breakfast in the morning."

"Of course, sir." Trask hurried out.

Knøfa returned to his bed. "Lights off." He clambered between the sheets and stared into the darkness. Did Skalar kill off the squibs? If so, why? That question, at least, answered itself. Of course he'd done it for the hematium. But that was only good for ship parts. Why would he need so much of it? Clearly, he didn't succeed in taking it all, or HHU would have no reason to be there now. But he might've gotten a good haul. Where would he have stashed it? Not at the Consortium main base. Too risky. Somewhere off-world, then. A base on another colony? On a non-colony world? Had HHU found it? Was that why they were now claiming Iridos?

He frowned. He'd talk to Tsurin about this tomorrow. Maybe. On second thought, she counted too much on the goodness of other people. Maybe he'd keep this to himself a little longer.

chapter 26

<u>Pelarr, Zebalu</u>

THE HUM OF THE HOVERCAR through her open window lulled Bika nearer to a daze than was safe for a driver. She switched to auto-nav, entered the destination, and watched the scenery pass as the car drove them toward the temporary housing complex by the port. Beside her, Botha stared out the window on his side of the craft, his shoulders slumped. Since their arrival in Pelarr three days ago, they'd searched every place in the city they could think might have a use for the Cartel's new worker force. No Bregainans were found at the brothels, the salt processing plants, the furriers and tanneries. Botha recognized no familiar faces among the grounds crews or trash pickup. They'd just come from the oceanfront, where they'd peeked in at the salvage processing and the zoo, and even browsed the "champions" on display at the gladiatorial arena before the next big competitions.

No luck. So much for any report she might share with Rizzo.

Bika frowned. Maybe Hannah had sent them to another city on Zebalu. Before she'd archived his harvest, she'd gotten enough from

Angus to know plenty of places on this water-centric world that could use temporary workers for large, periodic jobs. Could they search them all? Small though the landmasses were, Zebalu held so many. She and Botha were only two seekers.

What if the Cartel hadn't brought them to Zebalu at all? There was a disheartening notion. Bika gritted her teeth. It wasn't possible to search every city on eleven other worlds, but for Botha, she'd damn sure try. Not sure where they'd get the credits for all that, though. The colonials did insist on payment for use of their resources. She couldn't blame them for that. If Rizzo wanted Bika to go that far, the Syndicate would need to pay her way.

She peeked at Botha, who hadn't spoken in hours. "Maybe we should move to another city tomorrow, Na'apa. Try there."

He nodded.

What would he say to her as inspiration? To keep her spirits up? Something about the water, or a boat. No words came to mind, and she left him to his thoughts. Sometimes, she knew, the best support came from just being there.

The city unfolded as they passed by. Memories from past experience told her what she saw. A pleasure house there. A gaming house next to that. A public transport depot. A recycling and composting station, like so many others around the city. Small markets every few blocks. The Cartel hunkered on the other side of the city, above the cliffs at the east end of Pelarr's coastline. Except for a quick stop at the nearby salt storage warehouses to ensure the villagers weren't working there, she'd avoided that area. They wouldn't know who she was, not with this mask. Still, she didn't want to risk it. Hannah wouldn't let her escape a second time.

She braced her elbow on the open window frame while they rode past the city center housing. Tall, blocky buildings sat one after the other, side by side, row after row. It reminded her of the Northside District in New Canaan, when she'd gone searching for Nyros. These structures appeared newer, more well-kept, yet each resembled all the others. Humans worked hard to be unique individuals. It seemed a contradiction that they'd settle for such homogeneous living spaces. The scenery blurred into monotony when the next blocks brought more of the same, in smaller versions, set farther apart, with more greenery surrounding the buildings.

Bika kept reliving moments from the Cartel's snatch in Bregaina. Maybe Botha and Rizzo were right. Maybe she couldn't have stopped the tragedy. Even if they hadn't come to Bregaina that day, the villagers would've been grabbed. Except Botha wouldn't have seen it play out. And if Alira had stayed on Onlebaar alone, Botha, too, might've been taken or killed. No, she wouldn't have come through that unscathed.

Outside, the scenery changed to a more industrial setting. Late afternoon light cast shadows between the rows of warehouses, where large ground transports loaded and unloaded their cargo. Ahead, the block of temporary housing rose above other structures save the port itself. She'd be glad to get to their room, and order some food. Would Botha eat, or would he skip yet another meal?

The craft's high-pitched hum lulled her again. The road before them unfurled with the same sights she'd seen every morning and evening for the last three days, the same clamor of city sounds, the same metallic tang carried on the breeze from so many ships in port. Bika wrinkled her nose and closed the window just as she noticed a new sound. She frowned. Where was that coming from?

Ah. A crew crawled over, under, and around the recycling center near their building to clean and service the units. A transport sat near the road, where some of the workers dropped off debris or picked up supplies. The car slowed, ready to stop should pedestrians come into the street. Bika had not seen crews cleaning the units before. Perhaps it was a cyclical process, done on a periodic schedule where crews made rounds of the units throughout the city.

As they drew alongside the transport, a woman stepped out from behind the large vehicle. Afternoon light shone on her beautiful, clear, defiant features—Bika's face. The woman outside the hovercar, the *real* Bika, caught sight of the Bika inside the vehicle, too. She stopped moving and stared.

The Bika in the car rolled past the recycling center, her heart slamming against her ribs. "Botha."

No response.

"*Botha!*"

"Yes?" His voice sounded dull, automatic.

"I found them."

"What?" He lit up, his head on a swivel. "Where?" Then he saw her behind them.

The wail that came from his lips might have been joy or grief. Bika the driver wasn't sure which.

"I'm going back," she said.

"No!" he said, the word ripped from his throat. "You are not ready for this, Gelaboot. How many harvests will it take to free them?"

"I can't do nothing!" she shouted. "They're *right there*!"

Botha made a tortured sound, half wail, half laugh. "Yes, but you will be no good to my people *or* yours if you are a babbling mess, or even dead."

Bika cringed. "You're right. But there is one thing I can do, and no one has to die." She resumed control of the vehicle, turned the car around, and drove toward the transport. Bika the laborer still stood there, busied by exchanging one load for another. "Can you drive this craft, Na'apa?"

"Yes, but—"

"Okay, when I get out, you take my place. I'll send Bika to you."

"But you are Bika."

She ignored him. "When she gets in, take her to the room, pack our things, and stay put. If I'm not there by this time tomorrow, take her home. I'll catch up."

He stared at her, his eyes wide with apparent alarm.

"Trust me." She smiled and stopped the car on the street by the transport. Other vehicles swerved around her. She searched for the slavers, but didn't see them. She'd have to take the chance.

She got out of the car and approached the real Bika, who looked her up and down, mouth agape, skin ashen. "Wie is jy?" she whispered.

Bika the driver winked. "I'm a friend of Botha's." She took the real Bika's load in her own arms. "Go. He's waiting."

Her gaze, glittering with tears, shot to the car. "Botha is here?"

Bika the driver gently shoved the real Bika in the direction of the vehicle. "*Go,*" she said. "We'll get one shot at this." Bika the driver hiked up the boxes in her arms and walked toward the recyclers.

One part of her mind listened for the whine of the departing car, but the rest raced forward. At the recycler, small ladders had been set up at each open hatch. Laborers came and went with armloads of supplies—or whatever was in her crates—and passed them to other workers inside the machine. She swept the immediate area for a door where someone awaited her. One of them, a man, waved to hurry her along.

Yele. Botha's other partner.

Her stomach twisted. How could she help one, and not the other? Voices rose, and she squashed them. No time to meditate just now so

SHUT UP

At the top of the ladder, Yele claimed the crates and set them aside. "What took you so long?" he said, his voice fearful. "You know the guard will punish us if we don't finish on time."

The band around her gut twisted tighter. She was about to get Yele punished even harder. "Sorry," she muttered, faking Bika's accent as best she could. She knew almost nothing of the real Bika. Yele would soon know she wasn't his mate.

He picked up two boxes. "Take these to the truck and come help me finish in here."

"I'll do that part." She pushed the boxes at him. "You take those to the transport. I'll meet you there."

"But we aren't finished."

"They don't know that do they?" she asked. "If we don't finish on time, they'll know right away. But if we don't complete the job, the only way they'll know is if they come and inspect it. Will they do that?"

"I don't know, but—"

"Then let's gamble on the sure thing." She pushed the boxes at him once more, gently, ignoring his confused expression. "Take these to the truck. I'll be there shortly." She beamed what she hoped was a beatific Bika smile, and he frowned, then stepped out of the machine. Once he was down the ladder, she examined her surroundings. This was the only door in and out of this compartment, and Yele had done an excellent job of cleaning its blades, teeth, and gears. How did he not think they were finished?

She peered outside the door. The other two-member teams were also finishing, bringing the last of their supplies to the vehicle. Two supervisors rounded them up and began loading them in the truck. Yele stood outside, still waiting for her, and the view tore at her heart, shredding her with the knowledge that she couldn't save them both. But if he didn't go soon, if he alerted the guards to her absence, even this much would be for naught. She waved at him to go without her, then ducked into the shadows of the machine. A moment later, a mechanical whine came from deep in the recycler unit, and the door began to close.

Her heart took flight, and she leaped to the outside ledge, morphing to match her surroundings as she went. On the narrow surface she wobbled, her arms pinwheeling before she fell, shifting her camouflage as fast as she could. The ground beneath caught her at a hard angle, and she heard the pop when her shoulder snapped out of its socket. Pain shot through her body, and she rolled beneath the recycler to hide from the cameras while struggling to maintain her dermal patterns.

Breathe, she told herself through the shrieking agony. In through the nose, out through the mouth. Nice and slow.

When next she checked, Yele was inside the departing transport with the others. The guards hadn't noticed Bika's absence yet. Good.

Breathe…

When the site was empty, she rolled over on her belly and put the dislocated shoulder against the ground, rolling onto it by degrees to pressure the joint into place. The resounding pop when it snapped back echoed in her ears, and the world went gray. She laid still while her body healed itself.

A long while later, she sat up and took in her surroundings. Several humans came toward the machine with their recyclables. She stilled her movements and refreshed her disguise to match the deepened shadows of approaching night. When they were gone, she picked through the memories of those individuals on idents they'd brought with them from Bregaina, chose one—a male named Abeo—who had died the night of the raid, and shifted, then set off for Botha and Bika's room.

chapter 27

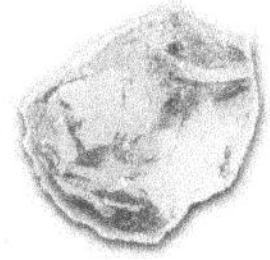

Tuneloras, Saacharis
<u>Syndicate Trader Base, Zen Garden Courtyard</u>

RIZZO STOOD ATOP THE DARK stepping stones that bisected the pale pebble bed. She'd smoothed the pea gravel first and drawn ripples around each of the dark gray boulders in the chill pre-dawn air. Now, she dragged the wide teeth of the rake, creating wave patterns alongside the meandering path. The early hour made the setting even darker than usual for Tuneloras, but small footlights lined the border of the bed, and stone lanterns flickered with simulated torchlight, making the shadows of Rizzo's waves and ripples dance across the bed.

To one side, she heard the soft hiss of a door opening and closing. Whoever it was—probably Bailey—held their silence while Rizzo finished her work. She stopped, checking the results of her labor. Overall, satisfactory. The new bench, of a deep reddish simwood, sat near another boulder, this one planted with a small, trailing vine whose leaves were spherical, like green berries. Carefully tended moss colored the ground outside the pebble bed a vibrant green.

She scratched her chin. Bits of resin on her fingers from her latest bonsai work still smelled of evergreen and peat, making her nose twitch.

"What is it?" she said.

Bailey came up beside her. "We received word from one of our Clan contacts."

"The unammi prisoner is dead."

"No," Bailey said. "Not yet. Not that our people know of. But they report rumors that the unammi could change shape, take human form, or even become invisible. And they can affect people around them with some sort of mind-bending abilities."

So those secrets were out, at least. Rizzo grunted. Knøfa would not stop at one unammi. This was only the beginning of a much bigger mess. Did Baldric know yet? "Is that all?"

"No, ma'am. Knøfa has his people working to create a viable device that can detect unammi even when they are disguised as humans."

Rizzo's gaze snapped around and she stared at her second. "Has he succeeded?"

Bailey peered at her with a dawning expression.

She'd figured it out. Rizzo could see it on her face.

"You already knew about them," Bailey said, her voice hushed. "That they could do these things."

Rizzo gripped her second's shoulders. "Has he succeeded?"

Bailey shook her head, her long black hair swinging over one shoulder to brush like silk against Rizzo's arm. "I don't think so. But you know it's only a matter of time until he does."

Rizzo released her. "Maybe. But it'll take time, and without an unammi prisoner to test it, they can't know whether or not it's functional." Would tech like that work on them? *Could* it? A chill raced up her spine. "Send our contact a coded response. Keep track of the Clan's progress on that project. If they're getting close to success, sabotage it. Do not let them complete that device."

Bailey nodded, but did not leave.

"Was there something else?"

"Are you going to send word to Admiral Baldric?"

Rizzo went cold. "Why would I do that?"

Bailey closed her eyes, looked down. After a moment, she turned to Rizzo. "Don't you know by now that I would keep any secret for you? Carry out any mission? Do anything you asked of me, no matter the consequences?" She stepped closer, leaned toward Rizzo. "Don't you know—"

"Stop." Rizzo's voice came out husky, low. She shuddered, cleared her throat, and took a deep breath. She should've seen this coming. Probably did and chose to ignore it. Because the truth was…

Well. The truth was inconvenient at the moment.

"Yes," she said. "I know. But I told you this wasn't my secret to share. Unless they confide in you, my lips are sealed."

"And what about the rest?"

Rizzo stared at this woman she'd known so long, who she trusted with her faction. Her life. Oh, there were so many things she could say right now. "The rest is irrelevant."

Bailey's eyes went wide with unmistakable hurt, their pain stabbing through Rizzo.

"Emotional entanglements are a danger for faction leadership, Captain," Rizzo said, her voice softer. "They cloud the issues. Blind us to threats. Make us vulnerable."

A mote of hope lit Bailey's countenance. "But if we weren't in the Syndicate—"

"Irrelevant." Rizzo tried to soften the word with a gentle voice. "We *are* the Syndicate. Therefore, anything I feel for you," she said, one corner of her mouth lifting ever so slightly in a suggestion of a smile, "must remain unspoken. Is that clear, Captain?"

"Understood, Admiral." A single tear trembled on Bailey's cheek, and Rizzo brushed it away. Bailey coughed, stepped back, and straightened. "I'll get that message to our Clan contact." She started to leave.

"Bailey."

Her second pivoted at the low call.

Rizzo sighed. "You aren't wrong. About any of it."

Bailey's features cleared. She nodded and left Rizzo standing alone in the garden.

chapter 28

ABEO STUMBLED TO BOTHA'S ROOM and leaned on the door comm.

"Yes?" Bika's voice.

"It's Abeo."

Her shout resounded through the hall behind him, and Abeo cringed to think who might hear. The door slid open. Bika's smile was a beacon of joy. She grabbed Abeo in a tight embrace, almost weeping.

"Jy is veilig! Jy leef! Ag my vriend…"

Abeo wished Galen were here to translate. He wrapped tentative arms around Bika.

Behind her, Botha grimaced.

"Bika," he said, "bly stil…kom terug in die kamer in…"

She snapped something in their language over her shoulder but wouldn't release Abeo until he dropped his arms.

"We should go inside," Abeo said.

Bika released him, but didn't move out of the way. She stared up at him, a touch of uncertainty behind her happiness. She spoke, but he didn't know her words, and she frowned at Botha, her confusion clear.

"Kom terug, Bika. Come, Abeo." Botha said.

The baba's soothing tone washed over the three of them. It helped, but what Abeo needed right now—what *Alira* needed—was a bit of quiet. The mood at that moment said "quiet" was not in the plan.

Bika finally allowed Abeo to enter, and they moved into the room. When the door was closed behind them, Botha tried to get Bika to sit, but she slapped his hands and shouted at him, then waited for Abeo's explanation.

"Bika…" How the hell was he going to explain this? He hadn't considered this kind of fallout before he'd acted, but what else could he have done? Leave her there? No. Never. He'd figure something out. "I am not who you think I am."

She scoffed, rattled off a lot of words Abeo didn't understand. Botha tried to help, but she laughed as though they were teasing her. Several attempts by Botha to explain, none of which were in English, set her jaw tight with annoyance.

"Bika," Abeo said, his tone low, his voice soft.

She stopped and gave him her full attention as if finally this joke would be over.

Botha gripped both sides of his head. Bika still smiled, but seemed no longer certain this was a game. She blinked, touched his arm.

He pulled her down on the edge of the bed with him. "Bika, you know how you saw a woman who looked just like you out there on the street? And she sent you here with Botha and took your place?"

She nodded. "Yes."

"That was me."

Her smile faltered.

"Just as I was able to be you, I am now Abeo."

Bika took that in, trying to understand. "Is Abeo here? Will you send him home, too, and take his place?"

Botha squatted beside her. "No, Bika. Abeo has died."

"Nee. Ek glo jou nie." Her features went slack, then clamped down tight, as if Abeo and Botha had betrayed her. She rose from the bed, repeating her words again and again, her voice growing louder each time. Botha stepped between her and the door, trying to calm her, but she slapped and beat at him, her fists pummeling his shoulders and chest. He took every blow without a sound until she crumpled, curled in on herself, and began to wail.

Botha caught her when she fell, lowered them both to the floor, held her, rocked her. He, too, wept as he spoke to her, but Abeo did not know what he said. For a long time, they sat like that, grieving together all that had been lost the night of the snatch.

Abeo watched, felt the rustle of Alira's Companion nearby, and took comfort in that presence despite the pangs of guilt and sorrow that pierced his own heart. No matter what Rizzo had said that night, Alira would always blame herself for the attack on Botha's village. Abeo wrapped his arms around himself as if to block out the cold, the fear, the pain. It didn't help.

He didn't know how long they sat that way. Night had fallen by the time Bika's wails ceased. She quietly wept a while longer before she sat up on the floor before Abeo. Her eyes, staring up at him, were puffy, tinged with reddish purple on her brown skin. Abeo didn't know her well enough to be sure, but he thought she held her shoulders stiff, her jaw tight.

"If you are not Abeo, then who are you?"

What harm would it do to trust her with a small truth? Maybe it would nudge her toward acceptance. "My true name is Alira, but you know me as Eli."

She scoffed and glared at Botha. His expression sent her gaze back to Abeo's. "Then why do you not wear your own face? How is it possible for you to appear as Abeo? You even bear the birthmark on your cheek, as he did. What magic is this?"

Botha leaned forward to stroke her hair. "It is true, Bika. All the days and nights I was gone, I was helping Eli," he gestured, "at Onlebaar. I told you I needed to throw my friend a rope, remember?"

She babbled in their language, but the moment she stopped, Botha went on in English.

"Eli is like the water."

She huffed. Spat something at him in their own tongue.

"There are many types of water, are there not? Rains," he said, "monsoons, droughts, floods. Oceans, lakes, rivers. All wear different faces. We call them different names, but they are water, just the same."

"But he looked like me," she shouted. "And now he is Abeo. And in the village he was Eli. How? This is not possible. People cannot just—"

Her eyes widened, whites glaring against her now blanched flesh as she made the connection. "Jy is 'n *gees*?" She scrambled up from the floor and lurched toward the door and Botha had to stop her.

"No, Bika," Botha soothed, raising his own voice enough to make Abeo cringe. "He is no spirit." He shushed her, calming her in their own tongue.

When she calmed, barely, he went on, careful to stay between her and escape. "Eli is not a ghost. He is not a demon. But he is not human. His people can change their shape, wear any disguise, as you know. But he is no threat to us. No threat to our village. He is a friend. He saved me from the slavers that night. He saved Oni after she fell and would not wake up. He helped many others that night. He saved you here, in this viper's den. Can you not see?"

She peered at him, still confused, but angry. She swung her focus to Abeo. "Why would you do this? Trick people that way? How can we trust you if we don't know your true face?"

"Because there are humans who hunt my kind. Who would hurt us or kill us for sport or for science. There aren't many of us left, Bika. If we don't hide, we will die." He stood up from the bed. She scrambled away from him, out of his reach, as if he would harm her. Abeo sighed. "I promise I'm no threat to you. But you can't tell anyone about this. You can't tell the other villagers."

"Ag nee," she exclaimed. "I won't help you deceive my people. I won't keep that big a secret from my family or friends or neighbors. If such a one as you will be staying among them, Bregainans deserve to know what you are."

Botha tried to explain, but she would hear none of it. Again, she tried to get past Botha. Again, he had to stop her. She turned her anger on Abeo.

"You see? This is your evil. Botha of before Eli would never have stopped me from leaving. Now you have poisoned him with your tricks."

Abeo stepped closer, and Bika recoiled as if Abeo's touch would soil her.

"Bika, it isn't just for me that I ask you to keep this secret. All my people, the old and the young and everyone else, will be in danger, too, as will yours."

She stilled, her gaze boring into him, searching for truth, maybe. "What is this? What do you mean?"

Abeo ground his teeth. "The people who hunt my kind will do whatever it takes to find us. If they know I've been to your village, they'll come after all of you in search of me. You'll never be safe," he said, hating every word, every apparent threat that croaked forth from his throat.

The color leeched from Bika's cheeks as she retreated until she ran out of space and cringed against the far wall.

Abeo despised himself, recoiled at the fact that he had brought this on them, regretted ever meeting Botha even though without him, Alira would likely be dead by now. Better that than this.

Even though his words were no empty threat and Botha knew it, he glared at Abeo as he reached for Bika, shushing her, trying to calm the storm they all knew was coming.

When it hit, Bika whirled on Botha. "You brought this adder among us," she shrieked. "You did this to our village. To *me*!" The rest of her words, spoken in their language, were lost on Abeo. Botha's manner alternated between pleading and annoyance, contrition and reasoning, as he tried to console and calm her.

Abeo's whole body thrummed with tension and fear. What if someone in a nearby room called for help? In his natural form, Alira's skin would have been streaked with white. Abeo felt himself slipping toward the edge, a place he dared not go. He needed to get control of himself. Now.

He curled up on the floor behind the door, as far from their fight as he could get and reached inside himself, pushed his mind into the spaces between the shouts while maintaining enough balance to hold his shifted form. As Botha's teachings began to work their magic, Abeo's shoulders relaxed. His heart rate slowed. His body calmed. After what felt like hours, the shouting stopped. When Abeo opened his eyes, Bika was staring at him. She stood next to Botha, her hand clenching his in a tight grip. Could Botha still feel his fingers?

He got to his feet, his movements calm and unhurried, and waited to see what would happen next.

"I am sorry for my words," Bika said. "This has never happened before to me. It needs new thing learning. I will do better next time." She gawped at Abeo, her posture above her own feet like that of a wild bird, ready to take flight at the first sign of danger.

Abeo's heart sank. "I frighten you."

"Yes," she said, breathless. "I do not know how you do what you do. But it must be a terrible thing to be hunted like animals, to live in fear and not wear your own face. I would not want a life like that. I will keep your secret, for your people and for my own."

A chill ran through him. He knew what he asked of her, but he had no choice.

He nodded. "Thank you."

chapter 29

Haven, Danua
<u>Clan Trader Base, Operations Center</u>

VOICES TALKING OVER ONE ANOTHER jumbled into a confusing tangle around Knøfa as he made his way around the circular room. He knew each station's task, had worked many of them himself in his youth under Tsurin's tutelage. An inner ring of desks hugged the main control core at the center of the room, while a double-sided outer band spanned the larger part of the space. On this level, each station controlled intrabase communications, to keep a finger on the pulse of everyday functions and tasks. Up one level, the same setup housed comm interchanges with the Danua Coalition's businesses as well as other planetary exchanges. Above that would be Transit Control, overseeing ship and shuttle traffic in and out of the base's airspace and landing bay.

He stood behind each worker, observing them for a moment before moving on to the next. A part of his focus, though, was in the medfac with the squib. Doctors had reported moments ago that they'd delivered the trigger shot that would cause the squib's body to release its ova. In thirty-six hours, they would harvest the product. One week later, they would implant all the viable embryos.

Even though he'd not been the sperm donor, in a way this would make him a father. The idea made him snort, which made the young crewman in front of him twitch.

His wristcom chirped and he touched it. "Yes."

"Trask here, sir. I'm on my way to Ops now. Do you have a minute to speak privately?"

"Yes. I'll meet you in Admiral Tsurin's medfac room. Two minutes."

"Very good, sir," Trask said. "On my way."

Knøfa hadn't covered all the stations yet, but he could start with those on his next inspection. He set out for the lift. This running of the base during Tsurin's recovery hadn't been as difficult as he had expected. She always told him there was more to the job than could be seen at a single glance, but he wasn't sure he agreed.

When the lift arrived at his floor, he stepped on, set it for the medfac, and resumed his thoughts.

Maybe it was because Tsurin had been training him from the age of four to take on this role. She was a good teacher, not just explaining things to him, but throwing him into the fray and showing him how to work his way out. Like the time she had sent him on a raiding party with one of her experienced crews with instructions for the captain to give Knøfa a bit of responsibility in both the flying of the craft and the looting of the site. He'd been proud of himself that day, and though he hadn't scored the largest haul, he had found the only bit of shiny that led the Clan to a new business contact.

Or the time Tsurin had brought to his quarters both a woman and a man from one of the Clan's brothels. She'd explained to him what they were for and left him with them, with the understanding that she would expect a report on the experience later. He never did figure that one out. He'd heard other officers of all genders talk of their sexual exploits but never understood the appeal. What those two had done to him had been more clinical than anything else. When he'd reported to her that he had endured, more than enjoyed it, she'd dismissed the subject and never brought it up again.

The lift stopped and Knøfa stepped off. Trask approached from the other end of the corridor.

"Admiral," Trask began, "I—"

Knøfa stopped him. "Wait until we're with Tsurin. Let her hear this at the same time you tell me."

Trask's expression shifted, but Knøfa ignored it. He couldn't understand it, so why let it bother him? The captain fell in beside him and they walked together in the direction of the medfac.

In Tsurin's room, Knøfa chased out the med techs before greeting Tsurin. She seemed better today. Her eyes were clearer, her smile not so twisted even though they still had those tubes in her nose. Was she sitting up higher in the bed? He didn't mention it in case she wasn't. He didn't want to discourage her.

"Trask has news for us."

"Oh?" she said.

The captain's attention shifted from Knøfa to the bed, then he cleared his throat. "Word is out that we had an unammi prisoner in custody."

Knøfa stilled. "Do they know of our plans for it and the surrogates?"

"The report didn't make that clear, sir."

"Who sent this news? From where?" Knøfa's ears began to ring.

"Stay calm," Tsurin said.

He stopped her with a gesture.

Trask squinted at the bed before answering. "From Rubene, sir. One of our people working in the Federation faction."

"And where," Knøfa heard his voice growing louder, "did *they* get this information?"

"Unknown." Trask shifted, moving marginally closer to the door. "But the intel would've had to come from inside our base. No one else knew."

"So, someone in the Clan has betrayed us?" Knøfa stepped closer to Trask. "Is that what you're telling me, Captain?"

"That's my guess, sir." Trask swallowed, his skin a shade paler than it had been a moment earlier.

That meant he was afraid. Even Knøfa knew that. Tsurin's past lessons whispered in his memory. Don't scare him. Frightened people do stupid things.

Knøfa lowered his voice as he swiveled to the bed. "This is your doing."

Her mouth fell open. "What are you talking about?"

He pointed at her. "I told you last year we should run loyalty spot checks every few months." His jaw worked as he struggled to contain his frustration. "You said I was being paranoid. You said you trusted everyone with access to valuable faction information. If you'd listened to me then, this would not have happened."

Tsurin rolled her eyes. "You *are* being paranoid. This kind of thing happens in factions. They keep tabs on us. We keep track of them. If someone gave an untrustworthy crewman access to that classified data, it wasn't me. But I doubt it was something as official as a spy. It's more likely that one of the med crews or surgeons said something to someone else and they were overheard, and the rumor mill took over. Word like that travels fast among Traders." She scowled at him. "It isn't that big a deal, Knøfa. Let it go."

"Not—" Knøfa blinked at her. "Not a big deal?" He scoffed, pointed at the world in general. "If word is out that I ran tests on a squib—"

"Unammi," she corrected.

He raised his voice. "On a *squib*, and that the *squib* then died, I'm not likely to trick another into my brig, am I? And if word gets out that I'm holding a hybrid brat in custody, what do you think will come of *that*?"

He waved toward the bed. "Do you believe this?" he said to Trask. "She thinks I'm being paranoid."

"Knøfa, calm down," Tsurin began.

Knøfa cut her off. "No, *you* calm down. You've been lying here on your back for months now, while I've been running the show. I've worked hard to keep it in shape on your behalf, but you have no idea of all that's happened since your accident. Apparently, I'm not the only one who's been trying to keep you informed, but it's like you always said. There's a lot that doesn't end up in a report, right?"

She drew a breath.

"And even now, now that you're better, you stay in that bed and let me do all the work. Well fine. If that's the way you want to play it, I'm done being your second. As of now, I am assuming control of the Danua Clan. You no longer get any say in the decisions of this faction."

He glared at Trask, stabbing a finger in the man's direction. "You are now the official second in command of the Clan. Congratulations."

Knøfa faced the bed once more, where Tsurin stared at him in shock. "I always respected you. But I'm done with that too." He spun and raged out the door with Trask close behind. He pushed through the corridor so fast that crewmen in front of him pressed themselves against the walls. It sounded as if Trask was almost running to keep up.

Knøfa had been loyal to Tsurin since he was four years old. He'd listened to everything she said, carried out every order or instruction she'd ever given. Heeded every lesson and tried to incorporate them into his working style. For her to talk to him like that, especially in front of Trask, was over the top, even for his commanding officer.

Well, no longer.

He stormed through the corridors and up the lift to the observation deck. Here, in the topmost level of the Clan's operations center, he could see in every direction—past the walls of the faction's base, past Tsurin's disregard, past everyone's low expectations of Knøfa, the not-quite-right officer. He'd show Tsurin. He'd show them all.

A gentle sound reminded him that Trask had not been dismissed. Knøfa spoke at the windows. "Do you have any idea, Captain, who this spy might be?"

"Not yet, sir," Trask said, his voice low. "But I'll figure it out."

Knøfa nodded. "You do that. Get security involved. Get the whole damn base involved, if that's what it takes. Bring me this spy."

"I give you my word." Trask cleared his throat. "There is one other matter."

Knøfa turned away from the window. Trask stood well out of reach. Maybe he was smarter than Knøfa had given him credit for. "What is it?"

"Your techs have a good start on the detection device for the unammi."

Huh. A ray of light in this storm. "When will they begin testing?"

"Well," Trask said, his features twisting, "there's the rub. They've based it on the unammi's genetic structure so it should, theoretically, be able to tell the difference between unammi cellular structures and human ones. But…"

Knøfa waited. "Spit it out, Trask."

"There's no way to test it, Admiral." He shrugged. "The techs designed and built a prototype and pointed it at random humans, but of course they got no surprises. And yes, it showed a positive reading when they pointed it at our unammi patient in the medfac, but that won't tell them if it would 'see' her in a human form. Without a subject we know is disguised as a human, they can't tell whether it would work the way you want."

Damn it. He needed another squib. Or a shipload. For an animal that could heal almost instantly, the one he'd found broke too easily. Unless…Would the device detect the hybrid offspring, even if they appeared human? He frowned. Even if it would, they couldn't run a test like that for months yet.

"Very well. Tell them to keep at it. And find me some test subjects. Dismissed."

He might have been wrong about Skalar being involved, but the theory made sense. Harajüd House wasn't about to go into another world and just take over like that. Only a Trader would do that. Unless Skalar had done it *for* HHU, and they then removed him so he couldn't talk.

If only he knew what they'd done with all the squibs.

chapter 30

<u>Bregaina, Bejami</u>

ELI SET THE JUMPER DOWN on the landing platform with a noticeable thump. He'd need a lot more practice if he was ever to be as good a pilot as Rizzo. At the moment, he couldn't bring himself to care much. He thanked Na'Staani they'd made it off Zebalu. But the memory of Yele standing by that transport in Pelarr, waiting in vain for his partner, arose once more to play on the viewscreen of his closed lids. Throughout their trip, Yele's expression of betrayal, of abandonment, had haunted Eli until he wasn't sure he would be able to rest ever again.

Outside, villagers poled their boats toward the ship, coming to welcome them. So few! Had they lost that many? Bika's cheeks gleamed with tears. She regarded him, her visage shifting between joy and fear.

Alira's Companion rustled in Eli's mind, that uncomfortable harbinger of impending Change he'd come to recognize. He wished it wasn't so familiar.

He replayed moments from the fight in Pelarr, the struggle to convince Bika to keep his secret. She'd said little on the way home, clung to Botha's hand every minute of their trip. But the only other time she'd shown open fear was after they left Bel-Rhovan's landport behind, and Abeo had shifted to Eli's form in the jumper. He'd warned her not to watch, but she did it anyway. She didn't speak for a long time.

"Are you ready?" Eli asked Bika.

She stared out at the approaching boats. "When you came to me in Pelarr, and helped me escape those menserowers who stole me from my home, why did you not save Yele, too?" She brought her focus to bear on him. "Or the others?"

"Bika," Botha began.

Bika held up a finger. "I want Eli to explain."

Eli shrugged. "Because I'm only one person. I would need to wear their faces and save them one at a time. And it would only be a matter of time before they caught me." He reached out to her, but she ignored the gesture. "I'll go back for the rest of them, Bika. It might not be soon because I'll need help to do it. But I will bring them home as soon as I can. I promise."

She turned, pain bright in her eyes, and nodded. "Good." She stood up, opened the hatch, and jumped down to meet the others crowding up the ladders.

"Oh, my friend," Botha said in a weary voice, "you have done it now."

Eli frowned. "Have I?"

Botha laughed. "You do not make a promise to Bika unless you know you can carry it out." He got to his feet and, at the hatch, spoke over his shoulder. "I would not want to be you if you fail." He followed Bika out to the platform.

Eli didn't want to be himself either. But he had meant what he said. Every word.

chapter 31

New Canaan, Harajüd
En Route to Dagons Public House

AT THE BASE GATE, CREW waved Admiral Baldric through without question. Thrace made a note to mention it to Sa'abah. Yes, her features were distinct enough to be recognizable, but so were Skalar's. Remember where that had gotten him. Thrace didn't expect any unammi to come through impersonating her, but one never knew. And even if it wasn't a real problem, they should never relax security. Not for the admiral, or anyone else.

She drove, windows down, between the base admin building and the Consortium's industrial facility. The bay wasn't visible from ground level at this distance even after she veered toward the city center, but it lay close enough to scent the cool evening breeze with the heavy tang of salt. She still hadn't managed to tour the bay or visit Shamashu Island. There was never enough time.

New Canaan never really shut down. None of the colony worlds did. But on Harajüd, with tourism one of its top industries, every major city's heart beat strong at all hours of the long days and nights. Traffic always flowed. Pedestrians always filled the sidewalks. Businesses, especially those like Dagons, never closed.

Just outside the city center market, Thrace followed the roundabout to North Market, then parked in the admiral's reserved space in front of the pub. Early in her faction leadership, it would've been unwise for her to travel alone like this. Now, though, she'd made a place for herself in the Consortium. Crew actually seemed to like her—mostly, anyway. Promoting Mira had been a good idea. She had all the makings of a good second and, one day, a good admiral. But Thrace couldn't yet trust her with the secret of the unammi. With Thrace's own identity. The time would come when Thrace couldn't run the faction herself, for whatever reason, and its leadership would change. She hadn't decided yet how she would deal with that inevitability, except to know the unammi situation would need to be resolved by then. She just hoped they could find a reasonable solution that worked for everyone, but she had a feeling this meeting with Kilbee was about that very subject. The suspicion left her uneasy and cold.

Most businesses these days had the more efficient entryways that slid into the walls, rather than requiring floor space for a door that would swing in or out. Dagons had gone with the old way, using a realwood door salvaged from an old building that dated to the early days of this colony's founding. Heavy as it was, the thing swung easily on thick hinges without so much as a squeak. Not that you would hear something like that in the din that blasted from the opening. Inside, patrons surrounded the stools at the bar, stood talking on the spiral staircase near the rear wall, and clustered at the rails in the gallery. In a momentary gap between passing customers, Thrace caught a glimpse of Kilbee at her table. He'd beat her here. Was probably already eating fries.

She nodded at one of the wait staff, and at one of the bartenders as she threaded her way through the crowd to the stairs. There, the chatting clientele pressed to one side to allow her passage, watching as she climbed. She was used to that now. What she couldn't get comfortable with was the emotions they felt when they saw her. Most viewed the admiral of a Trader faction—any Trader faction—as a cold-hearted criminal who would gut you without a second thought. And Thrace had to admit there were sound foundations beneath those rumors. But even while she knew she might need to resort to that at some point, she planned never to choose violence first. For her, it would be a last resort. Still, she could see where a fearsome reputation could work in her favor.

As long as she could maintain it, anyway. Alira hadn't been wrong about everything she claimed while sitting in Skalar's chair. Letting others see her weaken or hesitate would pit her facade. Best to let them think the worst of her.

She reached the admiral's table and sat across from Kilbee. "I see you started without me."

He shoved another few fries in his mouth and spoke around them. "I wish we could grow potatoes at the outpost. Then I could eat these any time I wanted."

"If you ate them every day, they wouldn't be special."

His expression said he didn't agree.

The server brought her a glass of water with a pitcher for refills. When she'd gone, Thrace activated the privacy screen. "What's the latest at the base?"

"It isn't the base I'm here about," he said, chewing the last of his fries. He wiped his fingers before resting his elbows on the table. "The council knows about our findings, about the new worlds we located."

Thrace scowled. "Who told them?"

Kilbee sucked his teeth. "I did."

She drooped, her shoulders sagging. "Why?"

"Because they have a right to know. And because we both know they won't be safe on Earth forever."

He was right, but she hated that fact. She pressed her lips together and felt for his emotions. He was on the defensive, expecting her to be angry. Ready to meet her challenges to his actions. And while he'd taken that action for the right reasons, he still second-guessed his own decision since if the council took the survivors to a distant world, he might never see his ama again. He and Rakalesh didn't usually view things in the same light, but he would miss her if she left.

"What did they say when you told them?"

He scanned the crowded bar. "They're inclined to go with one of the new options. They said it would be—let me see if I can get the wording right—'better for the rest of the survivors if the possibility of a strange new life wasn't so tantalizingly close.'"

Thrace waited. He wasn't finished yet.

"You know, I'm trying to see it from their perspective. I understand their reasoning. Oh, who am I kidding?" He brought his gaze to Thrace's face. "They don't all feel this way. Rakalesh and Dyson are swaying those who are uncertain. I'd guarantee that. So it's really those two who're behind that attitude." He looked down at the table. "The longer I work in this capacity, as liaison between you and them, the more I sympathize with what Alira had been saying all along. Their recalcitrance may yet be the end of the unammi. But they don't see it. They won't, because change is uncomfortable. It's unknown. It's new. And they fear anything that doesn't fit their expectations."

Thrace leaned toward to him. "Did you tell Rakalesh your misgivings?"

"Yes," he said. "I also pointed out that further dividing our population was going to diminish our viability as a species, and that they'd only just begun to regrow the irolium. If they move, they'll need to start all over. I wondered aloud at my ama whether the irolium would even grow from scratch, with so many fewer of the unammi to spark the symbiosis."

"What did she say?" Thrace fought to keep her hands still, instead of clenching them together.

He laughed, a sound not of amusement, but of disbelief. "She told me I was worrying over nothing. That it would be fine. The unammi had always been fine. She continues to insist that they'll be better off far apart from human worlds."

Thrace drew an uneven breath. Though she supposed she could see the appeal of moving far, far away, this news unsettled her. That kind of distance would make resupplying themselves with irolium a far more difficult task. Perhaps that was part of Rakalesh's and Dyson's thinking— hang the threat of deprivation over those who'd fallen from favor, as she'd been expecting them to do. Given the frightening possibility that would present, outcasts and mitigants might do whatever the council dictated.

"Is our experiment showing any results?"

"No," he said. "Not yet."

Thrace sighed. "Then maybe we can at least convince them to leave behind a large enough portion of the remaining crystals that we won't need to resupply before it does."

Kilbee's mouth twitched up at one corner. "That's a thin hope."

She shrugged. "Better than none at all. And who knows? Maybe they'll decide to stay on Earth after all." She touched the digital menu and placed an order.

"What are you getting?" he asked.

"More fries, enough for both of us." She grinned. "Humans call them comfort food. Let's find out if they're right."

chapter 32

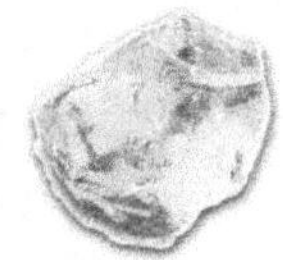

Haven, Danua
<u>Clan Trader Base, Admiral Knøfa's Office</u>

KNØFA SURVEYED THE WORKSPACE TSURIN had used ever since she'd taken over the admiralty from Henri. She had made changes to its setup then, moved the furniture to suit her working habits, hung a few trinkets on the walls, set personal mementos on the desk. He remembered the rug in front of the seating area, the one that used to be in her quarters when she was still a captain. She'd told him she bought it on Rubene, but he knew she'd taken it from his parents' house the same night she took him away from their bodies. He'd always marveled that she didn't think he would recognize it. He'd been young, not stupid.

He surveyed what was now his own office. He hadn't understood Tsurin's desire to rearrange things. He would not do so. This setup was familiar to him. He'd worked here with her on more projects and operations than he could count. Its layout and placement of necessary items was second nature at this point. Moving it would require an adjustment period to refamiliarize himself with the changes. Inefficient. A waste of time for something as ridiculous as aesthetics.

No thank you.

The scene from yesterday in the medfac played in his mind like a worn out holo, glitchy and dim. He may have outgrown his old mentor, but that didn't mean everything she'd ever taught him lost its value. She'd drilled into him throughout his life that he shouldn't make hasty decisions. He didn't always listen, but this time it might be a good idea. So, he'd waited a full day, thirty hours in which he'd played and replayed the way she'd spoken to him in front of his second, with flashbacks into all the instances where she'd overruled his reasonable suggestions and good ideas. He had told her repeatedly that it was unwise to put so much faith in her crew when they were all technically criminals. Now, her trust had fouled his plans. As if his project for the squib and whatever progeny he might wrest from the otherwise useless meat of its body weren't already on a tight schedule. The medfac was harvesting its ova, but that didn't help him now. He needed another adult. Except, if word reached the other squibs that he was using them this way, he'd never trick one into his medfac.

That is, *if* he could even find one. Or know it was a squib when he saw it.

At least he could stop obsessing about a cure for Tsurin. He'd done the right thing. He didn't need her any longer. Neither did the Clan. Maybe with him at the helm instead of Tsurin, with her bleeding heart and all those lines she would never cross, he could finally push this faction out of the dregs and into the competition.

"TICS, identify."

A small chitter sounded. Then, "Voice identity matches Knøfa, captain and second in command."

"Find Admiral Tsurin."

"Admiral Tsurin is in MedFac 13."

"Classify health status of Admiral Tsurin."

A rustling chitter ran on for a few seconds. "Admiral Tsurin's symptoms include persistent coma, absence of any detectable brainstem reflexes, and lack of independent ability to breathe. These criteria, when present together, denote a diagnosis of brain death. Therefore, her health status is legally classified as deceased."

He knew better. She'd been awake and talking. Still, the TICS classification served his purposes.

The door chimed.

"Confirmed. Transfer all base command override authorization and command clearance to me, effective immediately."

This time, the chitter lasted a bit longer.

The door chimed again. Knøfa ignored it.

"Transfer complete."

"TICS, identify."

"Voice identity matches Knøfa, admiral and commanding officer."

"Notify all medical staff that they are to cease support activity on Tsurin's body at once." If she didn't die from *that*, he could always move her to the brig. Or take care of her himself. "Once her body ceases autonomic function, they are to transfer her remains to the crematorium and carry out the necessary disposal. Report to me when this is completed."

"Acknowledged." Another chitter, and the TICS went silent.

The door chimed a third time. "Come." He rounded her desk— correction, *his* desk—and sat down. Hmm. On second thought, he actually might swap out this chair for his own larger one.

Trask stepped in and approached the desk. "Knew I'd find you in here, sir."

Knøfa peered at him. "Why wouldn't you? It's my office."

His captain nodded once as if that was all the explanation he needed. "I have news on the Iridos situation."

Tsurin would tell him to offer Trask a seat. Knøfa ignored the mental nudge. She wasn't giving him orders any longer. "Well?"

"You were right about Skalar. He sent Crow with an armada to buy hematium from the Iridosians, but they refused. Crow's people wiped the city off the surface, killed the natives, then went in and took a hauler full of the ore."

Knøfa scowled. "Killed them all?"

"As far as anyone knows, yes, sir. But…" Trask twisted his head to one side with a small grimace. "Apparently, the op didn't go as well as they hoped. The Iridosians had some sort of weapon that wiped out half the armada, and when the crews went down to the surface to start mining, they all went nuts."

"Explain."

"They started fights, heard voices, saw things that weren't there, that sort of thing."

Like his crew had done when Knøfa first put his own squib in the brig.

"A significant percentage of the Consortium crew didn't make it. Either they killed each other, or the radiation from LADRAS got to them faster than it should have." Trask frowned. "Doesn't make any sense."

But it did. Didn't it? His squib prisoner could change its appearance, hide in plain sight, heal at an incredible rate, traits he assumed were common to its kind. If its ability to affect human mental states was also on that list of special gifts for all of them, Trask's news would imply some of those on the surface survived, at least long enough to poison Crow's crew against one another. It would also make holding more than one in his brig a little trickier than he'd expected. Not a problem, yet. He had to find them first. If there were any left, that is.

"What else?"

"That's all for now, sir." Trask raised an eyebrow. "How did you know Skalar was involved?"

"How did you not?" Knøfa regarded his second. "HHU has been closely allied with the Consortium for at least a decade. Maybe more." He counted on his fingers. "The hematium shipments began slowing down. Consortium leadership vanished to gods only know where. And now the colonial government is in control of that resource. It's a simple equation."

"Of course, sir."

"What did you learn about this new admiral?"

"Thrace Baldric," Trask said, his voice crisp. "No one ever heard of her before. She showed up with Skalar one day and took over for Crow. A couple of months later, Skalar was gone, too. She *says* she doesn't know where he is." He spread his hands out as if to suggest the inference was obvious.

"How did the crew take the change in command?" Knøfa wondered at this in his own situation, too, though so far nothing had changed.

"There were some issues in the beginning. No surprise there, but they seem to have taken to Baldric. I hear she's quite charismatic. Most of them support her now."

Knøfa grunted. "But not everyone. Not the person who's feeding you this information."

Trask gave a small shrug.

"Who's her second?"

"Captain Mira Cohen, a longtime Consortium crewman recently promoted to Captain and installed as next in line. I didn't get much about her. Even though she's been in the faction for years, she never got far until now. She's probably green in matters of leadership, but that's a guess."

The admiral tapped on the desk. "If Skalar took a hauler full of hematium from Iridos, chances are he didn't hide it on his own home base. So where'd he put it?"

"Good question, sir."

If it was him, Knøfa would hide it as far off the normal trade routes as possible, to stop someone from tripping over it by accident. But Tsurin taught him that all the rocky planets and moons in this quadrant had been thoroughly explored. Some still served as mining camps or might be used for off-planet storage or, in some cases, held off-planet medfacs for treatment of contagious disease. A few might serve as a shadowy faction rendezvous where no party wanted to advertise their participation in the action. Knøfa would bet on one of those as the most likely candidate. But which one?

"Very well," Knøfa said. "I have three tasks for you. First, find out where Skalar hid the hematium he took. If you can, find out why he wanted it."

"Yes, sir."

"Second, I want to know what happened to Skalar. If he's still alive, where is he? If he's dead, when and how?"

"Yes, sir."

"And third…" Knøfa squinted up at his second, his teeth clamped together, "I want a full report on this Baldric person. Where she came from. Where she trained. Where she originated. I want to know her specialty, how she walked in off the street and took over the biggest, most powerful faction on twelve worlds without anyone even knowing what was happening until it was over. Find out how she is charming her crew, and all those in HHU's corporate body. Anything that will help me understand who she is and how she operates, I want to know it."

"You've got it, sir. I'll see what I can dig up."

"Good," Knøfa said. "Dismissed."

Trask was halfway out the door before Knøfa stopped him.

"Yes sir?" Trask said.

"One other thing," Knøfa said. "Send someone after my desk chair in my old office and have them bring it here immediately. This thing is too dainty for my behind."

He thought for a second that Trask was amused. But the admiral must've been wrong because though the captain's face did twist and contort, he never did laugh.

chapter 33

THE BLARE OF A HORN almost knocked Alira from her bed. A cool night breeze blew through the low vents in the domed structure, bringing the brackish smell of wet mud. The tide was out, then. Shifting to Eli's form, she stumbled to his feet. Many lights filtered through the window port, muted by the privacy screen in the plaz. All flickered from the direction of the communal platform.

Eli hurried out of the guesthouse and down the ladder to the walkway, his mind racing between possibilities. Another snatch? So soon? He'd heard no ships. Was someone hurt? If so, at least Eli could help. His soft-soled shoes whispered across the boards as he hurried through the gloom to the crowded platform. Voices raised in the Bregainan tongue set Eli's heart racing. Whatever was going on had stirred people's emotions to a near frenzy.

He climbed the ladder as fast as he could work his legs and found the villagers crowded around one woman who pointed at Botha, then at the guesthouse, while she spoke in a loud voice. Botha's hands were up, palms out, as if to placate or calm her, but it wasn't working. Not even close. It even appeared to be making the woman angrier. Bika stood to one side, her arms crossed, her emotions tangled across a confusing mask Eli could not interpret. He frowned, stepped closer. He must've made a sound because those Bregainans nearest him whirled, their faces going blank, their ranks parting as more and more of the villagers saw that he had joined them. Silence fell like a heavy fog, dampening the mood even further, until the shouting woman saw Eli standing there. Her mouth pinched into a pucker.

It was Jaru, one of Botha's and Bika's other partners. No one spoke. In the nearby marsh, a night bird trilled. Everyone stared at Eli. A chill crept up his spine.

"Am I intruding?" He didn't need his harvested voices to tell him that was a foolish question. Nor did he need to be a reader to know what they were arguing about.

"Yes." Jaru started toward him, her expression wrathful. "You and all the trouble you bring."

"Jaru!" Botha said with a chiding tone. He moved closer to her. "You are being unfair. Eli did not bring those menserowers here. We were fortunate he was here when they came. He knew who they were, and he helped us bring Bika home." He gestured to Bika who looked at Jaru, then at Eli, then at the platform before her feet.

"How did he know who they were unless he is one of them?" Jaru said, her voice echoing off the shelters and the marsh mud. She shot Eli a hostile glare, and spun to Botha, waving in Eli's direction. "Nothing like this ever happened until *he* showed up."

Murmurs of agreement and anger rumbled among the assembled villagers.

Again, Jaru threw a belligerent sneer at Eli before casting her gaze on the others. "Some of us were taken, like Bika and Yele. Many were injured, like Oni." She pointed at her partner, who stood beside Bika. "Others were killed. The spirit of our village is sick, like a festering wound that cannot heal until the poison is removed. He," she pointed at Eli, "needs to go. Tonight. Now."

Eli's throat tightened, making it hard to swallow. He forced himself to stay calm. This all felt so familiar. He'd hoped to find a home here, or at least a place he could visit and find moments of peace, as Galen had so often done. But Jaru had a point. Upheaval seemed to have latched onto him, to follow him wherever he went. The last thing he wanted to do was bring it here, among Botha's people.

For once, Botha got angry. "You can't just—"

"It's okay," Eli said, just loud enough to be heard over the other voices. He regarded Jaru and the others in the crowd. "I hear you. This is your village. It's understandable that you would want to feel safe in your homes."

His glance landed on Bika, who would not meet his eyes, before he fixed on Botha. "I'll be gone within the hour." He descended the ladder amid a sudden, jarring silence. His legs, stiff and wooden in their movements, carried him in a lurching stride along the walkways. His ears rang. His mind scattered in many directions at once, making no progress toward any specific destination. Where would he go? What would he do next? He couldn't go to Earth. Rizzo didn't want him. His presence at the Consortium would be problematic for Galen. Zebalu wasn't safe for him or anyone else, apparently.

He'd almost gotten to the guesthouse before the din rose among the villagers. He tuned it out as he climbed the ladder to the guesthouse and packed his minimal belongings. When he finished, he stood in the center of the large room, breathing in the smell of the marsh, listening to the night sounds, the babble of the villagers behind that. He had not spent enough time here to truly love it as Galen did. But the way Botha talked of Bregaina, the joy he conveyed when he told stories of life here—the bh'tati crop, or the scavenging of muil eggs, or whatever—had roused in Eli a longing for some place where he could belong. Where he could feel welcome, respected, even loved.

Maybe that place didn't exist.

He went outside, then down the ladder. The tide was turning. Puddles and trills of water seeped into rivulets in the mud where they gleamed in the ambient light from the torches and stars. Eli had heard the villagers say that it came in fast, so he hurried across the walkways, his feet splashing at the last, to climb up to the landing platform.

Botha stood at the top, touched by the light of the stars, his features cast in shadows.

Eli waited for him to speak.

At last, Botha sighed and reached out. "Ah, Gelaboot."

Eli slung his slight pack over one shoulder and grasped Botha's hands with his own.

"I am sorry this has happened. It is not right that they burden you with their troubles. But my voice is only one among many. I cannot change their decision, though I tried."

"Don't worry, Botha." Eli touched Botha's shoulder. "It's not the first time I've been asked to leave a place. It won't be the last. I'm used to it. Besides, it's time I was on my feet. Back in the game, so to speak."

Botha's teeth shone in the darkness, but not in a smile. "Are you sure? My rope reached you once. It might not work a second time."

"You did more than throw me a rope, my friend. You taught me how to patch my own boat." He squeezed Botha's shoulder, then let go. "Now that Hannah has shown us her plan, I need to find what resources I can to stop her. And I made Bika a promise. I intend to keep it." Botha looked so sad. Eli hated that he had to ask one more favor. "Please don't report Abeo's death just yet. It's my only way out of here."

Lips pressed tight, Botha cleared his throat. "Row that boat quickly, Gelaboot. The others will report the deaths in three days."

"That's long enough." Eli jerked a thumb over his shoulder at the rented jumper they'd brought from the Bel-Rhovan landport. "I assume you will allow me to take that to the city?"

Botha nodded but didn't speak. Perhaps he couldn't. Eli had to swallow the lump in his own throat to push the words out.

"I'll pack up the rest of our things at the camp and leave yours there for you to pick up. You'll need to let Rizzo know when you do so she can retrieve the hab."

Botha nodded.

Eli watched him for a long time, remembering their moments on the island, all the lessons the elder had taught whether he'd intended to or not, the joy in his laughter, the love in his eyes. Then Eli boarded the jumper, fired it up, and flew north into the night.

Part Three

chapter 34

Tuneloras, Saacharis
<u>Syndicate Trader Base, Admiral Rizzo's Office</u>

LATE AFTERNOON LIGHT FILTERED THROUGH the gray haze that was Tuneloras' sky, casting a dim glow into the Zen garden ten stories below. Fullspec lights across the ceiling in the office, set at fifty percent for the moment, cast Rizzo's shadow across the window before her. She caressed the small woodcut. Lourdes had given it to her, a gift to bring strength, courage, and perseverance in Turizomi's new life as a free adult. Its familiar feel—the hye-won-hye burned into one side, the sanded edges worn smooth by her touch over the years, the small pits and gouges it had gathered in all that time—always brought a measure of comfort. Where was Lourdes now? Was she still alive? Had she freed other child slaves after she'd freed Rizzo, and did she ever know how Rizzo felt about her?

The sound of the door chime broke the silence. "Enter," Rizzo called. She watched the reflection in the plaz to see who it was, though she already knew. Bailey, responding to her summons. Good. The captain stood just inside the door, long hair swinging free. Rizzo liked it that way.

She returned the woodcut to its shelf.

"I've seen you hold that before," Bailey said. "What is it?"

Rizzo's gaze fell on her and, for a moment, she almost told her. About the woodcut. About Lourdes. About her childhood. Then she looked across the office at her desk, and the waiting communique. "Another time. We've received word on changes in the Clan, but it's complicated. Multilayered. The unammi are involved. It's time you knew as much about that situation as I can share. Sit."

Bailey chose one of the seats at the table, near Rizzo, and sat forward, as if her whole body were focused on the admiral's words.

"You remember Skalar's attack on Iridos?"

Bailey's features twisted. "Yes."

"Some of them escaped and are in hiding."

"More than just a few of the pilots?"

"Yes."

"That's good, then, that some of them made it out. Right? But why would they need to—" The captain's confused expression shifted as she pieced it together. "Because of Knøfa's prisoner. Because of what he learned they can do."

"Yes and no." Rizzo paced to the window, staring out at the skyline of the city beyond the base walls. "They went into hiding because they knew someone like Knøfa could discover their secrets. We humans," she said, her tone lower, "are a curious lot. We leave no mystery unprodded."

"Not all of us," Bailey said. "Not you."

"Indeed." Rizzo regarded her second. "But they also couldn't chance Skalar's people finding them."

Bailey nodded. "This is why you wouldn't tell me what was happening. You're protecting them."

Her statement didn't require an answer and Rizzo didn't offer one. "Intel now says Knøfa has learned about Skalar's attack, and that some of the unammi still live. He's searching for them."

"Is he likely to find their hiding place?"

Rizzo heard the note of alarm in her captain's voice. Lourdes's voice whispered an old adage in her mind, and Rizzo murmured it aloud. "A determined dog will always unearth the bone."

"We can't allow that," Bailey said. "What are we going to do?"

"We?"

Bailey shrugged. "Of course."

"I don't know. Yet." Rizzo pulled the seat next to her captain's and sat to face her. "Baldric needs to know there are people in her command, crew from Skalar's regime, who are loose-lipped. They'll sink her."

"And her surviving people."

Despite herself, Rizzo peered at Bailey with pride. Not much got past her. Only one of the many reasons Rizzo had promoted her. Trained her. Groomed her. "You'll make a fine admiral."

"Not anytime soon, I hope."

"This new Clan admiral concerns me." Rizzo slumped in her seat. "Tsurin was injured on a snatch-and-grab. I still don't know if Knøfa did it himself or had it done, or what actually transpired, but she finally died."

Bailey winced. "I'm sorry to hear that. I know you admired her."

"I did." Rizzo frowned, stared into the space between them. "Our contact says they kept her on life-support for months, even knowing she could never recover." A shudder went through her at the thought of living as a lump in a bed, vulnerable and burdensome. "She would've hated that. And…" She locked eyes with Bailey. "…so would I. Don't ever do that to me."

Bailey leaned forward, one hand on the table near Rizzo's. "Never."

The admiral pushed herself up straighter in her chair. "I'm glad for her sake that it's over. But her death means Knøfa is now in full charge of the Clan. That doesn't bode well for anyone."

"What can I do?"

Rizzo pulled her lips to one side. How much of what they were doing had been reported to Knøfa? Did he know Rizzo was working with Baldric, or helping the unammi? "I don't doubt Knøfa has contacts in Tuneloras. Probably in the Syndicate. If we are going to get further involved in helping the unammi, we can't take the chance that our actions will be reported to that faction. Whoever they are, we need them gone. Find them for me. Any sources that might feed him info, root them out. Bring me their names." She pinned Bailey with her stare. "Recon only. Take no action against them."

"Understood." Bailey rose. "Should I contact Admiral Baldric for you? Fill her in?"

"No." Rizzo glanced at her desk, the communique set up and ready to record. "That's for me to do. Your assignment is complicated enough without adding unammi drama." She gave Bailey a hint of smile. "Perhaps next time. Dismissed."

Once Bailey left, Rizzo rose, crossed her office, and stood before the desk. She'd hoped the unammi situation would resolve itself, but that didn't appear to be possible. With Knøfa actively searching for them, she would need to do whatever was necessary to help the survivors stay a step ahead of him. At least this problem couldn't be heaped on Alira's narrow shoulders.

The admiral grunted in wry amusement.

"TICS, begin recording, voice only." She drew in a long breath. "This information is urgent and should be delivered personally with all possible haste to Admiral Thrace Baldric at the Consortium base in New Canaan. Knøfa is now in full control of the Clan. He has learned of Skalar's actions with regard to our mutual friends, as well as the fact that those he seeks are now in hiding, and he is on the hunt. He is also attempting to devise a mechanical means to detect disguised individuals. I don't know if he has yet succeeded. I advise all possible evasive maneuvers, as soon as you can." She shuddered at the potential ramifications of this latest development. "If I can help, Baldric should let me know at once. Rizzo out. TICS, end recording. Encrypt with iron cypher. Authorization TR94VXY37. Complete encryption and send to Harajüd agent NY743."

"Acknowledged." A soft chitter followed. "Message sent."

She stared across the office long after the TICS went silent. She didn't know how many of the unammi had survived Crow's armada, but if they were in hiding somewhere other than Iridos, then they might no longer have access to their weapons. That would explain why Alira and Galen now sought weapons contractors, though there would be no way to complete a deliverable system soon enough to be of help in this situation. When Knøfa found them—and no doubt he would—they would be vulnerable, exposed.

Rizzo knew all too well how that felt, to be at the mercy of someone larger, stronger, and with better resources. She'd been snatched when she was only ten. Seven years later, Lourdes had freed her. That day, Rizzo had vowed never again to allow herself to be backed into that position, that she would take her own life rather than repeat that experience.

Yet that night in Bregaina, as she'd fought to protect the running, screaming villagers from the snatchers, she'd felt the same sense of frustration and fear as when she was ten. She'd stood on the platform in the baba's village, helpless to do more than slash her blade at armored Cartel crew members cabled to their ships for easy extraction.

She ground her teeth and clenched her fists. Those snatched villagers were citizens of Bejami, it's true, but without their identifications they would have no resources to comm for help or book passage for travel, even to another city, in a first step toward regaining their freedom. More than likely, they'd been warned that efforts to resist would result in harm not to them, but to loved ones. Friends, or family. Other villagers who had been taken. Perhaps their children. Combine all that with limited sustenance, interrupted sleep, and the trauma of the snatch itself, and even the adult villagers would soon be as helpless as young Turizomi had been at ten years of age. How many other villagers on Bejami had lived through a scene like that one in Bregaina? Bejami was a world of isolated pockets of habitation. The other worlds had their share, too. Hannah wouldn't stop with one raid.

Neither would Knøfa. A life of slavery was bad enough, but if Knøfa found the unammi, he'd take as many of them as he could. Word had already leaked about their special abilities. In a matter of months, if not sooner, all the colonies would know. Knøfa would not be the only one to want those abilities for humans. Depending on how many unammi remained when they were found, the consequences could be as devastating as a serious genetic bottleneck for the unammi species at best, extinction at worst.

Bailey had been right. They could not—Rizzo *would* not—allow that to happen.

chapter 35

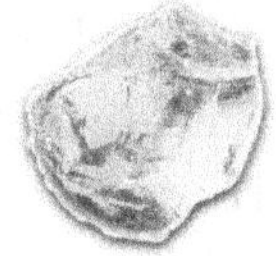

Haven, Danua
<u>Clan Trader Base, Interview Room 3</u>

KNØFA WATCHED THROUGH THE PRIVACY window as the workers filed into the room on the other side of the pane. All had been cleaned and patched, their few wounds tended and healing. These were all adults. He'd insisted on that when he agreed to the deal with Admiral Dupré. He had enough problems without the added burden of children on the base. They were necessary, of course, for the continuation of the species. But their charm was lost on him. How anyone could find them cute or amusing remained a mystery.

Except for the squib hybrids. Their appeal lay in what they could teach him.

Those projects carried the promise of profit in the future. Here and now, the product focused on full-grown workers. Of the twelve he offered, ten had come from Hannah's raids—seven from Bejami and three from Ranafta. The remaining two originated right here on Danua, and were legitimate indentures, indebted to the Clan for gambling past their means.

Those two might eventually clear their debts and rejoin their families. The others, whose debts accrued from the cost of their capture, plus their daily expenses of food, shelter, medicine, and clothing, might be indentured for life. The colonials were only willing to pay so much for their temporary contracts, and the Clan required a profit to make them worthwhile in the first place. For these workers, the math never edged into the black, but as long as the Clan made a profit, Knøfa didn't care. They would be a continuing resource for revenue.

Beside him stood the colonial negotiator, Seije Alanko. Middle-aged, maybe sixty or so. White hair. Shorter than Knøfa, but then so was everyone else. Long face, long fingers, long legs, hooked nose. She had yet to smile, which was odd. She peered through the window, arms crossed.

"What are you feeding them?" she asked, her voice coarse, gravelly.

"Food." Why was that important? "All the basics."

She gestured. "They're a bit thin. I worry that they won't be up to the tasks for which we contract them."

"Which are?"

"At the moment," she said, "charsten factory work. Production on the textiles. If that works out, we'd shift them to the seracology farms. Beetle population is up, so silk production is on the rise. After that, more factory work, preparing the fibers, cleaning the machines, that sort of thing."

"That's nothing." Knøfa scoffed. "These workers are more than adequate to those tasks."

She raised a brow at him. "It's tougher than you think. Long hours on one's feet, bending at slight angles to reach the equipment or the beetle habitats or whatever. It'll age them quickly if they aren't up to it."

"The contract's satisfaction clause makes it clear you can bring them back within thirty days if that proves to be the case." His lip curled at her expensive silk garb and charsten leather boots. If their negotiators could afford to dress so, then the board members of Danua Textiles could certainly afford his workers. "My per-month price is firm."

Her features tightened. "Very well. We'll take them on that trial basis. If we keep them more than one month, the contract will be renewable each standard year."

"Done. TICS, prepare the contract with the agreed details, and display it here for completion and signature." A soft acknowledgement and chitter preceded the appearance of the contract in the plaz before them.

Alanko indicated the projected document with a prim wave. "I'd like to read it once more before we sign."

"Be my guest." Knøfa gave her some space. His wristcom chirped. He touched it. "Yes."

"Admiral," Trask said, "I need to see you."

"Meet me in IR3. We can speak when I finish here."

"On my way."

Knøfa leaned against the wall by the door as Alanko scrolled through page after page of text. He didn't need to read it. He already knew it by heart. Tsurin had taught him from his early days in the Clan the necessity of contractual agreements, how their integration into every aspect of colonial life on the charter worlds had become de rigueur in the early colonial period of colonization. Now they were an accepted part of business, and the signing of one an almost sacred act. His gaze flicked to the bottle of wine and two glasses on the small table, ready to recognize the formalization of an agreement.

The door slid open and Trask stepped inside.

"What is it?" Knøfa asked.

Trask glanced at Alanko. "It can wait, sir."

Across the room, Alanko reached the signature page. "Very well, Admiral. I accept your terms. Shall we complete the contract?"

Knøfa rejoined her before the display. "After you."

She touched her finger to the surface and scrawled her signature with a flourish. When she finished, Knøfa added his own to the page in beautiful script. "TICS, affirm and secure this agreement between The Clan and Danua Textiles."

A soft chitter, then, "Affirmed and secured."

"Send a copy to Seije Alanko and to the records director at Danua Textiles, and ensure the agreement is entered into the colonial register."

"Acknowledged. Copies sent. Record entered. Agreement is completed."

At the table, Knøfa poured two small glasses of wine. He rarely indulged. Didn't like the flavor of alcohol much. But this tiny taste sealed the ceremony and could not be skipped.

"To our mutual benefit," he said.

She touched her glass to his and they both drank.

"A pleasure doing business with you, Negotiator Alanko. Now," he gestured toward the door, "if you'll excuse me, another pressing matter requires my presence. The crewman in the corridor will see you out."

When she was gone, Trask moved to his side. "I put out word that we were searching for a hidden Consortium base where Skalar might've stored off-the-books hauls. I implied the possibility of payment for information that led us to this place, said reward payable upon proof of the intel's veracity."

Knøfa squinted. "How much of a reward did you promise?"

"I didn't give a set figure, sir. But," Trask said, "it may have worked. An ex-Consortium crewman contacted one of my people earlier today, said she knew about an old off-the-map hiding place Skalar used on various occasions. She hinted that Skalar's crew left a hauler full of hematium there a couple of months before he went missing."

The admiral stared at his second. "And did she know where we can find it?"

"My crewman believed she did. And," Trask said, "she also pointed out that there had been some unusual activity surrounding that base ever since, especially since Admiral Baldric took over. And she's made it off-limits to anyone outside her hand-picked crew, most of whom my contact never heard of before."

Knøfa narrowed his eyes. "Squibs?"

"Hard to say," Trask said, lifting a shoulder. "But no one had heard of Baldric before either, until she showed up with Skalar after the incident on Iridos. I can't help but wonder if there's a connection, sir."

Was Baldric a squib? Trask said she'd won over most of the Consortium crew. More mind-manipulation? Anyone manning Baldric's secret base would have to be impersonating humans then. Otherwise, this informant would've known what they were. Knøfa frowned. How many were even now hiding on one of the Clan bases or posts, with no one the wiser?

He peered at his second. Was Trask even human at all? Probably. It seemed unlikely that a squib in hiding would bring him the location of other squibs. Unless it was a diversion, or some other trick to mislead and send him in the wrong direction. But the only way to find out was to explore this lead.

"Very well," Knøfa said. "Talk to this person. Report to me."

"Will do, sir." Trask walked out of the room and left Knøfa standing alone.

chapter 36

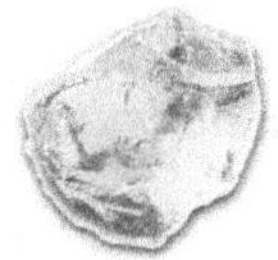

ELI FOLLOWED THRACE AS SHE pushed through into her office, her back and shoulders as stiff as her jaw had been during their whole trip from the landport to the base. She hadn't taken his story well, had been shocked that Botha's people had banished Eli. Her only comment, muttered through clenched teeth, had been to wonder how he could alienate even the most compassionate and reasonable people.

Eli didn't argue. He'd entertained the same curious thought himself even though he knew this one wasn't his fault, that the Bregainans had simply landed on him as a convenient scapegoat. He didn't blame them. His appearance, or Botha's weeks of absence from their village on his behalf, were the only variables they could point to in their lives, after which they could say, "Here, this is when everything changed."

Nor had Thrace been happy to hear they'd found nothing useful on the new Cartel admiral's slave trade. They'd have to go about that another way.

Thrace poured water for them both, then they sat in the realwood chairs in the seating area. Skalar had prided himself with wasteful objects such as these chairs, each one carved from a single tree on Bejami—illegal as hell, but no one ever called him on it.

Eli rubbed the polished grain of the chair's arm. "Didn't you say you weren't going to keep these?"

"I wasn't. I still may not. But no fate seems less wasteful or disrespectful than any other. Throwing them out, burning them, selling them, all are just as ignoble an end. I may donate them to a museum. I haven't decided. But you aren't here about these monstrosities." She watched Eli over the rim of her glass. "What will you do now?"

"I don't know." He set his glass on the table between them. "I don't suppose you have a place for me in the Consortium?"

Thrace flinched. "And what happens if Skalar or Crow show up?"

"They won't."

"You don't know that." Thrace scowled. "I've worked too hard to get this faction under control and win the confidence of the crew to risk that kind of interference." Her gaze softened. "I'm sorry, but no. You can't stay here. Not on the base. And I wouldn't recommend showing either of the former Consortium leaders' faces anywhere on Harajüd, either. Chief Downing has them on a 'wanted' list."

"You reported me."

"No," Thrace corrected, "I reported *them*. As you suggested. Remember? You aren't responsible for their crimes."

"Aren't I?"

"You aren't responsible for *all* their crimes."

Despite himself, he smiled. "Fair enough. But to be honest," he said, sobering, "I don't know what to do with myself."

Thrace's mouth twisted to one side, but she didn't fidget with anxiety.

It had been a long while since he'd seen his i'shin fret that way. Thrace had changed so much, grown more confident and self-assured since they'd left Iridos together. So had Eli, but in very different ways. Would the two of them ever find their way back to one another? His throat pinched, making it hard to swallow.

"I—" Thrace began. Her wristcom chirped, and she touched it. "Yes?"

"Admiral, Spencer Kilbee is here. Shall I send him in?"

"Yes. Please do." Thrace looked at Eli. "Let's resume this topic when he's gone."

The minute the door closed behind Kilbee, Thrace gestured in his direction. "You were just here three days ago. You haven't even had time to make your next delivery."

He eyed Eli—maybe remembering him from the holovid of Elisul at the outpost.

"It's me, Tiral," Eli said. "Alira."

Surprise flashed over his features, as clearly displayed as if she'd seen the gray in his skin.

"Ah. Glad you're well." Kilbee turned to Thrace. "I was on the way to Rubene when I got a comm from the outpost."

"I thought we agreed that base wouldn't use long-range comms." Eli frowned. "That's like waving a flag and begging to be tracked."

"Unless," Kilbee said, "it's urgent."

Thrace squinted at him. "Bad news?"

"Depends on your definition of 'bad'," he said. "A small group has split from the main population of survivors and moved through the underground passage to the nearby city."

Eli lurched to his feet. "Because of pressure by the council?"

"Yep."

"Damn it." Eli pounded on the arm of the chair. "They're going to—"

"Stop." Thrace glared at Eli, her voice full of command. "Weren't we just discussing this?"

Eli bit back his frustration. She was right. Not his place. Not anymore.

She held his gaze another moment then fixed her attention on Kilbee. "If they're in the neighboring tunnels, they aren't shielded. Correct?"

"That's right." He shoved his hands in his pockets. "We can start on building new shields or expanding the current ones to include the new city, but it'll take time. And you can bet this won't be the end of it. You know I'm right."

Thrace folded her arms, fingers tapping.

Eli's mind raced. Someone needed to point out Rakalesh's mistake. Again. As if it might make a difference this time, when it hadn't done so all those others. Probably should *not* be Alira, though. Rakalesh had little to say to Eli's host. What would Thrace do?

"Tell them to start on new shields," Thrace said. "How many left the main tunnels?"

"More than a hundred. For now," Kilbee said.

Almost a third of them. The whole surviving unammi population was falling apart, splintering like a shattered wooden beam. Nyros had so often tried to convince his wayward sister that the unammi's rigid strictures gave them a firm framework on which to hang the other layers of their society. He'd insisted that their resistance to change gave them the strength to withstand anything that might break them. But their uncompromising attitude also meant they would break before ever bending. Alira had tried to tell them. Now her predictions were coming true. He wished more than anything that she had been wrong.

Kilbee cleared his throat. "At least three want out altogether. I promised I'd come and get them."

Behind him, Thrace spoke. "How practiced are those three at a convincing human facade?"

"Unknown. But I'll check them out, run them through the paces, when I—"

"No," Thrace said.

Eli gawked. "No?"

She ignored him. "Tell the outpost to extract them and begin training them to live among humans while you complete your runs on the usual schedule. Test them when you're there. Bring them when you come for your next run. I'll set up a place for them by then."

When Kilbee was gone, Thrace resumed her seat. "I know where you could put your specific talents to use."

Eli perched on the edge of the other chair. "In the Consortium?"

"Only in part," she said. "You'd need to convince Rizzo to get involved, too. And maybe her allies, as well."

"Go on."

"What if you were a liaison between the divergent unammi who want to live among humans, and the Trader factions or the human colonies where they want to live?"

He blinked. "Explain."

"We can't keep placing those leaving Earth in the Consortium. Rizzo can't give them all a role in the Syndicate. They're going to need to spill over into the human cities. I've been making friends with some of the leaders in the colonial government of late, but outcasts from Earth will need someone aware of who and what they are to help them make the transition, to help them find a place to live, a place to work. Someone who can show them how colonial credits work, how to shop in the city markets. A contact who can answer their questions about this life." She tilted her head toward him. "Why not you?"

"Me? I've never done any of those things. I'd be as lost as they were."

"Would you?" Thrace's lips curled up at the corners. "You're right, at least in part. Alira never lived among humans off-base or held a colonial job. Alira never had to worry about credits or shopping. But what about your other harvests? I'd bet there's a wealth of information in there you could draw from to help your unammi kin."

Eli got up so fast he almost tripped over the legs of the chair. "You can't be serious."

"Why not?" Thrace relaxed in the massive chair and peered up at Eli.

"Wha…" How to respond? "A few minutes ago, you were worried that Skalar or Crow would show up."

"And you assured me they would not. A month or two ago, I would never have asked. You've come a long way since then. Maybe you should start trying to poke around in the knowledge your human harvests hold without freeing them or letting them drive the ship, so to speak. Wasn't that part of Botha's plan from the start?"

"I don't know." Eli paced. "Maybe. Even if it was," he looked at Thrace, "we never got that far before the snatch, and suddenly he's not my mentor any longer. I'm on my own."

"So?"

So? How could Thrace not see the obvious danger here? He was still sputtering, trying to put his dismay into words when Thrace's wristcom chirped.

"Yes."

"Front gate here, Admiral. You have a visitor. He says to tell you it's about your mutual friends, ma'am."

Thrace and Eli exchanged a frown. "Who sent him?"

A pause, then, "A recent ally who attended a social function with you in Bregaina."

"Rizzo," Eli hissed.

Thrace stood, her movement slow, precise. "Send him in with an escort."

"Yes, ma'am."

She moved around the Bejami chair to her desk, where she could assume her role for this stranger. She stood for a moment, staring out over the city where darkness had begun to fall. Lights were winking on in the parks, along the streets, in the buildings. Here, too, lights brightened almost as if on cue. Eli moved beside her.

"TICS," Thrace said, "set nanopanel to clear."

The system chittered and another view of the darkening cityscape emerged on the wall.

"What do you think it could be?" he asked.

"We'll know in a few minutes," she said, her voice soft, almost a whisper.

They watched the skyline along the bay deepen with shades of crimson radiance as Lakaya sank toward the horizon. Clouds formed, plumping on the coastal breeze as it blew inland, their wisps blazing in the dying light before their glory faded.

By the time security chimed Thrace's door, the western horizon held only a dull afterglow that wavered and darkened into the purple night sky.

"Do you want me to leave?" Eli asked.

"No." Her voice sounded strange, faraway. "This may involve you as much as it does me. Besides, if you decide to take my suggestion, the news may be of use to you." She turned to face the door. "Come," she called.

A slender young man entered, followed by the security escort from the gate. "I'll be right outside, ma'am."

Thrace nodded, then invited the visitor to sit.

"Thank you, ma'am," he said, "but I won't be staying that long."

"Very well." She lowered herself into her seat with deliberate precision. "I'm Admiral Baldric. And you are?"

"I'm Nori," he said, his voice lilting and soft. "Admiral Rizzo sent me with an urgent message. She says to tell you Knøfa is now in full charge of the Clan, and that he knows about what Skalar did to your mutual friends. He knows the survivors are hiding, and he is hunting them as we speak."

A shiver raced through Eli, chilling him to his bones. He pressed trembling fingers to his mouth.

Thrace's rich brown hue leeched from her cheeks, leaving her a little gray. She gripped the chair's armrests.

"Knøfa is also trying to create tech that can detect your friends even when they are in disguise," Nori continued. "Rizzo doesn't know if he has succeeded. She recommends immediate evasion, as soon as possible, and said to tell you that if she can help, you should let her know at once."

A stark silence filled the space around them while Eli and Thrace absorbed what her messenger had revealed.

"Is that the entire message?" Thrace said, at last.

"Yes, ma'am."

She stood. "Very well. Thank you, Nori. You've done well. Please pass my thanks to your admiral. I'll let her know if we need any assistance in this matter." She touched her wristcom and the door slid open, admitting the security crewman. "My officer will see you to the gate."

Thrace waited until he was gone, then sank into her chair. "It's only a matter of time until he finds them."

"That doesn't make any sense." Eli frowned at her. "Rizzo told us Knøfa was a threat, I understand that much. But if he found out that Skalar ordered the attack on Iridos, why doesn't he think we're all dead? Why is he searching for the rest of us?"

"Does it matter?"

"That's a ridiculous question."

"The result is the same," she said. "We must stop him."

He clenched his fists. "What aren't you telling me?"

Thrace sighed. "Knøfa has an unammi prisoner."

Eli tried to say…something. Anything. No words came.

"He knows most of what we can do," Thrace said, lines of strain evident around her mouth. "The healing, the morphing, maybe all of it."

"How long have you known?" Eli said, forcing the sounds past the catch in his throat.

"Five or six weeks. I can't remember exactly."

That long? "Who is it?" He barely recognized his own voice. "Who is Knøfa torturing?"

"We don't know." Thrace took a step toward Eli. "We assume—"

"Who is 'we'? Who else knew of this?"

Thrace winced. "Rizzo and Botha."

Eli's eyes widened. "Botha knew? All that time on Onlebaar, he *knew*?"

"No." Thrace moved closer. "Rizzo and I came to the island to tell you, but you were out walking. We told Botha. He and Rizzo didn't know if you were strong enough to take the news."

"What did you think?"

"I didn't know," she said. "I wanted to tell you, but then we went to Bregaina, and the snatchers came, and you and Botha left for Pelarr, and the chance just never came. There was always something else happening."

Somehow, he managed to stay upright, despite feeling like he'd been kicked in the stomach. Rizzo's reticence he could understand. She didn't know Alira well enough to know what she could and could not take. Botha had watched her grow stronger, going from a quivering mass of flesh to someone who managed to save one of his villagers from a slave trade. Still, he had seen Alira at her worst, so Eli could almost understand why he would doubt her resilience.

But Thrace?

Eli swallowed his hurt. He needed to be objective. Galen had seen Alira fall a long way. He had been beside her while she came apart bit by delusional bit. He'd stood by as long as he could, held his faith for her until she rounded on him one too many times. They'd barely seen one another since Botha took Alira to Onlebaar, and she hadn't had enough time to demonstrate her reclamation of sanity, so perhaps Galen's uncertainty could be forgiven.

His silence must've gone on too long.

"We couldn't tell you," Thrace said, her voice sounding defensive, "until we were sure you wouldn't go after them. I'm sorry, but you know I'm right."

What would Alira have done, had they told her of all this? Maybe nothing. And maybe, instead of being in Bregaina when the snatchers came, she would've been on her way to Danua even knowing the odds. She'd known it would be nigh impossible to retrieve their irolium, too, and yet somehow she'd managed it.

But Thrace was right. No matter how wrenching the knowledge that an unammi was suffering, he couldn't pull off a rescue. Sacrificing himself to a hopeless cause wouldn't have helped anyone and would've given Knøfa another prisoner.

"Perhaps it's better I didn't know," Eli murmured.

Thrace leaned forward. "I didn't hear you."

Her words grounded Eli in the moment and he stared at his i'shin. "What about now, Thrace? Where do we stand now, you and I?"

Thrace drew in a long breath and blew it out at a slow, measured rate. He waited for her to fidget. For her to say the words that would bring them together.

Instead, she shrugged. "So much has changed. Neither of us is the same as when we came here from Iridos. The situation grows more complex by the hour. The future is uncertain at best, for us as individuals, for our people as a whole and," she gestured toward the door, "now it seems even for our species. So honestly, I don't know where we stand. I suppose we see what happens tomorrow, and the day after that."

He swallowed the lump forming in his throat and mourned all they had lost. Thank Na'Staani this form's skin would not reveal his grief and confusion in this moment, even though Thrace would feel it anyway.

So ironic that for her whole life, Alira had championed the benefits of change and now, now that Eli swam in changes so deep that they threatened to drown him, he would give anything to embrace the familiar. The known.

He wrapped his arms around himself, fought for calm, listened to the sounds in Thrace's office and to the spaces between them. He couldn't afford to walk away from this person, not with things as they were for the unammi, but beyond that he didn't want to. Even if they could no longer be i'shin, Galen and Alira would always have a bond that went beyond friendship.

"Are you okay?"

Her voice nudged him out of his reverie. "I'll be fine."

"Good. We have things to do. TICS," she said, "connect me to Spencer Kilbee."

Seconds later, he responded. "Yes, Admiral?"

"Where are you?"

"Just stepped off the base."

"Change of plan. Rendezvous with us in the landing bay immediately."

"On my way."

Thrace shot Eli a sidelong glance. "I'd say we need to go to Earth, don't you agree?" She went into her workroom, then returned with a TICS pad. She passed it to Eli. "Here. You'll be needing this."

He took it, still not sure what was happening, and she stepped past him, already moving to the door. "TICS, locate Captain Mira Cohen and tell her to meet me in the landing bay at once."

"Damn," Eli objected, still reeling from the revelations of the last few minutes as he shoved the pad into his pocket. "I just got here."

Thrace snorted at his discomfort and spoke over her shoulder.

"I should think you'd be getting used to living aboard a ship by now."

chapter 37

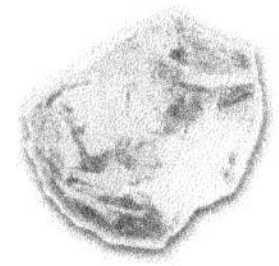

Haven, Danua
<u>Clan Trader Base, Admiral Knøfa's quarters</u>

THE FIRE IN FRONT OF him crackled and popped, producing as much heat as if it were real. More, in fact, since the simfire generator regulated its production based on the temperature of the room, and right now it was damn cold. Or maybe that was the coldness inside of him he felt, and he was confusing the inside with the outside. It had been a while since that had happened, but Tsurin used to be able to help him tell the difference. For a moment, he missed her calming, instructional presence. But she would chide him for time wasted on things he couldn't change. He'd chosen to let her go. He didn't regret the decision. Time to move on.

He stared at the flickering flames that licked and embraced the simwood and recalled the medfac's latest report. Of the fifteen squib eggs the medfac harvested, seven survived and accepted fertilization from human sperm samples. Surrogates were implanted a few hours ago. Now the next experiment phase began, as did yet another exercise in waiting. Best case, all seven would come to term, and he could test them each, one at a time. But he would need to first establish which of the young—what did one call squib offspring? Pups?—carried which squib traits.

Worst case, none would make it as far as, or through, the birth and he'd have just the one in his medfac. When asked whether they should remove its life support system, he'd said no. Even "dead," it could prove to be a valuable resource as a long-term donor.

His wristcom chirped, and he touched it. "Yes."

"Admiral," Trask said, "I have that news you asked me to bring."

Knøfa's gaze returned to the flames. "Is it going to be worth my time?"

"I believe so, sir. I questioned the informant myself. The intel seems genuine."

"Very well. My quarters."

A pause, then, "Are you…dressed, sir?"

"Yes. Why?"

"Well…last time you were…er…Never mind. I'm on my way."

Knøfa almost pushed himself out of the chair. Tsurin would say he should always look the part and, while he was dressed, his hair and clothing were disheveled from lounging in front of the fire. But he'd seen his admiral at her best and worst, and as Knøfa's second, Trask should get used to that, as well. He smoothed his tangled hair and straightened his shirt. That would have to do.

His door chimed. "Come," Knøfa said, grunting as he got to his feet.

Trask came closer to the admiral's chair, just out of reach. "I just got word that Rizzo learned of your interest in the Consortium's connection to Iridos."

Another cold streak crept through Knøfa, and he clamped his jaw tight before the anger could send him into a rage. He liked Trask. Sort of. Knøfa trusted the man. Or as close as Knøfa might ever get to that, after Tsurin had let him down. If he allowed himself to succumb to the wrath that tried, even now, to overtake him, he'd need a new second.

"What else?" His voice came out strained, as if there were a strap pulled tight around his throat. "You said you had a piece of information I'm after." It better be good news. Something to help tip his scales into balance.

"I've learned the location of the Consortium's secret base, sir."

Oh…oh yes. Yes, that would do just fine. The frost inside him began to thaw and he almost checked to see if he was melting on the floor. "Where?"

"Our informant says it's in the Sol system," Trask said, "in a subsurface base on the moon of old Earth."

"I thought that system had been contaminated. Some sort of biohazard."

"That it was, sir." Trask raised an eyebrow. "Of course that was centuries ago."

Knøfa stared, his mind racing over the implications of this intel. No one would've contemplated a search there, at a place so fraught with trauma and pain—for most people, anyway—let alone a place said to have killed off its last human inhabitants. How long ago did the colonies shut down their old world? He couldn't remember, but it was more than a few centuries, he was almost sure. How long would it take for a plague to die out? For the planetary environment to become safe?

Maybe a human plague would be no threat to squibs who could heal so fast. If Skalar's controversial outpost was there, that's where he'd find the squibs.

"You say the base isn't on the planet," Knøfa said. "It's on one of their planetary satellites."

"That's right, sir. And if I'm correct, Earth only had the one."

"TICS," Knøfa said, "what is the flight time between here and Earth?"

The system chittered. "At best speed, seven standard days."

He blinked, realized he was still staring at his second. "Send someone after the Syndicate mole. Whoever you send, also have them dig for whoever is talking about Clan business outside the Clan. I want everyone with loose lips gone, the faster the better."

Trask frowned. "You don't want me to do it, sir?"

"No." Knøfa started toward his sleeping alcove, speaking over his shoulder.

"With all due respect, Admiral," Trask said, "I am capable of carrying out a termination."

"I don't doubt that." Knøfa grabbed a pack from under a table by the bed and began to throw clothing into it. "But I want you here, running the base while I go squib-hunting. Set me up with Tsurin's command crew and have them prep the *Lysbringer*. I'll want to leave immediately."

Trask started for the door, but Knøfa stopped him. "Do it from here. I want you nearby in case there's anything else."

"Of course, sir." The captain touched his wristcom and began giving orders.

"TICS," Knøfa went on, "compile a research packet. Include all available information on the biohazard that killed off Earth's remaining population, most recent geological and atmospheric data for Earth and its satellite as well as all habitable worlds of any size in that system, and any human bases or structures still standing when Earth went dark. Calculate estimates on which, if any, of those structures or habitats might still be standing and what their status might be. Extrapolate from known details on Earth's remaining lifeforms and atmospheric data how long that planet's biohazard may take to be rendered inert."

"Acknowledged." A chitter followed. "Estimated compilation time required equals sixty-seven hours and fourteen minutes."

"Very well. Transfer calculations and compilation parameters to the TICS system on the *Lysbringer* and begin."

"Acknowledged." The TICS went silent.

"A little light reading, Admiral?" Trask said.

Knøfa peered at him. "Light? No. Interesting, yes." He bent, pulled out another armload of something and shoved it in the already full pack. "Watch that crew in the medfac while I'm gone. I don't want anyone pulling the life support on my squib."

"But…"

"What?" Knøfa still stared at Trask.

Trask's face twitched. "We've already taken her ova. The surrogates were implanted. Aren't we finished with her?"

"No. Not when I'm about to bring home some of its friends. Maybe even a male squib. Once I have enough for breeding stock, then we'll stop the support. Not until then."

Trask nodded.

Knøfa bent to his task. "I want you to personally oversee the preparations for this trip. Ensure plenty of water, supplies, food for at least two and a half weeks for me and the crew. I don't want to go hungry before we get home."

"What about food and water for the unammi?"

He stopped. The man had a point. No sense letting them starve on the trip to Danua. They wouldn't be much good to him if they weren't at their best. "Very well. Include at least a dozen extra mouths in the count."

"Will do, sir. I'll meet you in the landing bay in, say, an hour?"

"Make it thirty minutes." Knøfa raised a brow at his captain. "That's not a problem, is it?"

"No, sir," Trask said, though Knøfa could swear the man had gone a little pale. "No problem at all."

chapter 38

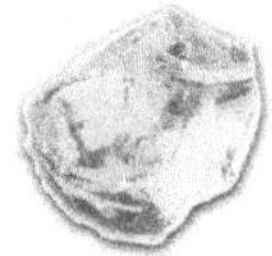

Aboard the Nebula
<u>On Approach to Consortium Outpost</u>

GALEN WATCHED FOR SIGNAL BLEED-through as they drew near. The outpost still ran dark. Good to know. "Shields are good at this end."

"For now," Tiral said. "Ship's instruments reported on the way in that solar activity is increasing and should peak in the next few hours. Once we land, we should stay underground as much as possible."

Alira spoke up. "Will that affect the shields?"

"The mechanisms for those are underground." Tiral shrugged. "We won't need to shut them down. But the flares may interfere with their output. It hasn't happened before, not since I've been here. But this storm is stronger than the others. We don't know what to expect."

"And the cities?" Galen asked. "Will it interfere with those, too?"

"The main city might experience intermittent bleed-through, but it won't fail entirely unless they take a direct hit. System predictions show the cities aren't in the zone of highest risk for ejections."

Galen considered the other ramifications. "How have solar storms historically affected our sensors?"

Tiral scowled. "They're hardened and shielded. They *should* be fine."

"Understood," Galen said. "Contact the base. Tell them we're coming in."

Tiral got on the comm.

"Start your checks on both cities while you're still outside the atmosphere," Galen told Alira. "Mark where they're first detectable. We need to know how to prepare."

"Got it." Lavender splayed across her skin. "You know they'll need to stick together in one city. I'm not sure I can convince them to do that." Her features twisted. "I'm not sure they'll listen to me about anything."

Her reticence dragged at his intentions. They didn't have time for doubt. "You need to try."

She nodded, determination in her straight back, the set of her shoulders, the colors in her display.

Galen watched her, torn between duty and selfishness. He wanted more than anything to just fly off someplace new with her and never step another foot into a leadership role. To spend the rest of their days in this life exploring together, finding new experiences, investigating new ideas. But if he'd learned anything from his unammi teachers, it was that his people came first. And in this situation, he had no trouble seeing that as fact. If they failed here, there would be no unammi left to put first.

He swallowed hard and turned to the controls to guide the ship into the small landing bay, his first time seeing it since repairs had been completed. No time to inspect it now, though. He'd see to that after this quandary was resolved.

Once they touched down, he set the engines on standby and pushed out of his seat. This would be his first crisis as admiral, but not as an unammi. The last time humans had approached an unammi city, calamity had followed. The knot in Galen's stomach tightened.

"Remember," he said as Alira came to take his place, "the controls are a little sticky on the—"

She grinned. "I remember. I should've had that repaired months ago. I left you with too many unresolved issues, didn't I?" She held out her hand.

He waved off her concern and touched her fingers, his eyes drinking in every detail of her face. "Be careful."

"You, too."

Galen met Tiral in the corridor. Together they walked away. Alira would be fine. They would all be fine. He had to keep believing that.

He and Tiral stepped off the ship and retreated into the sealed corridor leading out of the bay. Through the viewport, he watched the *Nebula* lift off and move toward Earth.

"She knows what she's doing," Tiral said beside him.

"Of course." Galen cleared his throat and led the way into the base. One of the other outcasts met them halfway to control, and Galen addressed her as they walked. "Report."

"No change since our last update. We're still keeping track of that solar event."

Galen stopped outside the door to control. "Did we get all the buoys repaired?"

The outcast glanced at Tiral, who sighed. "Yes. But let's hope no one scans them close enough to see the changes."

Slim hope of that. Without having met this Knøfa human, Galen had only Rizzo's estimation of the man on which to base an opinion. But he suspected if Knøfa came here, he probably wouldn't accept a surface view of anything. He'd dig deeper. And he would find them.

He should've armed this base weeks ago. They wouldn't have been ready in time for this, but at least they'd be closer to it. That would be a top priority when this was over, assuming they made it out the other side.

Galen entered the control room. "Come on, then. Let's fill everyone in on the situation, and get set up for a long vigil."

chapter 39

Tuneloras, Saacharis
<u>Syndicate Trader Base, Admiral Rizzo's Quarters</u>

THE CHIRP ROUSED RIZZO, AND she rolled over in the dark. "Yes."

"Admiral, ma'am, you should get down to medical on the double."

Rizzo grabbed a pullover shirt on her way to the living space. "What is it?"

A pause. "It's Captain Bailey, ma'am."

A dagger of fear pierced Rizzo's heart, the chill of its blade slicing up into her throat, down her arms, into her belly. "On my way."

She shoved her feet into shoes on the way and slid through the door even before the panel fully opened. In the corridor, she broke into a run. Crewmen hugged the walls as she passed, clearing her way. She tried to exercise Bindhu discipline to rein in her racing thoughts, to keep them tight, each in their own corner. Panic solved nothing. Wait and see. Evaluate and take informed action.

But this was Bailey. Rizzo's fear railed against her calming efforts, and by the time she reached the medical wing, she trembled atop a chasm of dread.

Then she rounded the corner. A trail of crimson blotches smeared the floor next to footprints and streaks along the wall from the other direction—the north landing bay where Bailey kept her ship—and Rizzo tipped over the edge, screaming in her mind while she continued forward with faltering steps.

The trail of blood led into the trauma center where a team worked frantically over an anonymous body in one nook. Rizzo approached on unsteady feet until she could see the smeared face. That long hair hung in a tangled mess of slick wet clumps. Her eyes were closed, one of them so horribly swollen it probably wouldn't open at all, even if Bailey were conscious. One of her arms lay twisted at a strange angle, the hand bent backward, its fingers splayed in all the wrong directions. The other arm had been scraped raw like she'd been dragged over rocks. Medics had sliced off her clothing to reveal a bubbling gash across her ribs, another just below them, and another in her side. So much blood…Reyes had bled like that in Rizzo's shower. They'd carried his body out in a box.

Bailey's chest rose and fell in hitching motions.

When she opened her unswollen eye and her head rose half a centimeter off the table, Rizzo flinched.

Bailey croaked something unintelligible, growing more agitated by the second. Doctors tried to calm her, but she ignored them. Instead, she reached for her admiral.

In a blink, Rizzo was at her side, gripping Bailey's bloody fingers like a lifeline, though she wasn't sure which of them she was trying to save. Maybe both. She leaned over, peered at Bailey. "Who?" Her gaze dropped to Bailey's lips, which formed two words over and over.

Knøfa's people.

Rizzo nodded. "Okay. I've got this. You rest."

Bailey shook her head, her matted hair flopping with the wild movement. No, she said. Finished. Finished. Then she collapsed on the table, her breathing shallow and rapid. A medic nudged Rizzo aside with mumbled apologies, and Rizzo stumbled away from the table, her chest heaving. She slapped a hand over her mouth and tasted Bailey's blood.

Another medic from the table hurried by, and Rizzo grabbed his arm. "Is she—"

He bared his teeth in a grimace that said far more than words. "It's pretty bad, ma'am. We'll do what we can." He gently pulled his arm free.

She backed up until she ran into the wall. Waves of hatred and fear threatened to swamp her. Hatred of Knøfa and his people because they'd brought this fight to *her* door and harmed *her* second on *her* turf. And fear because if Bailey died—

Rizzo turned from the nook where her second's life teetered, and dragged her mind into a related, but tangential direction where logic and reasoned actions would take hold. She could take care of this. Ensure that Knøfa or his minions never got another chance to harm anyone. Rizzo knew she was good at many things, but torture—that was her true forte. Esther had called it Rizzo's grim art. The night Esther had caught Turizomi standing bloody over the bodies of those two slavers who'd tried to kidnap her, Esther asked her if she'd enjoyed killing them. Turizomi had said yes. That they had deserved her blade, that it had given her joy to see them suffer, to know that she had stopped them from doing to anyone else what she'd endured for years. That given the chance, she would do it again.

Esther had compared it to what she'd heard others say came from a chemically induced euphoria. Over the next few months, she'd taught Turizomi that pursuing that kind of high, even in opposition to those who deserved it, would destroy her. Esther had been right. As admiral, Rizzo could find other ways to resolve lesser issues, even if she sometimes had to mete justice in order to set things right, like with the children in the mine. She'd done what she'd had to do with Reyes, but she had taken no pleasure in it. She couldn't afford that kind of self-indulgence.

This…

Rizzo clenched her jaw. This wasn't just any victim they'd harmed. This was Rizzo's second. Her most trusted friend and companion. Her—

She pressed bloody fingers to her mouth once more and closed her eyes until she stopped shaking. When she opened them again, she knew one thing for certain. If Bailey died, Rizzo would take great pleasure in making Knøfa pay.

chapter 40

<u>**Earth**</u>

THE NEBULA CLOSED IN ON the region of her people's city, and Alira slowed. Her viewscreen showed quite a different sight, so many months after her last visit to this place. Then, bits of color had dotted the rocky landscape, but now a thin blanket of white covered the land, softening its angles and curves in a deceptive way. Not like the snow in Onlebaar where she could sink up to her knees, deeper if she wasn't cautious. She set the ship on a flat spot near the entrance to the caverns and shut down the engines, reluctant to leave her warm seat to face the cold. Not the weather. She could resist a chill wind. No, she dreaded Rakalesh's reception. She shivered and took a moment to build her strength before she left.

She'd taken three steps before Rakalesh came through the tunnel entrance onto the surface, draped in a hooded cloak that would protect her delicate skin from this world's star. Tiral must've brought that garment—possibly a whole shipment of them—for his ama and her people. Morphing would've protected them just as well. Better, perhaps. But Rakalesh would never permit such a profanity in her city. Alira sighed and chose not to shift her own form and antagonize the elder just yet. Alira needed her compliant.

She almost snorted. As if *that* would happen.

Twenty paces from the nose of her ship, Alira stopped and waited. Rakalesh's movements looked…slower. Laborious as if, even in this lighter gravity, her steps came harder. More determined, as if the elder had to will her feet to move forward.

When she'd drawn near enough, Rakalesh stopped. "How dare you come here?"

Alira sneered. "You never change."

"That is the point. But you can't seem to grasp that concept, which is why you are not welcome among us."

"Evolution is necessary for the continuation of the species, Na'ama. You know this." Alira peered at the red streaks on Rakalesh's flesh. But the anger displayed there lost some of its bite to the lavender and white speckles of doubt and fear. "Whether or not you want to admit it, that natural process of change made us who we are. Without it, we would still be human."

Rakalesh stepped closer, her features set into a composed mask. "Everything that has happened is *your* fault," she said, the venom in her voice making her display redundant. "You might not have brought the sh'toi down on us, but you and your words and your promotion of sedition among the survivors has led us to this crisis. Half the people here." She waved to one side as if indicating the entire landscape. "A quarter there." Another wave at the sky. "The rest scattered to the stars." She glared at Alira with shaded silver eyes, their hatred piercing and colder than the wind on this open plain. "You did this to us. I am glad Lurien is not here to see it."

Alira flinched. She forced herself to remain calm as Botha had taught her, and worked to quiet the voices. "I didn't come here to fight."

"Good. Then you can leave." Rakalesh moved toward the city.

"I came here to warn you."

Rakalesh stopped. "Of what?"

"A human has discovered our secrets."

The elder swung around, her face splashed with white. "What did you say?"

"He captured an unammi stranded on Danua." Alira pushed the words out fast. "My sources tell me he tortured them, ran experiments on them. Kept them alive through it all. As far as we know, he's still doing it. He knows at least some of what we can do."

"Who is it?"

"We don't know. We couldn't get close enough to find out. But Na'ama," she stepped closer, "now he's searching for others. He will come here. He'll find all of you, unless you hide."

Rakalesh's covered head shook, not in negation but in apparent fear. "No. No, Tiral and those you set against us are protecting us. He explained they have shielded the city. No one will see us as long as we stay under the surface."

"As long as their ships don't land, that's true for you and those still in these tunnels," Alira nodded at the cliff behind the elder. "But the others, the ones who left and went through to the next city, they aren't hidden. The humans will find them. They need to rejoin your group."

The elder's glower recurred, though doubt leaked through her trembling facade in traitorous lavender and blue blotches. "Impossible. That would tear the rest of us apart. Let them go to the outpost. Let those you've twisted to your agenda protect them there."

"Na'ama," Alira began, stepping forward.

The elder recoiled, gaping at Alira as if she were a monster. Perhaps she was, in a sense.

Alira frowned but stayed where she was. "Na'ama, do you remember dragging me into meditation space with you after I'd harvested the first few humans?"

Rakalesh only stared at her.

"You said then that you admired my courage, that I had blossomed toward fullness. You also said you couldn't imagine living with those other voices in your mind all the time. Do you remember?"

The elder's jaw worked. Her mouth drew into a thin line. Red began to creep in.

"When I went to Harajüd, to the Consortium, the voice of Skalar—its former leader and one of my harvests—spoke of his traditions and rules, how I should run the faction as he would have. I listened and, with his guidance, enforced compliance among the crew with no mercy. No leniency. No probing for a better way. No room for change." She pointed at Rakalesh. "You and Skalar had much in common, except he killed rebels outright. You send them to a slow death."

Anger surged across Rakalesh's display. "I won't listen—"

"You need to hear this. Doing things Skalar's way made his people resist and act out even more than they would have otherwise. His enforced rule nearly destroyed the faction, and it came very close to destroying me. The council's unwillingness to foster or promote or even allow natural change and growth among the surviving unammi is killing us all."

"That's ridiculous," Rakalesh said. "The unammi are strong. We will get through this, just as we have every other crisis." But her blue speckles betrayed her.

"You can't keep dividing the population," Alira said, "separating outcasts from the main body of our people or mitigating unrelenting individuals without flinging us past a genetic bottleneck in the direction of total extinction."

She stepped close, grasped Rakalesh's arm in a sudden, tight grip that widened the elder's eyes beneath her hood.

"This danger is at your door, Na'ama. I see the end of the unammi, and it wears a face—not just the human one I came to warn you of, but the one before me right now, and the ones that sit on the council with self-righteous indignation and declare as anathema all lifestyles different from their own." She pulled Rakalesh closer, until they were nose-to-nose. "Don't do this. Revise the council's direction. Reintegrate the others into the populace and cooperate with one another to find a way forward that will work for everyone, or the unammi will not survive."

"You keep saying that," Rakalesh said, pushing her words through lips gone white.

Alira squeezed Rakalesh's arm. "Because you won't *listen*."

Skin blanched, upper body flinching from this perceived threat, Rakalesh stared at Alira. The elder's breaths came fast and hard, and for just a second, Alira was glad she'd at least gotten the councilor's undivided attention.

But it was over too quickly. Rakalesh jerked her arm free and retreated, stumbling over the rocky ground until she was out of reach. She rubbed her arm where Alira had grasped it, and suddenly, Alira saw the bend in the elder's spine, the slump to her shoulders. The lines on her flesh where the colors no longer reached bright fingers of light. How had she not seen this before?

"You speak as if you know my trials," the elder said, her voice trembling. "You don't. You had someone telling you what to do, at least. A guide. You've not led a population through a trauma where they lost more than half their number, as well as their homes, their way of life, everything they've ever known. You've not led the survivors through a diaspora to an unknown world where everything must be created anew. You call the councilors self-righteous, and then insist you know what's best for us, that abandoning our familiar traditions, our one last bit of home, is in our best interest, when you don't know. You're not even one of us, and you haven't been for a long time. So go on with your life of change, Alira. Take your ideas and your advice and your suggestions on what we need to do, and go. Leave us alone."

She turned her back on Alira. "And if you aren't going to contribute the genetic material I've requested for so long," she said over her shoulder, "then stay away from us. What little energy I have left belongs to my people. I won't waste any more of it on you." Then she departed, her gait slow and proud, though unsteady.

How long would it be before she required aid? Did she already? Rakalesh was the oldest of them. She was never going to relent, much less change. Alira would need to find another way.

Rakalesh retreated into the tunnel and the rock rolled in front of the door.

Alira reentered the *Nebula*, lifted off, and flew toward the splitters' city.

chapter 41

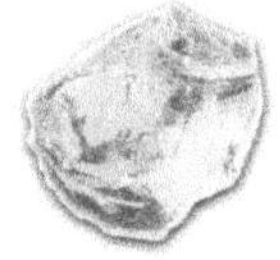

Tuneloras, Saacharis
<u>Syndicate Trader Base, MedFac 3</u>

RIZZO STOOD AT THE FOOT of Bailey's bed. Her arms crossed over her chest, gripping her own arms above the elbows. She needed to keep from clenching her fists and taking out her rage on a wall, a desk or, say, another admiral. If Bailey would just wake up, Rizzo could leave, go to the gym and expend some of her energy on the heavy bag or a partner's practice mitts. Until then, she kept vigil and hoped.

A nicked lung and a shallow blade wound to Bailey's kidney had been the worst of the many intrusions into her body, but the amount of blood she'd lost making it to the base had nearly cost her life. She'd survived the first three hours, which the medics said were the most crucial. Still, they offered no guarantees.

Too bad that little troublemaker wasn't nearby, the one with so many personas that all pricked against Rizzo's neatly ordered world like a thorn in her shoe. The Syndicate's new ally certainly dragged behind her a good share of havoc, but she was also a gifted healer. Rizzo would give anything for that talent just now.

Surgeons had hacked off Bailey's hair above her shoulders—she'd hate that—but hadn't yet washed it. Rizzo wanted them to do it, but they insisted the captain be saved further stress until she could heal. Now she lay covered with a loose gown, and a light blanket, her head elevated, cropped hair spread on the pillow like a dark halo, her broken arm and hand in a stasis cast anchored to a frame on the bed. Sensors relayed her body's readings to a screen on the wall. Traces of dried blood still lingered on her neck and under her fingernails or crusted around the roots of her hair. Her face, now a deep purplish blue, had swollen. Rizzo wouldn't have recognized her second if she'd happened upon Bailey without prior knowledge of who she was.

Rizzo took note of these clinical details, logging each of them for later reference tomorrow, or the next day, or the day after, so she could recognize Bailey's recovery, and celebrate every small step. Memory of that morning in the Zen garden, when Bailey had professed her feelings, hovered at the edges of Rizzo's thoughts. If only she had said aloud what she'd known in her heart to be true. She moved to the side of the bed, and willed her captain to recover so they could replay that moment. She reached out to brush aside a strand of Bailey's hair.

Her wristcom chirped. She froze. She should just ignore it. But what if it had to do with Bailey?

Rizzo stepped out of the room. "Yes."

"Admiral," Jukka said, "you've received a special delivery marked 'urgent.' Given the attack on Captain Bailey, I'm holding it at the gate pending your approval to bring it on base."

Rizzo's mouth went dry. "How large is it?"

"It's a refrigerated packet, ma'am," Jukka said in a deadpan tone. "About the size of a head."

His words rang in her ears. "Bring it to my office, Captain."

Jukka hesitated. "Are you sure, ma'am? I could open it here—"

"He doesn't want to kill me. He wants to hurt me," she said. And his efforts were working. "Bring it yourself."

"Yes, ma'am. Five minutes."

Rizzo peered through the viewpane at Bailey's damaged body. She was still beautiful, even in all her brokenness. "I will end this," Rizzo whispered. "One way or another."

She left the medfac, moving through the corridors at a slower pace than when she'd first come last night. The passages she knew so well blurred by until she arrived at her own office. Outside, the city lay in typical gray Tuneloras haze, lights here and there even during the day. When the door buzzed, she called out entry. Jukka entered with the box. She already knew what it held, but they opened it together atop the table where she and Bailey had so often spent hours working some task or another. When the wrapping was undone, and the crate cracked open, Rizzo looked inside.

Jukka had been right. The eyes of her Clan informant stared up at her, their irises a muted gray glassed over by death.

The agent left behind a sick mother, two younger sisters, and a toddler. She'd shared a brief holo of the child's first steps the last time she'd been home for a visit. How long ago was that? Four months? Six? She'd been full of pride for her boy. Rizzo asked the agent then if she wanted a job closer to home, but she'd said no. Not until she'd finished this tour. She'd had her sight set on an officer's position.

Now she stared, unseeing, at the ceiling and her child would grow up motherless. An orphan, like Turizomi had been.

No, not like Turi. Rizzo would see to that.

"Enough," Rizzo muttered.

Jukka held his silence.

Rizzo straightened her shoulders. "Notify her family. See that they are on our rolls and well cared for."

"Of course, ma'am."

"I want her remains cremated, the ashes neutralized, then buried on the grounds."

"Any memorial, ma'am?"

"Yes," Rizzo said. "If I recall correctly, she loved trees. Plant a rusucre sapling with her and ensure installation of a bench nearby. Choose the tree's placement so as to plan for its growth. We don't want it blocking critical views from any of our strategic windows."

"Will do. Is that all?"

"One more thing." She picked up the crate. "TICS, record a message for Captain Michael Trask of the Danua Clan. Begin." When the system chittered acknowledgement, she moved behind the desk, reached into the crate, pulled out the officer's head, and held it up.

"Did you do this?" she asked. "We all keep tabs on one another, Trask. The Clan had two informants here, and I planned to scare them and send them packing before they nearly killed my second. Needless to say, they won't be returning to Danua."

She placed the body part in its crate with care. "Are you so eager to alienate or even kill those with whom you could be allied instead? No one wins in that kind of game." She placed her palms flat on the desktop as she stared at nothing in particular. "It was always my impression that none of us sought a faction war, but perhaps I was wrong. Maybe Knøfa wants exactly that."

She raised her gaze to the recording, so she'd be glaring directly at him when he viewed the message. "What of you? Tsurin always spoke well of you, but now I don't know what to think. Your admiral is determined to enslave or torture an entire race of beings in pursuit of a few extra credits or points on some imaginary scale that no one but Knøfa is watching. You've done nothing to stop it, so I need to ask. Is that what you signed up for? If not, then why the hell are you just standing there?"

She leaned closer to the recording, her movements slow, deliberate. "If Knøfa is left unchecked, he will destroy your faction, and perhaps the entire Trader network." She raised a brow, pointed at the camera. "You can do better, Michael Trask. Take the Clan. Make it your own. Stop him before he goes too far." Rizzo stared into the holocam a moment more. "End recording. Encode to play only at the sound of Michael Trask's voice command to do so."

A soft chitter. "Acknowledged."

"Send message."

Another chitter, and the office fell silent. Across the room, Jukka stood slack-jawed. "You know what you just did."

"I do." She took a deep breath. Knøfa had started this. She would finish it, indirectly if possible, hand-to-hand if necessary. "I'm counting on Tsurin's judgment of this Trask person. Let's hope I'm not wrong." She held out the crate.

"Jukka," she said before he could get to the door.

He paused. "Yes, admiral?"

"If I ever go rogue like Knøfa has, if I—" She stopped, cleared her throat. "If I start randomly maiming or killing people over power plays or some other such stupid rationalization, promise me you'll push Bailey into my seat, as I've just done to Trask."

"Of course. But," he said, "I can't even imagine the circumstance that would make you act like that man."

She frowned. "You can't know that. Running a faction takes its toll."

"Maybe," he said. "But from what I've heard, Knøfa didn't start on solid ground. He was always going to go south."

The vote of confidence felt good. Hopefully he was right. "Thank you, Jukka. Dismissed."

When he was gone, she went to the window and tried to trace events to the point when things started to go so wrong in her life, both on base and off. No matter what route she took, it all pointed to that night in New Canaan when she'd gone to kill Skalar, and instead saddled herself with a project she hadn't wanted but couldn't seem to shake. As much as Rizzo wanted to lay the blame for all her problems at that little instigator's feet and claim that ever since she fell into Rizzo's life, everything had changed, she knew it wasn't Alira's fault. For all Rizzo knew, she was safe on Bejami now and still working with Botha.

No. This was on Knøfa. On the Clan. And if Trask wouldn't make it right, Rizzo would.

chapter 42

<u>**Earth**</u>

ALIRA COULDN'T SHAKE THE SUDDEN clarity of Rakalesh's stooped form, the impression of weakness that had clouded Alira's vision of that elder's endless strength. In the last two seasons, Rakalesh had seen the unammi through challenges that would've overwhelmed others, even those many seasons younger. Could Alira have done any better? Maybe not, but her way would've at least been different. In the end, though, it didn't matter. Her strengths and sacrifices had been needed elsewhere. She'd played her role. Apparently, she was still doing so.

She followed Tiral's directions to the splitters' city, flying slowly, mindfully. How should she present her case to the splitters? Would they welcome her interference? Maybe they, with their different view on change and adaptation, would be willing to go with her to the outpost until this threat was past? She could only hope.

Below and around the *Nebula*, rocky terrain lay dusted with snow, thicker in patches where the winds had pushed it into small drifts. Most of the route before and behind her lay open, like the canyon between the unammi's domed city and the open plains where she'd loved to windwalk. Except here, time and weather had moved the walls farther apart, lowered their barriers, opened the way. Now, a large mound rose to her left, while the cliffs lined the horizon on her right, their ridges folded around canyons of their own. The plain between the *Nebula* and the cliffs held scattered rock pillars with their odd, pockmarked surfaces. Above her stretched deepening shades of blue. When she'd first viewed this place, she had feared that wide, open space. Now it was a beloved thing, that sky. Any sky. She'd taken it too much for granted while Skalar drove her actions.

She veered toward the rise where Tiral had told her to find the surface opening, and threaded her way between the pillars. Ahead stood the debris from a long-ago rockslide, the cliff face above a deeper shade of rusty brown, as if the wound had not yet healed. The entry should be…

There. She saw the darker shadow at the base, near the jumbled stones and standing outside, three figures. Galen must've told them she was coming. There was no place to hide the ship. Instead, she settled it between two of the pillars near the rockslide. By the time she shut it down and stepped out the hatch, the others awaited her.

The first person she saw was Trumo. He rushed to her, unashamedly embracing her and showing his affection in dermal displays and actions. She didn't recognize the others, one youngling a few seasons older than Trumo, and one frem, but neither seemed to disapprove of Trumo's emotional exhibition. Alira sighed and returned the youngling's hug. Maybe there would be hope for her people after all.

When he finally released her, she realized he'd grown taller. Two seasons—over half a standard year in human measures—had made such a difference!

"It's good to see you, chithe."

"I missed you," he said, his small body lit with bright yellow streaks and veins of golden hues. He pointed up at the sky. "We should go inside, though. This world's star burns our skin if we aren't careful."

She raised a brow at him. "And you don't use it as a reason to practice your shifting?"

"Sometimes," Trumo said. "But not too often. I'm told I should take my time, not be too eager yet."

"That's wise advice." She touched his face.

"This is Ceala," he said, gesturing to the female frem. "She took over my care after my ama was killed in the attack. And this is Folmir, Ceala's other youngling. My new brother."

"Aes te nalya, Ceala, Folmir," Alira said.

They responded almost in unison. "Nalena t'staani, Alira." Folmir stepped closer. "It's an honor to meet you. We speak your name in our city, Na'ama."

Alira blinked. "You speak…what?"

"You didn't know?" Trumo's colors swirled. "The other council said we couldn't talk about you. Even say your name. They—"

Ceala touched his shoulder. "Basu'tao. Alira has come a long way. I'm sure she's tired."

"It's okay," Alira said, her words slow, thoughtful. The council and their ridiculous rules. Why would they forbid her very name? What would that solve? She nodded at the sky. "But Trumo has a point. And I have much to tell you. All of you."

Ceala's face puckered, but she led the way inside. As they walked, Trumo took up a position on one side of her, and Folmir took the other side. It felt like an escort, but one she was proud to endure. She smiled down at Trumo. "You look much better than the last time we talked."

"I am," he said. "I like my new family. Life is better here than in that other city."

"Oh?" Alira said. "Can you tell me why?"

His lips pulled to one side. "Here, I don't need to hide my happy."

A small seed of light took root in Alira and sent out the first cautious tendrils. How could she make them rejoin the traditionalists with their suffocating rules and enforced compliance? Even if Rakalesh would've allowed it, Trumo's "happy" and Folmir's hope were sparks Alira would never want to douse.

It would need to be the outpost, then. At least until they could extend the shields. "Ceala," she asked, "how many are here in this city?"

"One hundred and fifty-seven," Ceala said, "frem and younglings."

Too many to take in one trip. Or in one ship. Alira would have to make multiple passes or call down Tiral and one or two of the others to help transport them all off the surface. That would take time, something she wasn't sure they had. That resource was slipping past them like sands in the wind, moving faster than they could track, its sting every bit as sharp.

Alira frowned. There had to be another answer. They stepped into the shadow of the entry and were swallowed by the tunnels.

chapter 43

Aboard the Lysbringer
<u>En Route to Consortium Outpost</u>

THE SLUR OF MOTION ON the viewscreen resolved into a focused visual of stars in unfamiliar arrangements. Knøfa made a mental note to download star maps, if this trip proved fruitful. For now, he leaned toward the viewscreen, more intent on the planetary system before them.

"Report."

"We're approaching Earth and its satellite, sir. Solar activity is ramping up, but we should be fine," the navigator said over his shoulder. "Warning buoys are lighting up our boards, though."

"Biohazard?"

"Yes, sir. They say we should keep a distance outside the lunar orbit."

Knøfa puckered his lips. His research indicated the plague organisms would not have reached outside the atmosphere unless carried there by humans in the atmo of their ships, as had happened on the last colony world to be settled by humans. What was it called? Oh yes. Nidahn. But studies also revealed a distinct lack of clarity in persistence of such a virulent plague, especially one without hosts on which to feed. No one knew—thus TICS could not predict—whether it would still be present. The buoys were supposed to be programmed to change their message if and when the planet again became safe, but at last check, many years ago, they'd still been issuing the same warning his ship received now. No one had been curious enough to land and find out for sure, and most other orbiting bodies in this system had been scraped clean of any valuable resources long before that. Thus no one had come here since.

No one except Skalar. Did he know something Knøfa did not?

"Time?"

"Estimate three minutes, sir."

"Begin scanning for life forms."

chapter 44

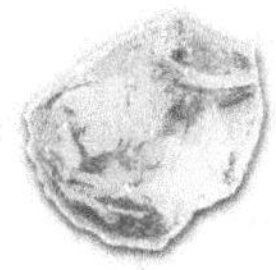

<u>Consortium Outpost</u>

GALEN'S SENSES TWISTED, AS IF someone had reached inside him to skew his sense of balance. He stumbled and fell against the console in the control room. Before he could investigate the source of his disorientation, a crewman shouted an alarm.

"Human ship on sensors!"

Galen blinked. So soon? "Designation?"

"Command class. Danua Clan."

"Jam sensors," Galen said. Shields had been up ever since he and Tiral had arrived, so they should be invisible. But just in case they hadn't already detected life signs, the jammer would make ping-backs to their ship look and sound like natural emissions from the heightened solar activity—just enough negation to make them think there was nothing to see here, and they should move along.

He pushed himself upright and stood behind the crewmen at the controls. "How are we doing?"

"We're ghosts," one said. "They don't see us."

The humans hadn't seen them *yet*. Galen's heart thumped wildly. But they would be discovered if the storm caused system failure and their cloak dissolved. He paced. The crew on this base and the unammi on the planet below—so much was at stake. His stomach knotted, and he fought the urge to wring his hands. Alira had known, going in, that he wouldn't be able to warn her if this happened. Those on Earth's surface were too far away to reach through the joinedmind, and he couldn't use comms. Even if the outpost's jammers didn't interfere with his own transmissions, the Clan's ship would see the signal. See *them*.

"What's the status of the buoys?"

"They're still online," one crewman said. "So far as I can tell, all show red, set to warn."

"And the storm won't affect those?"

"No. They're built with static hardware. Hardened. They've been there for centuries, through countless solar storms. If they're still broadcasting after all that time, they'll be fine now. Any repairs we had to make also meet that standard."

He hoped she was right. Might the mitigants be capable of offering any assistance in a group defense? Because if that ship landed, they would need every last individual's contribution in order to fight off its humans. Galen had never directed such an endeavor, but he had never learned how. He would rectify that lack as soon as possible. In fact, if they were still breathing after this encounter, he would make sure each of them, including himself, practiced that critical skill daily.

He called through the joinedmind to Tiral. He should be here for this.

chapter 45

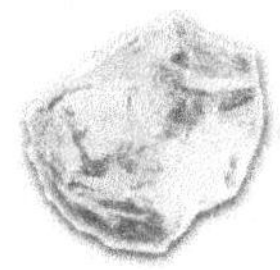

Aboard the Lysbringer
<u>Above the Consortium Outpost</u>

KNØFA STARED AT THE VIEWSCREEN. If the buoys were right, he couldn't imagine even Skalar would risk his crew on a base this close to a plague zone. But if readings were positive, he'd need a bigger ship. The *Lysbringer* wasn't built for attack. Its intention as a command ship used mostly for personal travel or recon meant it carried limited firepower—two non-nuclear missiles and a couple of defensive weapons big enough to allow them to escape a hot encounter, but not enough to lay siege or take over a site.

"No life signs detected on the satellite, sir."

"And our readings are reliable?" he said. "Solar activity isn't fucking with us?"

"No, sir. Everything's green, so far."

"Scan for hematium." That, at least, he could investigate for himself, should they find any trace. "TICS, show me a surface map of the planetary satellite below from the most recent historical data."

A soft chitter preceded the appearance of a holoprojection in the middle of the bridge space. Knøfa rose and walked closer and peered at the craters and antiquated satellite tech littering the moon's surface. He grasped the edges of the projection and examined it bit by bit, as he'd done at least six times during the journey so far. Each time, he caught something he hadn't noticed before.

"Negative, sir. No signs of hematium."

Knøfa frowned. "Nothing at all?"

"No, sir."

He reviewed the holo again. He'd come all this way for *nothing*? Trask said he'd believed the informant. So, if the hematium wasn't here…

"TICS, show me a surface image of Earth from the most recent historical data." He already knew what he'd see, but he reviewed it anyway, inspecting every landmass, expanding it to better see the islands. What if the informant had gotten the planetary system right, but the specific orbiting body wrong? It's conceivable that Skalar had his crew deliver it to Earth's surface wearing hazmat suits to protect them from the virus. Hematium shed radiation tox. Chances are it would also shed biological organisms. Or perhaps irradiation—after retrieval—would cleanse the metal of all biologicals hitching a ride from Earth's biosphere. It's not a chance most people would take. But could Skalar have done so? *Would* he?

Knøfa squinted at the projected image before him. Hiding that metal—which would not just make him one of the richest, most powerful individuals in all the charter worlds if he could pull it off but would also hide evidence of what he'd done on Iridos—in a place where no one would think to look…yeah. That sounded exactly like something Skalar would've done.

He stepped back from the projection but continued to stare at it. Maybe the pathogens that started Earth's plague wouldn't have lasted long without viable hosts. But it was just as likely that the plague was still virulent. Some viruses were known to embed themselves in natural bacteria. If that were the case here, the virus could've holed up like a stowaway, hidden until new hosts made themselves available. He'd not been able to determine which of these pathogens had been the culprit on old Earth.

Still, he'd traveled for over seven days to get to this podunk place. If he went home without at least checking out the possibility, he'd always wonder if he'd missed something. No harm in running a few scans.

He dispelled the holoimage and resumed his seat. "Helm, get us closer to the planet."

chapter 46

TIRAL ENTERED CONTROL JUST AS one of the crewmen reported, "They're going in."

"Toward Earth?" Galen asked.

"Yes."

Galen's hands clenched, and he shot a look at Tiral, who'd gone white. "They won't go past the buoys. Right?"

"Let's hope not," Tiral said, his voice tight.

Images of the Iridosian pockmarked surface, the unammi's shattered and melted domes, flashed through Galen's mind like waking nightmares. That time the humans had brought an armada, but a large unammi population had been onsite to fight the humans' advances. There might be only one ship this time—at least for now—but there were far fewer unammi, split into even smaller groups over a wide region, to negate Knøfa's efforts and take his ship down. Would they all be able to reach him? He hoped so, because if Knøfa found them there, and got away to bring reinforcements, the unammi would have no choice but to evacuate in a very short window of time. Given the tensions between the traditionalists and the splitters and outcasts right now, it would be an extremely difficult, if not impossible task.

Either way, at this distance from the planet, Galen and his crew could do nothing but wait. With the sensors on the sunward side of this moon shut down due to the solar storm, they couldn't even keep track of the ship. That helpless feeling vibrated his senses as if someone had struck a huge bell. His flesh twitched. His ears rang. The same acrid taste coated his tongue as when Yoloron had told him the younglings might dim, or the unammi frem might be sterile.

A chitter from the controls yanked Galen's attention to the crewman manning that post. "What is it?"

"Um," she said, "I think there's a problem."

chapter 47

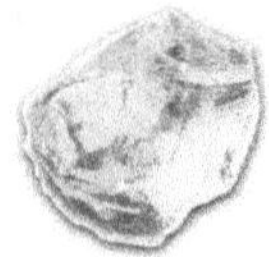

Aboard the Lysbringer
<u>**On Approach to Earth**</u>

"SIR, WE'RE STILL GETTING MULTIPLE warnings from the buoys in this vicinity."

Knøfa scowled. "How far apart are these things? Show me the grid."

A holoprojection spread out in the air before him, and he got to his feet. Red dots, representing the buoys, spread around the surface of the planet like a cloud of barrens flies around an ørkhund's leavings. Damn. He opened his mouth to order hematium scans when something in the display flickered. He squinted. Moved closer. One of the red dots changed to green, then to red. A moment later, it winked green, then red. He pointed. "Check that buoy. Tell me what you see."

"I'll need to move us a little closer, sir, to get a good reading."

"Do it." The red dot blinked several more times before setting into a stable red state. Knøfa frowned at the other dots, watching for them to blink. None did.

"Well?" he demanded.

"Coming to it now, sir." The crewman ran her test. "Results show intermittent patterns of signal degradation, sir. Looks like it's in the process of failing."

"Is it the storm?"

"I don't think so, sir," she said. "If it was, it'd be affecting all of them."

"Scan one of the others."

She did so. "That's weird," she said.

"What do you see?" Knøfa said, coming to stand behind her.

"These internals," she said, her words slow as if she was uncertain about her conclusion. "They're…newer than the other one. Not all of it, just parts, like it was repaired after it was built and deployed."

"How long after?" Knøfa pressed. "Still ancient tech?"

"No, sir," she said, frowning at him. "This is new hardware."

"What about the others? How many are like that?"

This time the silence lasted longer. Knøfa clenched his jaw. He needed to be patient.

"A lot of them, sir," she said at last.

Knøfa spun to face the holoimage. "Scan the atmosphere for microbes. Tell me what you see. TICS, show me Earth's surface as it is now."

A projection of the planet below took shape in front of him, this time a live image of the blue and green world.

"No harmful microorganisms, sir."

Her voice sounded strange, and he considered her wide-eyed expression. It didn't help. He still didn't know what it meant.

"Check it again. Let's be certain."

The second result, and the third, both returned the same verdict. Whatever plague had chased humans from this world millennia ago, it wasn't here now.

Knøfa dispelled the projection and took his seat once more.

"Viewscreen on. Helm, take us closer to the surface. Begin searching for any structures, signs of a base, hematium, anything you wouldn't expect to see on an abandoned planet."

He had to admit, it was a clever move. Let everyone think it's still deadly so Skalar could keep it for himself. He almost smiled in admiration. Instead, he gripped the armrests on his chair so hard they bent.

That's where Skalar's base would be. Down there.

chapter 48

Earth

ONCE INSIDE, CEALA SENT THE younglings to their educators and led the way through the twisting passages. Alira followed, looking around at those making a home in these ancient tunnels, apart from the council and their strictures. Many watched her pass, spoke her name, their displays awash in yellow, gold, and tan even as they showed clear excitement in their faces, and in their hurried steps to greet her or follow her small group to their chosen gathering place.

After a lifetime of others ignoring or ridiculing her, and months of hiding behind a mask never intended for her, the renown sat uneasy in Alira's middle like an unsettled meal. She nodded, acknowledged the greetings, but directed her concentration elsewhere.

The tunnels here, reminiscent of the traditionalists' city, had their own character and shape. The passages were narrower, the ceilings a bit lower, though the same structural mechanisms had been used in the larger spaces to stabilize the whole network. Floors had been worn smooth by the passage of seasons upon seasons of feet, first human and now unammi.

Alira had wished so many times that she could live among her people, that she could return to the rites, the Tellings, and the teachings—minus the conformity bits. Here, in the splitters' city, she could do it. It'd take time to acclimate to all the recognition, true. But that just meant they accepted her as she was. *As she was.* Finally, she could come home. She could belong, at last.

Alira's arms flushed with yellow spots. "What are you going to do about supplying irolium for the new city?"

"The council has promised us our own seedstones." Ceala grimaced. "We can't keep splitting like this. Soon there won't be enough seedstones to go around, nor enough unammi nearby them to spark the symbiosis."

She was right. It was baffling that Rakalesh couldn't see it. Was the councilor simply too weary, too worn to make rational judgments? Alira pressed her lips together. That might explain Rakalesh's refusal, but not Dyson's. Who else on the council was blocking the necessary changes?

"We've discussed forming our own council," Ceala said. "Nearly everyone has agreed it would be best. Most even suggested the same individuals to serve, but we want to make a few revisions to the old council structure."

"Like what?"

Ceala shrugged. "Periodic shifts to new council members, so that no one is required to serve more than three seasons in a row. It would allow those who've served a chance to rest from their duty and create openings for change as we grow and adapt to this new home."

Alira smiled. "Were you suggested to serve on the first round?"

Ceala's skin flooded with yellow and speckles of gray surprise. "Yes. How did you know?"

"I—"

Both of them froze, along with other frem in the corridor, as the call to assist came through the joinedmind. A chill swept through Alira at the threat—a human ship. Knøfa's people. It had to be them. They'd come sooner than she'd expected. Her fear deepened, flushing her skin white. This city was unshielded. The humans would see them, see her ship.

Already, her people worked together to push the intruders away, make them leave, but that was a mistake. If that ship's crew left Earth with the knowledge that there were unammi here, that the environment was safe, the unammi survivors would be forced to leave. Again. They couldn't allow that. The ship and its crew must be taken down.

The thought spiked terror in her. Would she harvest them all? Even worse, was Knøfa among them? Rizzo had warned Alira, told her to avoid this very situation. She had barely endured Bellamy. If Rizzo was right, and Alira harvested Knøfa, she might not make it through that kind of nightmare a second time.

But what choice did she have?

Inhaling deeply, Alira reached through the joinedmind. When she found Rakalesh, she shared the knowledge with her, with everyone, that the humans could not be allowed to leave. *We need to kill them all. We can't—*

A ripple passed through the joinedmind, like a stone dropped in a pond. The wave touched every unammi, sending shivers along the lines of connection. When it got to Alira, it had doubled in size. Tripled. It washed over her, driving her out with a physical sensation as if someone had planted a hand on her chest and shoved her.

She stood beside the other frem who, still connected, worked at their task. Speckles of gray dotted those around her. That had *never* been done as far as she knew. Rakalesh? Dyson? Both? All the councilors? The people were so few right now—they couldn't afford to eject even one mind in this endeavor. And if they let that ship leave…

Alira shuddered. The others needed to heed her message. But she didn't dare distract them from their essential focus. She hesitated, torn, while the struggle played out around her. The survival of her species depended on her choice.

Part Four

chapter 49

Aboard the Lysbringer
<u>Earth</u>

"NO SIGN OF HEMATIUM, SIR, but…" The crewman paused.

"Well?" Knøfa pressed.

"Correction. I do see hematium in a minuscule quantity, sir."

He scowled at her. "How much?"

She hesitated. "About what you might expect to find in the mechanical parts on a small interstel craft, sir." She raised her gaze to his. "A command-class, maybe. Or recon. Same size as this one."

A ship? Knøfa leaned forward. "Designation?"

"One minute, sir." She accessed her panel. "Consortium. The *Nebula.*"

Ah! He knew it. He *knew* it! "Life signs?"

"Mostly animals and plants, sir, but—" She halted, her voice cut off as if she'd sliced away the words with her knife. "Wait, there's something else. Not human, though. Squibs, maybe?"

Knøfa lurched out of his seat. "How many?"

"Ship counts one hundred and fifty-eight, but I'm not certain," she said, her words slow. "One of them reads odd, like I can't tell if it's just one person."

He chewed on that for a minute. He'd expected to find Skalar's outpost here, and a couple cargo holds full of hematium. If this base was manned entirely by squibs, then that Baldric person had to be one of them and—*was Skalar a squib, too?*

"What about weapons?" Knøfa barked. "Anything on scans?"

"No, sir, not as far as I can see."

Knøfa frowned. The informant's story detailed what had happened to Crow's armada. Maybe their defensive systems weren't set up yet? Maybe they trusted that humans wouldn't come here? Or maybe...

Could that have been connected to the squibs' abilities to mess with people's minds? Maybe it wasn't just thoughts and visuals they could affect. Maybe they could do things to physical matter, too.

Was that even *possible*?

Either way, Knøfa didn't want to take chances, but he wasn't leaving just yet. If he planned to come back later and grab a shipload of squibs, he'd need more information. A lay of the land.

"Get me closer to that ship," Knøfa said. "And look alive. I'd like to not get killed today."

chapter 50

<u>Earth</u>

ALIRA BRUSHED THE EDGES OF the joinedmind to sense its intent, which still worked to make the intruder depart. She ground her teeth. Through their connection, she could sense Knøfa's ship at a distance, approaching on a first recon pass. They seemed untouched, unaffected. How long did the unammi have before the ship left orbit?

She nudged her way in once more, this time with greater subtlety. As she delved deeper, she encouraged those connections she sensed nearby to a deadlier goal. Like a drop of ink in a bowl of water, her influence seeped through the group's web, convincing the others that the ship's escape meant their doom. In slow measure, the unammi's efforts turned toward finding and increasing flaws in the ship before it could escape.

This time, the ripple that came racing through the joinedmind slammed into Alira so hard she stumbled into the wall. When she tried to rejoin them again, she hit a block. Again and again, she pressed against the barrier only to be rebuffed. She screamed, her fists clenched before her, the red hues of her anger and frustration reflected off the walls, the frem nearby, the floor. If she could reach Rakalesh now, she would shake her, make her listen, show her the folly of this plan.

The rustling that so often preceded her Companion's appearance registered just before Alira felt his presence. From across the tunnel, he watched her.

"Do something!" she said.

Her Companion shifted through its forms in rapid succession, the shapes nearly blending into a single amorphous figure. Alira felt a buzz along her skin, as if the Iri were almost physical, their energy bleeding through the barriers between their world and hers. The voice, when it came, was not that of Elisul, but of many voices speaking in unison, all in her mind.

You may not survive.

She shook her head. "Can't help that. It's me or all of them."

The Companion shifted and buzzed, as if thinking. Weighing the outcome.

The others will see your harvests. They will know what you are.

"No. I'll hide them, as I've done in the past."

They will see Us, too. We cannot be hidden. We are too many.

Alira flinched. She hadn't considered that. She brushed the edges of the joinedmind once more, checking progress. Some of the unammi were pushing to destroy the ship, while others worked to send it away. With their focus divided so, they wouldn't succeed at either.

She nailed her Companion with a desperate glare. "I don't care what it costs me! Just help us! Help *me* help us!"

Her Companion shifted, shifted, shifted, then faded out of her view.

She reeled as if slapped, her inability to effect the necessary change dragging a bellow from her throat. There had to be a way. But she saw none. With a wail, she hunkered down, squeezed her eyes shut, and waited for it to be over.

chapter 51

Aboard the Lysbringer
<u>Earth</u>

"SIR, EXTERNAL COMMS JUST WENT down."

"Irrelevant. We can fix comms once we leave here." He paced the bridge, arms crossed. "Stay on point. How far are we from that ship?"

"Coming up on the port side now, sir."

"Give me visual," Knøfa said. "And start recording. I want current environmental and geological readings, as well as a topographical layout before we leave."

The planet surface appeared in the holovid, the nearby ground passing too quickly to make out. Cliffs rushed past them. Odd pinnacle-like formations dotted the plain on both sides. A light layer of snow covered most of what he could see. So this would be their winter.

"Sir! Two squibs on the surface, sir!"

"Where? I don't see—"

The holo enlarged, zoomed in close. "There!"

He sucked in a breath. Two blue idiots raced from the cliff face toward the ship. "Are there catchnets onboard?"

"Affirmative."

"Take us down closer. Hurry." The ship dipped lower as Knøfa stabbed a finger at the coms officer. "Tell the hold crew to grab those squibs."

The crewman babbled into the comm and received a hasty reply. The squibs grew larger in the holovid as the ship approached. He'd grab the rest later, but these two would at least be a start.

The visual blinked as they drew near the running squibs, who'd reversed direction to race toward the cliff.

"What just happened?"

"Unknown, sir." A crewman peered at the console. "Some sort of interference. A pretty massive solar flare let loose from the star's surface a few minutes ago. It could be playing havoc with our tech."

"Fix it. I need that data."

"Trying, sir." A sheen of sweat on the man's brow glistened in the bridge lights as he worked.

The holo stuttered, its image warped, twisting the squibs to one side before it winked out.

"Get it back!"

The frantic crewman worked the controls. He grimaced, even as he attempted a fix. "I'm not sure what's wrong, sir. Without a reason for the glitch, I don't know what to repair." Sweat dripped from his hair onto his clothing.

"Keep trying." Knøfa's neck was so tight it creaked. "Did we get the squibs?"

The officer spoke into the comm, waited. "Yes, sir. We got them."

"Good. See that they are isolated in the brig immediately." He couldn't take the chance they could create this same kind of havoc from *inside* the ship. They were busy enough already. "Are we still recording?"

"Unknown, sir," another crewman said. "I can't tell without the vid."

Knøfa growled, a low guttural sound that vibrated his chest. He forced himself to sit still and remain calm. It was entirely possible, maybe even probable, that the glitches were not their fault. Still, he wanted to throttle them. He couldn't afford to kill his crew just now.

"Turn us around. Get me to that ship. At least we already know where that is."

chapter 52

<u>Consortium Outpost</u>

GALEN PRESSED HIS LIPS TOGETHER. He needed those weapons *now*.

He dove into the joinedmind, called everyone together as best he could without ever having done it before, and directed his concentration toward Earth. Together, the outcasts and mitigants reached out for the larger group of unammi, who he had no doubt were working to disable that ship. If they could add their efforts to those in the new city, they might have a better chance.

But the city was too distant, outside their range. Alira and the others were on their own.

Galen released the focus and sighed. He hadn't expected it to work, but they had to try.

"Tiral," he said, his voice low, "when this is over, we will arm this base, and we will arm the city below. Whether the main city wants weapons or not, we need a way to stop this from happening again."

"Indeed." Tiral did not look up. There was no point. Whatever happened on Earth, it was out of their control.

<h1 style="text-align:center">chapter 53</h1>

Aboard the Lysbringer
<u>**Earth**</u>

AN ALARM SOUNDED ON THE bridge, a steady beep that shoved needles of annoyance into Knøfa's brain.

"Report. And shut off that noise."

The sound stopped, but his ears kept ringing.

"There's a pressure leak, sir. Level two aft."

That presented a problem. "Send a crew to seal it."

"On it, sir."

This made the third technical glitch in the last few minutes. Was this the solar storm, as his crew thought? Or were the squibs doing this? Some sort of shield tech that would screw with his ship? Could this be an enhanced version of his prisoner's ability to mess with his crew? Probably. But given a choice, he'd hope for something he could affect. "Check for shields."

"Nothing I see, sir. If they've got one, it's not tech I recognize."

"Where's that ship?"

Helm squinted at his panel, then nodded. "We should be over it in sixty seconds, sir."

Fine. He'd hoped to run another scan, get more information. But the squibs were making his life difficult at the moment. Maybe he could distract their efforts.

"Give me weapons hot."

Ten seconds. "Go, sir."

"Ready missile one to fire on the Consortium ship's coordinates on my mark." He counted down the seconds. "Mark."

"Missile away, sir."

"How's that pressure leak?"

"Still working on it, sir," the crewman said, "but they're close to having it sealed. Pressure is stabilizing."

Good. It looked like they'd need more ships.

Of course, Skalar had sent a whole armada.

Still, Knøfa was not prepared to land or do anything more than peep, grab, and run. If the squibs were behind his ship's faults, he needed to put some distance between them and find the limit of their reach.

"Helm, get us out of here."

He felt the shift in direction and speed as they shot toward the sky.

chapter 54

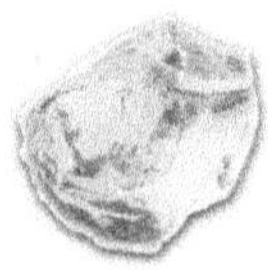

<u>**Earth**</u>

THE BLAST RATTLED THE CAVERNS around her, shaking those nearby out of the joinedmind. Flashbacks of their city on Iridos chilled her and, from the white flush on everyone in sight, them as well. It was happening again. Unless she could stop it.

Alira steadied herself and shouted to those who could hear. "Help me! We can't let them leave!"

Once more she brushed the edges of the now-shaky joinedmind, and as she did, she felt her Companion return. Its presence, so close it raised bumps on her skin, whispered in its many voices like the murmur of a crowded space before it merged with her. *Into* her.

She froze, fear icing her limbs and tightening her throat. The voices of before, of her harvests, were nothing to this mass. She could not find the silence, as if there was no space between the murmurings. No end to their essence. Heart hammering behind her ribs, throat so tight she could not speak, she squeezed her eyes shut and held her breath. Any moment now, it would come—that plunge into the babbling blackness of insanity.

But the Iri only waited, watched, feeling and experiencing through her senses. She opened her eyes to find the other unammi around her all staring, open-mouthed, as if they had seen, truly *seen*, her for the first time.

They will know what you are.

Alira blinked. Too late to worry about that now. She dove into the joinedmind, bumped against the barrier, pushed her way into it, then shoved past it. Blasted through.

And saw what all the rest of her people, shocked to stillness now in the midst of their efforts, had seen. Two unammi younglings scooped up by the ship, a replay of the Bregainan snatch in miniature.

ah, no! who?

Iri whispers rose in volume before an image of Trumo and Folmir shone to all those connected. The wail that burst from her own throat matched Ceala's and others', deeper in the caverns, grief that magnified and reverberated through the joinedmind. Pain knotted in Alira's chest and rippled through her body as if Knøfa had reached into her and pulled out the last good thing left. Her ama was lost. Nyros and Ijydin were lost. Her place in unammi society, her city, her *world,* all lost. Now Trumo—

his little face, shining up at her in class…

his search for belonging, so similar to her own…

his embrace in the healers' caverns on Iridos…

his clear trust that she would make things right…

how terrified Trumo and Folmir would be right now…

Why in all the worlds did they go onto the surface? Surely they'd seen there was a crisis going on with the frem! Unless they were already separated from the others when the emergency call went out? She cast about for a way to save them, but in the time it would take her to reach the *Nebula,* assuming it was still intact after that blast, Knøfa's ship would escape. Images of what would await them in Knøfa's custody twisted in her imagination until she thought she might be sick. She could not let that happen.

They had no choice now.

Her connection to the joinedmind rang with Iri voices as she shot an urgent message through the unammi collective. Their combined rage at the human ship veered the focus of a few, then more, and finally all to deadly intent directed outward at the escaping human ship, their energy joining hers as she reached out to the craft. She had directed energy before in the rites, but never like this. Between the energies of her people, the images of Trumo and Folmir, and the whispers and surge of the Iri, the power blasting through her threatened to overwhelm her senses.

But there was no time to think about that. She pushed aside the fear, the doubt, the fact that they were deliberately sacrificing two of their younglings, even the knowledge that the unammi would rise or fall based on their actions in this moment. Instead, she reached the craft in her mind, far up in the atmosphere, and pulled the others with her as she flew through the ship's structure, seeking the easiest flaw she could find. As it rose toward the upper atmosphere, the heat of its ascension added to the unammi's efforts and began to pull the ship apart. A small extraneous part flew off and fell away. The backup sensor array. A hull plate.

hurry!

The outer hatch on an airlock. Sensor arrays. And then the leak the unammi had already effected earlier, its internal patch as yet incomplete. Alira wrapped her will around the edges of that break and pulled with all the might she could drag from the joinedmind—including her Companion—at the molecular connections in the hull.

chapter 55

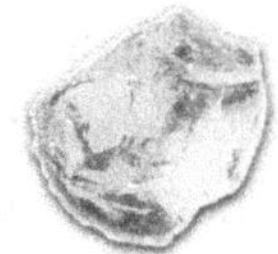

Aboard the Lysbringer
<u>Earth</u>

NO ALARMS SOUNDED, BUT LIGHTS flashed across the board as crew members shouted critical reports, punctuated by creaks and groans from the ship itself.

"What was that?" Knøfa called.

"Which one, sir?" The officer's panic thrummed in every word. "Hull plates, sensor arrays…we're losing external parts faster than I can keep track!"

"Helm," Knøfa growled. "What's our position?"

"Approaching upper atmosphere, sir!"

"Go faster!"

"I'm trying, sir," the officer shouted. "Engineering's not responding to my commands! They—"

Another loud *pop* interrupted.

"That was the outer hatch on the main airlock, sir!" someone yelled. "And the primary sensor array—"

A loud hiss bled through the crew's shouts.

"Report," Knøfa bellowed.

"Losing pressure, sir! It's that hull breach from earlier. The patch is pulling apart from the outside!"

This was the squibs. The crew needed to move this ship faster, get them out of here, and rethink coming back with an armada. There had to be another way.

Knøfa drew breath to bellow an order just as the seals around the bridge cracked and vented. All the air left the bridge in a deafening whoosh.

In the silence that followed, the slice of darkness before him spread. His crew floated up from their seats, their eyes wide and mouths working like fish on the dock, and he rose with them, his mind registering every detail until his lungs popped inside his chest. The blackness around him seeped inside, and he knew no more.

chapter 56

<u>Earth</u>

THE WHISPERS IN ALIRA'S MIND faded into a distant hiss that sounded like air escaping from the human ship. It had almost reached the outer atmosphere, and she screamed as she pulled more from the others in the joinedmind than they'd thought possible, channeling the eruption of power through her own connection to the Iri and to the ship until the seams burst open, the whole side of the ship separated at the plate junctions. Bodies began to spill from the ruptures, which multiplied as the ship kept going, and before it could jump to interstel, what remained of the twisted ruin exploded, its pieces thrust outward in every direction.

Her scream died with the breath that had fed it, and she dropped to her knees. Others around her stirred, blinked, and moved toward her, but the last thing she saw before the world went dark was Elisul, standing across the tunnel.

chapter 57

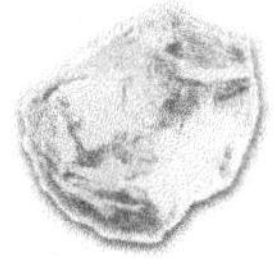

Tuneloras, Saacharis
Syndicate Trader Base, MedFac 3

RIZZO STIRRED IN THE SEAT, which was just uncomfortable enough to make sleep an impossibility. As she'd hoped. She pushed against the armrests, sitting more upright. Across the room, Bailey's machines kept track of her vitals while medicines kept her sedated. She needed the rest, if she was to heal. Med crew said she'd beaten the odds already and Rizzo hoped they were right. But she had seen wounds and blood loss like that before. It hadn't usually ended well.

She settled in for a brief doze. Her message to Trask had surely been seen by now. She could only imagine what sort of upheaval that might spark, but if it served the purpose for which she'd intended it, the result would be worth the trouble.

Just as she drifted into a doze, her wristcom vibrated. She activated the earbud and murmured a response. "Yes."

"This is your requested notification that an incoming message has been received from Admiral Bardo of the Levyron Order," the TICS reported in her ear.

"Put visual through to MedFac 3," Rizzo said as she sat up. "Keep audio on my earbud."

TICS chittered, then her childhood friend's image materialized between her chair and the bed. His gold-flecked eyes held more crinkles at their corners than the last time she'd seen him. An admiral's life would do that to a person, although in Bardo's case they were more likely to be laugh lines than anything else. His shaggy hair held more gray but that one lock hung in his face, as usual. He hadn't even bothered to stand up to record the message. Instead, he sat slouched in his chair, one foot up on the desk, an antique acoustic guitar cradled in his arms. He strummed it as he spoke.

"Turi," he crooned in tune with the made-up music. "Oh Turi. Hmm mmm mmm…" His fixation shifted away from the camera, down to his beloved instrument. He continued playing while he hummed.

Rizzo sighed. If one wanted to communicate with Bardo, one accepted his oddities. Everybody had them. His were all musical.

After a couple more bars, he stopped, his fingers flat on the strings, and beamed at the camera. "It was good to hear your voice. Sorry to learn about the Bregainans, though. Did you have friends there? Were they among those taken? If so, point me in the right direction, and I'll break some bones." He swung the guitar to the side and placed it in its stand with a delicate touch, then planted his elbows on the desk with casual grace.

"Of course, I can take on a weapons project. You know me. Always ready with the paying jobs. You were so mysterious about it, I look forward to hearing the details. I'm at your service." His stare pierced the camera. "And I am absolutely in on anything that involves stopping the slave trade, no matter what they call it. I haven't forgotten the day my best friend in the world was snatched," he said, his smile tight, his poise shadowed by ghosts. "It took me over thirty years to find you again. So yeah. Whatever you need, I'm your guy."

He squinted into the camera. "Your message makes me wonder about that jacked load of child slaves from the Cartel four months ago. Was that you? And another strange coincidence—I heard Harajüd House took over Iridos after the unammi abandoned it. Rumor says they found a bunch of kids inside the mine, all dead from radiation poisoning. They also found traces of human remains scattered just outside the ruined city, presumably the adult supervising crew, all dead from what appeared to be an explosion of some kind." He tapped his jaw. "Now what would make me think you played a part in that?

"If so, good for you." He winked, then picked up his guitar. "I expect you are working out the details of the collaboration you've got in mind, but meanwhile I'll monitor my channels. See what I can find. Let me know when you wanna meet." He paused, his demeanor serious for a change. "It would be really, *really* good to see you, Turi." Then he grinned, strummed a bit, and the message ended.

Rizzo blinked at the space where his image had been. On the other side of it, in the bed, Bailey's eyes were open—even the swollen one, though by barely a slit. Rizzo lurched out of her chair and made it to the bedside in three long strides.

Bailey seemed to follow her movements, so this was no fluke. She was awake. She licked her lips and tried to speak but could only whisper.

Rizzo leaned in to hear.

Bailey turned her head on the pillow with laborious effort, pointing her gaze more directly at Rizzo. "Bardo doesn't comm. What's up?"

She'd seen the holovid, then. Rizzo shrugged. "Nothing that can't wait."

"He's still an imp."

"Heart and soul." Rizzo's mouth twitched at the corner.

"That was," Bailey said, her words slow, "almost a smile."

"Get well and I might do it more often."

"I'm working on it." She didn't speak for a moment, then focused as best she could on Rizzo's face. "How bad?"

"Bad enough." Rizzo scowled. "Thought I was going to lose you."

Bailey's cheek twitched on the least bruised side. "No chance. I'm here to stay."

"Good. Now get some rest. That's an order."

"Aye, ma'am." Bailey closed her eyes and relaxed. A few seconds later, her breathing deepened.

Once she was asleep, Rizzo slipped a hand under her second's free one, brushed its back with her thumb, and allowed herself to hope.

chapter 58

<u>Earth</u>

THE NEBULA, OR WHAT REMAINED of it, sat in a crater, surrounded and partially buried by rubble from the rock pillars that had flanked it. She hadn't yet commed the outpost to let them know the end result of the encounter, but probably Rakalesh or someone in the traditionalists' city had done so.

A summons came through the joinedmind. Alira ignored it. The only thought she could hold for more than a few seconds was that other than the shifting of light and shadows across the rubble, this scene was like a miniature reminder of the surface on Iridos after the armada's attack.

"How did the Clan find us here?" She surveyed the damage. When no reply came, she peeked at her silent Companion. Ah. The laconic treatment. She sighed and paced around the crater in search of any salvage, arms wrapped around herself. Doubtful she'd find anything in that charred mess. "He must've gotten some intel about the outpost, or he would never have come here."

At least this ship had fired only the one missile, and a small one at that. Otherwise, some of the tunnels might have collapsed. The entry, though damaged, was now cleared of rockfall, and usable once more. A few repairs continued farther inside, but no unammi had been killed—at least, not in the caverns.

Only Trumo and Folmir. That fresh loss clenched her heart, purpled her skin.

Ah Trumo.

Thank Na'Staani she hadn't harvested any more human memories. She'd awakened sick with worry, only to find her internal landscape was quiet once more—except for echoes of that incessant whisper of voices, as if she'd stood in a busy port building amid passing travelers all talking among themselves.

"Was that the Iri I heard in there?" She glanced at her Companion. "When you joined with me, I heard so many voices. Was that you? All of you?"

The Companion shifted through its panoply in slow motion, so that she could almost make out each form before it morphed into the next. No response came and she moved on, staring over the plain around the crater. The snow, out there, still lay white along the ground.

"Maybe," she said, speaking as much to herself as to It, "my experience with the harvesting sickness prepared me for the merging. I don't know." She swung to see the tunnel entry, jagged and broken. Now, its opening sat clogged with unammi, all staring at her as she walked around this hole and spoke to someone they could not see. Their displays spanned the spectrum of colors, sometimes all at once. "It didn't prepare me for *that*, though you did warn me." Their reception had been odd enough before, when she'd first arrived.

Now...

Alira kicked a pebble into the hole. She wasn't quite sure what they'd seen in her. Maybe all her harvests, both human and unammi, maybe the Iri's voices and energy, maybe all of it. Whatever the reason, since the joinedmind, not one of them had spoken to her as they would have before that. If they addressed her at all, it was with hushed tones, and a lowered gaze, or with stark white skin, their limbs trembling all the while. Would they ever see her as one of them again?

Probably not. Some of the traditionalists never had, anyway. This would only ground their claims in reality. She watched them watching her until she could no longer stomach their fascination. She drifted toward the plain in search of a bit of distance. She hadn't gotten far when she heard an approaching sound. Someone was coming.

Ceala.

Damn. She didn't want to talk now. But she couldn't walk away from another unammi who'd lost her own youngling in this attack. She steeled herself for the encounter as Ceala drew near.

"Na'ama Alira," she said, her head bowed in respect, her skin mottled purple and white.

"Ceala," Alira responded, her voice soft. "Look at me."

She raised her chin and met Alira's eyes.

"You need not fear me," Alira said. She reached out. "We are One, remember? And we are both shattered by the loss of Trumo and Folmir."

Ceala touched her palm to Alira's, flickers of yellow dotting her skin. "It's true. I know you were not Trumo's ama. But you are still as wounded by his loss as am I by the loss of them both."

Blue and purple washed over Alira's arms. "Wynaes bejhul. They were so young, not even finished with their training." The words came automatically. What training? Without the guilds…

"I…" Ceala swallowed hard. "…wanted to share something with you that might help."

Alira gestured for her to go on.

"Both younglings were curious, more so than was good for them, sometimes." Ceala rubbed her palms together. "I found it difficult to chastise them, but they were always into something beyond their skill set." Speckles of tan affection accompanied the purple of mourning on her skin. "I know of at least two occasions when they snuck onto a pilot's ship while it sat on the surface before those frem learned to secure the vessels as soon as they exited them. I think they almost fired Tiral's weapons that first time before he caught them." A small frown darkened her features, then was gone. "Luckily, no one was hurt."

Alira stared at her. "How did the council not know of this?"

"I protected them as much as I could," Ceala said. "But they were quite intent on their goal, and I don't think even the council could've deterred them."

"What goal?" Trumo had never mentioned anything like that to her.

Ceala regarded her. "They wanted to follow in your footsteps, to be like you, a hero to our people."

Murmurs rose in Alira's head, and she shoved them down. "Me? A hero?"

"Yes, of course," Ceala said. "You went among the humans at great risk to yourself to find our pilots and bring them home. You found all our irolium and brought it to us so that we wouldn't dim. You found this new world for our survivors, a place where we can thrive and grow. And if not for you, those humans would've evaded us and spread the word of our presence here." She smiled. "Of course, the younglings want to emulate your courage and boldness. If I were younger, I might do the same."

"But—"

"That's why I think," Ceala went on, "that Trumo and Folmir were trying to get to your ship so that they could assist in the defense of the city."

Alira opened her mouth, but no words would come. Her Companion shifted slowly through its array of forms, its rustling a soft sound in the background. If she'd been around more, been more present for Trumo, she could've seen this coming, pinched that flower before it blossomed.

But no. Botha would say a single boat can't row in two directions, or something like that. She'd had her role to fill, and she'd done what she needed to do. She supposed Trumo had done the same, and in that at least, he *was* like her.

"Thank you for telling me," Alira said at last. She reached for Ceala. "Do you blame Trumo for leading Folmir to his death?" Did she blame Alira, too?

"Oh no," Ceala said, taking Alira's hand. "Not at all. I knew my youngling well. Trumo didn't talk him into anything. Folmir did this because it's what he wanted. I'm proud of them both. What they did was a noble, selfless act, even if they died in the effort. Their names will be remembered by our people."

A shout from the tunnel intruded. Rakalesh waved at them from the entrance.

Alira groaned. She didn't want to deal with recriminations, especially with the younglings taken. She'd done what she had to do, what Rakalesh *should* have done to start with.

And now, with these revelations Ceala had shared—

No. The council would get no apology from Alira.

"I need to go," she said.

"Of course." Ceala touched Alira's shoulder. "I hope you'll stay long enough to call their names with us."

"I will." Alira said, starting toward the splitters' city. Toward Rakalesh and the others, who shrank at her approach. Her Companion shifted at her side.

When she reached Rakalesh, she continued past without stopping. "What are you doing here, of all places? I thought you would be among the traditionalists, where you're most comfortable."

"You ignored my call," Rakalesh said, "so I came through the connecting passages."

"Why?"

"Because it's a shorter route than the surface one."

"No," Alira clarified, "I mean, why did you call? What do you want?"

"I need to speak to you," Rakalesh said. She touched Alira's arm. "Can we please stop? Go somewhere more private?"

Alira stopped, her Companion still at her side. "Let them hear us. I harbor no more secrets."

The elder's eyes searched Alira's face. If Rakalesh sought regret or shame, she would be disappointed. At last, her shoulders sagged.

"Very well. I am tired. I can't fight this any longer. I don't even want to." Rakalesh appeared even more aged than she had before. Alira certainly felt older. They'd all been through a lot in the last cycle.

"What does that mean?"

The elder met her gaze. "I will fully endorse the changes you've been suggesting your whole life."

"But," Alira frowned, "didn't you already make those suggestions to the Council? Aren't they already cross-training the frem?"

"Yes." Rakalesh's jaw tightened. "But several of the councilors…opposed those activities. Their obvious disapproval has made the population somewhat less than enthusiastic about participating in new training."

"'Several councilors,'" Alira quoted. "You mean you and Dyson."

"Yes." Rakalesh stood taller, not a whit of blue or lavender in her skin.

Alira's Companion shifted to Elisul's form, a whisper of Its multitudes brushing her mind. "You did this on purpose, to discourage the changes we all knew were necessary?"

"Changes *you* say are essential." Red speckles dappled Rakalesh's face. "*You* aren't on the council. *You* aren't responsible for the well-being of our people. It isn't *you* who would deal with the fallout if those changes brought disaster."

Some of the nearby unammi pressed closer, clearly listening to this exchange. Confusion and curiosity mingled in their displays.

Gray surprise flushed Alira's arms, followed by soft red, then blue as she stared at the councilor. She should've known. If those ideas hadn't been stifled, if they'd taken root long ago, Trumo and Folmir would have been safe with the others, behind a shield. Knøfa never would have found any of them. Rakalesh would need to deal with those consequences one day.

"Let me guess." Alira peered at the councilor. "You and Dyson are also the ones who decided my very name was anathema. You know what? Forget it." Alira waved away anything the elder might have said. She had no fight left in her at the moment. "It doesn't matter. What does the council say now? Will they encourage the cross-training and all the rest?"

Rakalesh shot a quick side glance at the others nearby who witnessed this drama unfolding. "Without my or Dyson's vote to stymie it, the council has passed the changes into our laws. And you're apparently a hero, now. Even I couldn't stop them from speaking your name." Her mouth puckered like she'd bitten into a rotten fruit. "Congratulations. You've won."

Alira gritted her teeth, red speckling her arms. "You speak as if we were competing in a game. This isn't about you or me, or whose suggestions for changes make it through a council vote. It's not even a debate over whether change is good or bad for our people."

She stepped closer to the elder, red flooding the skin of her arms. "Trumo and Folmir are dead. This," Alira gestured at the city and people around them, "all of *this* is about our survival, about what's best for the unammi. Especially now. No one *wins* unless we *all* do."

Silence filled the passage around them, save for the shuffling of feet, the low murmur of voices as others gathered, and the rustling of Rakalesh's wrap when she shifted.

Then the impact of the elder's other comment sunk in. Alira frowned. "Wait, what do you mean without your vote? Without Dyson's? Why didn't you vote?"

"We're stepping down." Rakalesh seemed to shrink, to draw into herself and take up less space. "The council will appoint replacements. But now that the others have seen your harvests, seen your direct connection to the Iri, to that kind of power, they won't be easily dissuaded from following you, regardless of what any other logic or reason might argue."

Alira nearly laughed before she took in the expectant faces around them. Would they listen to her? *Should* they? The very thought was ludicrous.

Wasn't it?

"I don't want to be followed."

"You may not have a choice. Without our traditional foundations on which to build, they will seek the first support structure they can find. You stand out."

The crowd parted and a trio of frem approached from deeper in the tunnels. "Your pardon, Na'ama, but we need your guidance in one of the repairs."

Rakalesh nodded. "I'll be right there."

The frem's skin dotted with pink. "Apologies, Rakalesh. I was speaking to Na'ama Alira."

Alira blinked. "Me?"

"Yes, Na'ama." The frem kept their gaze lowered.

The Companion shifted for a moment into Elisul's form—*They will see you*—before reverting.

Sudden green veins of duty spread through the lavender unhappiness in Rakalesh's skin. "Of course," she said, as if the words had been dragged unwilling from her throat. Her silver eyes met Alira's. "You see? My time is past."

Alira gaped at her. "How do you always manage to make everything about yourself? Don't you even care that Trumo and Folmir are lost? That Ceala is grieving?"

"Of course I do," Rakalesh said. The red was back. "But I couldn't stop it from happening."

"Yes," Alira said, fists clenched. "You could have. *We* could have. If we had destroyed that ship before it even got close—"

"I'm not having this discussion with you, especially not here and now. What's done is done. I am through defending my actions." She scanned the gray and red dermal displays of those witnesses who heard every word. "You claim to want what is best for our people. Did you mean it?"

"Yes, of course." Alira shrugged. "But—"

"Then the others," Rakalesh said, "require your leadership."

Alira glared daggers at the elder, then let it go. There was no point in arguing. "Are you coming?"

She followed the other frem to a rockfall beneath where her ship had been. Daylight filtered through a hole in the ceiling. Alira consulted with the frem working the site and advised them to seal off this chamber for safety's sake. They could find a passage around it, if necessary.

When she finished, another frem approached with a request that she oversee their stores and supplies. Behind that one, two others waited their chance to speak to her. Rakalesh watched from the sidelines. The Companion was nowhere to be seen, but It wouldn't have gone far. She gave instructions to the waiting frem and broke from them to approach the elder.

"Let's walk," she murmured, "before they give me ten more tasks."

Amusement flickered across Rakalesh's skin, but to her credit she made no comment. They moved through the outer chambers to the subsurface tunnel that would lead to the traditionalists' city, passing others who all stopped to peek through their lashes or who peered around corners. Alira did her best to ignore the scrutiny. "What will happen to the two cities? Will they merge into one?"

"That will be up to the new council," Rakalesh said.

"Those here in the new group told me they'd considered forming their own council."

"Then perhaps they will reach a decision between them," Rakalesh said. "It's no longer my concern. But," she said, "it might be yours."

Alira tried once more to imagine living here, among her people, with irolium growing from the caverns, performing the rites and Tellings, deciding with her kin how they could best move forward. Together. "What if the splitters want to stay here?"

"The other councilors already discussed this." Rakalesh focused straight ahead, as if she didn't want to see the adoration—and awe—for Alira in those around them. "If that is their decision, we'll provide seedstones and a supply of irolium, which they can replenish at will, for as long as it lasts. But we all know that the new growth of irolium from the established seedstones will grow faster with more of us nearby."

"Yet knowing this, you still chose to divide us more and more." Alira tried to keep the anger from her voice, but her red speckles showed her opinion. That's one thing she liked about being in a human form. No one outside her skin knew what she was thinking or feeling unless she chose to share it.

"Think what you will. Given the information available at the time, I did what I believed was best."

As Alira had done. Not every decision worked out the way you wanted, expected, or hoped. *Let it go*, she told herself.

"Will you keep the human base up there in our sky?" Rakalesh said.

"Seems prudent, wouldn't you say?"

"It didn't help us much this time."

"Next time it will." Alira said. "We'll update the sensors and give one or both cities access to the data, so you can see a threat coming before it's on top of you, we hope. And the buoys would be enough for most other humans. Not sure why they didn't work this time. I'll check with Galen and find out."

"He's on his way to retrieve you," Rakalesh said. "If you still want to go. With the changes we're incorporating, you might find a place here where you could make your home. Provide a new Founder's Daughter and raise her among her own kind."

How quickly the Councilor's attitude had changed! Less than a day ago she'd told Alira to leave them alone. They neared the passage to the neighboring city. This far from the main bevy of chambers, no one else stood nearby to hear. "I'm not sure I want to give a daughter that kind of legacy."

"What?" Rakalesh's flesh stippled with white. "Why?"

"Because I wouldn't wish this kind of challenge on anyone. The harvests keep the Founder's Daughter at a distance from everyone else. You assured me that the others couldn't cope with knowing about the harvester, and insisted I keep that part of myself secret. I believed you. I did what you said. But every time I followed your advice, the walls around me grew thicker, and the door smaller. The more souls I harvested, the more isolated I became. It's not fun, nor is it likely to change anytime soon, especially now that they see me for who I am. Why should I do that to my own daughter? And anyway, the one time in all our history where we could've used that harvested knowledge, none of you wanted any part of me. What was the point?"

Alira took Rakalesh's arm and pulled her into motion. "Besides, even if I remain around to train a daughter, there are so few unammi left. Our society is falling apart, everyone going separate ways." She'd talked about change, yes. But not to this degree. Nyros's voice echoed in her memory, observations about how a single change would beget others until the whole was no longer recognizable. He'd been right. "Lurien was the last harvester who could've reseeded the knowledge of the guilds, now that most of them are lost. If the new council is going to cross-train the younglings as they grow into frem, then the guilds may no longer serve a function in the new society. I just don't see the point to having a harvester any longer."

Whispers rose inside her, the throng of Iri brought by her Companion.

Yes, there is. The Companion spoke with Eli's voice. *Your line is our connection to this world. Without you, we will have no way to communicate with your people.*

"Or maybe I'll make more than one so they can share the responsibility. And I don't imagine the harvesters will be a secret any longer. Perhaps that'll be good for all our people, to know the knowledge of their kin isn't lost." Alira squinted at Rakalesh, who still appeared to be in shock. "I will say we should stop adjusting the younglings when they are ready to become frem."

"But…" Rakalesh struggled to form a question under this onslaught of unwelcome information. "Why?" she said at last.

They reached the passage to Rakalesh's city. Alira faced the elder, tried to see her as a person, not an adversary. "Aes te nalya, Rakalesh. Safe journey home."

"Nalena t'staani." Rakalesh's response was automatic. She waited, but when it was clear Alira would not answer her question, she turned toward home. The passage, long and narrow, winked and flashed with the reflected colors of the elder's confusion.

Alira watched for a time. So many choices before her. Like the twists and curves in the passages of this city, each would take her in a new direction. She had no way to know which was the best option. She could only pick one and play it out.

She smiled. For the first time in a long while, she found herself excited about tomorrow.

chapter 59

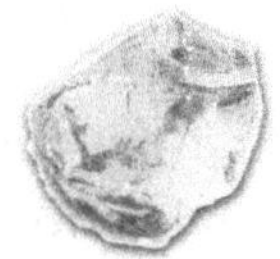

New Canaan, Harajüd
Consortium Trader Base, Admiral Baldric's Office

IT HAD BEEN NINE DAYS since the confrontation on Earth. All the way to Harajüd, Galen had struggled to absorb and understand all the changes happening in the unammi city. Alira, too, had seemed preoccupied and distant the whole trip. Something major had happened during the Earth-side clash with the Clan ship, but she hadn't yet discussed it with him.

Even with all that time on the ship to think, Thrace's return to her human role in the Consortium yesterday felt so surreal, like her reality had shifted in some significant way and she still fought to keep her balance.

The door chimed. Thrace left her workroom but spared a backward glance before securing the door behind her. She wasn't ready for this confrontation, but apparently she had no choice.

"Come." She crossed to her desk as Mira entered with Harlan close behind.

True to his pattern, Harlan barged in front of Mira, his features full of suspicion.

"Did you know the Iridosians could make themselves look human?"

Thrace didn't need to fake her expression of shock. Mira, too, stood agape.

"Did Skalar know this? Was he running genetic experiments on them?" Harlan scoffed. "I wouldn't put it past a Trader admiral to keep information like this close to the vest, but I'd hoped HHU and the Consortium were forming a more open relationship, so here's your chance to come clean. Are you holding out on us?"

"Chief," Thrace managed, "I assure you the Consortium is not, and as far as I know never did, run genetic or any other experiments on the unammi. I can't speak for Skalar, but I would *never* do such a thing."

He squinted at her, tight lines around his mouth conveying his doubt better than any words might.

She lowered herself into her seat to hide the trembling in her legs. "What makes you say they can take human form? Did you see one doing this?"

Harlan rubbed his stubbled jaw, hesitating as if he was unwilling to share.

"You seem a bit dazed," Thrace said. "Would you like a cup of coffee?"

His eyes lit up, just like she'd known they would. He grunted a reluctant yes, and she commed Andrea to bring three cups.

"Chairman Roucharde got word from Danuagov," Harlan said as he sank into a chair. "The Clan had a prisoner, an Iridosian—unammi, whatever—they found somewhere. Our source didn't know where, but probably on Danua. The barrens there aren't suitable for much human habitation, so they're ideal for hiding."

Thrace went cold. "Danuagov knew the Clan had an unammi prisoner, and did nothing?"

"They said they just learned of it yesterday, after the Iridosian died."

"I see." Thrace couldn't disguise the tremor in her voice. Her throat was too tight. She'd known this would be the end result, would've wished death on whoever it was even sooner to save them the suffering. But what had the humans done with the body? She wanted to ask, but a question like that would raise issues she didn't want to address.

Mira studied her. Questions sprouted in the captain's mind. Thrace could feel them from here, even over the distraction of the frustrated chief.

Harlan rubbed the bridge of his nose. "But see, that's a security issue. If the Iridosians can look human, they could be anyone. Anywhere. Hell, for all I know *you* could be one."

Mira's gaze shifted to Harlan, then to Thrace.

The captain's questions blossomed into fullness, her suspicion clouding Thrace's concentration. Hopefully, Mira would keep it to herself, for now. One curious human at a time, please.

"Excuse me?" she said. "Do you really think I'm an unammi?" Thank Na'Staani her voice didn't quaver with fear.

He grunted. "No. But you could be. So how would we know if they're coming and going in our colonies? If they aren't registered…" He broke off his own statement. "But they'd have to be, wouldn't they? They would need human backgrounds, human idents, human records." He focused on Thrace. "And the best place for them to get something like that is through a Trader faction."

"I thought the unammi were isolationists. They didn't mingle with humans. Why would they even want to come here," Mira said, "or any human colony? And weren't they all killed anyway, when Skalar sent that armada?"

"Yes." Thrace kept her manner neutral. "As far as I know, there were no survivors on Iridos. If the Clan found one, it must've been a fluke."

The door chimed, and Andrea brought in their coffee. Thrace did not miss Harlan's near ecstatic reaction when he drank. He savored the mouthful before swallowing.

"Fluke or not, if any others are out there, they'll come to you or your colleagues for help. Will you let me know when they do?"

Thrace suppressed a shudder. The man was dead serious. And she could see in him human tendencies to indicate that treatment of unammi in his or HHU's care would be little better than what Knøfa had demonstrated. Not that she would deliver unammi to him in any case. Still.

"Of course," she lied. She was getting better at this admiral thing. "But why is this such a fear? I mean, I understand that you want to know the reality of who is coming and going in your colony. You're responsible for security, after all. It's just that the unammi never seemed like a threat. Why does this worry you so?"

He sipped the hot coffee and watched her for a minute. "There's more."

A knot formed in Thrace's throat, and she didn't try to speak. Instead, she leaned forward, elbows on the desk, and gestured for him to go on.

"Danuagov says they can disappear altogether, just match their skin colors to blend into the surroundings so you can't even see them. They can apparently also heal with superhuman speed and can affect the minds and actions of those around them."

Thrace had never felt so grateful to be wearing a human face.

"Those things alone are enough to raise my hackles," Harlan said, "because I can't help but wonder what they might do with those abilities. What if Skalar didn't kill them all? What if some of them got out? We know so little about the Iridosians or their ethics, we don't know what to expect from them. What if they hold a grudge against all humans now? That fear might be baseless, but until I know for sure, it's my job to worry."

She knew all about worrying. Her own position, and those of Spencer Kilbee and the unammi she'd helped place here and on other worlds, had been tenuous before Knøfa found that pilot. Now that their secrets had been revealed to humans, unammi everywhere would be at even greater risk.

Harlan took another sip, and shifted in his seat, as if warming to his topic. "But even that isn't the whole issue here. What could we do with that kind of knowledge? I mean, sure, we could use that accelerated healing skill in all sorts of applications, which would be beneficial to a lot of people on a lot of worlds. But be honest, if not with me, then with yourself. If you knew how the Iridosians could shift their skin patterns to hide, you Traders would use it to create camouflage for your ships or bases, wouldn't you? You worry me enough already without adding that pressure." He laughed, and tipped his cup, finishing his coffee.

She hadn't touched her own cup. "I can see how all of that would be of concern to someone in your position."

Mira was a bit shellshocked and more than a little suspicious. "What will HHU and Danuagov do now?"

He shrugged and stood. "That's not up to me, at least not yet. But I hear the Clan had started development a couple months ago on some sort of device to help them 'see' an Iridosian in human form."

Thrace's breath caught. "Oh?" Damn it. She'd hoped that project would have failed by now. "Do they have a prototype yet?"

"I dunno." He sighed, then pinned her with a glare. "But I won't forget your promise to me. Any Iridosians come to you, you come to me."

She stood. "I'll certainly notify you at once of any rogue unammi bent on harming HHU in any way."

His eyes narrowed, as if he'd caught that she didn't exactly say what he wanted her to, but it must have been close enough. He nodded. Mira followed him out, frowning as she left the office. She knew something was up. Thrace may need to confide in her second sooner than she'd planned.

She counted seconds. At twenty, she called, "You can come out now."

The door opened, revealing Eli on the other side. "So it's over." His voice trembled. "Whoever it was, they're no longer suffering."

Thrace sank into her seat. She'd been keeping thoughts of the prisoner at a distance. In the beginning, she'd done it so that she wouldn't reveal the secret to Alira. Later, she'd ignored it because she was too busy to allow the distraction. Now…

An ache began behind her ribs, spreading up into her chest and down into her belly. She grimaced. Grieving would have to wait a little while longer. She still needed to deal with Eli.

"Are you going to tell me," she said, "what happened on Earth?"

Eli walked to the window, his teeth worrying at his bottom lip.

"It must've been something big," Thrace said, nudging him toward a response, "to make our people act so strange, so deferential to you."

He peered out at the city, but she'd bet credits he wasn't seeing the structures or the people or the island or the bay.

Several moments passed in silence. Apparently, Eli had no intention of answering. Would he ever tell her? It was clear he needed to talk. So much had happened in such a short time, and he had packed it down inside him, locking it away where it could eat at him slowly. The time when Alira would have confided in Galen with ease and confidence was past. How should she deal with this new person? This changed Eli?

A part of her wanted to wrap her arms around him, convince him to stay here and make a life in New Canaan so they could at least see one another more often. Yet she observed as he wrestled with some inner turmoil, the struggle playing out on his face. Were his harvested voices clamoring? Was he on the verge of losing control? She hadn't forgotten how bad it got the last time, how close he'd come—behind Skalar's mask—to ruin for himself, for her, and for all their people.

Those memories stayed her hand, silenced her tongue. No. As badly as she wanted him, she didn't yet trust the calm. As long as he was here, she would watch.

And wait.

chapter 60

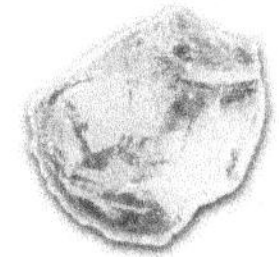

ELI DIDN'T FEEL LIKE THINKING about Earth. Instead, he replayed memories from his harvests, images of the two Danua pilots in their various interactions on the human worlds. Hard as it was to accept, it was probably best they'd kept Alira in the dark. Knøfa's prisoner would never have expected a rescue attempt. They would've echoed Nyros's words. Pilots were expendable. And if Alira had gone after them and gotten herself killed, she wouldn't have been there to stop the snatchers from taking Botha, or to keep Knøfa's ship from escaping with knowledge of their whereabouts and two of their younglings. She wouldn't have been able to save Trumo and Folmir from that doomed pilot's fate.

Eli wondered again who the prisoner had been.

"Was Knøfa among those humans who came to Earth?" he asked.

"I don't know," Thrace said. "Probably. Rumor is that he hasn't been seen in more than three weeks."

"If Chief Downing knows about us," Eli murmured, "then word is spreading. Danuagov will share it with all the colonies." He still stared out the window. New Canaan, below, carried out its business as it always did, people small as insects crawling through its streets and buildings, working its waterfront, interacting with one another. Did they know, yet, of the magical unammi? "We can no longer wear our true forms on human worlds. Or among humans at all."

He hugged himself, gripping his upper arms. This wasn't news, exactly. It'd been true since Crow's ships flattened the city. But Alira had always held some small hope that humans would make it right, that she could one day be herself there, among those aliens who valued the uniqueness of individuals. Knøfa had stolen even that potential future.

Thrace stood beside Eli, but said nothing. Galen had always known when to speak and when to stay quiet. In this case, anything Thrace might say would be superfluous.

"Is this why you asked me to be a liaison before we went to Earth?" he asked. "Because you knew this would be an issue going forward?"

"That, and Rakalesh was alienating so many of those on Earth, bringing them to live among the humans seemed a better alternative to mitigation." She touched his arm. "They still need someone to help them acclimate. And you can travel as Eli Sullivan now. Or one of your other new names and personas."

"Yes." Distracted, Eli patted his pocket where his new identicards rested in their special case. He tried to imagine Downing's explosion if he realized Thrace was already providing false idents to unammi. "It's funny."

"What is?"

He drew a deep breath and let it out. Red faces flooded his memory. Red frem standing over Alira in the grove while she gathered rufesh for the kitchens, something they all could've done, but chose not to. Those frem had mocked her, despised her, wanted her gone.

"I was an outcast long before I left Iridos," Eli said.

"And that amuses you?"

Eli rested his forehead on the window. White faces replaced the red ones in his thoughts. All those frem in the splitters' city surrounding Alira because she'd done something they could not. Those frem had followed her around like younglings in the birthing house, waiting for her to perform some miracle.

Neither Alira would ever fit with her own kind.

"When I went to Earth this last time," he said, ignoring Thrace's question, "I actually believed for a minute that I could go home. That *we* could go home."

"Why?"

The shock in Thrace's voice was almost as telling as gray skin.

"Because in the splitters' city, they accepted me for who I am. Or rather," he said, "they did. Before Knøfa came."

Eli was no empath, yet even *he* could feel Thrace wanting to ask for more. "But then I merged with the Iri, shoved my way into the joinedmind, and convinced them to kill the ship rather than send it away."

"You—" Thrace touched Eli's arm. "—merged—"

He nodded against the plaz. "It was the only way we could do what needed to be done." White faces. Staring. Afraid of him. Of her. Of *them*.

"And the others saw? They knew what—" Her words stopped as abruptly as if she'd sliced them off with her blade.

Eli straightened, met her wide gaze. "That's why they were strange. Later."

She dropped her arm and gawked at him.

"Rakalesh tried to convince me to take her seat on the council."

"She wha…"

"Don't worry." Eli smiled. "I declined the honor. But the gist of it all is that I'm now at quite a loss as to what I should do with myself. Your offer of a position as liaison sounds intriguing. If I can't be Alira, I might as well be someone else. At least that way, I can help our people in the short term." No need for Alira to hang around them and see their fearful reactions, all of them watching when they thought she couldn't see. Better to help them from a distance.

"Indeed." Thrace, apparently still taking in this news, studied him. What was she looking for? Not that it mattered. He'd come too far to worry now about what others thought. That part of Alira had been burned out in the merging.

For that small thing, he was glad.

"It would definitely help the outcasts and relapsed mitigants, and the others who just want out." Thrace gave half a grin. "But there's also another reason."

"What's that?"

"It's about time we started putting our own contacts and messengers in other cities, especially Danua and Zebalu, to gather intel and keep us informed. We'll need to keep a constant vigil on the new Clan and Cartel admirals."

"Isn't that a bit risky, especially if Harlan's intel about the detection devices is accurate? What if our people are discovered? Unammi spies when our race was rumored to be extinct?"

"I think Rizzo has agents working to sabotage that project." Thrace shrugged. "But we'll be careful. We'll train our people well in the art of human mimicry and camouflage and start them out in low-risk positions."

Eli frowned. "And how am I going to help with that?"

"Ask Skalar."

Eli huffed an unamused laugh. Another suggestion that he access his harvests. From Thrace, of all people. After everything they'd been through.

"If you want me to help settle our people among the humans, I'll need to weave those efforts into my search for Botha's and Bika's people. I made them a promise." He still heard the wails of the Bregainans, echoes that might follow him the rest of his life.

Thrace's expression went blank, and she retreated from the window.

Eli squinted at her. "What?"

"Yeah. About that…" She fidgeted for a moment.

Eli closed the distance between them and stepped in front of her. *"What?"*

She peered at him, so clearly worried he could almost see the veins and blotches of color in her skin.

"I got word from Rizzo earlier today," Thrace said. "Her people found a group of the snatched villagers."

"How many?" Images from that night in Bregaina played out in Eli's head. "Does Rizzo know? Where are they?"

Thrace grasped his hand. "You are not responsible for their safe return, Alira—"

"My name is Eli. Where are they?"

"I knew you'd go after them yourself," Thrace said. "You always did take the world on your shoulders."

"Don't change the subject."

With a sigh, she released him. "They're with a group of slaves on Zebalu, up in the Jaudgin region, harvesting ikanne."

Human memories surfaced, images of an icy, frozen wasteland. "Probably without proper protection and safety gear."

Thrace didn't respond.

He started for the door.

"Where are you going?" she called.

"Where do you think?" he snapped.

She caught him before the door slid open. "Stop," she said. "Think this through before you go charging to the rescue—"

"I gave Bika my word." He scowled at her, his chest tight. "I am *not* going to leave them there—"

"No, of course not." Thrace gestured. "But you'll have a better chance of success if you take time to form a plan. Consult some maps, gather some intel on ikanne harvesting and what it involves. At least then you'll know what you're walking into."

The longer he left them there, the greater their health hazard, especially if some of the elders were on this crew. But Thrace had a point.

"Okay. But I won't wait more than a day, if that."

"Understood." She led him to the seating area. "By the way, this is a perfect example of why I think the liaison position should be yours."

What did one of those things have to do with the other? He dropped onto the Bejami chair. "I don't see the connection."

"Both projects will involve travel," she said, "finding allies, forming connections. You can search for Botha's people while you're settling your own."

"Maybe." His thoughts swam with ideas, plans, potential problems and obstacles, not to mention all the details he'd need to keep straight to pull off either job, let alone both of them. What if the voices took over? What if he lost his focus and some of the Bregainans or even some of the outcasts died because of it? What if—

"Either of those projects would be a full slate for any one person." He grimaced. "I already made Bika a promise—"

"I know."

"—so if you also want me to serve as liaison, I'm going to need help with coordinating it all."

Her eyes narrowed.

He shifted in his seat. "You're already seeking alliances with the other factions, aren't you?"

"Yes. Why?"

"Maybe you can merge the liaison structure into your own outreach on behalf of the faction. I can be the in-person contact while you set up meets, organize, and manage the program from here, using other faction allies to lengthen our reach. We can communicate via—"

"—No," Thrace said. "I can help, yes, and I'll certainly let you know of any contacts that seem opportune, but I won't take charge of it."

"Why not?"

She spread her arms wide. "You should already know the answer. You ran this faction for a while. This base, its operations, the outpost, not to mention all the other satellite bases under Consortium control? That's all I can manage. I don't dare push my luck. If we lose this faction…" She leaned closer and winked. "That's why I suggested it to *you*, even before that showdown on Earth. Besides, a new contact will expect to speak to the same person each time you communicate. It wouldn't build trust or confidence to have multiple contacts, at least in the beginning."

Thrace had good points. Still, after so many massive failures in prior endeavors, having him assume a major role felt…risky.

Yet something inside Eli whispered. Encouraged. Urged. A thousand voices, a hundred thousand. Millions. He'd come through the harvesting sickness and survived. He'd merged with the Iri and lived to dream of it later. If anyone was going to take on this challenge, why not him? Besides, such a life would allow him to truly fulfill the role of the Founder's Daughter and share this world with his Companion.

He pressed his lips together. Between the unammi pilot and Trader voices among his harvests, he'd know most of the loopholes in HHU's or other corpgov structures to help find housing and jobs for those Thrace sent his way. But to be an effective liaison, or to find Bika's people, he'd need to familiarize himself with other cities, other worlds. That scared him.

It also excited him.

Maybe he could spread it out a bit. Get help from others. Like, say, Rizzo.

"Might be better," he said, almost to himself, "if some of our people stay on the move. We can't afford to settle them all in one place. They could even help search for the Bregainans."

"Excellent ideas. We'll have to find a way to supply them with irolium."

"I hope we have enough seedstones," he said.

"I had an idea on that."

"Tell me," he said.

"Maybe," Thrace said, "you could ask Elisul to intervene on our behalf in that regard."

Eli blinked. "Intervene how?"

"What if the Iri could spread into other surfaces besides stone? The seedstones could be used in smaller portions to spread colonies of Iri wherever our people roam. They could grow in ships, in habs, in colonial quarters, any place the Iri can find a foothold and provide the symbiotic exchange with smaller populations to spark growth of the irolium." Thrace's smile grew, along with a glimmer of hope. "Maybe they'll even be able to develop at a faster rate from different surfaces. The crystals might well be smaller, but even a thin layer, still connected to the Iri, would be sufficient for a single unammi, or a small group."

Could they do that? *Would* they? He scanned the office. No hint of his Companion, except a rustle in his mind. "It's a good idea. I'll ask."

"So." She crossed her arms. "You never gave me an answer, when I asked you about this liaison thing before. You always tried to deflect, so I'm asking one more time. What do you say?"

Thrace displayed such confidence now. The way she stood her ground…that kind of admiral would be a good ally for anyone taking on such a role as she was suggesting. Even if they moved the surviving unammi off Earth to a new location, even if the outpost was no longer necessary for their safety, having a friend in charge of the largest Trader faction would be critical to everything this new role could hope to accomplish.

"I say I need to speak to Rizzo. But first," he pointed at her, "I need a plan to get to Bika's people on Zebalu, and a new TICS pad. Knøfa blew up mine."

chapter 61

Tuneloras, Saacharis
<u>Syndicate Trader Base, Admiral Rizzo's Office</u>

RIZZO LISTENED TO THE RAMBLING messages in her incoming communiques list. Every one of them had to do with supply chain issues or satellite base matters, or perhaps with one of the Syndicate businesses around Tuneloras. She mentally logged the action items from each, while she stared out the window, but the majority of her thoughts remained on Bailey. In the two weeks since she'd come home wounded and dancing on the edge of death, the captain had made a remarkable recovery. Even the medics told her to slow down, there was no race to win here. But Bailey would be Bailey, and the second in command of the Syndicate had never been one to put something off if she could do it today.

Just one more reason why the admiral would be lost without her.

Rizzo had found it both freeing and terrifying to admit to herself that she had feelings for her second. They hadn't yet had The Conversation that needed to happen. The one where Rizzo described—as if she needed to—the risks inherent in any potential intra-faction relationship. Where she explained that they could not be open about it, and why. Where she offered Bailey one last chance to walk away from it with no hard feelings and no questions asked. It was that last part that worried her the most. Now that she had admitted to herself how she felt, would she be able to accept it if Bailey declined her affections?

She squared her shoulders. Of course she would. She wouldn't like it, but she'd dealt with deadlier blows than that.

The comm unit still rambled. She hadn't heard a single thing it said in the last few minutes. Wait, had that message just said something about Michael Trask? "TICS, pause playback." She peered at the holo. It *did* look like him.

The door chimed. "Enter," she called.

Bailey walked in. She used a cane to do so but still, she was upright and mobile. After all her time in the medfac, she must've been glad to get out of that bed, and out of that room.

Rizzo came toward her. "Do the med techs know you're loose and carousing?"

Bailey's smile was still lopsided but improving. "Carousing. Hah, if only." She limped farther in.

Rizzo gestured at the desk and walked beside her, but did not insult her by offering to help.

"Actually," Bailey said as she eased into the chair, "I'm a free woman. They released me a few minutes ago. And I'm supposed to walk every day. So yes. They do know."

"I don't see a cast on your arm," Rizzo noted.

"Nope. All healed." She grinned up at Rizzo. The worst of the bruising was gone, leaving only the greenish-yellow discoloration behind, but the flesh still puffed out more than it should. Her short hair hung free around her face. "They did the best they could with the torso injuries, but apparently soft tissue can sometimes take longer to heal than bones. Docs tell me I should be all healed in another week or two."

Rizzo nodded, unable to stop watching Bailey. Unable to forget how close she'd come to…

She cleared her throat. "Good. You are needed around here."

Bailey pointed at the holo. "Isn't that Michael Trask?"

Rizzo swung her gaze around. "I think so." She squinted at his short dark hair graying at the temples, brown eyes that tipped up at the outer corners, square jaw. "I was about to replay the message. Interested?"

"Yes, ma'am."

"TICS," Rizzo said, sitting next to Bailey, "replay current message from the beginning."

The holo blinked, and the man's deep voice rumbled through the audio. "Admiral Rizzo, I received your communique and thought long and hard about how I should respond. You were right about me. I was not a fan of the things Knøfa did. I've always felt he was a disgrace to this faction. Tsurin couldn't see it. She had a blind spot where he was concerned."

He shook his head. "I don't know what Knøfa wanted, to be honest, but I am not in the market for a faction war. And I did *not,*" he pounded a fist on his desk, "have anything to do with whatever happened to your people. I give my word." He grimaced. "But one does not easily stand against that man. Not if they want to survive the encounter. I carefully considered what I would do when he returned so as to avoid more trouble like that package you received, or what happened to your second. But an attempted coup would've cost too much, not just for me, but for the faction. It's likely I would've left the Clan and moved on to other things." He looked at the camera. "However, as it happens, Knøfa is missing. No one has seen or heard from him in three weeks. I'm not even sure where he went, only that he said he was going 'squib hunting'—his words, not mine."

He sat back in his seat, displaying a bit more of his lean torso.

"Seems I wasn't the only one to notice his absence. Things got tense around here recently. I had to flex some muscle. But I'm now in charge. If Knøfa ever shows up…" His lips tightened for a second. "Well, I'll tackle that if it happens. Meanwhile…"

Trask's features twitched. "I know you've heard by now that Knøfa had an Iridosian prisoner. One of our crewmembers found her hiding in a barrens cave, and Tsurin went in alone to coax her out. We don't know what happened after that, but when Knøfa finally went in after Tsurin, she was unconscious. She never woke up. Knøfa took her off life support a month ago." Trask swallowed hard. "But he kept the unammi alive, ran genetic and…reproductive…experiments, even after she lost all brain function."

Bailey gasped. Rizzo's hands clenched into fists.

"I took the prisoner off life support the moment I assumed control of the base, just before I freed most of the slaves Knøfa had in his possession." He paused, his eyes working to pierce the holographic veil, spanning the distance to lock onto Rizzo. "On a related note," he said, his words pointed, heavy with meaning, "the few slaves I kept are pregnant. I've moved them to a safe house on the northeast coast of Mjolnir Island, but I didn't want to release them with no means to care for themselves or their babies, especially since they are carrying…" He stopped again, as if unsure how to phrase his next words. "…delicate cargo. Very special."

Rizzo blinked. That couldn't mean what she thought it did. Could it?

"I know you have no love of slaving, so I wanted you to hear from me that I do not intend to continue that practice. However, it may be best if these women did not go home, at least not yet. They need temporary shelter, where they can either have a medfac end their pregnancies with ample discretion, if they choose, or carry to term in relative seclusion. I cannot leave Haven just now to ensure these women's evacuation to a safe location. Perhaps you can assist them?

"This is laying a lot at your door, I know. If I could see to it myself, I would. The things Knøfa did after the barrens incident were deplorable. It's going to take me a while to clean up his mess. In the meantime," he brought his face closer to the camera, "you said something about allies. Are you offering the Syndicate in that regard? Because I'm interested. I believe the next move is yours."

The holo stopped, filling her office with silence.

She stared at the space where Trask's image had been, her brain frantically connecting dots in search of alternative meanings. Knøfa had a female unammi prisoner. He was running reproductive experiments. No mention was made of a male unammi prisoner. Several of his slaves were now pregnant with "delicate cargo." She did the math over and over, trying—and failing—to find some other outcome to the equation.

Knøfa crossed an unammi with a human.

"I don't even want to say what I'm thinking," Bailey said, her voice low, hesitant. "I mean…I wouldn't have expected a pairing like that would be possible."

Rizzo grunted. Such a thing had never entered her realm of consideration. Until now. What had Knøfa been thinking? Stupid question. He wanted to see if it could be done. Maybe it was to, as he might word it, enlarge his herd, or perhaps learn whether the unammi traits could be bred into humans. No matter his reasons, if he'd gone hunting, he hadn't finished experimenting. He'd wanted to take no chances, either, just in case these cross-pregnancies didn't work out.

Apparently, he'd taken on a beast larger than his trap would hold. The Syndicate agent on Danua had reported that Knofa's prisoner could affect people at a distance. After experiencing that from a single unammi in his brig, he should've known better.

"TICS, send Jukka Braithwaite to my office at once."

Bailey tucked a lock of hair behind her ear. "You're going after those women."

Rizzo tried to imagine leaving just when Bailey was finally on the mend. The tug of angst was more than she wanted to confront right now. She trusted her crew. They would get it done. "No. I'm needed here. But," she frowned, "if he said he was going 'squib-hunting,' then he found out where the unammi are hiding. That can't be a good thing. I need to know where he got that information."

"Don't you know where they are?"

"No. And I never asked. That's a precious commodity to the unammi, maybe their last shield. Now that their secrets are out, they'll be in constant hiding." Trask had said he didn't know where Knøfa went. It was possible he was telling the truth. But did she believe him? She didn't know. Yet.

"And you want to help them," Bailey said.

"Yes."

As usual, her second seemed to peer past the surface of her skin and see into her mind.

"Okay then," Bailey said at last. "Where do we start?"

chapter 62

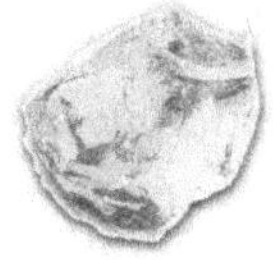

<u>**Near Jaudgin, Zebalu**</u>

THE WOMAN STUMBLED OUT OF the icy water and wiped her face. Others followed, trembling from the cold despite the thermal suits they'd been given. Three days of this work had taken one life already—one of Botha's people, and the loss still ached in her chest. She hoped they wouldn't lose more, but fingers, toes, and lips of those nearby showed a bluish-gray tinge to their normal brown hue. She frowned at their guards, both of whom watched from a distance, settled beside a heating unit they did not choose to share. No need to police the workers any closer. Who could run or fight when their limbs were nearly frozen?

She shifted her shoulders to swing the gathering pouch from her back and pulled the strap over her head, taking care to not damage the delicate shellfish inside. Already, four cases of ikanne sat sealed and ready for shipment. This latest dive's crop, once all the workers' pouches had been emptied, should fill the fifth. She leaned into the briny smell above the open case and slid her pouch along the top of the ikanne inside. Her catch eased out to join their siblings with a soft, brittle clatter before she stepped aside to give space to the other workers.

At the water's edge, one of the older slaves tripped, fell, and another stopped to help. Even if she didn't already know them from that ill-fated gathering in Bregaina, it would be clear from their ease in interaction that these two knew each other. In fact, many of these workers did, as most had come from the same place. What would it be like, to feel at home or at ease with a group of people, to have a real family, whether of the blood or of the heart? Especially in these horrific circumstances, that would be a comfort.

A low rumble caught her attention. The guards stood, closing up their heater and pulling their coats tighter around their necks and ears. A ship approached from the west, flying low over the water. In seconds, it hovered over the flat land and settled nearby on the rocky shore.

One of the guards shouted as the last slave, the one who had fallen, emptied his pouch. Some of the other slaves sealed the case, and they worked together to carry the haul, box by box, to the ship. The rest disassembled the habs in which they'd slept. No cots to haul out, since they'd slept on the cold floor with thin blankets. The guards packed their own hab, all food supplies, and the heater.

Once all their gear and the crates of ikanne had been stowed and secured, guards gestured for the slaves to get aboard. They hurried out of the frigid air and onto the ship without complaint. Not that protests would gain them anything other than maybe a fist to the face. She followed last and sat at the end near the door, the coldest spot in the hold. Let the others get warm. She would deal in her own way.

The slaves rubbed their hands to stimulate blood flow and avoid frostbite. How many of them would lose digits? How long before the Cartel brought another group here to do this work, maybe from another village like Bregaina? How long before another slave succumbed to the glacial waters while diving without adequate insulation to protect them from the cold?

With no window, she could only guess how far out they were, but it was time. She'd seen enough. She dipped into a hidden pocket in the leg seam on her suit and pulled out the small blue stone, a chip really, small and flat enough to go unnoticed. At least half a dozen other fragments hid in similar pockets tight enough to keep them secure in the water, but small enough to avoid detection. She'd avoided accessing their energy thus far. Now, at her touch, the blue chip glowed. She wrapped her fingers around its light, which faded within seconds.

She opened her fist to find a dull, gray stone cracked into bits and shards. She dropped them on the floor of the ship and set to work on the guards. The one nearest her at the rear of the hold already dozed, propped against the interior hull of the ship. The other, near the cockpit, skimmed something of interest on his TICS pad. As she stared, he blinked, rubbed his eyes, continued reading. Soon, his cheeks twitched. He touched his temple and groaned before his TICS pad fell. He slumped over then slipped to the deck.

A murmur among the others rose like the hum of bees in a hive and she quickly shushed them. Workers nudged each other, pointing, until all of them focused on her.

The sleeping guard was easier, but the only sign of a change was that his chin dropped to his chest. Not dead. Not yet. But soon.

She teetered on the wall between decisions. Her remaining stone chips might be necessary for the ride home. Better to save those and disable the pilot another way. She rose, crept forward to one of the fallen guards, and released the snap holding his stunner to his belt. At the opening which led to the cockpit, she hesitated. The weapon she'd grabbed, a basic defensive tool that required physical touch to transfer the charge, fell short of what she'd hoped for but would have to do. So far, only luck kept the pilot from seeing what had happened behind him. She dropped to her knees and eased around the frame behind his seat, reaching up with the stunner toward his torso.

At the last minute, he turned to view something to one side, and saw her crouched so near, holding the weapon. He yelled something she didn't catch, punched something on the controls

the manual actuator

grabbed the lever, and banked the ship hard, throwing her off-balance. Workers in the hold yelped as they were tossed around. She struggled to right herself, no longer concerned with stealth, and concentrated only on touching the prod to any available spot on his body, but he flew with every trick he'd apparently learned as a pilot, spiraling down at breakneck speed only to pull out at the last moment before they hit water, banking and swerving, rising and twisting the craft without a thought for the safety of anyone aboard other than himself.

She grasped the empty seat beside him, anchoring herself as best she could, and hung on.

Forget the stunner. She'd do it her way. She concentrated solely on him, pulling at his threads of consciousness, diverting the path of neurons in his brain until he slumped, semi-conscious onto the stick, sending the ship into a sharp dive.

She shouted, bringing one, then two others forward to help her pull his unconscious form out of the seat so she could gain control of the craft which fought her as if enamored of its freefall. When she pulled it out at last, the aft fin of the craft dipped into the Cara'antra Sea. A brief spray of freezing water shot up behind them.

She increased altitude by a few meters. "I need a little help here."

Two people came forward.

"I'm going to slow as much as I can. Tell the others to hold on, then open the hatch and throw the guards into the water."

"But there is no land nearby," one of them said. "They'll drown."

"No. They'll freeze to death," she said. "Do you care?"

He shook his head. A moment later, she heard the hatch open, the whistling rush of wind and, barely detectable beneath that, three splashes of water, then the hatch closed and all she could hear was the joy of her fellow workers. She grinned, a small acknowledgement of her success, and flew on to her meeting with Kilbee. He would transport these people to Bregaina. She could almost see Botha's excitement when Kilbee brought the villagers to their home, along with others who belonged elsewhere. The Bregainans would help them get wherever they wanted to go.

Her humor dimmed, replaced by a frown. Even with the plan she— rather, Eli and Thrace—had put together, it had taken longer than expected to infiltrate this group. She hoped that snag wouldn't cost them too much. Not that Kilbee would mind. He would wait forever, if she asked him to.

But every moment she delayed, others suffered. She needed to speed things up, though she wasn't sure how.

Maybe Rizzo would have some ideas. That was her next stop, after a vessel change. With intel garnered through that ally, she could plan her next rescue.

She wasn't finished yet. In fact, she was just getting started.

chapter 63

Tuneloras, Saacharis
<u>Syndicate Trader Base, Admiral Rizzo's Office</u>

A LARGE HOLODISPLAY FILLED THE air above Rizzo's desk. She and Bailey inspected this initial design for a surface-to-air missile delivery system. The concept had flitted through Rizzo's mind in-between crises ever since she'd gone to Bejami with Galen. After Bardo's comm and Galen's final confirmation of the order, she'd begun to draft the plans, tweaking and improvising as she went. This would need to be new. Shieldable. Adaptable, especially since there was no telling where the unammi would be using it. She'd put the final touches on it this morning.

Bailey leaned on her cane and examined the blueprint with critical eyes. "That propulsion system," she said, pointing. "I've not seen that before. New?"

"Yes. And designed to be interchangeable with alternatives, depending on where they plan to use it. Baldric says this first one will be installed on a planetoid with little atmosphere."

"Ah," Bailey said. "That makes sense, then." She manipulated the design holo, examining it from every angle before pointing at one specific detail. "I wonder if we could shave a few kilos off the weight here, by—"

The TICS chittered.

Rizzo straightened. "Yes."

"Admiral, there's someone at the gate to see you, ma'am. An Eli Sullivan."

Less than a standard day after Trask's message. Still, it was unlikely that either Eli or Thrace would know about the new Clan admiral's revelation yet. Trask wasn't stupid enough to share with multiple contacts the fact that he held pregnant women carrying "special" cargo just waiting for pickup. Besides, the last Rizzo had seen Eli, he had not known of Knøfa's prisoner.

"Send him in with an escort."

"Yes, ma'am."

"You look concerned," Bailey said. "Is this anyone I know?"

Rizzo's second already knew the basics of this situation, even more than Eli did in some cases. But if Alira was going to be a regular visitor, as it seemed she would, Rizzo needed to bring Bailey all the way in. Both of those in command of the Syndicate needed to be on the same page. She'd make it right with the unammi later.

"You've met her."

Bailey frowned. "Her? Eli Sullivan is female?"

Rizzo closed the holodisplay and gestured to a seat, then took her own. "Remember Esther, who came here with the children from the Cartel?"

"Yes."

"Same person," Rizzo said.

Realization dawned. "Unammi?"

"Unammi."

"So, it's true, then," Bailey said, a touch of wonder in her voice. "They can look human."

The door buzzed, and Rizzo raised a brow. "Judge for yourself. Come."

Eli came in, saw Bailey, and stopped.

"I thought we would be alone."

Rizzo stood. "You remember my second, Captain Bailey Madden. Bailey, this is Eli Sullivan."

Bailey got to her feet with the help of her cane. "It's an honor."

Eli acknowledged her greeting then focused on Rizzo. "This is a private matter, as you know."

"Bailey is my right hand," she said, "and in control of this faction when I'm unavailable. If the Syndicate is to get involved any further with you and your people, she needs to be fully informed. If that doesn't work for you," she said, "I'll understand."

He hesitated.

After a moment, Rizzo leaned forward on the desk. "Eli. Do you trust me?"

He stared at her. "I do."

"I trust Bailey. She's a good person to have in your corner, and you need all the friends you can get right now."

He let out a breath. "Very well. I came to update you, and to ask for your help."

"Of course you did. Join us." Rizzo resumed her seat. Bailey sank down as well—gratefully, if Rizzo wasn't mistaken.

"Knøfa found our hiding place," he said as he sat. "His people came after us."

Ah. As she'd suspected. "And you took those pieces off the board?"

"We had to. If they'd escaped knowing where we are—"

The tone of his voice told Rizzo Eli wasn't happy about it.

"I understand the reasoning. But I was under the impression," Rizzo said, "you needed weapons." Otherwise, she'd not have blueprints on her TICS system right now. The Syndicate could be using the time to better serve clients who could pay more, and who were a lot less annoying.

He grimaced, as if caught in a compromising position. "We do."

"Then how—" Rizzo began.

"Rizzo, do you trust me?" he said, mimicking her own words of moments before.

She ground her teeth. Thrace had said Eli—Alira, whoever she was at any given moment—could be dangerous, even from a distance. And the

Syndicate agent had said the unammi in Knøfa's brig had frightened Clan crew with what it could do. Were all unammi like that? Rizzo had seen for herself the healing abilities Eli and Thrace had exhibited that night in the Baba's village. Were these…gifts…related? If so, how far could they take it? How far *would* they take it?

Clearly, the unammi had more than a few secrets. With all they'd been through since Skalar's attacks, it was understandable why they'd be loath to trust another human. She was not about to pressure Eli into an even more vulnerable position than he already was.

"Very well. One question," she said. "You participated?"

"Yes."

"Are you…" Rizzo considered how best to say it. "…still yourself?"

"Yes. They were too distant to affect me."

Rizzo glanced at Bailey's clearly confused expression. "I'll fill you in on that later, Captain. For now, just take in as much as you can."

"Of course, ma'am."

"Some of our people," Eli said, "have opted to leave the city. Live among humans. But they have no more concept of how that's done than I did when I left Iridos. I and others will work with them, teach them what they need to know before they settle on the colony worlds. But we'll need allies among the humans who can be trusted. People like you and," he swung his gaze to include Bailey, "the captain."

"The Syndicate will help you wherever we can," Rizzo said. "I've also reached out to Bardo and Georgeanne, as I promised. They could be trusted, eventually. But I didn't mention the unammi, only the potential for a weapons job. You'll need to think of some way to pay for this. I'm fairly sure neither of them will do it out of the kindness of their hearts."

Bailey made a sound that was almost a laugh before she regained control. "Sorry. Just trying to imagine Admiral Georgeanne doing something for free."

"The Syndicate will at least need our expenses reimbursed. If there is need for further payment," Rizzo gestured, "we can work out an arrangement."

"That's good to hear," Eli said, "though I don't know where we'd get credits to pay. We'll figure out a way. But I was hoping you would take charge of the project, maybe add other side efforts like trying to bring Botha's people home. I could assist, especially with the unammi…" He stopped when he saw Rizzo's reaction.

"No," she said. "Not because I don't want to help. But the Syndicate and its businesses are my first priority. Such a project as you propose is a full-time responsibility, too big to add to my load." Did Eli yet know about Knøfa's prisoner? If not, he was about to learn. He needed to know, and he seemed more able, now, to deal with that news, as well as her latest intel from Trask. Once she told him about the mothers, Eli would feel differently. More driven to take this on himself. She had no doubt. "This task is for you."

Eli dropped his chin. "I knew you were going to say that."

Of course he did. It was the obvious choice, though he didn't know it yet.

"I don't trust myself," he said. "You know this will require killing. No matter how I try to avoid it, someone somewhere will push me into it. What happens then? How do I know I won't be a weakness to the whole project?"

"You didn't stumble when you killed the Cartel snatcher in Bregaina. You'll be fine."

Bailey shifted in her seat. "I know I'm not up to speed yet, but if you are unammi, you can look like a different person—or the same one— depending on the needs of the scenario. Am I right?"

"Yes." He blinked. "I can do that, given adequate privacy. It would be unwise to shift in public view."

"Then," Bailey said, "aren't you the best person for the role based on that alone? If you need to stay hidden, then you can arrange to pass unnoticed in land and space ports, through any city structures or public transport, renting private transport, all the things a human with only one countenance can't do. We can make disguises for ourselves, it's true. Good ones, yes. But those take time and resources that may not be available on the spur of the moment, and will never be as reliable as your ability to be just another face in a crowd."

"Rizzo pointed that out once before."

Bailey shrugged, then winced, her movements still a little stiff. "I'm not surprised. The Syndicate, and probably the Consortium, could provide you with all the idents you would need."

Rizzo peered at her second. Not for the first time, she was grateful to have Bailey on her side, especially now as she jumped in without preamble or hesitation. She'd always been able to work either a negotiation or a blade with equal dexterity and professionalism.

Eli's weary air made her scowl. Was that part of his facade? Or was it a natural consequence of carrying too many burdens? She'd like to save him the additional worries of the surrogates, but if her suspicions were correct, none of the Syndicate's assets or resources would be adequate to the task of caring for their children, especially if they carried the same abilities as Alira and Galen. She shuddered inwardly at the thought of infants with such uncontrolled gifts being tended solely by humans.

No. This problem was one for Eli and his people, though they would no doubt require assistance from some quarter. Maybe more than one.

"I'll set the seeds for an alliance with Bardo and Georgeanne," she said, "and later introduce you to them. You'll need to be patient. These things take time. I'm still working on the new Clan admiral, Michael Trask." Trask, of all people, should be willing to help in any way possible. The unammi's most recent threat was partly on his faction's shoulders.

Eli came to full alert. "What happened to Knøfa?"

"Trask said he went after your people," she said. "Perhaps he was on the ship you destroyed. No one knows."

Eli looked away. "What is this Trask person like?"

"We don't know yet. He's been in the background at the Clan, but Tsurin spoke well of him." She teetered on the brink of revealing her doubts about him. Maybe later. No sense raising a specter against the man until she could learn more. Rizzo narrowed her eyes. "I'll find out whether we can trust him. If so, I'll let you know."

He nodded, his pain obvious no matter how he tried to hide it. She couldn't even imagine what Eli—or his host—had been through.

"I know, now, that Knøfa had an unammi prisoner."

"Yes," Rizzo said.

"You knew about this, but you said nothing."

"I didn't think you—"

"It's okay," he said. "I understand that part. Did you also know Knøfa's prisoner had died?"

Rizzo noted Bailey's surprise. "Yes."

"It was hard to hear this news from a stranger, one who sees Thrace and probably me as a threat. I can't speak for Thrace, but I would've preferred to hear it from a friend. Why didn't you tell us?"

"I know it's hard to lose someone," she said, "especially like that. But you shouldn't have needed me or anyone else to tell you what was clear from the start. That unfortunate unammi was never going to survive Knøfa's attentions."

Eli swallowed hard, nodded. "At least they aren't suffering any more. I just wish I'd known who it was, so we could properly mourn."

"Indeed," Rizzo said. "But additional details have come in. News you've likely not yet heard."

His eyes widened.

She wasn't comfortable with this turn of events. How would Eli take it? "You know Knøfa experimented on the prisoner, who was apparently female."

Recognition dawned on Eli's face and he swallowed hard.

That piece of information told him who it was. Rizzo sighed. "He also crossed her with a human somehow."

"He wh—" A storm of conflict twisted Eli's features. "But if she's dead—" He covered his mouth as if afraid he would be sick.

"The embryos were created outside her body and implanted into human surrogates. At least," she said, "that is my suspicion. All I know for sure is that Knøfa ran reproductive tests on the prisoner—"

"Bishtari." Eli's voice choked on the word. He swallowed. "If the prisoner was a female pilot stuck on Danua, then her name was Bishtari."

Bailey hung her head.

"Very well," Rizzo said. "I know Knøfa ran reproductive tests on Bishtari, but I don't know the specifics. My informant then went on to say there were pregnant human females carrying 'special' cargo in a Clan safehouse, and suggested I get them out of there." She paused. "I infer from his phrasing that the fetuses are an unammi-human hybrid."

Eli lurched to his feet, skin still pale. "We have to—"

"I've already sent a team." She watched his shaking hands. "I know this is not good news."

"Ah Bishtari…Livuce'ba wenaes bujhul," Eli murmured. He hugged himself.

Bailey met her gaze and waited with an unspoken question Rizzo read quite well. *What are we going to do?*

"Eli," Rizzo said, "assuming the surrogates are willing to carry the fetuses to term, will you take these women to your people so they can give birth there?"

"What?" he blurted, whirling. "No! They wouldn't be welcome there, I promise you."

No. Rizzo imagined that would be asking too much after all the humans had done to the unammi.

"Would you prefer that the women abort the fetuses?"

He frowned. "Unammi females are able to choose whether their mating results in a youngling." He regarded them both. "I understand human females cannot do this, but even if they could, this would be different. It was not their own bodies that produced the ova."

"No," Bailey replied.

"All corpgovs," Rizzo said, "offer medical procedures that remove the gestating fetus, if the mother so wishes. Doctors on this base can, as well."

He paced to the window, still hugging himself. Rizzo didn't remember seeing him do that before. But then she'd never seen him deal with this particular kind of stress in their brief history. Despite all the trouble this person had brought into her life, she would've spared him this decision if she could.

Except it wasn't up to her.

"My human passengers know of this procedure," he said. "It is something they would normally consider, given the circumstances."

Did he just access his harvests and not fall apart? Did he even recognize that he'd done that?

Bailey squinted at Eli. She hadn't missed that reference to passengers. She and Rizzo would have a lot to talk about later.

Eli missed the exchange. "Neither Bishtari nor these women," he continued, "had any say in the matter before this was done to them. Bishtari would say ask them what they want." He stared out the plaz a moment longer. "This is an unprecedented event, a meeting of our peoples, yours and mine. These younglings could be the beginning of a whole new evolutionary path for all of us."

"Eli," Bailey said, her voice hesitant, "you say your people won't accept humans in their midst. How will they feel about children who are half-human?"

An odd shadow passed over Eli before he got the mask in place once more. "I don't know. But I've no doubt it would take time to adjust them to the idea."

"Humans are likely to be the same," Bailey said. "I'm ashamed to say that our species is not very accepting of anything that isn't like us. You have some experience with that, I'm sure."

Rizzo nodded. "Not to mention that even if these babes appear completely human, if they are born with abilities like yours or Bishtari's, they'll never be safe among my kind."

His arms dropped to his sides. "Are you saying we *should* end them?"

"Not at all." Rizzo came around the desk to sit on the front edge, closer to her guest. "But it's best to ensure you're aware of the obstacles along all possible paths. Saving them, raising them, won't be easy on you, on their surrogate mothers, or on the children."

"I can't be the one to raise them. You know that, Rizzo," he said. "But I also can't, I *won't* believe we should destroy them based solely on their genetic heritage.

"Then what would you advise we do with the surrogates, if they choose to carry and bear these babies?"

A slight wrinkle creased his brow. "What will happen if I leave them in your care?"

"If the babes were human, there would be no issue. I would put their mothers in a safehouse until they gave birth and care for them until the mothers can fill a job here in the Syndicate or take their leave." She sighed. "But as you said, these are special embryos, who would need unammi caregivers. Humans are not equipped to manage their particular needs.

Besides, assuming they come to term, decisions on what happens to them after they are born could well impact your surviving people. This needs to be between you and the surrogates."

He huffed a sound, half grunt, half groan. "I've already promised to free the rest of the snatched Bregainans and to serve as liaison for unammi living on human worlds. I can't be there for these mothers and fulfill those other promises, as well. It's too much."

"Then recruit a team to help you. Sympathetic humans, and others among your own people."

"I think you and Thrace have more confidence in me than is warranted," he said.

"You're stronger than you realize. You've come far already."

"And I've made enormous mistakes," he said. "People died because I didn't know what I was doing."

"More still live because you were there. Like Oni." Rizzo peered at him. "What would Baba advise?"

Eli laughed, though it sounded forced. "Probably something like 'you can't know if the boat will float unless you put it in the water.'"

"Then perhaps it's time you tested that boat and patched any holes."

"Why don't you stay here, on base," Bailey said, "until the surrogates arrive? You can speak to them then and decide together."

"How long will that take?"

"They left here yesterday," Rizzo said. "Assuming no delays, it's at least seven days before they reenter the base."

His jaw worked as though he were chewing on that thought. "Let me think about it."

chapter 64

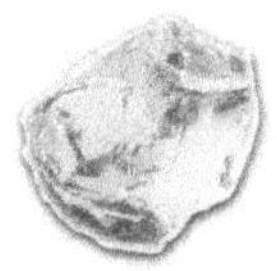

New Canaan, Harajüd
<u>Consortium Trader Base, Admiral Baldric's Office</u>

"ENSURE THE WHOLE SHIPMENT GETS to its intended destination," Thrace said. "Follow up with the buyers in a week. If they're missing any part of their order, I want to know at once."

"Got it, ma'am." Mira sat in the chair, her body stiff, unyielding. "Was there anything else?"

Thrace withheld the grimace she wanted to display. Her second had been stewing in silence ever since Harlan was there. Seven days ago? No, eight. It isn't like she could tell Mira about her admiral's origins. Not yet, anyway. Thrace had a good feeling about the captain, but not good enough to reveal such a sensitive secret. Not until Thrace could get to know her much better.

"Actually, yes," Thrace said. "I have yet to hear from some of the agents Skalar had placed on the other colonies, or in the other factions. I'm not ready to believe they've broken faith or left the Consortium. Maybe they're still watching me to see which direction I'll go before they surface." She shrugged. "But we can't continue business as usual without that intel. I'd like your input on who we should install as assets in the other factions."

Thrace felt confusion coming off the woman in waves.

"Are you sure you want my opinion on such a top-secret thing, ma'am?"

"Of course," Thrace said. "You hold knowledge of this crew that goes beyond my own. Once you suggest names, I'll review their records, past accomplishments and jobs, and other pertinent details before making the decisions. I have the utmost confidence in you." She paused. "Why?"

"No reason," Mira said. "Was that all, ma'am?"

Thrace sighed. "Yes. Thank you, Mira."

The captain walked toward the door. Halfway across the room, she stopped. "Actually, ma'am, now that you ask, I was under the impression you didn't trust me yet, and it's disappointing. I thought we were past that."

"Why would you think I didn't trust you, Mira?"

"Because last week, you practically fainted when Downing told us about the sq—unammi. I think you knew already, ma'am. I think there's something going on. I think you know more than you want to let on, and you haven't felt like you could share that intel with me." Mira stopped and lifted her chin, her chest puffed out even though she would probably run if Thrace said "boo."

Here it was. The thing Thrace had known was coming. The thing Mira wanted that Thrace could not give. Yet. She rose from her chair, and walked to the seating area, gesturing for Mira to take a seat. "Let's chat, shall we?"

Mira looked doubtful, but she perched on the edge of a Bejami chair.

Thrace sat in the other realwood chair and twisted to face Mira. The captain *felt* trustworthy. But Thrace couldn't yet chance it. She peered at the officer and chose her words.

"If Kisle told you something in confidence, something that would carry big consequences if it got out, would you tell anyone else that secret?"

"No," she said. "Of course not."

"Not even me?"

Mira winced. It was obvious that she felt the trap. But she couldn't yield. "No. Not unless it posed a danger to the faction."

"Oh?" Thrace squinted at her. "You would tell me then, without even asking Kisle? What if Kisle asked you not to do so?"

Her officer frowned.

"This is my dilemma, Captain." Thrace kept her voice even, non-confrontational. "You are correct in assuming that there is something going on, something related to the unammi."

Mira watched her. Thrace could feel her waiting for an answer.

"I can't tell you what it is," she said, "That isn't because I don't trust you, but because it isn't my secret alone. It's a complicated, delicate, multilayered situation that involves some of the other factions. Everyone involved is working hard to keep it quiet. The fewer people who know about it, the safer it'll be, so no. I can't share it."

"Other factions. Rizzo? Is that why her second came here? Why she sent a message?" Mira brought one foot up in the chair. "Is the Consortium involved in it, too?"

Thrace allowed a small smile to touch her mouth. "Now see, that's one of the things I can't discuss with you. Yet. It isn't my place to make that decision, any more than it would be yours to reveal Kisle's secret."

She didn't like it. That much was plain from Mira's expression, even if her emotions weren't churning so hard Thrace could almost *hear* them. But after a moment, she relented. "Okay."

"Does that satisfy you, for now?"

"Mostly," Mira said. "I have to admit, I wondered if you were going to tell me *you* were an unammi."

Thrace's heartbeat stuttered, and she was grateful Mira could not see her dermal display. She leaned a little closer. "If I were, it would certainly be something to keep close to the vest. Especially after what happened with Knøfa. But how wise do you really think it would be for an unammi hiding in plain sight to reach out to other factions for assistance?"

All the air went out of Mira, along with waves of relief. "Not very, I suppose. I don't agree with what Knøfa did, but I kind of understand why he did it. Or at least why I *think* he did. Imagine how far human medicine could advance, if we knew how the unammi do the things rumors claim. I mean…"

Thrace's throat went dry. "What if it were you who'd found the unammi, Mira? What would you have done?"

Mira studied her. "Is this a test, ma'am?"

"I honestly want to know."

The captain's shoulders tensed. She searched Thrace's features, then looked away as if thinking hard. Her brows drew closer together, and she rested against the chair's far armrest, one foot still in her chair. "I dunno," she said. "I guess it would depend on the situation."

"How so?"

Mira chewed her lip. "Hypothetically, if I found a single unammi in hiding, I'd do whatever I could to help them, no matter what. It's like you said to Chief Downing. Some profits aren't worth what's required to make them."

"But…" Thrace gestured, encouraging her captain to continue.

"What if there was some sort of plague, like the one that chased our ancestors from Earth in the first place?" Mira said, caught up in the thought experiment. "What if thousands or even millions of humans were dying, and we had a chance to save them by experimenting on and maybe even killing one unammi? Wouldn't that be the necessary thing? To work toward the good of the many, rather than save one?"

Thrace's breath hitched. Just for a second. Mira didn't seem to notice.

"Hmmm. Okay. I see your point," Thrace said, not taking her eyes off the captain. "What if the roles were reversed, though?"

"Ma'am?"

"What if thousands of unammi were dying, and there was a chance to save them by experimenting on or killing a single human?"

Mira's frown returned. "But humans don't have any special abilities."

"Maybe. But let's assume, for the sake of discussion, that they do. That the human had some elusive thing the unammi needed to survive. Would the same 'good of the many' reasoning hold true then, too?"

The captain studied the wall behind Thrace. Her lack of an immediate response was, in itself, an answer.

"Captain," Thrace said, keeping her tone soft as though she were imparting a lesson to a youngling, "either all sapients have an inherent right to dignity, or none do. It really is that simple."

Mira nodded slowly, but she wasn't finished gnawing that bone.

"Go on. You've plenty of work to do," Thrace said, "and I'm keeping you from your duties. Dismissed."

When the door closed behind Mira, Thrace dropped her head into her hands.

chapter 65

Tuneloras, Saacharis
<u>Syndicate Trader Base, Guest Quarters</u>

ALIRA SQUEEZED THE STONE, PULLING from it all the energy she could. A tingle raced through her arm, then faded. She opened her fist. The shining blue irolium crystal had lost all its color and cracked to dust. The survivors better get those seedstones going faster. She and those who helped her would need them as much as or more than those living in the new cities.

She dropped the bits into the disposal, thinking about Earth. Last she'd heard, the two councils, old and new, were in discussions about where to take the people from here. At least they were speaking to one another, instead of sniping. That alone was an improvement.

The comm in her temporary quarters chirped.

"Answer, voice only," she said.

"The surrogates are here and settled. Bailey is with them now," Rizzo said. "Are you ready?"

"As much as I can be. I…"

"What is it?" Rizzo said.

"I'm trying to decide what to wear." Alira almost laughed. She spoke of her masks as though they were jackets in her closet. When did that start? "Do you think they would speak more easily to a female or a male?"

"Female."

"Very well." Which one would she use? An old one? No, a new one. Better to build a persona specific to these new projects. One that would inspire trust and reassurance in the surrogates, as well as the humans who got involved with the new project. Did humans honor their elders, as the unammi did? She thought for a moment. "Give me five minutes, then Bailey can bring them in."

The comm fell silent.

Alira started the holorecorder and stood before her reflected image, sifting through ideas until one stood out. She watched her own short form adopt its amorphous, in-between state, then stretch and solidify into a taller, more defined shape. Dark, almost black eyes looked at her from her new, round face, its skin lined but with no distinguishing scars or marks. Gray hair sprouted from her scalp and fell past her slumped shoulders. Loose gray trousers and a long, supple tunic in pastel blue covered her soft, puffy form. She kept the big feet.

She examined the form, twisting to inspect it from all angles. Yes. Perfect. Not only would such a person evoke feelings of comfort among others, but she also could disappear in a crowd, even be dismissed as unimportant since an elderly female presented a lower threat potential.

She tweaked and adjusted small details in the disguise until she was satisfied with it, then committed it to memory. Several practice runs cemented the new appearance in her repertoire before the door chime sounded.

"One moment," she called. She squinted at her reflection. "What's your name?" she whispered. Both she and her reflection sized one another up, squatted down and stood up.

She stopped the holo and called, "Come."

The door swished open to admit Bailey and a small group of women.

"I am Booker," she said, then gestured. "Would you like to sit?"

Seven of them did, the human females carrying unammi—or part unammi—younglings. Booker suppressed a grimace. No one, neither human nor unammi, would want them. No one except her. She knew how it felt to be unwelcome.

Another woman stood apart, beside and slightly behind Bailey, near the door. Security, perhaps? Booker pulled a molded plaz chair over from the dining space and sat across from the women.

"Do you know why you are here?"

None did.

Booker glanced at Bailey.

"The admiral felt you could explain it better than she could," she said.

Of course she did. These situations would be easier if she could access Cesar's abilities, or sense as Galen could what turmoil seethed inside the surrogates.

She couldn't tell them the full truth. Not yet. If she did, and they opted to terminate, they would be security risks. She couldn't take that chance.

"You already know you've been impregnated," she said. "Yes?"

They fidgeted, restless in their seats, then nodded.

"Admiral Knøfa, of the Danua Clan, conducted speculative research on one of his prisoners, and implanted the resulting embryos into your bodies. The fetuses you carry are..." Booker weighed her words. "...prototypes created from his findings."

Their voices rose in dismay, overlapping one another. Bailey's blue gaze met her own.

"Are you going to make us carry these experiments," one woman said, almost spitting the word, "through to the end?" Her angry focus swung from Booker to Bailey. "Are you taking Knøfa's place?"

"No," Booker said. "Absolutely not. It is your decision."

The woman who'd spoken pushed shaggy black hair out of her face, then stood and stared hard at Booker. "I want no part of a genetic experiment. Count me out." She turned to Bailey. "Where is the closest med facility?"

"The Syndicate's facilities will help," Bailey said, "if that's your choice."

"It is." The woman spun to the other surrogates. "What about the rest of you?" Three more rose in agreement.

Four down. Booker wasn't sure which choice would be the better option for the other three. If they carried out the pregnancies, no one knew what challenges they would confront either before or after the births. It would likely be difficult for all concerned.

She couldn't ignore the fact that if the mothers carried to term, the younglings could potentially grow into frem who could bridge the gap between the humans and the unammi so that the unammi would no longer need to remain in hiding. Still, what were the chances that, once recognized for who and what they were, the hybrid younglings would be seen only as a means to an end for greedy humans? Probably good, or even high. It would be difficult for them to bridge any gaps in the shadow of that threat.

Booker sighed. There was no way to know that kind of thing in advance. She'd need to prepare for all possibilities, and hope for the best.

In the meantime, she would have to find a way to conceal the younglings and their mothers, either in unammi or human society. Somehow.

If the surrogates aborted, the unammi would lose that potential bridge, but Booker would no longer be responsible for their well-being. They could resume their lives, and Booker could worry only about Bika's people, and the promises Eli had made.

Either way carried pros and cons. What would Bishtari want them to do?

Booker swallowed a lump in her throat.

"What of you?" she said to the others.

One of them, long brown curls constrained by a band, pinned Booker with a look. "I don't like the idea of aborting unless there's a problem with the fetus. But how do we know the babies will be…" she hesitated, "…okay when they're born?"

Bailey stepped in. "We don't. But how is that different from any other birth? We'll run regular scans and prenatal tests to catch anything major prior to the birthing, but even they don't always see every potential problem."

The woman with the curls consulted the other two surrogates who still sat with her. They murmured among themselves and finally agreed to proceed.

Bailey instructed the woman beside her to escort the other four surrogates to the medfac for their procedures.

When they were gone, Booker peered at the three who remained. "Are you certain about this?" She leaned forward, elbows on her knees. "These babies are more unique than you know, but I can't tell you the rest unless you commit to follow this through and tell no one."

One of the women, her short blond hair unruly and in need of washing, scooted forward to the edge of her seat. "I'll do it. But will we be required to mother the children, too?" She winced in front of the others. "I'm not sure I'd make a good mom."

"That will be up to you," Booker said. "But we hope you'll stay and at least be part of the little one's life."

The third woman's gaze locked on Booker's. "I'm here for the duration," she said. "You got us loose from the Clan, and vowed to free us whether or not we help you, so I'm in. We owe you."

"No," Bailey said. "You don't. Base your decision on what *you* want."

The woman swallowed. "I have. I'll do it."

"So will I," said the curly haired surrogate.

If Booker explained the rest, she was committed. They would know about the babes, assuming any ever made it to and through birth. What would she do if any of them changed their minds before then? She hoped she wouldn't have to—

Well. No sense going there yet.

She told them of the Fall of Iridos, the destruction Captain Crow had wrought there, and that as far as the human colonies knew, no unammi had survived, until Knøfa found one in hiding on Danua and imprisoned her.

It took only seconds for the connection to click. Their expressions ranged from sympathy, to confusion, to shock.

"Our babies," said the blond woman, "are Iridosian?"

"Half-unammi. But yes." Booker held her breath.

"So," the woman with the curls said, "if we carry these babies to term, they could be the last of the Iridosians?"

"As Booker explained," Bailey said, stepping forward, "Crow believed there were no survivors at all. The one from Knøfa's experiments must've been a pilot, stranded on Danua. It's possible there are others in hiding out there. We just can't say."

The blonde said nothing, but her hands went to her belly in a protective gesture.

The third woman's lip quivered. Her gray eyes glistened with tears. "How awful! Why would they try to wipe out a whole species like that?"

"Only Crow could answer that," Booker said, working to keep her voice steady. "Are you still willing to proceed?"

"I've got so many questions," the woman with the curls said. "How will the genetic makeup of the fetuses affect the pregnancies? What can we expect through the gestation? What about the babies? What will they be like?"

"We honestly don't know," Booker said. "This kind of crossing has never been attempted. You three will be our examples. I do know an unammi gestation cycle is shorter than a human one. Whether that will change your term is unknown. We'll find out together."

"You keep saying 'unammi,'" the blonde said. "Do you mean the Iridosians?"

"That is the Iridosians' name for themselves," Bailey explained.

"I want to do this," the curly-haired surrogate said. "But I don't relish the idea of raising a half-human, half-Iridosian baby on my own, even on this base. And it sure as hell isn't going to happen in corpgov, or they'll make me and the baby into science experiments of their own." She looked from Booker to Bailey. "Even if they appear human, it's only a matter of time until medfacs find out they aren't. What are we supposed to do?"

"We haven't worked out all the details yet," Booker said. "We've known about your situation for only a short time. And we didn't know whether you would want to carry them to term. But if you go forward, we'll form a plan to support you and the babies and keep you all safe. You won't have to do this alone."

The woman frowned at Booker, then stared into space.

Alira hadn't even wanted to birth her *own* younglings. Booker couldn't imagine being asked to carry someone else's, especially knowing it wasn't fully one species or another. Of course, that revelation wouldn't be quite as upsetting for her, given what she knew about the connection between them. Still, she hoped she never had to make that choice.

What did Bailey think about all this? Booker made a mental note to ask her, later, if the opportunity arose.

"Okay." The woman with curls stared at Booker. "As long as you follow through on your promise, I'm good. If you betray me even once, or if I think I and the baby are in any danger, I'm out."

Yet another promise. Booker offered a strained smile. "Understood," she said. She considered each of them. "I know you'll have questions. Honestly, there aren't many answers yet. But we'll work with you throughout the duration. We'll figure this out together."

"I suggest taking some time," Bailey said, "to think about all this. It might be helpful if you're housed together so you can support one another. If you'll come with me, I'll get you settled."

The surrogates rose and followed Bailey toward the door.

"Captain," Booker said, "I need to speak to you and the admiral, first chance you have."

Bailey nodded, and led the surrogates out into the corridor.

Booker resumed her natural form, and Alira slumped in the plaz chair. That had gone better than she'd expected. Except…

Now what?

The curly haired woman—she *really* should've asked their names—had a point. They couldn't raise unammi children in any of the colonies. And the survivors on Earth would never welcome them, no matter how much they laxed their rules.

What was she going to do with these women? And how could she combine the effort of their care and maintenance with the obligations of her promise to Bika? Maybe that research the outcasts had done on alternate worlds would be useful now.

How would these hybrid younglings fare without irolium? What would the crystals do to their human genes? The Iri had evolved the unammi's human ancestors. Would the same thing happen here?

This was going to be a guessing game from the outset. If it were normal unammi younglings, she'd know what to expect. Better yet, they'd be surrounded by other females and younglings in the familial house, where even the newest mothers could be supported by those with more experience.

But here, with no idea of whether—or which—unammi traits would be dominant, there was no way to plan for contingencies. The human mothers wouldn't have any idea how to deal with infant unammi. Could they even endure it? Or would they give up when expectation and reality did not mesh?

Maybe she never should have encouraged them to proceed. Maybe she should've let them all terminate. It would've been easier on them. Easier on her.

Alira rubbed her face. How did she repeatedly manage to land in these kinds of situations?

Well, this time, she intended to enlist all the help she could find. She pushed up from the chair.

"TICS," she said, the pitch of her voice dropping as she shifted into Eli's form, "record message for Admiral Thrace Baldric, Consortium Trader base, New Canaan, Harajüd." At the ready tone, he continued. "Hello, Admiral. I've decided to take your advice and shoulder that project we spoke of. However," he said, smiling, "I'm sure it won't surprise you to learn that a few extra layers of complexity have been added to the plan, which means I'll need help. Who can you spare to work full time with me on this?"

The door chime sounded.

"TICS, pause recording. Who's at my door?"

"Captain Bailey," the system responded.

That was fast. "Resume recording." The system chittered, then she went on. "I'm currently in Tuneloras, the guest of Admiral Rizzo, and will wait here for your response. Aes te nalya."

He signed off, sent the message, then answered the door.

"Admiral Rizzo and I are ready to meet with you," Bailey said, gesturing.

Eli accompanied her down the corridor.

The captain walked in silence for a moment. "You handled that well," she finally said.

"Thank you," he said, "but as usual, I don't know what I'm doing. I just hope I can keep my promise to them. What are their names?"

"The woman with brown skin is Solji. The blonde is Miisa. And the one with the curls is Kaarina," Bailey said. "You won't be the only one keeping that promise. The Syndicate will help as much as we can." She fell silent as a couple of crewmen passed. When they were out of earshot, she glanced aside at him. "Thank you, for healing me."

He shrugged. "You mostly did that yourself, but you're welcome."

"Do you have a plan," Bailey asked, "for the Bregaina slaves?"

"Not exactly. That's why I want to talk to you and Rizzo. I could use your input."

They walked the rest of the way without speaking and were soon sitting before Rizzo's desk.

"If I'm going to fulfill my promise to Bika," Eli said, "and provide safe haven for the surrogates, I'm going to need a lot of help."

Rizzo scowled. "I've already told you I can't—"

"I know. I'm not talking about direct involvement," Eli said. "I meant supplies, ships, gear, and any trustworthy personnel you can spare long-term. You already know I can't pay you. Not yet. But that'll change. Soon."

"How?" Rizzo raised both brows. "You are in no position to gather credits without outside assistance. Setting up that kind of background and corpgov record would take a long while. Longer than we can stand to be without either the supplies you need or the credits to replace them. I've made promises, too. Syndicate obligations must come first. You can understand that, I'm sure."

"What if we could provide you with resources in exchange?" he asked. "Metals, stones, other raw materials the Syndicate could use in your regular industries?"

"Again, how?"

Eli watched her without speaking. He hadn't discussed this with the council. Hell, he hadn't discussed it with anyone. He wasn't at all sure they'd go along with it, but it was all he could think of. And it would be the beginning of payback for everything *else* Rizzo had done for the unammi so far.

"I can't agree to an arrangement," Rizzo said, "without knowing that kind of crucial detail."

"He can't tell us where he'll get these materials," Bailey said, "because that's where his people are."

Eli whirled to gape at her.

"Am I right?" Bailey said.

He sighed. "Yes."

"Eli," Rizzo said, her voice sharp, "stealing from any of the colonies is a very bad idea."

"You do it," he said. "All the time."

Bailey made a muffled sound that started like a laugh and transformed into a cough.

Rizzo paused. "Granted. But I have years of experience at this skill. You are more likely to be caught, and I can't allow the Syndicate—"

"It isn't one of the colonies."

"Then where?" Rizzo pressed.

"Do we need to know, ma'am?" Bailey asked. "The unammi can't take a chance on sharing that info."

"I understand that. I haven't asked before. But," she said to Eli, "now you are asking me to involve the Syndicate in ways that could bite us later. I can't take the chance—"

"It's okay." Eli stared at his own fingers, which clasped one another as if he were impersonating Galen. "You've told me you can be trusted, and I'm choosing to believe you. But you cannot come there, and you *cannot* let anyone else know. We'll never have another moment's peace, if you do."

"Agreed," Rizzo said.

"Of course," Bailey added.

Eli tried—and failed—to think of another way.

"The unammi survivors," he said at last, "are on Earth."

chapter 66

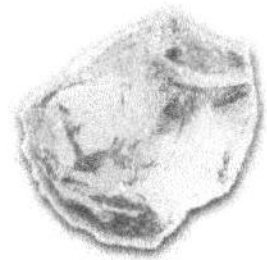

RIZZO BLINKED. EARTH? HAD HE said *Earth*?

"I'm sorry," she said through clenched teeth. "Did you just tell me that the unammi survivors are…" She struggled for adequate words. "That you've been traveling between a *plague-infested world* and the human colonies? *My base?*" Her voice rose, despite her efforts to keep it level. "That you are sitting here in my office at this moment, possibly infecting me and my second with a *deadly plague*?" She rose, slowly leaning forward on her desk. In her peripheral vision, Bailey also gawked at Eli, her mouth slightly ajar. "Is *that* what you are telling me?"

"Earth's biosphere is no longer contaminated." Eli said, voice low. "Whatever biohazards were there before, they're gone now. That's why you can't tell anyone. If humans as a whole learned of this, my people would be overrun."

"That's why you had to kill Knøfa," Bailey said, her voice soft. "You couldn't let him escape with that knowledge."

"That's right."

Rizzo frowned. Was it possible? Maybe. Perhaps the better question was whether it was likely.

"You ran scans? More than one?"

"Yes. Besides," Eli's features puckered, "how long did it take that Earth virus to overcome the remaining populations during the plague era?"

"I don't know." Rizzo couldn't remember the last time she'd done any research on humanity's birthplace. It never held any interest for her because it had nothing to offer her or her people. "It wasn't long, if I recall correctly."

"Exactly," Eli said. "The unammi have been there more than nine standard months. No one has gotten sick." He peered up at her. "I would never have risked your worlds, despite the disdain some humans hold for my people. Think a moment. You know this is true."

She sank slowly into her seat. "TICS, compile known information and extrapolated projections on the lifespans of biological hazards given a setting wherein there are no target species to spread and feed the infection."

"Consult records from all colonial systems?"

Rizzo hesitated. What if someone tracked her query? Unlikely, but possible. Would that lead them to conclusions which would threaten the unammi on Earth?

"TICS, belay that order. Cancel and delete request." She'd need to find another way to research the topic.

The TICS chittered and fell silent.

"Who else knows of this?" she asked.

"No one outside the unammi." Eli heaved a heavy breath. "I'm still not sure I was right to tell you. But as you pointed out, there's a price for your assistance in fulfilling my promise to Bika, and now to the surrogates. Trusting you is part of that. Just don't make me regret it."

She stared at his pale form, his long red hair, and tried to see Alira under the mask. What color would she be at this moment? One of these days, admiral and troublemaker would need to chat about those kinds of things. Despite the annoyance and disruptions Alira's presence always wrought, curiosity drove Rizzo to seek a greater understanding of these few remaining members of a threatened race.

"I'm not committing us to anything," Rizzo said. "But hypothetically, what kinds of supplies would you need?"

Eli seemed to consider the question. "Food that'll keep for a while, habs and some starting fuel resources, weapons for protection, basic tools for homesteading or whatever might arise, clothing, shoes, weather-related items. A few trustworthy helpers who won't ask questions or carry tales." He shook his head. "Probably a lot more but that's what comes to mind at the moment."

"Where will you set up?" Bailey asked. "Earth?"

"No. The unammi would never accept that."

"It's also too far from most of the colony worlds to make it a viable camp for your purposes," Rizzo said. "So where, then?"

He shrugged. "Honestly, I don't know. I haven't had enough time to come up with any options. What do you suggest?"

A few isolated moons might work for a while, but even those would be discovered eventually. Trader factions were known for using such out-of-the-way places for delivery drops and merchandise swaps. And any moons orbiting colony worlds would be too easily surveilled. Eli wouldn't want his camp to be under everyone's feet, but he also needed to be close enough to get help if and when he needed it.

Hopefully, the aid wouldn't always need to come from her. Eli needed more allies. A lot of them.

She'd need to do some research. Except the same hesitation that stopped her searching TICS records for viral life cycles also stayed her hand here. That sort of search could be traced or possibly trigger an alert in corpgov. It would be as good as breadcrumbs leading curious seekers straight to Eli's doorstep, so to speak.

"Wasn't there another plague world?" Bailey asked, her voice soft as if she was still processing Eli's revelation.

Rizzo watched her push a lock of hair behind her ear. "Go on."

"I vaguely remember a small colony," Bailey said, her words slow, deliberate, "settled after all the others. I believe it was connected to research? Or maybe a scientific community?" She frowned. "They weren't there long before a ship escaped Earth's quarantine and infected the settlers. I don't remember all the details, but if Earth is no longer a biohazard, maybe that world is safe now, too?"

"Where is it?" Eli asked, eagerness plain in his voice. "Do you know?"

"Not yet," Bailey said. "I'll have to examine the records to get the coordinates. But, we need to be careful. We don't want to leave any footprints behind in our searches or even draw attention to the subject of our search."

"My thoughts exactly." Rizzo squinted at her second. "Can you find out what we need to know without leaving a trail?"

"Yes ma'am." She nodded. "It won't be easy, but I'll get it done."

"Good. Get started immediately. Once we have a location, I'll check the current status of its biohazard myself." She leaned forward. "And while you're at it, start thinking of ways we can systematically obfuscate the existence of that world altogether. If it's a workable solution, we don't want anyone finding it by accident."

"On it." Bailey left the office.

Rizzo regarded Eli, quashing a feeling of admiration for him. Whoever he was at any given moment, he had upturned much of Rizzo's predictable world. Easy as it was to acknowledge only the aggravation, she had to admit to curiosity about how these promises Eli had made would work out. He was, in fact, playing the same role for Bika's people as Lourdes had played for young Turizomi all those years ago. If not for her, Turi would not have survived, and there would never have been an Admiral Rizzo. She wondered if Eli had any clue what was facing him.

"Thank you, Rizzo," Eli said.

"I haven't committed to anything, yet." She raised an eyebrow. "But just in case I do, tell me about these resources you can bring me from Earth."

chapter 67

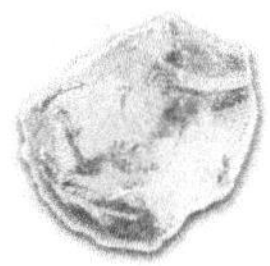

Tuneloras, Saacharis
<u>Syndicate Trader Base, Guest Quarters</u>

ALIRA STARED AT THE SIMULATED window in her quarters, showing an "outside" view with little of the bright daylight she'd seen on other human worlds. Tuneloras wasn't as dimly lit as the city on Iridos, but it was close, dark enough to spawn its own bioluminescent life forms. No wonder the lighting was so bright in Rizzo's office and here in Alira's quarters. It seemed humans needed specific wavelengths of electromagnetic radiation to maintain good mental health. Hah. They wouldn't have lasted long on Iridos.

The comm chirped.

"Answer, voice only. Yes?"

"We have news," Bailey said. "Shall I come by and escort you to the admiral's office?"

Finally! "Yes. Please," Alira said. "And thank you, Captain." She turned from the holoimage. Had Bailey's research been fruitful? Could Alira move forward, at last? So much depended on finding and starting a new colony, one off the humans' radar, where she could get started on these many projects she'd assumed. She'd spent all those seasons—years—on Iridos, trying to fit in, to find a role all her own among her people. Yet each one she tried had chafed, constricted so that it kept her from taking a full, deep breath, like a wrap tied too tightly around the chest. This, though…

Yes, it was scary. Yes, she worried she would be inadequate to the task. But the thought of abdicating the project before it even began triggered an ache deep inside her. She hadn't been able to save her own people. Even in a new home, they'd disagreed and pushed old agendas like they always had. But she could help the Bregainans. Bring them home. And along the way she could find the pilots, bring them to safety, without a council or a group of unammi telling her what was and wasn't part of the job. No one had ever done this before, unammi or human as far as she knew. She was free to take this new role and make it her own. She felt like she'd been waiting for this her whole life.

Maybe she had.

She morphed to her Eli form moments before the door chime sounded. Together, he and Bailey set off down the corridor.

"Did you find…it?" he asked.

Bailey smiled. "We did. And the admiral went there herself. It's safe."

"I was beginning to worry." Okay, that was a lie. Alira's worrying started long before now. "It's been more than a week since it first came up."

"Yes," Bailey said. "Finding it would've been easy. Covering my tracks was not. And then there was travel time to and from. But best not to discuss it out here. I trust our people, but I'd rather not risk yours on that basis."

Good point. Eager as he was to know what they discovered, he could hold out bit longer.

The minute the door closed behind them in the admiral's office, Rizzo focused on Eli.

"Nidahn is serviceable," she said. "Clean. And its location has been as obfuscated as Bailey could manage without drawing big targets on it, and on whoever you station there."

At last. A new home for her. A base of operations from which to fulfill her promises. "Bailey said you went there?"

"Yes."

"Did you land? Is it—"

"No," Rizzo said. "I only made a fly-by. But its atmosphere is clear of biohazards."

"You need to know it isn't ideal in terms of living conditions," Bailey advised.

Of course it wasn't. He sighed. "How so?"

The captain shrugged. "It's situated on the outer reaches of the habitable zone around its star, so it'll be colder. Polar regions would likely be too cold for humans," she added. "I'm not sure whether the unammi would be okay there. I expect the equatorial regions will be more liveable."

Eli considered her words. Iridos was colder than most human colonies, as well. "What about surface water? Could you tell if..." His voice trailed off. It could be paradise, but if there was no adequate water source, they'd need to keep searching.

"Yes," Rizzo said. "I saw a few large bodies while in flight, but scans showed other smaller ones as well—salt, fresh, and brackish sources, but that's irrelevant. We can provide solutions for water purification."

"Here," Bailey said, reaching for her TICS pad. "I'll send you what I found, and the data from the admiral's flyby."

Eli withdrew his pad. "Thank you." He checked Bailey's notes, then glanced up at Rizzo. "I'll need to see it in person."

"Of course," Rizzo said. "I would do the same. We can—"

The system chirped with an incoming communique. Rizzo checked it on her display. "This is from Admiral Georgeanne, marked urgent. I need to take it. Bailey?"

The captain stood. "Come on, Eli."

"What?" He lurched forward in his seat. "Wait...didn't you tell me you were going to reach out to her and Bardo about me? About the unammi? What if she's comming about that? I'd like to hear what she says."

"Eli—" Bailey tried to interrupt.

"Rizzo?" Eli pressed.

The admiral scowled. "Aid and assistance to the unammi is not the sole aspect of Syndicate business. I do have other tasks. You need to leave. If it's about you, I'll play it for you later."

"Wouldn't it be more efficient to listen to it now, and save yourself a repeat later?" Eli flashed his best winning smile. He'd been practicing.

Rizzo stood up slowly. "Out. Now."

"Aren't we working on building trust here?" he asked. "That needs to go both ways. I promise, if it isn't about the unammi, you can stop playback, and I'll leave before anything sensitive is revealed."

Rizzo's jaw worked, her stare hardened. After a moment, she muttered something Eli couldn't make out and shook her head. "You are going to drive me insane."

"You're in good company with that belief." Eli peered at her. "Right alongside my ama and the elders on the unammi council."

Rizzo cut her gaze to Bailey, but Eli was tired of receiving information after the fact. If this was about the unammi, he wanted to hear it firsthand for a change. If he always settled for being fed secondhand intel by go-betweens, they would never see him as a leader, as an equal. He needed to push for direct involvement. That's the only way these human alliances would work.

Finally, Rizzo relented. "TICS, receive communique from The Federation."

Bailey came to stand at Eli's side as the holo began.

A small woman with spikey brown hair appeared over Rizzo's desk, her lips parted in a grin. "Hey, Rizz. How's it hangin'? Thanks for the scoop about the unammi. I'd heard rumors that they have special…gifts, and that they can pass for human. Interesting. Raises a lot of questions, but if you're helping them, the Federation will step up. I'll expect to hear from them—her?—as soon as they can get to me. I also wanted to thank you for that update you sent. The information was timely. Saved me a lot of credits, and even more grief, so I owe you a solid. Thus my comm."

She moved closer to the holocam, her dark eyes gleaming. "Neither of us loves the slavers, but you have more reason to hate them than me. So, I wanted you to know my people found three slave groups on Zebalu. Two of them were working in—"

"TICS, pause."

Eli leapt to his feet. "What? Why? She's talking about—"

"You heard the part about the unammi. The slaves don't involve you. Out." She nodded at Bailey, who grasped Eli's arm.

He pulled away. "It *does* involve me. Weren't we just talking about helping Botha's people escape the Cartel's grasp?" Eli stepped forward, bumping into the desk. "You were there when it happened. You of all people should understand the depth of that promise I made to them."

"You don't know this is about the baba's people. It could be anyone."

"And that makes them less a target for rescue?" He almost sent a bryse, a nudge to encourage her to agree, but no. She was an ally. He would not interfere with her honest choices. Not by those means, anyway.

"Eli," Rizzo said through clenched teeth, "you—"

"Come on, Rizzo," he said, his voice soft. "What if it is Botha's people? His partners? What if it's children? I can help. Please let me help."

Rizzo made a sound in her throat, almost a growl. "You push me. Again."

He opened his mouth to respond.

"But you have a point," she said. "TICS, continue."

"—the fields, one along the northeastern plains of Kahari, and the other on the island of Silat. Those should be easy to get to, if they're still there. If you're going after them, let me know. I'll get you some updated information. The other group…"

Georgeanne sighed. She ran fingers through her spiked hair, mussing it further. "They're in a brothel in Matendarma, on the northern tip of Javandra. They won't be so easy to reach. I have a plan that I'm sure will work, but I can't do the pickup myself for…reasons I won't go into now. If I could, though, here's what I'd do.

"I'd send someone to Zebalu to assess the site. They'll need to know where the air intakes are for the building before they even get started. That's essential. Once they're familiar with the layout, and how to get in and out without being seen, they can set up some prolo smokers." George fixed her attention on the holocam. "If you've never seen that herb used in smoke form, you should know a little goes a long way. In this case, though, I'd want to produce enough smoke to drive everyone out of the building, so I'd use a lot. And I would tell my people to be out of the building well before the damn thing goes off. If they got hit with that smoke, they'd be useless to get anyone else out of there. Prolo fumigation won't hurt anyone, but it will induce a lot of coughing, runny noses, and watering eyes until it clears.

"Once the timers go off and the smoke gets into the building, everyone will come pouring out the doors. The smoke hangs around a while, but not forever, so a quick in and out would be the goal." She squinted at the holocam. "I'd be willing to bet brothel management sends the slaves out the rear exit, or via some other little-used passage so they don't have a chance to raise any calls for assistance with responding Zebalu emergency teams or whatnot.

"You already buy prolo from us, but so do a lot of other people, so its use shouldn't be an automatic connection to the Syndicate. Not sure what your supply levels are now. If you need more, send word. I'll get some to you quick as I can. It's always a guessing game going into a sitch like this one, but you already know that.

"Anyways, now we're even, more or less. Tell your unammi contacts to drop by the Federation for a chat. They should tell Claudio you sent them." She winked. "Ciao, baby."

The comm ended.

"Three groups." Eli stared at the space where Georgeanne's face had hovered. "I'm only one person."

Bailey grimaced.

"We cannot—" Rizzo began.

"I know." Eli waved off her protestation. "Just…processing the data. Don't worry. I'll figure it out." Somehow. Maybe Kilbee could grab one group and send one of the outcasts after the other. Eli, or one of Alira's other personas, could take on the brothel. "How long will it take to make those devices Georgeanne described?"

"A couple of hours," Bailey said. "Is that what you want to do?"

"Do you have a better suggestion?"

Bailey frowned. "No."

"Get started on those, Captain," Rizzo said. "I would expect only one or two air intakes, unless it's a large facility, which I doubt. I've been to that city. It's small, almost a village, populated mostly by seafaring workers. No tourism to speak of. Still, make four, just in case."

"Yes, ma'am," Bailey said on her way out.

Rizzo studied Eli. "Are you sure you can do this?"

"Ne. Bejhur asane," he murmured. No. I'm not ready. "I don't have a choice."

"Of course you do."

"No, I don't," he said, his voice low. "I made a promise."

Rizzo's expression was a confusing tangle Eli couldn't unwind just now.

"What?" he asked.

A small wrinkle lined her forehead, almost like the one Nyros used to get.

"You keep surprising me," she said. "I'll ask you one more time. Are you sure you can do this?"

Flashes from the night of the snatch flickered in his thoughts. The stark lights shining down on the platform. Bregainans being yanked up into the ships. Botha's wails, mingled with those of the remaining villagers. Botha had saved Alira's life. Even though the Bregainans had discarded Eli, he would do what he could to help them, no matter what it took.

Besides, if Nidahn worked out, as he expected, it could be a great base of operations to manage the slave rescues, as well as the other projects he'd taken on. If Rizzo would provide habs and everything else he needed to at least get started, he'd be well on his way to setting up a functional settlement. Now he just needed a support base and residents willing to work at a behind-the-scenes rebellion intent on upending slavery and other such detestable notions.

Heh. A rebellion. He laughed.

"Something's funny?" Rizzo asked.

"I've been a rebel all my life, I suppose, in the opinion of my people. But now, it occurs to me that establishing a settlement on Nidahn specifically for the purpose of saving rescued slaves and protecting the surviving unammi makes me a rebel in the human colonies, too." He laughed again. "It must be my destiny."

"Traders are the same." Rizzo said. "You didn't answer my question."

"Yes. I'm sure I can do this." Mostly. "But there's a lot to do to get started. I'm hoping you'll commit to those supplies I asked for, including any people to help us set up and run things on Nidahn. People whose knowledge of that world's safe status won't be a threat. Also, I need to contact Bardo and Georgeanne—you'll tell me how, I hope?—so I can start establishing communications with them."

"Very well. I'll send you their links and start rounding up some materials and people for the Nidahn jobsite." Rizzo rubbed her face, as if she'd been at her desk for days.

"Also," Eli said, "I'll be leaving as soon as Bailey can finish those devices."

"Isn't that rushing things?" She frowned. "It's a little less than two days to Zebalu from here. That doesn't give you time to put together a team."

Team. Right. Eli grinned. "Who says I'm going straight to Zebalu?

chapter 68

Aboard The Kukri
<u>**On Approach to Nidahn**</u>

ALIRA WATCHED THE VIEWSCREEN ON the older cargo ship. Before her, a frozen world hung suspended in the black of space, smaller than Earth, but brighter, too. Gleams of starlight reflected off its enormous caps of ice and snow at both poles, and highlighted lands approaching the equatorial zones, the only green patches she could see. Rizzo and Bailey had apparently been right. It would be colder here, but that made sense, given its position in this star system. Bailey had reported that no one ever again came here after the original colonists died out. That due to its infection status, not to mention its environment and the fact that all Nidahn resources could be more easily obtained elsewhere, the other human colonies had marked this world a cheap loss and forgotten all about it. That suited Alira's purposes just fine.

The key issue was to determine whether it would work for her needs now. She peered at the image. Lower temperatures wouldn't stop the outcasts from thriving. But what about any humans who chose to join them? And was it truly safe? Not that she didn't trust Rizzo. But something this important demanded she test the atmosphere for herself. That was the first order of business.

"TICS, scan for pathogenic bio-organisms in the atmosphere that would be hazardous to human life."

The system worked, then gave a reading similar to the one she'd seen when she'd first gone to Earth. She ran the tests twice, with each result the same. She even ran a calibration on the equipment to be sure it was fully functional, then ran another pass.

Nothing. Nada. Zip. Zilch.

okay crow…that's enough

Nidahn was as safe as Earth had been. These scans didn't even find as many of the similar microbes she'd seen there. Maybe the colder environment killed them off more effectively?

No way to know without years of study. She and her crew would not have time for that.

She dropped lower, entering the atmosphere and flying close enough to get a better look at the surface. North and south forays convinced her it would be best to remain in the equatorial region. Winter snows would surely come there, as she saw on one side of the abandoned world. But they would be milder than those at greater latitudes in either direction. Surely they could bring in supplies and equipment to prepare for that type of cold.

She flew for a while, taking in the view. Most shades of green seemed deeper here, darker than what she'd seen on Earth, Harajüd, or most of the other human worlds in her harvested memories. Large swaths of open land hugged the equator in a couple of places. Nearby, both north and south, regions of brown, black, and gray jutted at irregular intervals. Rock surfaces, maybe? Here and there, flashes of other colors—birds?— whizzed by on the viewscreen as she passed.

"TICS, check for surface regions within tolerances for human habitation."

The system chittered and she watched its holoprojection, comparing it to what she'd seen for herself. Readouts indicated at least two areas where high and low current temperatures rested comfortably within the range of those she'd felt on Saacharis. Rizzo's people, and other humans, should be fine here.

Several large water bodies glinted from the surface as she passed over the dayside. Quick readings told her most were freshwater. A few, mostly frozen under the ice and snow, read as brackish. Only those much larger bodies outside the continental land masses read as true saltwater. One large moon orbited the world, so tidal effects remained to be seen.

Alira nodded. Yes. This could work.

A few more scans marked the locations of areas with structures that resembled ruins. Kilbee—assuming he agreed to help set up the settlement here; she had yet to broach the topic with him—could assign teams to scout those when time permitted. Maybe there would be materials they could reuse in their own settlement. But what had they been before, when humans were still setting up this colony for research? What might her people find there when they searched?

How exciting it would be to set foot on this world before anyone else! To walk those ruins, as she'd done on Earth, and see them for herself! To dream of what this place might one day be, its role in the new projects and in the lives of those they could save!

But no. Those very people she sought to help needed her right now. She would need to leave the initial exploration to her setup crew and hear about it after the fact. She sent a quick comm to Rizzo about the world's acceptability and asked her to please deliver whatever supplies and materials she could manage.

Alira flew a few more moments, scouting and dreaming, then she set the coordinates for Zebalu and left Nidahn behind.

chapter 69

Surgappe Public House and Brothel
<u>**Matendarma, Zebalu**</u>

THE SMELL OF SALTED FISH, briny nets, and metallic crates crusted with barnacles permeated the air around the brothel. This close to the wharf, she had to wait for darkness to move. Business here didn't slow after Zebalu's star dropped below the horizon, but most activity would be centered on the front entrance where clientele, still reeking of their daily catch, would come seeking solace after hours of grueling work.

Alira matched her dermal display to a tangled patch of trees and undergrowth, whose shadows stretched across the pebbled lot behind the building's low structure. The combination provided concealment from curious eyes. She hoped Kilbee and his team were almost finished with their grabs on the other side of this world, and that they were already on their way to Bejami, where she would join them after she'd finished here. She had so much to tell Kilbee, things she'd not yet shared. So many details that could not be entrusted to a comm.

To keep herself occupied, she recalled her quick fly-by at Nidahn, trying to determine which location might be best suited to a new community. Such an odd realization, to know that no one had seen it in all these generations, that her people would be the first sapients to walk there since the original colonists had died out! Settling there would require a lot of exploration to find which of the available regions was the safest, the warmest. They'd also need to scope the boundaries of other wildlife and hopefully not interfere beyond what was necessary, test local plants to see which were safe and edible, and which should be avoided. She'd leave that last part to the medics and healers they would bring from other worlds.

She fantasized about ideas for the new world, and almost dozed off before shaking herself awake and shoring up her camouflage. Soon, she could sleep. Already, foot traffic had picked up at the front of the pub. Even with artificial lights, fisherfolk did not try to work through the night. Zebalu's oceans had minds of their own, like capricious siblings that took all a fisherman's plans and tossed them with the tide, then laughed at the troubles they had caused.

Colors began to creep across the darkening sky, painting the clouds at the western horizon in hues of gold, orange, red. Street lamps winked on in front of the pub and along the streets of the small town, but the one behind the pub, where she waited, did not. It would work again. After she finished here.

When the night's blackness reached sufficient depth, she adopted a human form and slipped Bailey's contraptions into her pockets. She crept from her hiding place, scuttled to the rear of the building, and reexamined the vents for the building's air circulation system. No change since yesterday. Inside all three, the low hum of airflow sounded, but only the largest one served as the main intake. She hunkered outside its access near the center of the structure and pulled two compact bundles from her pocket. Small, unobtrusive, but they would do the job. She lifted the cover without a squeak—she'd seen to that last night when she'd booby trapped the fan's electrical system—and crawled inside.

At once the air intake pulled at her crouched body as if to rush her pace. She ignored it. Took her time. She would only get one chance at this. Her shoulders and hips rubbed the sides, and she shifted to a smaller profile. Her weight, slight as it was in this form, pressed down on the thin metal floor of the horizontal air duct with hollow popping sounds and though there was no living space below, where others might hear, she slowed even more to avoid notice. Muffled sounds from the building's interior, those loud enough to be heard over the fan's noise, filtered through the branching channels of the intake. If she could hear them, they would hear her.

It seemed to take forever to get to the main ventilation unit. She peered through but saw nothing beyond the fan's spinning blades. With slow, measured movements, she slid flat and rolled onto her side to free her hands, one of which still gripped the packets. Small straps hung down from the center of each, strong enough to hold it in place for the time required, but fragile enough to be consumed in its task and leave nothing behind when all was done. She attached both to the mesh between the duct and the fan itself, ensuring they were secure, then followed the passage through the other side of the building.

The last part of the crawlspace narrowed further and, tempting as it was, she did not shift even smaller. Too much risk of the transformation being seen from outside. Instead, she wiggled forward, then wormed her way out of the opening at the end. Once outside, she checked her surroundings, crept across the lot to the trees, and crouched among the boles. From another pocket, she pulled a second device, poised her finger over the first switch, and pushed the button.

A minute passed. Then another. And another.

In the minute that followed, voices grew loud inside the building when its occupants began to throw open windows and doors. Thick black smoke escaped, first in tendrils then in clouds. People poured out the front of the structure, their voices raised in a clamor loud enough it might soon bring other curious villagers. She hoped—she *planned*—to be gone by then.

The door opened, spilling low light out into the lot. She hunkered down even further.

Four—no, five people hurried out, all coughing. One of them choked out words to someone silhouetted in the lighted doorway, then the door closed, and the fifth person herded the others farther from the building.

Closer to her hiding place. Close enough to see a few details, even in the darkness. Two women, and three men. All were swiping at tears from the smoke devices. Of the five, only one was fully dressed. The guard.

Damn it. She hadn't considered that. They'd need clothing. Alira pressed her lips together and frowned. She'd figure that out when she was finished here.

A quick touch on the second switch, and lights in the building went dark. Voices rose in confusion once more. The emergency lights came on almost at once, but the fans did not.

She squinted at the guard, who was still trying to clear his lungs of smoke. The moment his back was turned, she moved out of the trees, shifting to Booker as she went, and tapped him on the shoulder.

He whirled with a gasp, and stared, his mouth hanging open. "Who—"

She smiled. "Good night," she said, her voice almost pleasant, before she punched him as hard as she could.

The man grunted, while a spray of blood from his nose and a cut on his cheek spattered Booker's face. The blow lifted him off his feet and sent him flying at least two meters.

The four coughing, half-naked slaves watched his flight, slack-jawed, then gawked at Booker, their bodies varying shades of gray in the darkness.

"I'm a friend," she said. A siren wailed in the distance, moving in their direction. Booker glanced toward the front of the building—no one had taken an interest in them, yet—then at the slaves. "Ready to go home?"

chapter 70

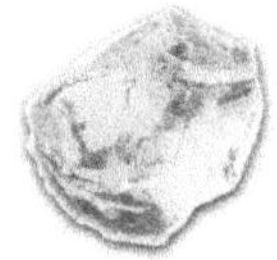

Stawanel Mountains
<u>Northwest of Bel-Rhovan, Bejami</u>

FROM THE MOUTH OF THE cave, a footpath—ledge, really—eased down to a plateau a few meters below and to one side, just large enough for a medium-sized jumper. Beyond, its edges dropped many hundreds of meters into the canyon, down to the river below. Booker stood just inside the cave, comfortable in the darkness. Wherever she went, she'd found safety in the shadows. Solace in their embrace. Behind her, in the deeper gloom, those she'd rescued from the brothel huddled outside her ship, which awaited delivery of the remaining Bregainans.

Bejami's satellite fly-by time approached. She peered up into the pale blue sky as if she could see it there. Instead, a flock of nagvël crossed before her. She hadn't seen them in so large a group before, and rarely at midday. Light glinted off their black plumage as they dipped lower, the mass moving in unison as if they could all hear one another's thoughts. It would be nice to have them come closer so she could see their red-tipped crests. Instead, they dove into the canyon and out of sight.

She saw the ship before she heard it, coming in low, hugging the curves of the mountains with skill and ease. Probably Kilbee, but she ducked into the shadows, just in case. The jumper dropped lower in the canyon, its sound betraying its presence, until it surged into view just shy of the plateau below. The craft lifted, swerved, and settled into the natural landing spot with a grace most pilots could only envy. Its engines dropped to standby, the hatch slid open, and a familiar face appeared.

He glanced up at the cavern. She stepped into the light, then raised a hand. He gave her a thumbs up and ducked inside his ship. The next people to emerge were the passengers, all of them rescues from his latest sweep on Zebalu. She waved them forward. A few hesitated at the narrow ledge. But that was the only thing that stood between them and freedom. The fall risk seemed somehow lessened by that fact, and she felt as proud of their courage as she would have if they'd been family.

In a way, they were.

When the first few reached the cavern, her own group met them with hugs and tears. Others arrived and joined in.

Kilbee came last, some little distance behind the others.

"I know you've missed each other," Booker said to the villagers, "and you've missed your home. I promise I'll take you there soon but Kilbee and I need to speak first."

They looked content to linger a while, hugging and catching up with one another.

Kilbee eyed her.

"Alira?" he murmured.

"The name is Booker. For now." She took his arm and led him to the far side of the cavern.

"You seem well," he said. "More settled."

She supposed he was right. But settled didn't always mean still. Booker had plenty of work in her future and, if he agreed to help, so did Kilbee. "Perhaps. But we'll get to that. What of our people? What of the city? How do they fare?"

"Now there's a tale," he said. "I hope you have no place to be for a while."

His voice held a lilt she'd not heard there before. He sounded…happy.

"The survivors are united now, in one group under one council made of individuals from both camps. And," he went on, "there are term limits now. No one serves on the council for life anymore."

"And your ama? How is she taking these changes?"

"Surprisingly well," he said. "She even speaks your name now."

Booker couldn't suppress a small laugh. "Will wonders ever cease?"

"I suspect that is your doing." Kilbee kicked a small stone, and it skittered off the ledge. "I don't know what you said to her after…well, after. That last time you were home. But it made a real difference in her."

Home. Earth would never be her home. Booker pushed the thought away.

"Your revelations during the rest of that visit changed everything else," he added.

"What do you mean?" As if she didn't know.

He gave her a strange look. "Everyone was already talking about what they saw in you during the joinedmind when you all took out Knøfa's ship. But your explanation of the Founder's Daughter, her purpose, the connection to the Iri, all of it…" He pressed his lips together as if he were still trying to grasp what it all meant. "Our people, our culture will never be the same."

"I am sorry for that," she said, her voice so low she wasn't sure he would hear her.

He turned her toward him. "No. Don't say that. Not ever. These changes you've wrought, they're things we should've done generations ago. You held up a giant mirror to us so that we could no longer ignore our mistakes. Sure, it might be hard to take those first stumbling steps into a new life but, in the end, we'll be better for it. Don't you see?"

A lump formed in her throat, and she swallowed hard. "I'll take your word for it. Now tell me more. You talk of change. Like what?" She strolled to the cavern's entrance and he followed beside.

"Where to start?" Kilbee pondered for a minute. "Maybe the most exciting thing is that the new council has decided to follow your suggestion that we no longer adjust the younglings. After you explained how that modification would impede their communication with the Iri, both councils—before they even combined—had made the choice to abandon that practice."

"Excellent!" Booker grinned.

"Also, mitigation has been abolished."

She grasped his arm. "Really?"

"Yes. I wasn't there for the council meeting where that decision was made, but I heard later that they discussed where our people would be now if mitigation had worked on you before we ever left Iridos. We probably would not have survived." He pinned his gaze to hers. "The councilors wondered aloud what other resources they may have squandered by mitigating so many of our people.

"But," he said, "you already knew mitigation isn't always forever. The new council has also set up a small group of frem, mostly healers, who are working to help those mitigants who hadn't already relapsed. They hope to revert them to a more normal state, but it's never been done. They aren't sure they'll be successful."

"Will they try to keep individuals from leaving the city?" she asked. "Or will those who do so still be outcast?"

"Nope. They're smart enough to see it's unstoppable. They've accepted all of us as full citizens, even approved your suggestion of a new guild, one that can train interested frem for service among the humans. The pilots on the outpost will be part of that guild, now."

"That's wonderful news," she said. Maybe some of those newly trained unammi could become the watchers Thrace had requested.

"There's just one other thing."

Her shoulders tensed. "I'm listening."

"The council held a lottery," Kilbee said, "to determine who would carry the genetic samples you finally gave them."

A lottery. She made an amused sound, part laugh, part grunt. One of Booker's human harvests had read an old, old story about such a thing, where the loser was sacrificed to ensure fertile crops, or some such thing. "Who lost?"

"You misunderstand," he said.

She frowned at him.

"The lottery was all volunteer. More than half the female frem in the unified city vied for the honor of carrying your younglings. Three women won."

Three. Booker didn't miss the irony. Three human surrogates, three unammi surrogates.

"The council hopes," he said, "you'll visit them often, and that when the time comes to share your harvests—hopefully, many long years from now—you'll be among them to do so."

"What?" Booker stared at him like he'd gone mad. "They want my human voices?" Of all the things she might've predicted, this wouldn't have been one of them.

"Of course. Just think how your Daughters can one day help unammi who venture into human worlds after our generation has rejoined Na'Staani!"

If only it were that simple. She'd barely survived the reapings herself. Of course, that wasn't quite a fair comparison. She'd been learning on the fly, with no guidance and no support. Her successors would have the entire unammi population for support. Still, Booker wasn't sure how she felt about bequeathing that experience to another, much less three others. "I'll think about it."

"Oh, and I almost forgot," Kilbee said, his voice casual, as if it were nothing. "They offered me a position on the council

She gasped. "Kilbee, that's wonderful! Congratulations! You can do so much good—"

"Not so fast."

She stopped. "What?"

"I turned them down."

Booker blinked. "You what?"

"I can't do that and be out here helping you. Thrace said you needed me. So," he said, "here I am."

"Oh, but it doesn't have to be you," she fumbled, "I mean, yes, I trust you. I love the idea of working with you again—on better terms, this time—but I can't ask you to give up a council seat for me. That's too much."

"You didn't ask me to do anything. I had a choice, and I made it. Edanor is taking over at the outpost. She's brilliant. She'll do a fantastic job, so I'm all yours. Now," he said. "When are you going to tell me your plan? I know you have one. What are we doing?"

Booker stared at this man who'd seen her at her worst and yet chose to believe in her best. What had she done to change his mind?

Whispers and a distant rustling caught her attention, and she looked over Kilbee's shoulder. Elisul didn't show up, but she felt him

> *them*

as if his

> *their*

breath was on her neck

> *this is right*

raising thrill bumps down her spine and across her shoulders.

She regarded Kilbee. "Are you sure?"

"Positive," he said.

She told him the whole story of the snatchers in Bregaina, how she and Botha had managed to find and rescue Bika, Bika's fear, the struggle to make her understand, and Eli's promise that he would not rest until the others from her village were also back home.

Kilbee whistled, peering at her as if he were a child listening to tales at an elder's knee. "That's who these people are? And the ones I picked up from you last time? Last month?"

"Yep."

"No wonder they received such a happy reception," he said. "Is this all of them?"

"I don't know. But it's been only two months. I'm just reaching the point where I can gather resources and set up a base of operations." That sensation of feeling inundated began to creep in again, as if she were drowning in responsibilities and promises, and she stifled it. No room for that now. "Thus, my request for assistance."

"What about Harajüd, or Saacharis for our base?" he said. "I'm sure Thrace or Rizzo would help—"

"No." She didn't miss his reference to "our" base. "Rizzo is going to help. But," Booker said, "we can't do it on a corporate world. We can't involve the colonies. It has to be isolated. Besides," she said, "we still aren't sure what happened to the missing pilots. I hope to search for them while I'm already on the hunt. And there's more."

She told him of Knøfa's experiments on Bishtari, watched him struggle with shock and grief for a few moments, then told him of the crossed fetuses, and the three human surrogates. She couldn't tell how he felt about that. Glad as she was for human skin sometimes, there were occasions when she would give a lot to see a person's dermal display.

They stood in silence for a moment while the others talked and laughed among themselves.

"You're going to help them?" Kilbee said. "These human surrogates?"

"That's the plan. Or part of it," she said. "Is that a sticking point for you? Because if it is—"

"No." His voice was quiet, but firm. "Bishtari was my friend. I want to help her younglings, even if they won't be fully unammi." He stared out at the sky. "I wonder how she would feel about that?"

"I've had the same thought."

"How do you know these younglings will even be viable, though? Isn't it possible they'll be…" He stopped.

"Freaks?" she asked. "Unnatural? Crow said similar things about us, you know. We need to be better than that. If they're nonviable, the fetuses won't make it to term. If they do, well," she shrugged. "We'll figure it out as we go. There's no template for this kind of thing."

"This is why you need an isolated world?"

"Mmmm…in part. Yes. But I also don't know what'll happen with my attempts to keep that promise to Bika. We need space of our own, in case it goes sideways. I won't risk another village." Like she'd done to Bregaina. She touched his arm. "Are you with me?"

"Yes," he said. No hesitation. "Absolutely. I'd bet some of the other outcasts and relapsed mitigants would be, too. Do you want me to pull up that list of alternative worlds the pilots researched before we left Iridos? Or after we arrived on Earth?"

"No," she said, a small smile lifting her cheeks. "Bailey had a suggestion that was exactly what we need." She told him of Nidahn, what she'd read, and what she'd seen for herself, and sent the coordinates to his TICS pad. "Rizzo has committed to helping us with gear and equipment, habs, even some ships. She's probably dropped off some of our supplies by now. Once I've made this delivery, I'll be visiting two potential allies, so I need you to go to the new site with a setup team and supervise the work. And oh, by the way," she said, as if she'd just remembered, "I may have promised Rizzo delivery of some of Earth's resources in exchange for the Syndicate's delivery of supplies and infrastructure. That won't be a problem, will it?"

"I doubt it. I'll ask when I go back, which probably ought to be soon." He squinted at her. "But this isn't just about your promise to Bika, or the missing pilots, is it? Not for you, anyway. If that's all it was, we wouldn't need a new settlement, would we?"

She laughed. The Bregainans and their new friends stood around outside the ship chattering with one another. They had plenty of stories to share, more than they could squeeze into these few moments. Their trial might be over, but their nightmares would probably linger a long while. She couldn't help them with that, but being among their own people would be a comfort, a support while they healed.

"It's okay. You don't have to tell me what it is. Maybe you aren't sure yourself. But," Kilbee shook his head without taking his eyes off her, "I know you, Booker, or at least I know the real you. There will always be another cause. And that's admirable. Just remember that if you use up all your own energy, there will be none left to save someone else." He gripped her shoulder. "Take a rest. You know what happens when you push yourself too hard. Besides, you've earned it."

"I will," she said. "I promise."

He didn't buy it, but he didn't pursue it. Instead, he changed the subject. "You should know that it got ugly on my latest run. Guards got pushy before I managed to kill them. We lost two people in that scuffle," he said, sorrow and anger as mixed in his tone as the colors would've been on his skin.

"Damn." That made three lost. It had probably been naive to think she could save them all, but that didn't stop her from mourning every loss. Thank Na'Staani Kilbee hadn't been killed. "If Cartel folk are watching for us now, then Hannah's taken notice of our strikes. She'll see that our efforts have been focused on the Bregainans. She's gonna come for them."

What was it about that faction that made it such an ongoing problem? Booker had heard horror stories about the old admiral, Virgil. And Alira had personal experience with both Bellamy and Hannah. She'd have to deal with that threat at some point, but not today.

Booker crossed her arms, as if she were cold. "I suppose I should tell Botha they need to move their village."

"Probably smart." Kilbee rubbed his jaw.

"They're going to hate leaving their home."

"I know. But better a new landscape than what'll happen if she finds them."

"Right." The villagers were still waiting for her. "I should go, then. Get the word to them sooner rather than later."

"Got it. I'll touch base with Rizzo to confirm her delivery of supplies and setup materials, then check out Nidahn before I go home." He laughed. "'Course, 'home' is a relative concept now, isn't it?" He sobered. "We might wanna think about a new name, though. Wouldn't be smart to call it by the old human name, not if we don't want trouble later."

"I think we should call it 'Nexus.' It'll serve as a connecting point," she said. "For all of us. Who knows? Maybe it'll even be instrumental in bringing humans and unammi together one day."

He snorted. "I know you've been right many times. But I hope you'll forgive my skepticism on that."

"Done." A small grin curled her lips before fading. "Be careful."

"Yeah. You, too."

He crossed the ledge with ease and entered his own ship.

When it was in flight and aimed at the horizon, she approached her waiting passengers, who still hugged and chattered, tears on every face. She swallowed hard. "Are you all okay?"

They nodded, their expressions telling her they were still stunned to finally be free.

"Good. Let's get aboard and strap in. I'll have you home soon." She didn't address what would come after. That was a job for their village elders.

Once everyone was seated, Booker stepped past the bulkhead and into the jumper's cockpit. She raised the ship off the ground a few centimeters and gradually pivoted toward the cavern's mouth. She exited the cave slowly to avoid passing avians, and then they were off. A few more hours and they would see Bregaina.

chapter 71

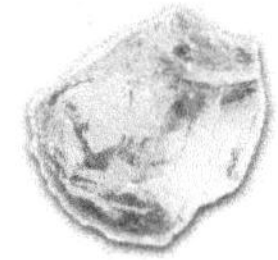

<u>Bregaina, Bejami</u>

THE MOMENT BOOKER'S CRAFT FLEW over the village, its inhabitants boiled out of their dwellings above the rising tide. By the time she landed, many boats were on their way. She settled the jumper in its docked status, shut down the engines, and swiveled in her seat.

"Welcome home."

They unbuckled and rushed her, each one touching her arms as she tried to exit the cockpit. "Thank you, thank you," they chanted, while she fought a lump in her throat. Then they were out the hatch and onto the platform, shouting for their loved ones, those they hadn't seen in more than two months. Those they had believed were lost. Their joyful reunions strummed something in Booker she'd thought long gone. It was all she could do to maintain her composure.

At the edge of the crowded waterway, Botha stood in his boat, his pole keeping him steady and motionless until the others had passed on their way to their own dwellings, their own families, bringing those rescues who came from different places along as if they were honored guests. His gaze flitted from one boat to the next before it landed on her form where she still stood atop the platform. When she was finally alone, he poled his way to the ladder and climbed up. At the top, he paused.

She came forward, her hands extended. "You are Botha?"

He nodded without speaking. He watched her, weighed her actions. Botha always saw far more than the surface of things. She should know.

"I'm Booker. Spencer Kilbee and Rizzo told me of you."

"Did they?" Botha's eyes sparkled like glints of daylight on the water. "They never mentioned you."

She managed to keep a straight face. "Perhaps it slipped their minds."

"Are they well?"

"Yes, but I bring a warning." She hated to give him this news.

"The snatchers will come again."

Her breath caught. He'd already realized this?

Silly question. Of course he had. Botha hadn't gotten to be a village elder by being stupid. "Yes. The Cartel will have noticed our pattern of hitting sites with Bregainan slaves."

"I saw this fish coming. It rippled the water." He tipped his shoulder toward the ladder. "Come and eat. Bika and the other families have prepared a feast, but you can understand if we don't gather in the communal space. You are welcome in our home."

Booker hesitated. "I should go."

He cocked his head. "You should stay." His smile peeked out from behind his stern stranger-face. "At least for a while."

"Okay." She locked down the jumper and followed him down the ladder to the boat.

He poled away from the platform in the direction of his own shared dome. "Your people have returned many of our folk," he said, his voice gentle, distant, "but some are still missing. Are they…" His voice trailed off, as if he didn't trust it to continue.

He wanted to ask about Yele. She didn't have to be a reader to know that. But he wouldn't do it. It wasn't in Botha to put his own wants before those of others in the village. Booker wished she could reassure him, but she'd not found Botha's partner again. Not yet. She hoped he still lived. If not, Bika and the others would surely blame Eli even more than they already did. He'd been *right there,* and—

Enough. She'd done what she could do under the circumstances. Besides, guilt would serve no purpose here. She pressed it down to settle uneasily in her chest. "We're still searching for the rest. It would be helpful if you could give us a list of names and physical descriptions of everyone still absent." She cleared her throat. "I do know, though, that not all of them survived. One of Kilbee's ops took five lives. Two of those were from your village. Another rescue grabbed workers toiling in frigid waters. One of your villagers succumbed to the cold."

He didn't speak.

She sighed. "I'm sorry we could not save them, too."

He swung to regard her. "Don't be sorry, Booker. They have gone shining to join with the air, the water, the trees, the land. They will be remembered."

As they neared Botha's domed dwelling, voices raised in celebration reached her ears. Somewhere, farther afield, a drumbeat started and was joined by a flute. They reached the ladder at her host's platform and climbed up to be greeted by Bika. "Botha convinced you to stay. This makes me happy. Come! Eat! There is plenty to share." Bika took Botha's arm and drew him aside, leaving Booker to fend for herself.

The central room of the dome reached high above those gathered. Muggy as it was, the structure of the building was such that hot air rose to be vented at the top, while cooler air came in near the floor. Booker felt as if she were standing in a breeze.

A table stretched the length of the space and groaned beneath the weight of so much food. Villagers made rounds of the table, circling it to access all the edibles then standing aside with friends and family. Others came or went through the door. Similar scenes were likely playing out in other homes throughout the village.

One of those she'd brought home from the brothel stood across the room talking to a small group. At one point, he gestured at Booker. The others with him all stared at her. She responded with a smile, but suddenly the room seemed too crowded, the air too thick with the smell of rich foods, the joy too palpable, the awkwardness unbearable. Booker hurried for the door and the platform beyond. She needed a moment alone.

The afternoon waned, sending shadows across the village, one dome's shade stretching across the next, shapes of swaying marsh grasses dancing alongside. Long-legged wading birds lifted off at her presence, flying toward distant marsh trees where they would roost for the night, high off the ground in relative safety.

It would be nice to join them. As if escape, for her, would be that easy. Far more clever predators sought her and those who helped her cause.

A sound announced Botha's approach, and he came to stand beside her.

"You did not eat."

"I'm not hungry."

"A celebration means feasting." He pointed at the water, where something jumped and splashed. "You see? Even the fishes join in."

"What are they doing?" Booker grinned.

"Hunting. Insects come closer to the water at night, searching for their own meals." He watched a moment, then raised his gaze to take in the whole scene, as if memorizing its every detail. "Beautiful, is it not? I will miss it."

His grief swelled in his expression, his body language. Its presence filled the space between and around them until she could not help but breathe it in. A dagger of pain shot through her. It wasn't entirely her fault his people needed to move, but it was she who had brought the warning about Hannah's wrath. He had already reached the same conclusion, true. Still, she felt responsible.

"But," he said, winking at her, "we will make a new home, someplace where animals will be more of a threat than the snatchers. Every place has its dangers but the lênask, at least, we can fight."

The pitch of his voice, the tilt of his head said he believed every word. But it would be hard leaving their home. Booker knew how that felt.

He peered closer at her, as if examining an odd insect. "Your face is unfamiliar," he said. "But I know you. Do I not?"

"I don't know how you would." A chill raised bumps along her arms. "This is my first time to Bregaina."

"Is it?" he said. "You remind me of a dear friend. Is she well?"

"I'm not sure I know who you mean."

"Mmm," Botha said. "I told her once that I did not know why the currents had carried her across my bow. Now, I do. If I had not met her, my life would be the poorer and my people still enslaved." He winked. "Give her our love when you see her.

"Now, come. Eat. Drink a cup or two of úta." His eyes appeared so innocent, except for that gleam of amusement.

She tried not to smile. "I don't consume alcohol."

"Ah." His lips twitched. "Neither does my friend. No matter. There are plenty of other juices to drink…Booker."

She ignored the slight emphasis on her name. "But I've heard mouth-watering tales of the savory, unfermented bh'tati. Might I try those?"

He laughed and led her back inside.

chapter 72

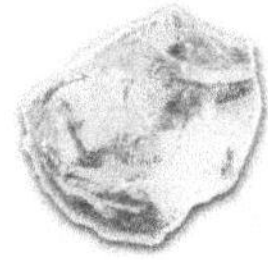

Aboard The Kukri

<u>On Approach to the Nexus Settlement, Nidahn</u>

STARS SLURRED THROUGH THEIR MILKY transition into distinct points of light as she brought the small cargo vessel out of interstel. Before her, the planet shone like a beacon, welcoming her home. Current tilt meant summer for the northern hemisphere, where the ice pack retreated, and marshy tundra exuded mists into the air to cloud the landscape.

Booker dove into the atmosphere, already looking forward to stepping on solid ground. Maybe she'd stay here a while this time. The settlement was the closest thing she had to a home, but it was only a couple of months into its development, nowhere near finished yet. Another pair of hands would be welcome. As she neared, light flashed in the small, unfrozen segment of turquoise ocean offshore near the encampment. She slowed, dropped her altitude, and came around to circle the hab compound below before settling into their landing site.

She sat in the *Kukri* even after the engines shut down, listening to its familiar creaks and groans. It was the first one Rizzo had provided, followed by several other, newer craft. The younger Nexus pilots preferred those, but Booker liked this one best. It always seemed to anticipate her needs as if they'd been long acquainted, though she'd used it first only a few months ago.

Someone banged on the hatch with a metallic tool, and she huffed a laugh. No subtlety in the Nexans, but then that was to be expected. Life was uncertain for them. They didn't want to waste a single minute. Booker understood that sentiment all too well.

She heaved herself out of the seat and opened the hatch. "Food supplies in hold one, medical in two, mechanical in three. Do you need help unloading?"

"No," said the man at the hatch. "We've got it. Spencer Kilbee is waiting for you in the compound."

Of course he was. Her nursemaid would make it his job to be here when her arrival was expected. It's just as well he'd picked a replacement to run the outpost, since he was hardly ever there anymore. She walked toward the settlement, holding an irolium chunk in her pocket. The path between the landing site and their cleared living space snaked through thick, wild growth. Trees, shrubs, vines, and wildflowers vied for space, while birds and some sort of fluttering, colorful insect pollenated the fruits. They were still testing those for edibility. Meanwhile, they'd been bringing in most of their own food, thanks in part to Rizzo, Georgeanne, and Bardo. Each of her meetings with the two new allies had gone well and promised to produce fruits of their own. She'd not shared with them the Nexus location yet. That piece of information was too precious. For now, she could only hope those humans would be as reliable and trustworthy as Rizzo, but she had a good feeling so far.

She stepped out of the woods into the compound. The edge of the clearing was sharp, as if it had been cut out of the forest with a knife. In fact, it had. She'd helped to clear the land herself, to widen the open space for their settlement and provide a buffer between the habs and the wooded areas. It hadn't been hard, but it had taken them over a week to finish. Another week for her cargo pilots to bring in the habs from Rizzo and Bardo. Georgeanne had sent food plants and medicines, which they used, and legal recreationals, which they did not. Those were offered in payment for the things they *did* need.

Kilbee stood between two of the habs, still in conversation with a couple of human crewmen. He finished whatever they were discussing as she drew near.

"How did it go?"

Booker shrugged. "Botha and his people are settling in at their new site. It's beautiful, and much safer. Snatchers could still get to them, but it wouldn't be easy. And it wouldn't be from the air. I had to get there by boat."

In the two months since she'd first shown this persona to Botha, Booker had been to Bregaina several times. This last visit, prior to returning to Nexus, she'd also brought Yele home. The vision of him climbing the ladder to his family's platform in the new village, the shouts and tears and hugs as Botha and his other partners greeted their loved one, would stay with her a long time. Her joy in bringing the last of the Bregainans home, great as it was, had been eclipsed by Bika's smile and Botha's meaningful nod.

Oh yeah. He knew who she was.

"And," Kilbee grinned, "snatchers would have to contend with the wildlife, too. Bregainans are accustomed to that. Cartel crew are not."

"True." She still hated that any of it had happened at all.

"Stop," he said, his tone soft.

"What?"

"Don't give me that. I see you grieving. It wasn't your fault," he said, touching her shoulder. "What happened to them.

Maybe not, but the Bregainans would always blame Eli.

"I know." She scanned the area. "Who's onsite, besides the usual crew?"

"Twelve humans, twenty-one outcasts and relapsed mitigants."

"Have any of them made the connection to this world's history?"

"No." Kilbee checked their immediate surroundings. "Far as they know, this is just some world none of the other colonies wanted."

"What about the humans who are here now? Do any of them know…" her voice trailed off.

"No." He dropped his voice. "We all keep to our human forms outside our habs. It seemed safer. I trust these humans, to a point. But this—"

"Good call." She touched his arm. "Rizzo knows. So does Bailey. The rest…" Booker paused. "The more of them that know, the less secure this site will be." Even the three surrogates who'd chosen to bear their special babes didn't know unammi were here on site. Not yet, anyway. That might change at some point. She hoped it would, but for now, Booker withheld that bit of truth from them.

Kilbee snapped his fingers. "I almost forgot," he said, "I have a surprise for you." He took off toward her hab, one of the few set in a smaller cleared patch beneath the forest canopy nearby.

She followed, greeting others who called to her along the way and pushing leaves out of the way as she walked.

Kilbee stood at the entry to her hab. "After you."

Frowning, Booker brushed past him and into the compact living space to find a small cluster of irolium growing on a seedstone attached near the top of her hab. The rush of energy filled her and, for a moment, her Companion's presence rustled in her mind. The Iri had been willing to try spreading into other surfaces besides stone. Perhaps they already did, on the worlds of those other beings her Companion had shown her in Its shifting form. How long would the Iri take, she wondered idly, to grow this cluster beyond its current size?

"It's perfect," she said. "Do you have one too?"

"Not here. On the outpost, they've started a fairly large growth. It was Galen's idea. And it appears to be working. We've set up a few others in scattered locations." He waved at the hab around her with a flourish. "But now you can stay here more often. Leave some work for the rest of us."

She stared up at the stones' soft glow, glad that it would not show through the opaque hab walls. "Won't the humans wonder what it is?"

"They've already asked. I told them it was something you found on an obscure world, that it was something you carried with you from place to place like a piece of home."

She shook her head. "You've built up quite the reputation for Booker."

"Only some of it is made up." He pointed at her cot. "Sleep. You need it."

"I will. Later." She gestured toward the compound. "There's work to be done. It might be nice to do simple labor for a while, instead of running ops."

He grimaced.

Her smile faded. "What?"

"Yeah. About that."

"What is it?" she pressed.

"Hannah's expanding her reach. Word is she sent a shipment of slaves to Ranafta a few days ago." He peered at her. "But your promise to Bika was fulfilled with this last run. No one would blame you if you pulled us off that part of the project."

Maybe Kilbee had a point. Still…

Booker thought about the situations she'd seen the Bregainans endure. Even now, she saw their faces when they were pulled out, and when this last group—and Yele—was reunited with their village. Galen had been right about humans. Even if some were bastards, like Crow or Bellamy or Knøfa, most were kind, benevolent souls just living their lives and leaving others to do the same. Those were the ones who became victims. Like the Bregainans. Could she really relax and leave them to their fates?

Her human voices murmured and she shushed them. She didn't need their input for this.

"Do we know exactly where they are? How many? All the pertinent details?"

"Not yet." He dropped his gaze. "You're not gonna stop, are you?"

Booker considered her response as she smoothed her hair, touched the fraying braids at each temple, the wrinkled wattle at her neck, the deep lines at the corners of her eyes. She liked this disguise. Its anonymity proved useful. And there were seven unammi pilots still unaccounted for. Someone should be working to find them. She supposed that would be her.

"No."

"Okay," he said, as if he'd know what her answer would be. "Well, we can't take any action until we get more details. I'm expecting an update soon."

"How are our special guests?"

He winced. "Two of them miscarried."

Her throat tightened. Her people couldn't even call the younglings' names, as they had done for Bishtari. "Which ones?"

"Solji," he said, "and Miisa."

"Were they…could you tell…"

"No." Kilbee's voice dropped to a murmur. "They were not well-formed, for either a human or an unammi fetus."

She heaved a sigh. Whether it was of relief or of mourning, she was not yet sure. "You disposed of the remains?"

"We did." He stood with arms akimbo. "Both of the women asked to stay on, be made part of the team. They had a pretty close friendship with Kaarina. Partly, I think they want to stay close to her, but I think they also feel strongly connected to what we're trying to do here. I told them I'd ask you." He squinted at her. "What do you want to do?"

"The readers confirmed their truthfulness, right? That they can be trusted?"

"As much as they can, yes. It isn't foolproof, though."

"Good enough for me. I say we welcome them. Let them make this their new home." She glanced in the direction of the makeshift camp. "It's not like we don't need the help."

She had so many mixed emotions about those lost younglings, about what they could've been. Maybe a visit to Solji and Miisa would help to comfort them. "What of Kaarina?"

"She's well. Working on one of the crews, as a matter of fact. Nothing that might risk the child."

"I'd like to see her, please."

He started to leave. At the door, he hesitated. "After you speak to her, will you please rest? Let your guard down? I'll send Betron with Kaarina. He can wait outside your door afterward and keep away anyone with questions so you can drop the mask for a while."

She almost said no. She didn't need a keeper, but with humans around it might be best to have someone outside to warn her if someone approached. It wouldn't do, at this point, for the others to discover she was unammi. "He has no other tasks to manage?"

"Nothing more important than this," Kilbee said. "Besides, in case you didn't know, he's one of your biggest fans. He'll be honored to do this."

"I'll think about it," she said, her mouth twitching toward a grin.

She walked around the small hab, refamiliarizing herself with its few furnishings and accoutrements, replaying scenes from her last few operations. She had yet to find anything so rewarding as the joy those Bregainans had shown when they were reunited with their families. No, she didn't expect to be stopping that work any time soon.

A sound at the door caught her attention as Kaarina ducked inside. Good thing the habs had some height to them. The surrogate stood taller than Booker. Brown curls tumbled down her back from the rough cap she wore for warmth. The woman's belly swelled beneath her outer clothing.

"Greetings," Booker said. "It's been a few months since we spoke at the Syndicate base. Do you remember me?"

"Yes," Kaarina said, her voice unsteady.

"Good. Are you comfortable here? Is there anything more we can do to help you feel at ease?"

Kaarina glanced around the hab. "No. I'm fine."

This did not seem like the same woman she'd met in the guest quarters on Rizzo's base. Booker tipped her head at the trembling woman. "Then why do I feel as though you are afraid?"

"Are they true? All the things people here say about you?"

Not that again. Booker muttered under her breath. She'd need to speak to Kilbee about that. At least Kaarina met Booker's eyes. She couldn't take it if the Nexus settlers started looking at her like her own people had done on Earth, after they killed Knøfa's ship.

"What things do they say about me?"

"That you overcame three Trader guards on a ship in transit and saved a whole crew of slaves."

What? Booker blinked. How had they known that was her? She wasn't wearing this persona then.

"That you hit another guard so hard he flew ten meters before hitting the ground and was killed instantly."

Booker almost laughed. Ten meters indeed. That guard had still been alive when she left.

"That you killed a Trader admiral and escaped another. That you stole a shipment of supplies from a corpgov and routed the food and materials here. That you—"

Booker gestured, and Kaarina fell silent.

"Some is true," Booker admitted. "Some is exaggerated. Some is patently false. But I am certainly nothing for you to fear. Have you changed your mind about this child?"

The woman frowned. "No. I understand why it's so special. But I suppose it frightened me when Solji and Miisa lost their babies. I just...I don't know what to expect. I've never had a baby before."

They had that in common, Kaarina and Booker. "And new things bring uncertainty."

"Yes."

Booker stepped closer, peering at the woman's abdomen. "How many weeks are you now?"

Kaarina's hand went to her belly. "About eighteen."

Human voices clamored in Booker's head. Too early for a human fetus to be this developed, this large. Not so for an unammi one. "Is this also part of why you are afraid?"

Kaarina's lips quivered. "Yes," she whispered.

"Do you mind if I..." Booker reached toward Kaarina.

"No." She dropped her arms to her sides.

Booker moved closer, touched Kaarina's clothing, tentative at first. When the mother did not object, Booker flattened her palm against the distended abdomen. Tendrils of her awareness reached into the woman's fruiting womb, seeking answers to Kaarina's questions, as well as her own. After a moment, she nodded.

"You're carrying twins." Booker wasn't sure whether this was good news or bad, but she—

Another awareness responded from Kaarina's womb, its touch so featherlight Booker might've imagined it. She reached in once more, trying to make contact, but felt nothing more from the babes.

Her arm fell to her side. She stepped back, staring at Kaarina's belly. Had she felt what she thought she had?

"What is it?" Kaarina said, both hands going to her abdomen as if to protect her unborn young. "Is something wrong?"

Booker dragged her gaze to Kaarina's and smiled.

"Nothing's wrong," she said. "Nothing at all."

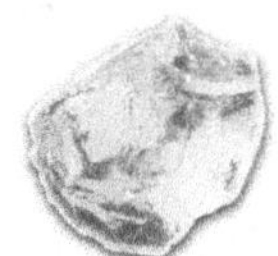

Did you enjoy this book? Please leave a rating and/or comment wherever books are reviewed and help others find and enjoy it, as well!

Sign up for Drema's newsletter!

You'll get occasional sneak peaks at upcoming stories, project updates, news on Drema's appearances, garden pictures, and cat news.

You'll also be the first to receive announcements about upcoming book releases, cover reveals, special promotions, and other juicy tidbits from Niveym Arts.

https://niveymarts.com/newsletter

You can also follow Drema on Facebook and BlueSky or subscribe to her blog for adventures in indie publishing, personal news and adventures, and other random posts.

Blog: https://www.dremadeoraich.com
Facebook: https://www.facebook.com/NiveymArtsLLC
BlueSky: @dremadeoraich.bsky.social

Acknowledgments

Though the Founder's Seed universe has more stories coming, *Driven*—book three in *this* series—was the completion of phase one in a long-term project. I owe thanks to many people for helping me bring it to your hands:

My beloved beta readers—Becky, Bob, David, Dylan, John, Lillith, Mary Lou, Michael, and Vince—for helping me identify plot holes, rough spots, and readability issues and who, by now, might be able to quote lengthy passages from the book as well as I can.

Grace Erin, John, Lauran, and Mary Lou for help in honing *Driven's* blurb to perfection—because all writers know that writing the perfect back-cover blurb is almost as hard as writing the whole book.

Thea Wallace of Lingo Whiz CC, for Afrikaans-English translation. Thanks for honing my rough Google translate versions of this beautiful language into realistic words and phrases correct for the story's context.

Jeff Coté, for teaching me the healing meditation process Botha uses in Alira's training.

My editor, Lauran Strait, who helped me smooth out all the unnecessary kinks, and who helped me decide which kinks were worth keeping.

My proofreader, Liesel Fitzgerald, for catching all the blips everyone else missed. Welcome to the TFS gang, Liesel!

Francis and the team at 100Covers who once again designed the perfect cover from my garbled concept notes.

My friends and associates who cheered me on as this long-overdue conclusion (of sorts) cranked toward the finish line.

And most especially B, for all the things, all the time, every day, everywhere. Thank you, Silly Man. I love you!

Special Note

Chapter eight makes reference to an Apple Blossom Meadery, which is my own invention. However, the Honey'd Spiced Apple mead mentioned in that same chapter is very real, very tasty (award-winning, in fact), and available through Starrlight Mead.

Check out Starrlight meads and ciders on their website. Better yet—next time you're in Pittsboro, North Carolina, look them up and arrange a tasting!

Starrlight Mead & Cider
130 Lorax Lane
Pittsboro, North Caroline 27312
984-312-5820
starrlightmead.com
info@starrlightmead.com

About the Author

Drema Deòraich is an award-winning author of speculative fiction that sometimes asks big questions. Her flash fiction, short stories, and novelettes have been published in numerous online journals, as well as a few semi-professional zines.

Her debut novel *Entheóphage*, a medical sci-fi/climate fiction novel, was published in 2022, and received the Literary Titan Gold Book Award in November of 2024. "Phagey" (as it is affectionately known by its fans) has become a subject of book club discussions in many places.

Her second novel, *Fallen*, first book in the science fantasy trilogy, *The Founder's Seed*, was released on May 1, 2024, and was awarded the Literary Titan Gold Book Award later that same year.

Broken, Drema's third release, was released in November of 2024, and continues the *Founder's Seed* saga.

Drema currently lives in Southeast Virginia with her husband, his two cats, and all her other characters. When time and mosquitoes permit, Drema works on transforming the lawn around their small home into more welcoming habitat for birds, butterflies, bees, and other wildlife. She also occasionally blogs about writing, ideas from Life that inspire her, environmental issues, ways to live more sustainably, and whatever else captures her fancy. Follow her writing posts at www.dremadeoraich.com, and her environmental posts at www.niveymarts.com.

Currently, Drema is hard at work on the first book in the Nexus trilogy, which takes place in The Founder's Seed universe, and continues the story begun in TFS. When not writing, she helps her legal-eagle boss save the world one case at a time, pets her husband's cats, plays games with her beloved B, or spends time in Nature, surrounded by flora and fauna.

Also by Drema Deòraich

Entheóphage
https://books2read.com/Entheophage

FALLEN
The Founder's Seed Trilogy Book 1
https://books2read.com/Fallen-The-Founders-Seed-1

BROKEN
The Founder's Seed Trilogy Book 2
https://books2read.com/Broken-The-Founders-Seed-2

~ • ~

Coming Soon:

(Title to be determined)
Book 1 of The Nexus Trilogy
(Still in progress)

"Cleanup Crew" (dark speculative fiction)
(Still in progress)

<h1 style="text-align:center">Appendix A</h1>

<h3 style="text-align:center">Characters List</h3>

Abeo (ah-BAY-oh)—Human. One of Botha's partners.

Alira (ah-LEE-rah)—Unammi. Has multiple human personae.

Bailey Madden—See Madden, Bailey.

Baldric, Thrace (BAHL-drihk, THRAES)—Unammi. Galen's primary human persona. Admiral in command of The Consortium Trader faction.

Bardo (BAR-doh)—Human. Admiral of The Order Trader faction. Childhood friend of Rizzo.

Bellamy (BEH-lah-mee)—Human. Past admiral of the Cartel Trader faction. Deceased. Now lives on as one of Alira's harvests.

Betron (beh-TROHN)—Unammi. One of Alira's biggest supporters.

Bika (BEE-kuh)—Human. Botha's primary partner.

Bishtari (bish-TAH-ree)—Unammi. Outcast pilot assigned to Danua.

Booker (BOOK-ur)—Unammi. One of Alira's human personas.

Botha (BOI-tah)—Human. Beloved elder in the village of Bregaina on the human colony world Bejami. Called "Baba" by some outside his village.

Braithwaite, Jukka (BRAYTH-wayt, JOO-kuh)—Human. Captain and head of security in The Syndicate Trader faction.

Ceala (see-AH-lah)—Unammi. Frem in disagreement with the Council. Folmir's mother.

Cesar (say-ZAHR)—Unammi. Killed in the Fall of Iridos. Now lives on as one of Alira's harvests.

Cohen, Kisle (KO-ehn, KYL)—Human. Mira Cohen's brother.

Cohen, Mira (KO-ehn, MEE-rah)—Human. First name Mira. Captain and second in command in The Consortium Trader faction.

Companion—Other. The ethereal multifaceted "entity" that represents the hive mind of all the Iri, not just on Iridos, but everywhere; appears to

Alira as Guide and Advisor. Only she can see him/them. See also "Iri" in the Glossary.

Crow—Originally human. Deceased. Now lives on as one of Alira's harvests.

Dawa, Tenzin (DAH-wah, TEHN-zihn)—Former human persona of Galen. Now abandoned.

Downing, Harlan (DOW-neeng, HAR-lehn)—Human. Security chief for Harajüd House Unlimited.

Dupré, Hannah (doo-PREE, HA-nuh)—Human. Admiral in command of The Cartel Trader faction.

Dyson (DI-suhn)—Unammi. One of the councilors on Iridos.

Edanor (EH-duh-nor)—Unammi. Pilot for the Consortium. Stationed at the outpost.

Elias Sullivan—See Sullivan, Elias.

Elisul (ee-LI-suhl)—The name given to The Founder by all unammi.

Esther (EH-stur)—Unammi. Was one of Ijydin's human personas. Now used occasionally by Alira.

Faraad (fah-RAHD)—Unammi. Outcast pilot assigned to Danua.

Folmir (FOHL-meer)—Unammi youngling now living on Earth.

Galen (GAY-lehn)—Unammi. Alira's lover and partner. Has used multiple human personae in the past but is currently using only Thrace Baldric.

Georgeanne (jorj-ANN)—Human. Admiral of the Federation Trader faction. Sometimes called George, but never to her face, except by a select few trusted individuals.

Hannah Dupré—See Dupré, Hannah.

Harlan Downing—See Downing, Harlan.

Henri (awn-REE)—Human. Deceased. Past Admiral of The Clan Trader faction. Admiral Tsurin's predecessor and mentor.

Ijydin (ee-JEE-dihn)—Unammi. Killed as a result of the attack on Iridos. Now lives on as one of Alira's harvests.

Jaru (JAH-roo)—Human. One of Botha's partners.

Jukka Braithwaite—See Braithewaite, Jukka.

Kaarina (kah-REE-nuh)—Human. Female slave purchased by Danua Clan to serve as a surrogate mother.

Kilbee, Spencer (KILL-bee, SPEHN-suhr)—Unammi. One of the human personas of Tiral. Serves as a merchant in the employ of the Consortium Trader faction.

Kisle—See Cohen, Kisle.

Knøfa (NEW-fuh)—Human. Acting Admiral in command of The Clan Trader faction.

Logan Roucharde—See Roucharde, Logan.

Lourdes (LOR-dehs)—Human. The woman who purchased young Turizomi (later known as Rizzo) from The Cartel, raised and educated her, then set her free.

Lurien (LOO-ree-ehn)—Unammi. Alira's mother. Killed in The Fall of Iridos.

Madden, Bailey (MAH-dehn, BAY-lee)—Human. Captain and second in command in The Syndicate Trader faction.

Michels, Luther (MI-kuhlz, LOO-thuhr)—Human. Deceased. Was Vice Chair of Saacharis Aggregate Mining. Did not survive questioning by Rizzo regarding his approval of child slaves in the mine.

Mira Cohen—See Cohen, Mira.

Miisa (MEE-sah)—Human. Female slave purchased by Danua Clan to serve as a surrogate mother.

Nyros (NEE-rohs)—Unammi. Alira's brother. Killed by Crow. Now lives on as one of Alira's harvests.

Oni (OH-nee)—Human. One of Botha's partners.

Rakalesh (rah-KAY-lehsh)—Unammi. One of the surviving unammi councilors.

Reyes, Thomas (RAY-ehz, TAH-muhs)—Human. Deceased. Was manager of the Gauri Metalb Mine on the human colony world of Saacharis. Did not survive questioning by Rizzo regarding his use of child slaves in the mine.

Rizzo (RIH-zoh)—Human. Known to a rare few by her childhood name of Turizomi. Admiral of The Syndicate Trader faction.

Rook—Human. Captain in The Cartel Trader faction. Deceased. Now lives on as one of Alira's harvests.

Roucharde, Logan (roo-SHARD, LOH-guhn)—Human. Chairman of the board of directors for Harajüd House Unlimited.

Sa'abah (sah-AH-bah)—Human. Captain and head of security in The Consortium Trader faction.

Skalar, Malcolm (skah-LAHR, MAL-cuhm)—Human. Admiral of The Consortium Trader faction. Deceased. Now lives on as one of Alira's harvests.

Solji (SOOL-jee)—Human. Female slave purchased by Danua Clan to serve as a surrogate mother.

Spencer Kilbee—See Kilbee, Spencer.

Sullivan, Elias (SUH-lih-vahn, ee-LI-uhs)—Human. First Founder of Iridos. Also the human face of the Companion when communicating with Alira, and (as Eli) a human persona of Alira when among humans.

Sweeney, Andrea (SWEE-nee, AHN-dree-uh)—Human. Adjutant to Admiral Thrace Baldric.

Tenzin—See Dawa, Tenzin.

Thrace Baldric—See Baldric, Thrace.

Tiral—Unammi. Pilot and outcast. Has multiple human personas, most commonly Spencer Kilbee.

Trask, Michael (TRASK, MI-kuhl)—Human. Second in command to Acting Admiral Knøfa.

Trumo (TROO-moh)—Unammi. A youngling with whom Alira feels a strong kinship.

Tsurin (TSOOR-ihn)—Human. Admiral of The Clan Trader faction. Injured by a cornered unammi pilot on Danua.

Turizomi (too-rih-ZOH-mee)—Human. Admiral Rizzo's birth name. This is not common knowledge.

Yele (YEH-leh)—Human. One of Botha's partners.

Yoloron (YOH-luh-rahn)—Unammi. An elder who serves on the Council and supports Alira's actions/beliefs.

Appendix B

Glossary

aes (AY-ehs) *Unameze* —Are. Can also be and often is merged with another part of the sentence (most often the adverb which qualifies or gives focus to the verb).

Aes te nalya (AY-es teh NAH-lee-yah) *Unameze*—We are one.

Ag nee! *Afrikaans*—Oh no! Expression of dismay/dread or negation.

Aggregate—Refers to Saacharis Aggregate Mining, the corporate governing body on the human colony world Saacharis.

atlish (AHT-lihsh) *Unameze*—Indigenous to Iridos. Large serpentine predator.

Baba (BAH-bah)—Father. Term of respect used by many humans as an honorific for tribal and village elders.

barrens, the—Regions common to certain latitudes both north and south on the human colony world Danua. Characteristics include cold and temperamental weather, rocky and hilly terrain, minimal stunted scrub, scattered caverns and barrows, and a few hardy wildlife species.

basu'tao (buh-SOO-tuh-ow) *Unameze*—Be still. Be quiet.

Bejami (beh-JAH-mee)—One of twelve colony worlds. Governed by the Bejami Trust. Not a planet, but a moon in orbit around a gas giant in the Emlacha star system (same as Rubene), though the Bregainans call the star Lynju. Bejami is home to the Mandoslóna prison continent. No space port. Single landport located in the capital city of Bel-Rhovan.

Bejhur asane (beh-ZHOOR AH-sah-nay) *Unameze*—I'm not ready.

Bel-Rhovan (behl-ROH-vahn)—Bejami's capital city. Smaller than most cities on other worlds. Bejami prefers to keep settlements small, but Bel-Rhovan comes close to breaking that rule/precept. Many tourist attractions here. Located on the continent of Dórucuin in the northern hemisphere.

bewondering *Afrikaans*—Admiration.

bh'tati (buh-TAH-tee)—Native to Bejami. Oceanic fruit of enormous seaweed forests in Dairnen Bay on the west coast of Dórucuin. Savory, salty, juicy. Center of the fruit is eaten raw or in stews. Pulp from layer between edible center and rubbery skin is used in pigments for tattoos, paints, dyes, etc. Rubbery skin is soaked in other fruit juices and allowed to ferment. Makes an alcoholic mead-like drink. (See úta.) Fruit is harvested by divers.

Bindhu (BIHN-doo)—Human spiritual practice. The word bindhu means dot, or point. In metaphysical terms, Bindhu is held to be the point at which creation begins and the point at which the many becomes the One. Beliefs consist mainly of peaceful coexistence and avoiding violence, unless there is no other option. Varying levels include paths to suit most practitioners: *Ashaan Path* encourages rigorous training of the body and mind until it is a finely honed instrument/weapon; *Shidara Path* espouses asceticism and withdrawal from daily life; and *Tuchani Path* explores sexuality as a route to enlightenment. All paths teach meditation. Bindhu practice expects this as a daily regimen.

Bly stil…kom terug in die kamer in… *Afrikaans*—Angry statement. Be quiet. Get back in the room.

Bregaina (breh-GAY-nuh) — Second largest village on Bejami. This is Botha's home. All buildings situated on platforms raised above the delta so that the tide can ebb and flow beneath them.

bryse (BREE-suh) *Unameze*—to "nudge" or gently "push" someone or something (at the cellular and atomic level) toward a desired outcome.

canara (cah-NAH-rah) *Unameze*—Flute-like instrument used on Iridos; made from roots and thick stems of the odasen plant.

Cartel, The—Trader faction located on the human colony world Zebalu. Run by Admiral Hannah Dupré.

charsten (SHAR-stehn)—Indigenous to Danua. A breed of cattle with long, silky fur prized for its use in textiles.

charter worlds—Human colony worlds that signed on to the Intercolonial Charter in their early formation. Charter worlds include all twelve known human colonies. Only one human colony never signed on to the Charter. See Nidahn.

chithe (CHEE-thay) *Unameze*—no direct translation; familiar pet nickname for a youngling; acknowledges connection to and concern for the child.

Clan, The—Trader faction located on the human colony world Danua. Run by Acting Admiral Knøfa, and his action second-in-command, Captain Michael Trask.

comm—Communique. Communication between two locations. Message can be recorded and sent over interstel distances, or it can be live, real-time exchange intraplanet. Can be verbal, holovisual, or both. Can also be text only, but this is rare.

Consortium, The—Trader faction located on the human colony world Harajüd. Run by Admiral Thrace Baldric (human persona of unammi Galen) and her second in command, Captain Mira Cohen.

corpgov—Human slang term. Refers to corporate governments on the human colony worlds. Sometimes morphs into similar slang specific to each world, like Danuagov.

cycle—Unammi measure of time on Iridos, equivalent to "day" in human vernacular. As it is tidally locked, it has no sunrise/sunset to determine day length.

Dagons Pub (DAY-guhnz)—Upscale public house located in New Canaan, Harajüd. Owned and operated by The Consortium Trader faction.

Danua (DAN-yoo-ah)—One of twelve colony worlds. Governed by Danua Textiles. Located in the Restelys star system. Three small moons. Home to The Danua Clan Trader faction, run by Admiral Tsurin and her second-in-command, Captain Knøfa. Temperate equatorial zones, skirted north and south by rocky barrens, rolling hills, and polar zones. One space port. One landport.

Fall of Iridos, The—Also called "The Fall." A term used by unammi survivors to refer to the attacks on Iridos by the Consortium's armada. The majority of their population was killed during or as a result of the attacks. The unammi's city was destroyed, and the survivors all eventually evacuated.

familial house—One of the guilds on Iridos. This is where all new mothers live with their offspring until the younglings are old enough to be separated from them.

Fashere (fah-SHEER)—One of twelve colony worlds. Governed by Fashere Enterprises. Located in the Jaunuit star system. Two small moons. One space port. One landport.

fealle sprite (FEEL sprite) *Unameze*—Indigenous to Iridos. Surface-dwelling, four-legged animal with short dun-colored fur and skin that blends in well to the sandy background for camouflage. Huge, double-lidded eyes. Powerful hind legs. Short, wide, stumpy tail. The animal's hearing is poor, but its eyesight is keen. It can spot the slightest move nearby and will instantly leap into the air to escape potential threats. The wind then carries it a short distance before it lands, scurries away, and burrows under the sand to wait out the threat.

Federation, The—Trader faction located on the human colony world Rubene. Run by Admiral Georgeanne (a.k.a. George) and second in command, Captain Claudio.

frem (FREHM) *Unameze*—Adult in service to the unammi; the opposite of youngling.

Founder, The—The person responsible for bringing the unammi to Iridos in the distant past. Revered and honored, along with the others who came with him in that era, by contemporary unammi. See Sullivan, Elias in Appendix A, Characters List.

Founder's Daughter—An unammi female conceived through a union of the high councilor and Elias Sullivan (the Founder). Sullivan donated seed generations ago, which was preserved in a sealed vault encrusted with irolium that genetically alters its DNA. Only a Founder's Daughter can harvest those who die in her presence. Founder's Daughters can absorb the memories and knowledge (but not the gifts) of those who die within their presence. Also called a soul harvester. See harvest.

Gadney (GAD-nee)—One of twelve colony worlds. Governed by the Gadney Farm League. Located in the Biziar star system. One small moon. One space port. One landport.

Geeste van lug *Afrikaans*—Spirits of Air! An expression of awe.

Gelaboot *Afrikaans*—A made-up word comprised of fragments taken from "gelapte" (patched) and "boot" (boat). Slang term used among Bregainans and other Bejami villagers to refer to someone who is healing from mental, psychological, or physical injuries or ailments.

hab (HAB)—Slang term for habitat. Usually refers to a temporary living shelter, usually used in short-term, transitional camp setups, but can be more structurally sound for long-term use.

Haradhalen (hah-RAH-deh-lehn)—A small continent just south of, and connected by ice to, the northern polar cap on Bejami.

Harajüd (hah-RAH-joohd)—One of twelve colony worlds. Governed by Harajüd House Unlimited (HHU). Located in the Lakaya star system.

Seven moons, all small, icy; the largest holds medical isolation facilities under a pressurized dome. The largest and most affluent of all the colonies. Home to The Consortium Trader faction. One of the first three exoplanets to be settled by colonists from Earth. Five space ports, as well as one space-based shipbuilding port and one space-based repair station. Two landports.

harvest, the—Iridosian special skill granted only to Founder's Daughters, one in each generation, always a genetic female. This individual harvests or absorbs the memories and personalities of those who die in their presence. The harvest is seen as sacred. Not all harvesters survive; a few are driven mad by their harvests. Some refer to a harvest or to harvested souls as a reaping.

harvesting malady, harvesting sickness—The gradual loss of identity in an unammi harvester when she cannot control the harvests, and the absorbed personalities take her over.

Haven (HAY-vehn)—Capital city of the human colony world Danua. Located on the continent of Storelandsør.

hematium (heh-MAH-tee-uhm)—Metal found only on Iridos; holds very unique qualities, like the ability to shed a radioactive charge, which make it essential in contemporary shipbuilding. Highly valuable to the human colonies.

HHU—Refers to Harajüd House Unlimited, the corporate governing body on the human colony world Harajüd.

Holovid (HAH-loh-vihd)—Holographic video or visual.

hovercar—Small, groundcar-sized personal transport. Does not make physical contact with the ground to move. Ground-bound. Engines make a higher-pitched humming sound.

hye-won-hye (SHIH-wahn-shih)—An ancient symbol from the Adinkra culture in West Africa of old Earth where, stories say, elders would walk on fiery coals without burning their feet. The icon means "That which cannot be burned" and is a symbol of toughness and imperishability, an encouragement to endure and overcome difficulties.

ikanne (ee-KAHN-nay)—colorful saltwater shellfish that thrive only along the northern shores of Matakri and across the channel along the southern shores of Utatikra on Zebalu. Very flavorful. A big seller on Zebalu, but they don't last long enough to ship off-world. Their delicate shells, however, are beautiful, rainbow-hued, and translucent when dried. Big sellers both on- and off-world.

Intercolonial Charter—An agreement drawn up and signed by governing bodies of all twelve human colony worlds. Initially drafted and confirmed by the first three human colonies to be settled in Earth Year 2687, the Charter governs the vast majority of human interrelations between the colonies, as well as what is acceptable and legal on any one of those worlds, including (but not limited to): ecological sustainability, intercolonial time measures (standard day/week/month/year), weaponry, languages, the sanctity of the Contract, citizenship, rights and privileges due all citizens, responsibilities of all citizens, medical and other systems of law, population growth, extradition, governance, etc.

interstel craft—Interplanetary and interstellar flight capable. Smaller and most mid-size vessels can dock at landports. Larger ships may only dock at space port.

Iri (IH-ree) *Unameze*—Subquantum beings that lived in the surface of the caverns on Iridos, as well as many other places in other realms, other worlds. It is thought that they are hive-based entities, and that they and those with whom they find a connection, like the unammi, live in symbiotic relationship. On Iridos, that symbiosis produced irolium stones, which introduced special qualities into the unammi. (See irolium) The Iri appear to Alira in multiple forms as Guide and Advisor. See entry for Companion in Appendix A, Characters List.

Iridos (IH-rih-dohs)—The original homeworld of the unammi. Now annexed by Harajüd House Unlimited. See Fall of Iridos.

irolium (ih-ROH-lee-uhm)—A blue stone that encrusted several caverns on Iridos before The Fall. The stone emits low-level, non-thermal magnetic radiation. This crystal is the source of unammi special gifts. Salvaged after The Fall and transported with the surviving unammi to their new city on Earth. Also shared with the outcasts in various locations.

i'shin (ee-SHEEN) *Unameze*—Familiar pet name for a beloved friend or lover, either gender. A shortened combination of "my heart."

jakkal (jah-KAHL)—Indigenous to Bejami. Medium-sized canine-type mammal. Travel, hunt, and live in social packs. Females make the rules. Young are raised by all.

Jy is 'n gees? *Afrikaans*—You are a spirit?

Jy is veilig! Jy leef! Ag my vriend! *Afrikaans*—You are safe! You live! Oh, my friend…

jumper—Usually small (though can be mid-sized) personal transports. Atmospheric craft capable of flight within a single planet's atmosphere;

not FTL capable. More functional than stylish. Makes a small whining sound.

Kom terug… *Afrikaans*—Come back.

Kris Cross, The—Syndicate ship, command class.

LADRAS (LAH-druhs)—Stands for "Limited Area Dispersal Radiation System." LADRAS missiles are illegal, as are all radioactive weapons, by the terms of the Interplanetary Charter.

Lakaya (luh-KEYE-uh)—G-class star central to the Harajüd planetary system.

lênask (leh-NASK)—Indigenous to Bejami. Large omnivorous primate. Lives in the trees among equatorial jungles. Sharp canine teeth, long, strong limbs. Will eat anything, including humans. Will also eat its own, if they are mortally injured or born with challenges that make them unlikely to survive. Screeches in whooping cries as it attacks. Sometimes hunts in packs.

Levyron (leh-VI-ruhn)—One of twelve colony worlds. Governed by the Levyron Institute. Located in the G'laudis star system. One small moon, which holds a biohazards medical facility beneath a dome. Home to The Order Trader faction. Levyron has an axial tilt of 157°, and a retrograde rotation. Visible in the night sky is the Finbeck Galactic Arm, which extends beyond Levyron. One space port. One landport.

Livuce'ba wenaes bujhul (lih-VOO-chee-bah wee-NAY-uhs buh-ZHOOL) *Unameze*—Traditional saying at a Rite of Mourning. No direct translation; closest meaning is "By your loss we are diminished."

Mandoslóna (man-duh-SLOH-nuh)—A prison continent found on Bejami; bordered in the north by jungles filled with voracious predators, and on the East, South, and West by vicious riptides and frigid waters. Home to life-sentenced prisoners from all twelve human colony worlds.

Mari Bay (MAH-ree)—Large bay located on the coast of New Canaan, Harajüd, between the Syrinaia coastline and Shamashu Island.

Matendarma (mah-tehn-DAHR-mah)—A small fishing village on the northernmost tip of Javandra, on Zebalu.

medfac (MEHD-fak)—Refers to a medical facility.

med tech (MEHD TEHK)—Refers to medical staff who work in a medfac.

menserower *Afrikaans*—Kidnapper. Literally, "people thief."

mitigant—An unammi frem who has proven to be problematic to unammi society in one way or another and has undergone the process of mitigation.

mitigation—A physical process undertaken by healers on Iridos to "reprogram" a frem's entire brain. Its purpose is to "fix" frem who cannot adjust to a life of service, or whose mental connections go awry due to some unforeseen problems in their physical makeup. It is also used to "fix" those who become problematic in unammi society, a tool to bring them into line with social expectations so that they do not foster discontent in others.

Mjolnir Island (MYOHL-neer)—Large land mass on the human colony world Danua, located off the eastern coast of Landetorr in the southern hemisphere. Northern half is in the fertile latitudes. Southern half is in the southern barrens.

muil—(MWEEL) Indigenous to Bejami. Small wading bird found along shorelines in equatorial regions; eats insects, small fish, crustaceans, worms, etc. Nests in large ground colonies just inland of the marsh. Small-bodied, stands up to 38 cm tall. Dull greenish grey backs and heads, pale grey bellies, mottled faces. Brownish yellow legs and bills, orange eyes.

muñise tree (moo-NYEE-suh) *Unameze*—Found only on Iridos. Tall, stately. Sturdy trunks with crusty, scale-like exterior surface (thicker on the windward side) to withstand sand and wind. All limbs are found at the top quarter of the tree, above the winds, and all angle up.

Musju (MOO-zhoo) *Unameze*—no direct translation; best approximation is "the flow" or "The Flow of Things as They Are." Comparable to the old Earth concept of the Tao. The unammi envision it in meditation or dream as a river or a stream, a body of water that has currents and eddies. It is the way of the Universe, of the Great Mind. Also used as a proper name given to the part of Na'Staani that directs the Flow.

My magtig! *Afrikaans*—No direct translation. An expression of amazement, similar to "Heavens above!"

nagvël (nahg-VEHL)—A medium-sized blackbird on Bejami. Stays near rivers and other watercourses. Glossy black feathers, wide wingspan, long tail, yellow eyes. Smallish crest atop the head that, when raised, arches gracefully toward its back in a spray of delicate, lacy, red-tipped feathers. Nighttime songs are the longest and most beautiful.

Nalena t'staani (nah-LAY-nah tih stah-AH-nee) *Unameze*—One is All; proper response to "Aes te nalya."

nanopanel—Large plaz panel chemically treated and infused with nanotech. Can be clear, like a window, or be set to project colored pattern displays, specific scenes from historical or contemporary vistas, or any visual that the programmer or user can adequately define.

napi (NAH-pee) *Unameze*—(verb) to respect.
> <u>Forms of use:</u>
> **Na** (NAH)—respected.
> **Na'ala** (nah AH-lah)—Respected elders, plural or genderless.
> **Na'ama** (nah AH-mah)—Respected female elder.
> **Na'apa** (nah AH-pah)—Respected male elder.
> **Na'frem** (nah FREHM)—respected adult (see frem).

nare *Afrikaans*—Nasty.

Na'Staani (nah stah-AH-nee) *Unameze*—Literally, "Respected All." Refers to The Great Mind, The All, The Universe, the unammi concept of All-That-Is, or the Divine.

ne (neh) *Unameze*—No.

Nee. Ek glo jou nie. *Afrikaans*—No. I don't believe you.

New Canaan (noo KAY-nahn)—Capital city on the human colony world Harajüd; located on the west coast of Syrinaia near the equator. Largest human city on any human colony world. Largest tourist city, numerous attractions, abundant industries.

Nidahn (nee-DAHN)—The thirteenth human colony, settled last in the human exodus from Earth. Quarantined when a plague ship made it there from Earth very early in its settlement. All Nidahn colonists died.

Outpost, The—secret off-world base owned/operated by the Consortium Trader base. Located on the moon of old Earth.

ørkhund (OORK-huhnd)—Indigenous to Danua. Small canine mammals, four-legged, large-eared, bright-eyed. Usually brownish in color to blend in with barrens soil/rocks/primary grasses. Native to Danua's barrens.

Pelarr (pee-LAHR)—Capitol city of the human colony world Zebalu. Located on the northern coast, near the western end of Duakela.

Pepita Public House (peh-PEE-tah)—Upscale public house on Saacharis. Owned and operated by The Syndicate Trader faction.

Phejoss (feh-JAHSS)—One of twelve colony worlds. Governed by The Phejoss Society. Located in the Nagapo star system. Luxury resort world, habitable only in the fringes of the large volcanic regions. No moon. One small space port. Two small landports.

pithasia (pee-THAY-zhah) *Unameze*—No direct translation. Similar to human concept of spirit. That portion of the Great Mind that is eternal, but which is tied to the DNA in a living physical body. Upon the death of the body, the bond is broken and the connection between the eternal and the mortal is disentangled, freeing the pithasia to reblend with the Mind, carrying its collected experiences and data for assimilation into the whole.

plaz—A non-toxic, plastic-like polymer used in place of glass in the human colony worlds. Far more pliable and versatile, more shatter-resistant, more easily constructed and transported, more heat- and cold-resistant than glass. Used in windows, doors, furniture, artwork, anywhere glass could be used, and other objects/uses besides. Few things in the colonies are still made from glass.

psuka beans (SOO-kuh)—Fruits of a vining plant native to Danua. Won't grow on most other worlds. Beans are large, bluish black when ripe, with a savory flavor. However, if they aren't prepared properly, they can cause gastric distress, stomach cramps, heartburn, etc. Many people avoid them for this reason.

Ranafta (rah-NAF-tah)—One of twelve colony worlds. Governed by the Ranafta Wildlife Preserve. Located in the Alama star system. One large moon, one small moon, minor ring system. Ranafta is home to many of the animals brought from old Earth, most of which have increased in size given the larger environment in which they are left to thrive. Two space ports. Two landports.

recreational(s)—Herbal or pharmaceutical substances used for recreational purposes. Mostly legal in all twelve colonies. Only a few are banned for serious safety reasons or because the botanical substances necessary to produce them are endangered.

respek *Afrikaans*—Respect.

Rubene (roo-BEE-nuh)—One of twelve colony worlds. Governed by Rubene Holding Company. Located in the Emlacha star system (same as Bejami). No moon. Home to The Federation Trader faction. One of the first three exoplanets to be settled by colonists from Earth. This is a green world, focused even more heavily than other colonies on sustainability and ecosystem-friendly practices. One space port. Two landports.

rufesh (ROO-fehsh) *Unameze*—Indigenous to Iridos. Opportunistic epiphyte that entangles tubers in the root systems of other plants and trees on Iridos. Lost to the unammi since The Fall.

rusucre tree (ROO-seh-cur)—Indigenous to Saacharis. Tallest trees on this world, but trunk and branches are thickly twisted and contorted. Bark is as pale grayish yellow as their leaves, which appear as thicker, overlapping scales that grow in thick tails at the ends of the branches and hang, willow-like, from the tree. Small seed cones hang near the end of the tail, and glow when ripe. Every centimeter of surface on this odd-looking tree is utilized in gathering light.

Saacharis (sah-KAH-rihs)—One of twelve colony worlds. Governed by Saacharis Aggregate Mining. Located in the Nadisa star system. Two moons. Sometimes dark on the planet's surface for hours when one or another eclipses the star; when both moons join in the eclipse, temperatures on the planet can drop significantly. Home to The Syndicate Trader faction. One of the first three exoplanets to be settled by colonists from Earth. Nadisa is larger and brighter than Sol of Old Earth. Yet the planet's thick upper atmosphere reflects back much of the harmful radiation and heat. Thus, the surface of Saacharis is dimmer, darker than other colonies. Two large space ports. Two landports.

season—Unammi measure of time on Iridos, used to denote a complete circuit of the planet around its star. Still used by unammi elders, even though they are no longer living on Iridos.

seedstones—Bits of stone embedded or encrusted with irolium, and therefore Iri, brought from Iridos and attached to cavern and tunnel surfaces in the new unammi city on Earth in the hope of establishing a new colony of Iri and thus irolium on Earth and elsewhere the unammi might settle.

Shamashu Island (SHA-mah-shoo)—Island off the coast of New Canaan, Harajüd at the mouth of Mari Bay. Mountainous on the western coast.

Shemonaea (sheh-moh-NAY-uh)—One of twelve colony worlds. Governed by The Shemonaea Fellowship of Seekers. Located in the Sakĕdris star system. No moon. First colonial world established and settled by colonists from other charter worlds; organized for the specific purpose of retreating from civilization in the search for spiritual meaning. No space port. One landport.

Shidara (shih-DAH-ruh)—See Bindhu.

shustithymia (shoo-stih-THEE-mee-uh)—a rare neurological disorder, usually genetic but in a few recorded cases, brought about by head trauma. Patients present with an inability to interpret varying facial expressions or body language, or to extrapolate their meanings; a total lack of compassion or empathy; inability to connect on a meaningful level with others. Few patients experience emotions other than confusion, obsession, and occasional—sometimes frequent—bouts of uncontrolled rage; some patients can be a danger to themselves or others. A significant portion of those with this disorder experience hallucinations. Can sometimes be controlled with medicines, but there is no cure.

shuttle—Small version of a passenger carrier; ferries passengers and travelers back and forth between the space port and the landport, or from one planetary city to another. Cannot be rented; passage available to anyone who can pay, or who is being transported by corpgov for work or other purpose.

sh'toi (shih-TOI) *Unameze*—No direct translation. Lowest form(s) of unintelligent life. Derogatory, insulting. Serves as singular and plural form.

silk beetle—Indigenous to Danua. Beetle-like insects that produce silky fibers. Highly prized for the famous silks and other expensive textiles produced from their efforts.

skimmer—Small personal craft same size and class as a jumper (though skimmers don't come in mid-size). Faster, sleeker, more elite. Stylish, functional, greater capacity for speed and distance. Still limited to atmospheric travel. Quieter than a jumper.

squib—Derogatory term used by some humans to describe an unammi.

standard time—Colonial measure of time created to standardize business practices between the various colony worlds, which all have varying natural day, week, month, and year lengths. Hours, minutes, and seconds remain the same as Earth time measures.
>   **one standard day** = 30 hours.
>   **one standard week** = 6 standard days.
>   **one standard month** = 30 standard days (5 standard weeks).
>   **one standard year** = 15 standard months (75 standard weeks).

stunner—Up-close weapon. Must touch the target. Depending on the setting, the weapon can simply stop the target or render it unconscious.

TICS (tihks)—Tachyon Interlink Control System. Used for inter- and intraplanetary communications, computer controls, personal memo systems, and numerous other purposes. Usually voice activated and/or controlled.

Tuneloras (too-NELL-oh-rah)—Capital city on the human colony world of Saacharis; located on the continent of Metaliven. Factories and mass-production industries are the biggest income providers here. Entire city is grungy. Dark. Large.

Tussen goeie vriende is daar altyd 'n kortpad. *Afrikaans*—Between good friends there is always a shortcut.

unammi (oo-NAH-mee) *Unameze*—the Iridosians' name for themselves.

úta (OO-tah)—Mead-like alcoholic beverage made from oceanic fruit on Bejami. See "bh'tati."

Verregaandor —

Wat het jou so lank gevat? *Afrikaans*—Colloquial phrase. Closest meaning is "What took you so long?"

Wie is jy? *Afrikaans*—Who are you?

Wynaes bejhul (ween-AY-uhs buh-ZHOOL) *Unameze*—We are diminished. A phrase used to express the loss of someone.

Ysigdo Channel (yih-ZIHG-doh)—Waterway on Bejami. Wide, frigid, and filled with deadly jellyfish, large predatorial fish, and other dangers. Currents are extremely swift, with strong undertow.

Zebalu (zeh-BAH-loo)—One of twelve colony worlds. Governed by The Zebalu Association. Located in the Rasuka star system. Three moons, one large with some atmosphere. Medical facilities located there under a dome. Home to The Cartel Trader faction. Three space ports. Two landports.